ANYONE BUT THE SUPERSTAR

SARA L. HUDSON

Boldwood

First published in Great Britain in 2024 by Boldwood Books Ltd.

Copyright © Sara L. Hudson, 2024

Cover Design by Head Design Ltd.

Cover Illustration: Shutterstock

The moral right of Sara L. Hudson to be identified as the author of this work has been asserted in accordance with the Copyright, Designs and Patents Act 1988.

All rights reserved. No part of this book may be reproduced in any form or by any electronic or mechanical means, including information storage and retrieval systems, without written permission from the author, except for the use of brief quotations in a book review.

This book is a work of fiction and, except in the case of historical fact, any resemblance to actual persons, living or dead, is purely coincidental.

Every effort has been made to obtain the necessary permissions with reference to copyright material, both illustrative and quoted. We apologise for any omissions in this respect and will be pleased to make the appropriate acknowledgements in any future edition.

A CIP catalogue record for this book is available from the British Library.

Paperback ISBN 978-1-83533-680-9

Large Print ISBN 978-1-83533-681-6

Hardback ISBN 978-1-83533-679-3

Ebook ISBN 978-1-83533-682-3

Kindle ISBN 978-1-83533-683-0

Audio CD ISBN 978-1-83533-674-8

MP3 CD ISBN 978-1-83533-675-5

Digital audio download ISBN 978-1-83533-676-2

Boldwood Books Ltd
23 Bowerdean Street
London SW6 3TN
www.boldwoodbooks.com

For Maggie.
Thank you for being such a badass.
(And for wearing lady-boss panties when I didn't want to.)

1
LIZ

My panties are wet for all the wrong reasons.

'Sorry, ma'am, there's a forty-minute wait.' The hostess points behind me at the picnic tables I passed on my way from the parking lot as I hurried from my rental car toward the salvation of the restaurant's air conditioning. 'But there *is* availability on the patio.'

It takes serious effort not to scoff at her suggestion as I pull at the front of my damp, cotton t-shirt.

Of course, there's room on the patio. Only crazy people would sit outside in ninety-eight-degree weather with a heat index of a 107.

And yet, when I follow to where she's pointing, I find a small crowd scattered around the restaurant's picnic tables.

This time, I can't hide the sound of incredulity as I survey the jean and boot clad customers acting like two free-standing water misters are sufficient to keep them from having heat stroke.

I mean, honestly, who wears long pants and boots in the middle of a record-breaking heat wave?

Texans, that's who.

But then again, from what I've seen so far of the Lone Star state since I landed yesterday –Texans *are* certifiable.

Take my sister-in-law, Bell. First, she married my (former) playboy brother Chase. Then she became obsessed with his pet sidekick – a hairless cat named Mike Hunt (see what he did there?). Obsessed enough to let the cat motorboat her on the regular as a form of affection.

It suddenly makes sense that Bell is Houston born and raised when I look at these crazy Texans *not* noticing the insufferable heat.

Yet as much as I love my sister-in-law, I'm not crazy. Or at least not Texas-level crazy.

Turning back to the hostess, I flash her a polite smile and prepare to do something I've never had to do in all my years in New York – put my name on a waitlist. 'Thanks, but—'

My phone buzzes. And while I would really like to ignore it, it may be from my boss, aka my professor, about the internship he arranged for me. One I'm due to start in three days. 'Excuse me a moment, please,' I tell the hostess, stepping aside and tugging my phone out of my jean shorts' back pocket.

The screen lights up with a text notification from my other sister-in-law, Alice. It may not be my professor, but as I consider Alice the nicest woman on the planet (how my eldest dour brother Thomas managed to score her is a complete mystery), I'd feel guilty not responding.

Opening the phone, I'm rewarded with a picture of both my brothers holding their respective cats – one hairless, one sasquatchian.

The cats, not my brothers.

I snort at their expressions. The cats' *and* my brothers'.

While my oldest brother Thomas has a strong dislike for Chase's sphinx – he and Mike both have nearly identical looks of disdain. Meanwhile, Chase mirrors Thomas' Bengal cat, King Richard (who Chase nicknamed King Dick Moore), adopting an expression of cuddly bliss.

My sisters-in-laws and I find great pleasure in talking behind my brothers' backs about how each of them personally chose a feline that reflects the brother they held a grudge against for years. Until recently. Until Bell and Alice.

Now they all get along. The brothers, not the cats.

Mike likes no one but Bell and me. He tolerates Chase.

Standing in the pub's small *indoor* waiting area for patrons, I can't help but physically feel how much I miss them as I look at the picture on my phone.

All of them.

In the year since I left (*cough* ran away *cough*), the Moores have not only grown by three – four if you include King Dick – but they've been doing things I'd always wished us Moores would've done more of when I was a kid – hang out as a family.

Too bad I'm no longer a Moore. Never was, really.

I'm about to sink into a pity party for one, something I've done far too often this past year, when a man sitting at the bar, wearing a slick suit (an anomaly in the casual pub/restaurant) catches my attention. He flashes his Piguet watch as he signals the bartender for his tab.

I don't stop to think what a man in a custom-cut suit and a one hundred grand watch is doing at Boondoggles Pub on the outskirts of Houston, Texas. Because as someone who, from the age of nineteen (thanks to an older friend's ID), has honed their drinking savvy in the busiest and most exclusive clubs in New York City, I know that hesitation costs when it comes to jockeying for position at the bar.

And my bar positioning skills are second to none.

By the time Business Suit has pocketed his credit card, I'm already in place, standing near the restroom hallway with a clear direct path to Business Suit's stool, waiting to swoop in.

My phone buzzes again. Thomas is calling.

Unlike Alice, or Chase's wife Bell, I don't feel as guilty letting my brothers' calls go to voicemail. Probably because, while neither Chase nor Thomas had a part in the paternity bomb my mother dropped on me a year ago (in tandem with the discovery that my *not*-father had embezzled my trust fund), they are a little too close to the reality that I'm not ready to face.

Plus, Alice and Bell send me cat pictures and funny gifs. Thomas, Chase and even my previously emotionally distant mother want to *talk*.

And after a year, I'm still not ready.

It's not that I'm in denial. I fully believe I'm not Stanley Winston Moore's daughter. And I'm well aware the man previously known as my father stole my part of the family's inheritance. In his eyes, I didn't deserve it. Plus, you know, he had mistresses to feed and shelter.

But knowing all of that is different to admitting it out loud. So I don't.

However, having been caught in a moment of weakness, probably brought on by hellish-heat, Texas culture shock, and acute anxiety over the *real* reason for my trip to Houston, I slide my thumb across my phone's screen.

'Liz?'

I smile at Thomas' serious baritone. 'Hey, bro.' Shifting to the side to let a waitress past, I keep my eyes on the bar and Business Suit.

'How are you?'

I open my mouth, ready to rebut his usual order to come home, when his question registers. My imperious brother asking how I've been smacks of Alice's influence. It's gotta be hard to maintain an aloof, asshole-ish demeanor when you live and sleep with a woman who's basically an angel reincarnated.

Deciding that if he's trying, then I should too. Clearing my throat, I keep my voice as agreeable as possible. 'I'm good, Thomas. You?'

'Hmmm.'

That is a usual Thomas response.

Chuckling away the surge of emotion I seem unable to shake today, I lean against the brick wall of the restroom hallway, still with a direct line of sight to where Business Suit leans in to say something to the guy next to him. A glance at the hostess stand has me hoping the two guys at the bar don't know each other. If they both leave, I'll have to compete with the couple that just arrived, who, like me, don't seem insane enough to sit outside.

Odds of the two guys at the bar knowing each other seem slim though, seeing as Business Suit's neighbor is sporting the same threadbare jeans and trucker hat that a lot of the surrounding locals are wearing. Together, they look like the human equivalent of oil and water.

Knowing my brother could hold world records in silence, I bridge the gap. 'How are Alice and Mary doing?'

'Fine.' He pauses, as if thinking. 'They'd be better if you moved back home.'

I'd give him credit for stepping back from giving his usual direct order and making a passive aggressive suggestion instead, except I'm pretty sure the credit should go to Alice.

I smirk, wondering if Alice made him swear to be nice before he called me. I'd bet my inheritance on it, if I had it to bet. But since I don't, I play the teasing little sister card. 'You know, Thomas, as much as I think Alice is a good influence on you, I'm still quite concerned about her intentions.'

Business Suit hands the guy something and then laughs at whatever the guy says before standing. As his shiny loafers hit the floor, I push off the wall, poised to move.

'Oh?' Thomas' tone suggests he's donned his usual superior expression. The one with a single eyebrow raised that used to remind me of our father. *His* father. 'What makes you think that?'

Business Suit is only two steps toward the door by the time I hop onto the vacant stool, my bare thigh halting my slide against the heavy, dark wood. Lifting my knees up, I balance on my jean shorts covered butt and shimmy fully onto the seat. 'Because if your wife truly took your feelings into consideration, she wouldn't be sending me pictures of you and your hairy pussy.'

The guy next to me chokes on his beer.

Thomas remains unfazed. 'Normally I would tell you not to say pussy, but I've been informed by said wife that as I don't reprimand Chase for the same vulgarity, I just end up sounding like a chauvinist asshole.'

'Whoa-ho, Tommy-kins.' I laugh at this heretofore unheard-of side of my stiff older brother. 'Pussy and asshole at the same time?' A bearded bartender double-takes as he walks past from the other side of the counter. 'Pint of cider and a water please,' I call to him before continuing my phone conversation. 'I take back what I said. Alice has been a *phenomenal* influence on you. Team Alice all the way.'

'Yes, well—' he sniffs '—you should be.'

We're silent for a beat. Thomas probably needing a moment to come to terms with sounding human. I use the time hang my purse on a conveniently placed knee-high hook under the bar.

Seemingly recovered, Thomas clears his throat. 'I also called to remind you of your niece's birthday next month.'

My smile turns wistful at the thought of Mary, my brother and Alice's adopted daughter. Unlike me as a child, Mary adores everything princess and spends most of her time wearing the poofy-style dresses I dreaded having to wear as part of New York City's social elite. To this day, ruffles give me chills, reminding me of the awkward family photoshoot sessions before gala events. Flashes of light from newspaper camera men, my 'father's' jovial laugh at being called a family man, before I was whisked away by whatever nanny or event caretaker on staff to a playroom that was more like a mausoleum where I and the rest of the elite's children would have to sit quietly until it was time for an exit photo op.

Shaking away the memory, I replace it with the video Alice sent me of Mary practicing her curtsies in a dress with at least three puffy petticoats, King Dick Moore clutched in her skinny arms. 'I won't forget.'

'And Chase wants you to know that Michael enjoyed the catnip-stuffed crocheted dildo you sent him.' Thomas snorts. 'He says he'll make sure to pay you back at some point in the future.'

I chuckle at the thought of my second eldest brother's hairless cat humping the one-of-a-kind cat toy I had made for him. Chase found out the hard way what catnip did to the neutered but still frisky Mike Hunt during his destination wedding trip to Vegas.

It isn't until Thomas and I say goodbye and I re-pocket my phone that I realize he never asked me where I was. Something Thomas *always* does.

I drum my fingertips on the bar.

Maybe Alice made him promise not to. Maybe he's given up trying to corral me home. Or maybe he already knows.

I frown at my warped reflection on the high polished countertop before laughing that last thought off.

There's no way he knows I'm in Texas. *I* didn't even know I was heading to Houston until last week when my former digital arts professor offered me an internship as his assistant while he worked as a storyboarder on a big-budgeted movie. I'd been all set to say no, having no clue what a storyboarder even was, until he mentioned I'd be working on site at NASA.

The bartender sets the water I ordered in front of me.

I know it's air-conditioned in here – thank God – but it's crowded and he's busy. And yet, even with a heavy beard and a thick, shaggy mop of hair, there isn't so much as a glisten of sweat on his brow. And he's wearing a *sweatshirt*.

Texans are nuts.

'Thanks.' I chug my water, eyeing the second bartender who's standing at the far end who also has a beard and a long-sleeve t-shirt with the pub's bulldog logo. Shaking my head, I lower my near-empty glass.

Who sports a beard in southeast Texas, which would be better described as the Devil's Taint?

'Devil's Taint?'

I jump in my seat, surprised that one, I said that last bit out loud, and two, the guy next to me heard it. Wiping an escaped water drop from the corner of my mouth with my hand, I turn to apologize, pausing when I realize this guy also has a beard.

Welp. This is awkward.

* * *

Felix

The hilariously vulgar-mouthed woman next to me sputters before turning pretty blue eyes my way. Eyes that widen as she looks at my face.

Merda. I had to open my mouth, didn't I? And not even a minute after Jack specifically told me to keep to my corner and stay quiet before he left, *despite* his parting gift of condoms that he found hilarious due to my recently self-declared celibacy.

If this woman recognizes me, I'm done for. I glance nervously around the bar, worried I've garnered too much attention just by looking somewhere else besides the lacquered wood bar that I've been hunched over for the last hour. I got too comfortable enjoying blissful anonymity. The papers don't think I'm arriving until on-set filming starts next week, and with the bearded, unkept look I've adopted since I started laying low in between studio shooting and location shooting, I planned to have one more night of normalcy before filming at NASA begins.

What I hadn't planned on was a hot – in both senses of the word – blonde woman making a weird connection between facial hair and Satan's small strip of skin residing between his testicles and asshole. Which came *after* her comment about a picture of someone's hairy pussy.

At this point, who *wouldn't* be intrigued?

'Ah, sorry about that.' She pulls at the front of her sweat-stained shirt and grimaces. 'I just don't get how Texans can stand this heat.' She waves a hand in my direction. 'Your, ah, beard looks great.'

Relieved at her mistaking me for a local, I can laugh at her blatant lie as I run a palm over the alternating patches of straight and kinked hair covering the lower half of my face.

I've played plenty of survivalist characters in my rise as the summer blockbuster action star, including the lead in a plane crash survival movie shot in the wilds of Canada. Each time, I was told by the film's stylist to grow out a beard, and each time, the facial hair was immediately nixed when I showed up on set looking like I had mange.

The bartender sets another glass in front of the woman beside me, this one full of cider.

'Thanks.' She points to the half-full pint in front of me. 'And whatever he's having. My tab.'

'Not necessary.' My glass is still cold against my palm. 'But thank you.' I promised Jack that the beer in front of me would be my last before I called the chauffeur for a ride to the hotel downtown.

'I insist.' She shrugs. 'An apology for the beard-taint comment.'

I nod with a small smile she probably can't see with my facial hair. I mean, I did make the one-beer promise *before* a woman slinging vulgarity like poetry took his seat.

My curse-poet shifts her body to face forward, then pauses, as if thinking. 'I'm Anne, by the way.' She turns toward me again and sticks out her hand. 'And you are?'

I sputter on my next sip, trying to think how to answer. The man on the other side of her catches my eye, his bright-green hat sitting high on his head. *John Deere* scrawled in yellow.

'John.' I take her hand. It's slender but when she pumps our hands up and down, I feel strength in her arm.

When she returns to her cider, I give her a subtle once-over.

Anne's trim, but fit. As someone who's trained every day for the past five years, I recognize the definition in her arms and the firmness in her long, tan legs sticking out from her cut-off denim shorts as being from some sort of fitness routine. And while her blue eyes close dreamily as she drinks her cider, I keep thinking about the crooked smile she flashed at my reaction to her obscene humor. That and her polite, 'and you are' introduction adds to the abundant collection of contradicting personality traits that I've noted in a short amount of time.

Jack always said character study was my strongest strength as an actor. That I could spend hours mulling over a person's actions, intent and motivation. I'd chalk up my unusual interest in Anne to that if it wasn't for my *other* head's interest.

A dimple pops on Anne's left cheek when she catches me staring. I don't need to have played the Man of Steel to know that the woman next to me could well be my kryptonite.

I know this because I do something I shouldn't. Something my agent and my publicist would advise against. And something my lawyers would most defiantly order me to cease. Raising my glass at my pretty and foul-mouthed neighbor, I clink it to hers. 'I think I'm going to need to hear everything about the wife with a penchant for sending pictures of, uh...' I glance around, more self-conscious of our surroundings than she seems to be and lower my voice to a whisper. 'Someone's heavily maned nether regions.'

Her smiles widens and the way my heart jumps reminds me of the time I BASE jumped off Shanghai Tower for what the movie critics define as my 'big break'. Which was before I became so famous studios insisted on hiring stuntmen, rather than risk the insurance payout if something were to happen to me. Before I had to grow out a beard to have a drink with a pretty girl at a bar without being accosted by strangers. And way before I realized the price of fame was the cost of having lawyers and public relations teams on call just to keep my personal life personal.

But when Anne clinks her glass back on mine, all that fades. 'Listen, Johnny-boy. If you want to know about something, you have to actually say it. Euphemisms are for the weak.' She shifts closer, her proximity bringing a sweet citrus scent that reminds me of my mother's kumquat trees. 'And just so you know, the wife in question is Alice, my sister-in-law, and the hairy pussy in question is my brother's. One of my brothers.' Finely arched, light-brown brows waggle lecherously. 'My other brother's pussy is bald.'

Years of improv classes fail me as I blink at her while my brain struggles to understand the words coming out of her mouth. 'Your brothers' pussies are hairy and bald?' The mental image that conjures gives me the shivers.

She drops her head back and laughs. It's loud, more of a cackle than a laugh. It also reveals a long column of throat. Both her inhibition and the exposed, pale freckles scattered along the curve where her neck meets her shoulder turn me on.

A rare occurrence during these past few stressful months.

Leaning back into her stool, Anne's laughter fades to a smirk. 'Don't say I didn't warn you.'

Ignoring her warning and all the others ringing in my head, I prop my elbow on the bar, bearded chin in hand. 'I'm all ears.'

* * *

Liz

'Mike Hunt is amazing.' John gapes at me in awe after I finish retelling just a few of my brothers' cat stories. 'Also, your family wins for most perverted pet pussy names.'

I raise my glass at him 'Excellent alliteration.' I take a long sip, my happy buzz having more to do with the man next to me than the two ciders I've had. 'Though in fairness to my niece, she wasn't aware of the unfortunate nickname for Richard when she bestowed it upon my brother's Bengal cat.'

John manages a small shrug, acknowledging the point. 'Yeah, but when you add in the fact that Richard's last name is Moore?' Small crinkles crease around his eyes. 'I feel like there was something serendipitous about it all.'

'Serendipitous, huh?' I chuckle while cringing internally at my slip-up.

While I would like to think that most people in Texas don't read the New York City gossip columns or society news, it would be just my luck to find one who does. One who could easily make the connection between the cat's last name and my brother's first. Thankfully, I introduced myself by my middle name. The name I've gone by this past year after I transferred schools to finish up my master's degree.

That, and with Chase's cat named Mike *Hunt*, hopefully John simply thinks King Dick's surname is autonomous and unconnected to the family.

Leaning toward me, crinkles still in place, John lowers his voice. 'Do you believe in serendipity, Anne?'

I snort, laughing a bit harder than I normally would in relief when John doesn't make the connection. 'If that's a pick-up line, Johnny-boy, you should be ashamed of yourself.'

'Yeah, that was lame.' He leans back, a smile crawling up the sides of his whiskered face. I'm almost blinded by a mouth full of neon-white teeth. He's laughed throughout our talk, but he must've been ducking his head because it's the first time I've gotten a full blast of his smile.

My suspicion that Johnny-boy is a diamond of a hottie under his rough of a beard continues to grow.

Interest peaked, I tilt my head, trying to get a better look at his face, which he's averted again, probably out of embarrassment for admitting he lacks pick-up game. Studying his profile, his thick lashes – lashes that women pay serious money to emulate – are backlit by one of the bar's pendant lights, as is his clear complexion. At least the bit not covered in hair. And when he cuts his eyes my way, I'm struck by how dark they are, how reflective.

How sexy.

Yep, just as I thought. Johnny-boy is one handsome man. Seriously so. A sense of familiarity hits me, and I lean closer as if that will help me understand it.

His eyes flit to mine, and seeing me near and intent, he looks away again, shifting the shoulder closest to me forward, as if embarrassed by my interest. 'Must be out of practice.' His laugh is less than enthusiastic.

I'd bet the money I used to have that there's a flush under his whiskers.

Regretting teasing him, I nudge his hitched shoulder with mine. 'I think I might believe in serendipity.'

He rolls his eyes but gives me a half-smile, if the twitch of his beard is any indication.

'Seriously.' I turn my near-empty glass in my hands. 'If I didn't, I wouldn't be here.' I tap a finger on the bar. 'Not just in the bar, but in Houston.'

'Yeah?' John turns to face me again, his embarrassment hopefully forgotten. 'Why are you here then?'

'Work.'

He nods, thankfully not probing further. 'Is work more exciting than hairless pussies?'

I choke on my next sip. 'Just one hairless cat.' I hold up a finger, laughing. 'Remember, Thomas' pussy has hair.'

'Ah, yes.' He nods, his solemnness cut short by a flash of white teeth. 'How could I have forgotten hairy King Dick Moore?'

The bartender stops again on the other side of the bar, making us snicker.

When our laughter fades, I nudge John with my shoulder again. 'Hey, if it makes you feel any better, I'm out of practice too.'

John's dark eyes glide over my hair, my chest, my legs and back up where he meets my eyes and scoffs. 'Uh huh.'

It's my turn to flush. But it isn't embarrassment that causes it.

His blatant disbelief boosts a confidence I hadn't realized I've been lacking.

It's been over a year since I've been on a date, let alone had sex. And the sex I had *before* my life imploded had been polite, awkward intercourse with men, boys really, who were too aware of who *my* father was, or *their* father was, to allow me to really let go. As if the details of my sex life might somehow get back to Stanley Winston Moore and I'd therefore be subject to ridicule and critique by failing to meet his elite and lofty standards once again.

Even now that I'm away from the constant scrutiny, I'm still holding myself back. Still dealing with the fallout of one present parent's past choices and one former parent's current ones. I've been so busy trying to figure out who I am, in addition to what I want to do, that I haven't flirted, dated or even indulged in anything other than too much self-pity this past year.

John finishes his beer, his throat working as he swallows the last drop.

But now... now I'm feeling all kinds of parched for the thirst I'd inadvertently denied myself.

'So, John.' I prop my elbow on the bar and face him.

I watch the right side of his lips quirk up. 'Yeah, Anne?'

'Since *you're* out of practice—'

He huffs a laugh.

'—and *I'm* out of practice,' I raise my feet to rest them on the bar stool's lower rung, my knees resting against his right thigh. 'Why don't we help each other out and practice together?'

He looks down at where our bodies touch, my thighs tightening under his gaze. 'It seems you've already started.' Resting his right hand on one of my knees pressed against him, he squeezes. 'That's what Texans call a false start.'

I snort, rolling my eyes at how stereotypical it is for a Texan to reference football. 'You throwing a flag?' Mentally, I pat myself on the back for knowing that tidbit of sports knowledge.

'Hell, no.' John signals the bartender for the tab. 'I may be out of practice but I'm not stupid.'

Unlike his previous drinking neighbor, John's raised arm reveals a smart watch. I guess even cowboys like to keep track of their steps.

When the bartender holds out a small clipboard with our bill, I shove some cash under the clip and hand it back before John can argue. It's the last of my travel money, but it's easier than trying to pay with a credit card that has a different name on it than the one I gave him. 'Just one of the things I like about you, John.'

Eyes on the bartender walking away with the money, he pauses as if he wants to argue, but then, as if thinking better of it, slides off the stool. 'Hopefully, there'll be a bunch more by the end of the night.' He holds out his hand. 'A night that involves a hotel room that *I'm* paying for.'

Thinking of my pitiful savings acquired from a year of teaching both Pilates and Paint and Sip art classes while finishing my master's degree, I slide my palm into his. 'Hotel room, huh? Sounds like a perfect place to get started on our practice.'

As if feeling shy, he ducks his head as he walks out of the bar with me, hiding another flash of teeth. 'Well, they do say practice makes perfect.'

2

FELIX

I make good choices. While my lawyers may disagree with me on that after my recent attempt to handle things myself, right now, with a pair of toned thighs wrapped around my head, I can say, irrefutably, that all of tonight's decisions that led me to this moment were fucking fantastic.

Anne grabs fistfuls of my hair as I dip my tongue inside her then flick.

'Yes.' Her hips move in tandem with my mouth. 'So good.'

Yes, it is. As is the sting of my scalp that tells me that while I may be out of practice when it comes to picking up women (mainly because I haven't had to do the picking up since my first movie released), I'm most definitely not out of touch when it comes to pleasing a woman.

Sliding two fingers inside her, I press up as I suck her clit.

'*Fuck.*'

Her whole body stiffens and my heartbeat, loud and fast, echoes in my head as her thighs tighten over my ears.

After a few tense seconds, during which I wonder if my neck muscles will hold out, her legs relax and settle on my shoulders.

'Damn, John.'

A stab of guilt hits me over the fake name and how I leaned into the whole native Texan identity. At first it was easy, donning a new persona, just as I've done multiple times before. But somehow, when the other person in the scene doesn't know it, it feels... shitty.

'I take back what I said about the beard.' Anne's voice comes out in breathy pants. 'Friction is my friend.'

My laughter chases away my thoughts and causes her legs to slide off my shaking shoulders. I can't remember the last time I laughed in bed with a woman. Most of the time, I felt like they were trying to pose for selfies between orgasms.

'A-plus, cowboy.' Anne, eyes closed, lips parted in dazed satisfaction on her face, is the hottest thing I've seen in a while.

Pushing her legs wider, I kiss my way up her body. A smile ever-present on my face as I caress the soft skin over toned muscles.

Her blush-colored nipples stiffen and pucker.

'Ah, *gatinha*.' A language I haven't spoken much in years falls from my lips. '*Tão doce*.' I flick my tongue across a hard bud.

'Mmmm.' Her eyes open in a few slow blinks, looking like a sleepy, blonde-haired, brown-eyed angel. 'I have no idea if you're talking about the weather or calling me a dirty girl—' she funnels her fingers through my overgrown hair, fisting control of my head once again and pushing it back down over her breast '—but either way, don't stop.'

An angel with a devil's mouth.

I let her guide me, but tilt my head back, wanting to watch her reactions to my tongue. Her smile rounds as my teeth graze her sensitive skin, her expression slackening when I suck. When she loses focus and closes her eyes once more to pleasure, I feel more accomplished than when I won my last People's Choice Award.

Pushing up off the mattress, I grab the strip of condoms my agent Jack thrust at me before he left the bar tonight and rip one off. He'd given them to me as a joke, knowing full well I'd sworn off women since—

No. Don't think about that.

If I start thinking about the shitstorm my life has been since the last time I let my guard down around a woman, it might impact my ability to put this condom on. And if that happened, I don't think my dick would ever forgive me.

Tearing the foil open, I position the condom over the tip.

'Hey, wait.'

I pause, halfway through rolling it on, as Anne struggles up to her elbows. Her eyes are glued to my dick, a frown marring her face.

Raising my hands up like a criminal surrendering their weapon, I play back our time together, wondering if I misread the signs. 'No pressure if you want to stop.' It takes all my acting skills to say that in a neutral, non-pleading tone. My raging hard-on a dead giveaway to my lies.

She rolls her eyes with a huff. 'Relax, Johnny-boy, I'm just throwing a flag on the play.' Up on her knees, she shoves me on my back with two hands.

My dick, happy to still be in the game, ignores the hard bounce. 'Unnecessary roughness?'

Head back, Anne's laugh is carefree. 'Nah. It's just my turn to take the field.' She climbs on top of me, the sight of her wet pussy as she throws her leg over nearly causing Felix junior to false start. 'I've never gotten to do this before.'

I blanche. 'You're a virgin?'

She drops a chin and levels me a look. 'No. Definitely not a rookie.' Glancing at the remaining three condoms in a strip by the edge of the bed, she plucks the partially rolled one off me. 'Just a quarterback who never got to call the shots before.'

I don't have time to translate what that means before she grabs my hard-on, pumping it up and down and licking her lips before kicking my legs open with her feet and settling between them.

'Here's the play.' One brow arches as she pumps her hand. 'You talk dirty to me in—' she tilts her head as if thinking '—whatever the hell language you spoke before.'

I bite my lip to concentrate on something other than how good her palm feels sliding up and down. 'Portuguese.' My voice nearly cracks.

'Yeah, that.' Her dimple pops with her next pump. 'And you can move my hair out of the way if you want a better view.' Her hand pauses at the top and squeezes.

'Fuck me.'

She smirks. 'Later.' Eyes on mine, she gives me another pump. 'But if you push my head down and make me gag, the only thing I'll be throwing won't be a flag, but you out of the hotel room.' She tilts her head to the side, blonde hair falling over one shoulder, the ends teasing the nipple I just sucked, a sexy, wicked smile playing on her lips. 'Got it, Johnny-boy?'

Going full method actor on her, I tip an imaginary cowboy hat. 'Yes, ma'am.'

* * *

Liz

Everything's bigger in Texas.

That's my first thought when I stretch my mouth wide enough to suck on Johnny-boy's dick without scraping it with my teeth. My second is *ugh*. The latex tang from where the condom had been is *not* pleasant.

But when I flatten my tongue and drag it up the underside of his dick and John's ass clenches with a groan, the ache in my jaw and the tang of rubber seems worth it.

Which, as someone who has never once enjoyed giving head, makes me think that maybe I should take tonight as a good omen. A sign that a fun, no strings attached night is exactly what I needed before putting the stop-avoiding-reality-and-meet-your-half-sister plan into action.

'*Tão bom.*' He shifts under me, his well-defined abs flexing with the movement. '*Você se sente tão bem.*'

John has been full of surprises since I sat beside him at the bar. The largest one being in my mouth. Others like his insanely defined body and his award-winning oral skills will also be immortalized in today's gratitude journal entry.

Bending his knees, John's legs tense as he murmurs in a language I can't understand, adding to the enjoyment of a job I'd always found arduous. Maybe it's because, for once, I have no fucks to give about his feelings, not sense of guilt of behaving like anything less than a lady, no worries about what tomorrow may bring.

Or maybe it's because even as I use my thumb and pointer finger to create a ring vice around his dick as I bob up and down, I take note of his fingers digging into the sheets and I know he's making every effort to respect the boundaries I laid out. Something even my past boyfriends failed to do, thinking I was too nice to stay mad, that I'd forgive them since it was easier than causing a fuss.

Annoyingly, I was and did.

So maybe my problem lately isn't that I'm ignoring my feelings, but rather that I'm stuck in them. Letting them control my actions rather than guide them.

My brother Chase always did say I was too much of a pushover when it came to the people I cared about.

Ew. Stop thinking about your brother, Liz. Gross.

Refocusing, I pause at the top to suck harder, the deep pull making John's ass lift off the bed. Dropping only when I release him with a pop.

'Você está me deixando louco.' John's voice, caressing my ears like a kiss, sends shivers down my spine.

I want to ask how he knows Portuguese but now isn't the time. It isn't even the night, or the guy. That's not why John and I are here. We're here to practice.

As if reading my thoughts, John's dick swells when I circle my tongue at the tip. Relaxing my jaw even more, I get to work.

It's not called a job for nothing.

Dipping back down, I hollow my cheeks and suck.

But just as he sweeps my hair back as I said he could, my lips start losing suction and my tongue starts to tingle.

I try to strengthen my pucker, but a line of drool escapes and the tingling sensation spreads to the roof of my mouth. 'Wait.' I let him go, this time without enough suction for a pop, and sit back on my haunches.

His hands go up again. 'Sorry.'

I'd laugh at him, all three appendages raised in surrender, if I wasn't so concerned with my sudden inability to feel my tongue. 'Sumpthing onng.' Panic sets in at my slurred speech.

John struggles up to his elbows. 'What did you say?'

'Sumpthing...' I reach up quickly, basically slapping myself in the mouth, but I barely feel it. Concentrating, I'm able to swallow the excess salvia pooling in my mouth and force a deep, shaky breath in through my nose, out through my mouth, just like I tell my Pilates class. Except instead of feeling relaxed, my entire body tightens when my exhale sounds like a pre-pubescent boy making fart noises.

'I ink I'm aving a toke.'

His previously vanished smile crinkles by his eyes reemerge between his brows. 'Toke?'

'*Toke!*' I jab a finger at my lips, where, in spite of my swallow, a drop of drool slides out of the corner of my mouth.

It takes a few more seconds, but my butchered word finally registers. 'Stroke?' John's eyes widen and his dick shrinks.

I slap my face *Home Alone* style. 'I an't eel ma ace!'

'Whoa, okay. Shit.' John, now fully limp, shifts back on the mattress so he can retract his legs from either side of my body.

I'm too panicked to move from my ass-on-heels blow-job hunch.

'Let's just calm down.'

My first thought is that the men of the world really need to realize once and for all that no woman, in the history of time, has ever calmed down just because a man told them too. My second is that John must be panicked too, because he doesn't realize the edge of the bed is—

'Fuck!'

I get a great shot of his taint and hard ass as he tumbles heels over beard off the bed.

Ignoring his idiocy for my more pressing concerns, I slide my legs out from under me and stand at the foot of the bed.

Struggling to his knees, John rests his arms on the mattress and frowns at me. 'What are you doing?'

Closing my eyes, I reach out my arms and then touch my finger to my nose. My pointer finger hits the target and I stretch my arm back out and try the other hand. Also good.

There's rustling of sheets and a crinkling of paper. 'Um, Anne?'

Ignoring him, I keep my eyes shut and lift one foot off the low-pile beige carpet. I remain perfectly still as I count to twenty. Even with my Pilate skills, I don't think I'd be able to do this if I was having a stroke. Lowering my foot, I open my eyes and frown at my perfectly balanced feet while my tongue lays heavy in my mouth.

What. The. Hell.

After a night that started off with humidity, anxiety and a smorgasbord of bearded Texans, I'd rallied my way into a buzz and an orgasm. I *thought* I'd win the night by riding a cowboy.

Instead, I can't feel my face.

'Anne?'

Sighing, I brace myself for more unhelpfulness and look in John's direction. Saliva drips down my chin, landing on my boob. *That*, I can feel.

Awesome.

'You're not having a stroke.' He's sitting on the edge of bed with nothing but a pillow in his lap and a grimace on his face. Neither his words nor his expression bring me comfort.

'But, ah, I think I know what happened.' John offers me the strip of remaining condoms. 'I swear I didn't know.'

Not bothering to ask questions that my mouth can't form, I snatch the condoms from him, wondering how they'll help me understand why I sound like the love child of Elmer Fud and Daffy Duck.

His deeply cut six-pack contracts as he shifts uncomfortably on the bed. *Guiltily*.

Lifting the condoms closer, I read the back of the tiny square foil packet and nearly choke on my unswallowed spit. 'Numbing cream?'

Except it doesn't sound like numbing cream. It sounds like 'ummin eam' and at full soprano.

I glare at the man across from me, the color draining from behind his mangey beard. 'Are oo uckin erious?'

* * *

Felix

I make horrible choices. Starting with hiring Jack, my former classmate and friend, as my manager. A manager who apparently buys condoms laced with numbing cream.

Anne wipes a line of drool off her chin and holds my gaze with a menace that only the finest actors playing the vilest humans have ever managed to do.

'Um, I can explain.' I point to the condoms in her hand. 'Those aren't mine.'

Her eyes narrow.

'Seriously.' I shift higher on the bed, feeling more vulnerable with just a pillow between us than I did while dressed with only a sock on my dick on a set full of people when I filmed my first love scene. 'My, uh, friend, Jack gave them to me. At the bar. He was the guy whose seat you took when he left.' I run a shaky hand through my hair. 'Really, I swear. He—'

'I unt ucking care a-bou ucking ack!' Anne whips my chest with the condom strip. 'I ant eel meh ace!' Flinging the strip at my face, she starts grabbing her clothes off the floor. 'I eed ta go ta a ospital.' With every attempt at a hard syllable, a burst of saliva sprays from her mouth.

Then my mind catches up to what she said.

My heart, first fast-paced from lust, then panic, sets a new beat per second record for extremely selfish reasons. 'I don't think there's any need to go to the hospital.' Standing, I grab my pants off the floor.

She sneers at me as she finishes pulling on her shorts and buttons them.

'Seriously.' I stumble into the side of the bed in my haste to pull on my jeans. 'They wouldn't put something poisonous on something that's meant to go on someone's dick.'

'I ouda a-whoa'd it!' She stomps her bare foot on the carpet, then grabs her bra, pocketing it, rather than putting it on. Like she's on a mission to get out of here as fast as possible.

Immediately, my mind goes to what the tabloids would say if this got out.

Action star Felix Jones arrives at hospital with unknown woman after sex accident.

Star suffers erectile disfunction with other woman just months after becoming official with girlfriend at Golden Globes.

Then to what Ron, my director would say. *You're fired.*

Swallowing back my panic, I try again. 'How about I get you an ice pack?'

'Wha da uck is un ice ack onna oo?' She stabs a finger toward her face. 'Iss alrea-y umb!'

'A heating pad?' My voice breaks teenager style. 'You could hop in the shower and let the hot water hit your face.'

Her expression blanks, as if replaying what I just said. Even I have to admit that was dumb as fuck.

I *think* she's sneering at me when another line of drool slides down her chin. 'In-thead a meh-ical twee-ment, oo wan me to otter-oard my-elf?'

I stare hard at her mouth, trying to make out what she's saying.

'Beh-cause ah oar pre-ma-or e-thack-oo-lathin.'

I might not have gotten the last word if she hadn't made an obvious and aggressive jerk-off hand gesture as she said it. 'I don't have a premature ejaculation problem!'

Her eye roll is cut short when she pulls her shirt over her head, mumbling something that I'm sure is less than complimentary. Once dressed, she slides on her sandals and my panic reaches new heights.

Quick-stepping, I move in front of the door. 'Don't go. Let's just wait a minute to see if the numbness subsides.'

'Ooove.' She's a vision with flushed skin and knotted sex hair. Like she was plucked straight from my dreams. A dream that turns nightmarish when her pretty eyes flatten into snake-like slits.

Scared shitless and knowing full well that I'm making things worse, I cross my arms over my chest and plant my feet. 'No.' My bravado is laughable as my hands shake under my biceps.

Anne, still glaring and apparently not the least bit intimidated, squares up to me while wiping moisture off her face with the back of her hand.

I can't tell if she's brushing away drool or tears. Either way, all my anxiousness and panic evaporate on a heavy sigh. I can blame Jack all I want, but I did this. This carefree, gorgeous woman was unlucky enough to think me a good time, and instead of living up to that expectation, all I did was scare her and possibly make her cry.

I'm an asshole.

Disgusted with myself, I hang my head, playing through what I need to do to try and make this right.

Get dressed, Google the nearest twenty-four-hour clinic. Call Jack.

If I'm recognized, so be it. One silver lining to the incident that started my personal life shitstorm a few months ago is that I now have a PR firm on payroll. If it leaks, hopefully they can handle it. And Camilla... well, there's no telling what she'll do, but hopefully, my lawyers will handle it.

But first, I need to apologize.

'Anne, I...' Looking up, I catch sight of fury-filled eyes before pain radiates between my legs and everything goes white. Air explodes from my lungs in a strangled moan and bile climbs up my throat as I drop to my knees.

Anne's small hands push me the rest of the way over until I'm lying on my side, gaping like a fish with my hands cupping my privates.

Stepping over my legs, she opens the door with one hand and flips me off with the other. 'Uck off, ass-ole.' Then she slides her phone out of her pocket and takes a picture of me – hurt, dumb-founded and half-naked – before slamming the door behind her.

Game. Over.

3
LIZ

'So, Anne, what do you think of NASA?'

'Ish b'gar an I ought.' I cringe in apology to Emily Durham, NASA's public relations manager. 'Orry.' Thankful that *this time* my incoherence is due to a mouthful of food and not a cock covered in numbing cream, I grab a cup of coffee from the table that the catering company set up for the first day of filming, forcing the stale, tasteless muffin down with a scalding sip. '*Uhh.*'

Emily's eyes widen in concern before she rushes to hand me a napkin.

Eyes watering, I use it to dab my eyes. 'I'm okay,' I wheeze out after a few shallow breaths. Which is kind of true. If you don't count the Urgent Care visit or my recent homelessness due to a housing issue between my college and the studio.

The past three days in Texas have been eventful, to say the least.

It seems since I'm here as my professor's assistant and not as a storyboarder the studio hired, film production housing doesn't apply to me. Nor does the shuttle that takes them to and from NASA. Both of which my professor failed to realize when he offered me the internship.

Not only did I have to find and pay for a hotel, but I needed to extend my car rental agreement since the hotels within walking distance of NASA charge astronomical rates.

Pun intended.

You'd think Houston would be overrun with hotels to choose from, but while NASA's address may be Houston, it's really located in the smaller suburb of Clear Lake. Houston made a narrow southern extension of the city's zip code so they could claim NASA as their own.

I guess 'Clear Lake, we have a problem', doesn't have the same ring to it.

The rhinestone hair clip holding back one side of Em's blonde bob sparkles in the overhead fluorescent lights as she scans the crowd of production team members gathered for the press junket.

I only just met the petite and sparkly NASA PR manager today during the morning tour. Despite her shorter than my average five-foot-six height and how every aspect of her outfit is shiny, sequined or glittered, the crew shifted uncomfortably under her glare as she imparted a welcome/warning on where they could and could not go during filming.

Most of the buildings we passed on the tour this morning need security access to enter, which Em 'kindly' reminded us that I and the rest of the Hollywood interlopers don't have. And even the ones we're allowed into, like the one we're standing in now, are chock-full of such state-of-the-art equipment that 'cost more than our lives'.

Having been warned, the film crew gathered for a press junket in one of what seems like hundreds of buildings on the acres and acres of land that make up Johnson Space Center. Em had the concrete flooring sectioned off with red tape to delineate what areas were off-limits to crew. She even made sure to point these areas out to everyone as soon as they entered in case they were color-blind.

The petite PR manager doesn't seem super enthused about Hollywood infiltrating NASA.

Even so, she was apparently too intrigued by her love of all things sparkly not to introduce herself to me afterwards so that she could get a closer look at my flip-sequin t-shirt.

Brush the sequins down and you have yourself a Bengal cat, a la King Dick Moore. Brush them up and it's an ugly beige gremlin. Or, you know, Mike Hunt. I found someone on Etsy who makes custom flip sequined shirts. And as I like to patron artists when I can, I bought one for me and one for everyone else in the family – stick-in-the-mud Thomas included.

My niece, Mary, is going to love it.

But that was *before* I realized I was going to need hotel and/or car money during my time in Texas.

Em raises her eyebrow at me as I pop another mini muffin into my mouth before looking over the smorgasbord that only a few people have touched. 'Hollywood does put out a better spread than Uncle Sam, I'll give you that.'

My face heats, all three muffins laying heavy in my stomach.

I could make a joke about my unusual gluttony, but I can't think of anything funnier than the truth. And yet, I'm pretty sure telling someone you just met that you cut your weekly food budget down to near-nothing because of possible homelessness due to a flighty professor and an Urgent Care co-pay I was forced to fork over thanks to possible numbing cream poisoning after ingesting said cream off a one-night stand's dick three nights ago isn't the best way to begin a new friendship.

Even if said someone covets sequined, interactive hairless pussy t-shirts.

Instead I go with a heavily pared-down truth. 'I skipped breakfast this morning.'

My brothers may have refunded the inheritance my 'father' stole from my account with their own funds, but I never felt right using it. I've only dipped into the replenished account when both my brothers decided on expensive destination weddings. I figured if Thomas and Chase decided to pledge their lives to someone in a five-star resort location then that's on them.

But using it to pay for my food and lodging so I can meet the other family member they didn't know I had? That seems like something I should be woman enough to take care of on my own. Especially as they don't know about her. The existence of my half-sister was something my mother only told me after I sat, silent and trance-like, for an hour in the family's 15,000 square foot Manhattan mansion after also being told I was illegitimate and broke.

Thankfully, oblivious to all this, Em just nods at my excuse and grabs her own cup of coffee, her reach setting off a disco-ball effect on the large expanse of cement floor from her stack of crystal bracelets.

She helps herself just in time. Soon we're both shuffling back from the catering table as the growing crew help themselves to food before it's taken away for the scheduled press junket.

There are various types of press junkets. There are the large ones put on in convention centers with tickets sold to fans, and there are small, intimate ones that only include reporters and the movie production's main principals—director and actors.

They're usually scheduled after filming is finished and before a movie's release. But as *this* movie will hold the record for most scenes shot on site at NASA, the studio's marketing department is trying to garner early interest.

And because of NASA being a government-secured site, the press junket crowd, which looks deceivingly small in the cavernous building, is made up from crew members who already received their security badges and select, pre-approved reporters.

One of the grips, a camera and light technician, bumps into a panel of switches on the mock International Space Station training module (clearly marked behind red tape), causing Em's gold flat to tap a staccato beat on the floor, her small foot making a larger than average noise in the football-field-sized building despite the murmuring crowd.

'The next few weeks are going to be such a pain in the ass.' Her flat freezes mid-tap and her sparkly glossed lips grimace in my direction. 'Uh, no offense.'

I hold up the hand still gripping the napkin. 'None taken. I can only imagine what needed to be contracted, signed and fought over during the whole filming agreement process.' Balling up the paper, I toss it in the trash. 'This is my first time on a movie set. I didn't even know what a storyboarder was until my professor offered me the internship.'

Part of the scholarship I was awarded when I transferred schools requires teaching assistant duties, but as I was too late to apply, there weren't any available. With this internship, I'm able to meet the required hours to graduate. Which means I won't have to reapply for another scholarship or take on extra shifts at both the Pilates gym and Paint and Sip studio.

And, of course, the film's NASA location makes the step I had been hesitating to take all that much easier. It was all too serendipitous to refuse.

Cringing at the reminder of douchebag Johnny and his bad pick-up line, I refocus on the real reason I'm in Texas and scan the cavernous building for a blonde woman with brown eyes and thick, black-framed glasses – the description of my half-sister.

But with half the crew local Texans and the other half California imports, nearly everyone is blonde, including myself.

And no one has glasses.

Ding. Em glances at her smart watch. 'Shoot.' Checking to make sure her rhinestone-collared blouse is neatly tucked into her metallic-pink, pleated, knee-length skirt, Em straightens as if readying for battle. 'That's my cue to go greet the VIPs.'

I get the feeling the tiny PR manager is fighting an eye roll.

'Have fun.' I manage to sound cheerful even though Em leaving means I'll be left on my own, looking as clueless as I feel. Everyone on the crew seems nice, but they also all know what they're doing.

'Fun?' Em snorts, grabbing her gold satchel bag off a shelf behind the red tape nearest the buffet table. 'I have a feeling that after just one day with Hollywood types, I'll be a lot more thankful for dealing with one of our astronauts causing an occasional tabloid ruckus.'

I hold back from asking after a particular astronaut ruckus, one about my sister that happened a few years go. Instead, I wish Em good luck as she hikes her bag onto her shoulder before setting off, leaving me to mentally pull up my big-girl panties and make my way through the crowd toward my professor.

I reach him just as a woman my age wearing a coral-colored halter top which pairs perfectly with her flawless tan gazes at Professor David Mirales like an enraptured puppy. 'Have you met Felix Jones before?'

'No, sadly, I haven't.' David shifts back to make room for me. 'But I heard from Ron that he's on site for the press junket.'

The crowd hums excitedly, whether from the intel David just gave them or the fact that he's on a first-name basis with the director, I'm not sure.

The director, Ron Allen, is David's friend from college. A fact I'm less awed by and more thankful for as their friendship provided me the internship and chance to meet my half-sister.

Coral Halter Top lifts her eyes to the tall guy next to her. 'Do you think all the rumors are true?'

The guy shrugs, his normal-sized t-shirt lifting above his belt. 'You never know, man.' His shoulders drop, lowering his shirt back down. 'I mean sure, celebrities date all the time, but these days the tabloids will print anything.'

'Yeah, but didn't he take her to an award ceremony after-party?' Coral Halter Top counters.

Tall guy shrugs.

'Guys, guys.' David holds up his hands as if to call a truce. 'If you'll spare an old man a moment to impart some advice?'

I'd bet the remaining limit on my credit card that David's lengthy pause has nothing to do with waiting for a collective answer and everything to do with soaking up their adoring gazes.

'While it's always good to be informed about the people you are working with—' Halter Top throws Tall Guy a haughty look '—it's also good not to believe anything you hear or see second hand. *Especially* in this business.'

The girl's haughty look falls and Tall Guy smirks.

Feeling the need to play peacekeeper, a habit long-engrained from a lifetime of doing the same for my brothers and our – *their* – father, I speak up. 'Who's Felix Jones, anyway?'

It works. The tension evaporates as all eyes turn to me, their corresponding mouths gaping.

'*Who* is Felix Jones?' A different, though equally tanned woman repeats my question in disbelief.

'Are you serious?' Halter Top adds.

'He's the biggest action star in Hollywood,' one of the group says.

'He's been in every summer blockbuster for the past five years,' another crew member is quick to inform me.

'I don't really watch action films.' Growing up, my weekends were filled with charity events and social gatherings that my parents deemed more appropriate. And when I finally had a say in my own schedule, I liked holing myself up in my room to draw or read more than going out with my classmates – fellow children of the social elite.

Also, living in the city with the largest US theater district, I found I'd much rather see a show on Broadway than a bunch of explosions on screen.

'Yeah, but he's the *lead actor* in the movie.' Tall Guy shakes his head. 'Didn't you do your research?'

Thanks for the judgment, Paul Bunyan. I will my skin not to reveal my embarrassment, but with the way my cheeks heat in the arctic air-conditioning and how Tall Guy shifts uncomfortably in his checkered Vans, I'm positive I failed.

I also fail at overcoming my long-learned unwillingness to speak up for myself. Because I *did* do my research.

I spent the small amount of time I had between David offering me the internship and leaving for Texas downloading and mastering all the necessary graphic design applications David uses for storyboarding. I may have switched my master's from art history to graphic design after I no longer felt the need to appease the man I once called father, but even with all the courses I've taken under my belt, I still have a lot to learn. I wanted to be as prepared as possible.

Because I *hate* being the center of attention. And nothing makes you the center of attention more than being caught unawares.

And yet, even with my late nights learning new stylus techniques and panel formatting, the group's shocked collective makes me feel like my time would've been better spent poring over back issues of *People* magazine instead.

David chuckles, thankfully drawing a few eyes his way. 'Anne is my student.' He drops a hand on my shoulder. 'She's here to earn hours toward her master's degree in graphic art.' He gives me a reassuring squeeze.

He may have good intentions, and I'm grateful he remembered to call me Anne and not Liz, but I can see the group retreat even further at the knowledge that I'm not really one of *them*.

Which is fine, I tell myself as I rescan the room for blonde hair and glasses.

I'm not here to make friends. Or to further a future career in Hollywood. I'm here to graduate and to figure out a way to introduce myself to a half-sister who knows nothing of my existence.

A half-sister who also happens to be the most famous astronaut at NASA – Dr Jackie Darling Lee.

* * *

Felix

'Yes, but do you have a cow?'

I stare at the curly-haired woman floating across the massive screen hung in the front of the most impressive room I've ever been in. 'I'm sorry?'

'A *cow*.' Julie Starr, aka Jules, aka, NASA's Starr, drops her chin to level a stare directly into the camera recording her from inside the International Space Station. 'Do. You. Have. One?'

Microphone in hand, I blink at the camera in front of me before turning to my manager/agent Jack for help.

I knew I'd be impressed when our morning VIP tour finished in the Mission Control, a place rife with both history and innovation, but I didn't know I'd be too awe-struck to make sense of the Q&A the film studio set up between its principle cast members and NASA's astronauts.

Jack just shrugs, his earlier expression of childlike excitement vanishing from his face the moment he realizes my eyes are on him.

He's been giving me attitude ever since he raced to my hotel room a few nights ago to find me half-dressed and icing my balls.

My gaze shifts to astronaut Vance Bodaway, aka Bodie to almost everyone. He's been our escort and tour guide around NASA this morning. He shakes his head, his long, black hair falling over the NASA patch on the left breast pocket of his blue jumpsuit.

'The cow is a key element to the female character's story arc,' Jules continues. 'And I should know since the character is basically me.'

Thankfully, my co-worker, Amanda Willis, takes the microphone. 'Ms Starr, it's an honor acting a role based on you.' She flashes her girl-next-door smile at the camera. The one she gave this year when accepting her most recent Golden Globe for best female actress in a comedy. 'It's a dream to bring a woman of your intelligence, talent and humor to the big screen for millions to see.'

I've never worked with Amanda before, seeing as she's Hollywood's rom-com queen and I'm its action star, but I've heard nice things. Which says a lot in a business full of vicious gossip.

'That's great to hear, Mandy.' Jules tilts her head at the camera. 'I can call you Mandy, can't I?'

Amanda smiles wide. 'I—'

'And I never understood why movies portray women as either smart or funny or sexy,' Jules continues. 'Why not all three?'

Recognizing that Jules' questions lean toward the rhetorical, Amanda just nods.

Jules presses the hand not holding the mic to her chest and her body continues to slowly rotate clockwise in front of the camera. '*I'm* all three.'

'So modest, our Starr,' Bodie mumbles, twisting his lips as if to keep from laughing.

Jules' expression turns contemplative. 'Do you know how to ride a Ducati, Mandy?'

'Umm...' Amanda's smile slips.

'Stop interrogating the celebrities, Starr.' Astronaut Luke Bisbee floats into view, his tall body running the length of the entire screen, knocking Jules into the curved wall. 'You know full well that Trish said her book was a work of fiction, any resemblances to people living or dead are completely coincidental.' He winks into the camera. 'At least that's what legal told us to say.'

The surrounding NASA employees continue to work at their consoles, each with multiple computers, all of them set up in grid-like rows facing the screen. And yet none of the workers look up from their stations, choosing to ignore the astronaut comedy show in front of them and the award-winning actors and director behind them.

Their disinterest reminds me that while a celebrity may command attention in the 'normal' world, here at NASA, the employees have bigger things to deal with.

Like the infiniteness of space.

Taking advantage of everyone's preoccupation with keeping the International Space Station running or Bodie and Luke's effort to rein in

Jules' attempt to add livestock and a motorcycle chase to the movie's cast and scene list, I back-step until I'm shoulder to shoulder with Jack.

'Did you find her?' My voice is barely audible over the astronauts' bickering on screen and the low murmurs of NASA employees speaking into their headsets as they work.

Jack keeps his eyes on the screen in front of him as he whispers in return. 'And just who might you be referring to?'

I roll my eyes at his continued blank expression. 'Don't play dumb.'

Jack examines his nails. 'Oh, you mean the one-night stand who left you naked and emasculated on the floor?'

I glance at the flight director whose desk is next to where we're standing. He doesn't so much as twitch over Jack's comment. Although seeing as he's busy overseeing every aspect of every person's job in this room, I'm not sure if that's because he's used to not visibly reacting or if Jack's voice hadn't carried.

Jack rocks back in the custom loafers I bought him for Christmas last year. 'Or do you mean the one who ghosted you after taking a nude photo of you?'

Seeing as Mission Control is kept at a near-frigid level due to all the computer equipment, I can't blame the heat climbing my neck on room temperature.

'No, I know.' Jack's eyes narrow. 'The woman who could get you on Ron Allen's shit list and therefore banned not only from the serious movies you want to start making, but from *all* future projects.'

Ron Allen, the director of this film, took a chance on me. After Jack and I begged him, of course.

I'm grateful for the action films that put me in the spotlight. It's just that, when I got into acting, I wanted to do more than just flash my abs and make quippy one-liners before jumping out of a helicopter. As the male lead, which is more of a side character in this female-focused romance, I'll get a chance to flex more than my biceps. I'll get to show Ron, and the movie audiences that I can be serious and funny without setting off or surviving an explosion every five minutes.

Narrowing my eyes right back at Jack, I take a deep, cold breath in through my nose. 'No.' My voice so low, I push my shoulder into Jack's to make sure he hears me. 'I mean the woman whose face you paralyzed by handing me a strip of numbing cream condoms like you're an erectile dysfunctional Santa Claus.'

His carefully groomed and fashionably stubbled jaw drops. 'I do *not* have erec—' He freezes, his eyes shifting around the room to the people startled at his elevated tone.

A question from the ISS brings everyone's attention back to the front.

Jack's breath tickles my ear. 'I do *not* have erectile dysfunction.' Straightening, Jack smooths down his tie. 'Those condoms were advertised as "for her pleasure" and—' his hand pauses over his chest as if making a vow '—I am nothing if not a giver.'

I manage to keep from laughing, and note, not for the first time, that Jack should be the one in front of a camera, not me.

'And no.' His voice back to a normal whisper as Luke answers the director's question about microgravity's effect on facial expressions and physical reaction time. 'I didn't find her.' Jack's hand reaches for the pocket where he usually keeps his phone.

Guilt creeps back in. Jack isn't a stereotypical agent or manager. He isn't constantly on his phone making calls and greasing wheels. I'm his only client. So knowing that he's anxious for his phone means one of two things. Either he's waiting to hear the latest from the PR firm about the expected release of my *semi*-nude photo, or he's fallen off the wagon again and needs a Candy Crush fix.

I slide my arm across his shoulders and give him a quick side hug.

Jack's been with me since the beginning of my career. Hell, before that. We grew up in the same town, went to the same high school. We even headed to LA together after college – him to go to law school, me to try and make it as an actor.

Two years later, when I got my first big job, Jack was the one who stepped in and handled the contracts. He's been my agent ever since.

He knows me. He knows my mom. He knows the truth about what's happening and he's done nothing but have my back through it all.

I don't want to add to his worry, but the memory of Anne, slacked-faced and tear-streaked, flashes in my mind for the millionth time since my nuts were kneed into my stomach. 'What if she was really hurt?'

It takes a second, but Jack catches on to who and what I mean, and, to his credit, his expression softens. 'We've already talked about this.'

The director laughs at something Luke says and Jack and I both smile as if we've been listening.

Jack drops a hand on my shoulder and whispers, '*You* have a bigger chance of having a sperm deficiency from her violent assault to your testicles than she does of having any lasting damage from the *infinitesimal* amount of numbing cream she may or may not have ingested.'

I can't help but chuckle at his phrasing, thankful my reaction matches the room's mood. 'Spoken like a lawyer.'

'Spoken like a celebrity manager.' He smiles back and drops his hand from my shoulder. 'And friend.'

Before I can rib him for our bromance moment, the sound of my name jerks me to attention.

'Isn't that right, Felix?' The director, Ron, looks at me expectantly.

Amanda hands me the receiver, her hand covering one end. 'You used to want to be an astronaut when you were younger,' she murmurs, saving me from looking like an ass for not paying attention.

Lifting the receiver, I give the camera set up in the center aisle a red-carpet smile. 'Yes.' I pause for a well-timed self-deprecating chuckle. 'However, I had to give up the dream when I realized I needed to not only take but *pass* Calculus.'

I get the expected chuckle.

And an unexcited aside. 'Yeah, and he gets more ass as a movie star.'

It's whispered, and in the din of keyboard clicking and soft murmurings, I can't tell where or who it came from. Jack's shoulders stiffen, so I know he heard it, but thankfully Ron is busy assuring Amanda that neither a cow nor a Ducati are necessary to harness her character's emotions throughout filming.

'But now I get to live the dream,' I continue, pretending I hadn't heard the dig and that it isn't just NASA's camera in my face, but all the paparazzi who are ever ready for me to slip up so they can post about it and get more social media clicks. 'All thanks to NASA allowing us to film an unprecedented number of scenes on site and even allow Amanda and me to train under the guidance of real astronauts.' I adjust my expression into one of humble gratitude. 'I want to thank you all for this unique opportunity and I promise you that we'll do all we can to ensure our film is as accurate as both NASA and Hollywood magic allows.'

It's a good performance, even getting even the hardcore NASA workers who hadn't shown any interest in us Hollywood interlopers to flash me an appreciative smile.

But just when I think I created the perfect segue to leave for the nearby press junket, Jules grabs the mic. 'If that's true then you really need a cow.'

4

LIZ

My gut is churning.

And it's not the three – okay, *five* – mini muffins I've consumed since waiting for the VIPs to arrive.

'He's coming!' Halter Top low-volume squeals, causing all the women, and some of the men, to straighten up, a few of them running a hand through their hair.

I'm aware of everything around me, but it's foggy, as if it's not happening a few feet from where I'm standing, my eyes glued to my phone.

Earlier, I excused myself from the group to do the *research* Tall Guy mentioned. And now, after Googling the cast of *Countdown*, I can't take my eyes off the image of the male lead.

I reread the caption beneath the photo:

Felix Jones at the premiere of *Shanghai's Salvation*.

I never saw *Shanghai's Salvation* or any of the other movies listed under the actor's filmography.

And yet the combination of short brown hair, parted on the side and quaffed with the perfect amount of product, up-tilted lips and deep brown eyes, which are bracketed with the ideal amount of smile lines, seems eerily familiar.

'Do you think he's as hot in real life and he is in his movies?' a crew member asks.

Another nudges the person beside them with their elbow. 'Remember when he was on *The Ellen Show* and he gave everyone in the audience an Xbox to commemorate his movie being turned into a game?'

'I wonder if the bulge behind his Calvins is as large as the billboard on Times Square makes it out to be, or if it's just photoshop?' someone ponders.

The crew's gossip, once it registers, eases the pinch in my chest.

Of course I've seen Felix Jones' eyes and lips before. I may not have watched any of his movies, but he *is* a celebrity. He's been on TV talk shows and commercials, and thanks to one of the gossip-savvy crew, I know his underwear billboard is hung in the middle of my home city.

Laughing at myself, I lower my phone. My past personal drama must've made me more anxious than I thought. During my year of self-discovering, I'm realizing I might be less carefree like my brother Chase and more paranoid like my other brother Thomas.

The door opens across the way and the crew goes quiet.

I lift up on my toes to get a glimpse of the incoming celebrities, but the gathered crowd, confined to the area *not* marked in red tape, is too large to see more than the tops of their heads as they enter.

The crew exclaims as one, each person having an opinion on the group entering the building.

'I knew he'd be just as hot as in the movies.'

'Whoa, Amanda looks amazing. I hear she does some sort of dance to keep in shape.'

'Do you think Felix wears lifts? I didn't think he'd be so tall.'

'Do you think the rumors are true, do you think the woman is dating—'

'All right, all right, settle down everyone,' a man's voice yells, quieting down the crew. 'For those who don't know, I'm Ron Allen, the director of *Countdown*. And the two next to me are its stars.'

There's a subtle shift in everyone's stance, as if making room for people to step forward.

'Hi, everyone, I'm Amanda Willis.' A woman's voice rings out in the cavernous building like a Broadway performer.

I put the face that came up in my Google search to it.

'I'm very much looking forward to working with everyone.'

I'm about to pocket my phone when Felix Jones speaks. 'And I'm Felix Jones.'

While a collective female sigh echoes, my hand tightens around my phone.

It can't be.

'And, like Amanda, I'm very happy to be here and to begin working with you.'

Doing the same as I did for Amanda, I conjure up the picture of Felix Jones from my phone. But instead of a perfectly quaffed and tuxedoed movie star, my imagination distorts until the man has a baseball cap and an unruly beard.

No. Not possible.

Using the hand not holding my phone in a screen-cracking grip, I brace myself on the side of the full-scale International Space Station mock-up and climb onto one of the large speaker boxes the crew set up earlier for the press junket. Red tape be damned.

Carefully, I circle-shuffle in my Birkenstocks until I'm looking over the crowd.

Em's there. The overhead lights reflect off her jeweled barrette, making her easily discernible despite her height. Next to her is Ron, a man of medium height that I recognize from a photo in my professor's office back in New York. Amanda Willis is next and then—

Tall Guy shifts in the crowd, blocking my view.

Fucking Tall Guy.

'I know you might want to get autographs or ask questions,' Ron says, the second part of his comment laced with meaning as his eyes move through the crowd, 'but remember, this is not the time. We're professionals here to do a job.'

Halter Top visibly deflates.

'I'm known to run a tight ship on my film sets, but I will be even more strict on this one.' Ron raises his arms, gesturing to our surroundings. 'This is NASA. A federal agency.' He nods at Em. 'They were nice enough to allow us here to capture the real, everyday life of the men and women of NASA and I, for one, don't want to fuck that up.' He smiles at the last, his expression easing some of the building tension. 'So, besides today—' he gestures at the journalists '—there will be no personal cellphones, laptops, cameras or tablets allowed during filming.' He waits for the collective groan to fade. 'Anyone caught not adhering to this rule will be dismissed on the spot.'

A woman steps next to Ron and goes over some of the same guidelines that Em went over earlier and adds in housing details that I wish were relevant to me. I'm about to hop off the speaker when Ron speaks up again.

'Now that that's over, I want to thank you all – crew and otherwise – for being here today.' Ron nods, his eyes a lot less scary when he's not threatening people. 'It's going to be a great time and an even better movie.'

Amanda raises a hand and adds her own, 'I'm so happy and thankful you all are here.'

'Yes, thank you.' Felix Jones, still hidden behind Tall Guy, speaks, his voice sending a chill of recognition down my spine. 'Or as my *mamãe* says, *obrigado*.'

I fight the sudden need to vomit masticated muffins all over NASA's billion-dollar training equipment less than a foot away.

While I can rationalize the familiarity of his face on my phone, and even the sense of déjà vu at his voice, I *can't* ignore the foreign language.

Not when it sounds *exactly* like the whispered naughty talk that had my toes curling and my vagina clenching before everything in my mouth went numb.

Ignoring the threat of muffin retribution, I tap my thumbs over my phone, clicking the link for the actor's personal bio. *Of Portuguese descent* glares at me from the white screen.

I suddenly have trouble breathing and swallowing. As if I'm suffering phantom numbness from my recent condom trauma.

Which makes sense as, when the crowd parts, and I finally get a look at the Oscar-nominated, two-time Golden Globe winner and People's Choice's most charming smile winner three years in a row, I don't see Felix Jones, male lead actor of *Countdown*.

I see a freshly shaven douche bag named Johnny.

5

FELIX

'Let's head toward the ISS mock-up.' Em, the public relations manager and, as it turns out, astronaut Luke Bisbee's wife, leads us farther into building nine.

For a petite woman, she pushes through the crowd in no time. Amanda, Jack and I follow behind, while Ron stops to speak with someone, hugging and clapping their back in greeting as if they haven't seen each other in a while. He's soon out of sight as the three of us are swallowed up by the crew.

Practiced smile in place, I nod as I walk, the crowd feeling larger and more imposing as we cut through it. Though I don't pause to meet anyone's eyes, I'm aware of the looks, the winks, the head tilts and scrutiny as I go.

It's something I've gotten used to over the years in the business. The curiosity. The lack of privacy. The public's growing sense of ownership over what would normally be boring, everyday aspects of a non-famous person's life with every film released.

I accidentally lock eyes with a brunette in a bright halter top and her smile, pulled unnaturally tight, almost makes me wince. Careful to avoid dropping my gaze to her impressive cleavage, I nod in return while I pass.

In my peripheral, I see a crew member elbow another in the side while whispering out of the corner of his mouth, making the other crew member smirk.

Sigh.

This is not Mission Control. These people are not exploring the infiniteness of space. While I may still be on NASA's grounds, the people in front of me now are pure Hollywood. Their business is show business. Which means they want to be up in *my* business.

They've probably all heard the recent rumors circulating from people they *think* are credible sources. People who've worked with me in the past or who have publicly declared me a friend in various interviews and soundbites, whether we've met before or not.

It only goes to show that you can't trust anyone in this business. Because the only ones who know what's happening are me, Jack, a bunch of lawyers and Camilla Branson.

Hopefully, my PR team, who has specific orders *not* to comment on my dating life, is correct in thinking that by having Jack secure me a role as a funny, romantic leading man, I'll be able to prove that I'm more than just a set of abs who can dismantle a bomb in thirty seconds. That I have range.

And if Ron, a prolific film director with various accolades to his name, likes what I can do here, he might keep me in mind for his other, more serious films as well. Spread the word to his considerable network of directors and producers with studio contracts that boast both mainstream films and art-house productions.

At the edge of the actual-sized International Space Station mock-up, a long fold-out table, draped in a black cloth, has been set up, a microphone in front of each of the four chairs.

I'd heard the writer of *Countdown to Love*, the novel the screenplay was adapted from, was going to attend the junket as well, but, looking around, I don't see anyone else stepping forward.

But who I do see has me stumbling over my feet as I pull Amanda's chair out for her.

'Whoa.' Amanda reaches over to help steady me. 'You all right?'

Bracing against the ISS structure, I jerk my gaze back toward the spot where I thought I saw… no. Instead of two condemning blue eyes, I'm met with the bony chest of an annoyingly tall crew member. Lifting my eyes to his, we frown at each other, both confused for different reasons. Shifting forward, then back, I try and fail to see around him.

Em clears her throat, her eyes superglued to my hand resting on the ISS mock-up.

Taking one last futile look, I drop my hand and shrug sheepishly. 'Ah, sorry about that.'

Em seems less than impressed with my apology.

Shaking off what must've been an anxiety-driven hallucination, I refocus on my co-star. 'After you.' I wave Amanda forward with a flash of my million-dollar-contract smile.

Her nostrils flare and I'm almost positive she's fighting an eye roll.

I may have overdone the smile.

'Be careful,' she murmurs before settling in her chair.

'Don't worry.' I ease back on the amount of teeth I'm showing and step over to my chair to her right. 'It wouldn't do for someone who does as many stunts as I do to be a klutz.'

'No.' Amanda averts her face from the cameras, throwing me a smirk that I'm pretty sure her image consultant would say was anything but the carefully curated girl-next-door look she's known for. 'I meant careful where you aim that smile.' A brow lifts to match the corner of her mouth. 'I think you might've just inadvertently impregnated someone.'

'For God's sake, don't joke about that,' Jack grumbles, moving behind both of our chairs to stand at my other side, almost like the protective detail he wanted to hire and that I'd nixed. 'That's all we need.' His eyes shift over the gathered reporters. 'A pregnancy rumor.'

Jack's expression makes me laugh more than the joke.

'Sorry, Amanda.' I sit beside her. 'I'll try and keep the smolder under wraps.'

She snorts then faces forward, her contradictory bright but demure smile ready for the cameras. 'You do that.'

Ron takes his seat to Amanda's left and the murmurs around us die down. He checks his watch and glances at the empty seat next to him. 'Well now, shall we start?' Ron adjusts his mic, holding his hand over it and murmuring, 'The sooner we get this over with, the sooner we can be done.'

Amanda and I share a smile.

Lowering his hands, Ron addresses the members of the press, front and center in the crowd. 'Who wants the first question?'

Every single reporter raises their hand.

* * *

Keep smiling. Just keep smiling.

Feeling very much like Dory swimming through a sea of naval mines, I loosen my shoulders and act unfazed as a reporter asks a question.

It's an art, really, this press thing. You need to give just enough of yourself to seem genuine, but not so much that you end up on a therapist's couch or a gossip blog. Or even more gossip blogs than usual, in my case.

'Miss Willis, any concerns as a romantic comedy veteran about your co-star's recent *action-packed* past?' It's been ten minutes and with most of the standard questions asked, I've started to notice a sharper edge to the reporters' queries as they begin to dig.

Ron's lips purse, his fingers drumming the table.

Out of the corner of my eye, Jack shifts in his loafers.

Amanda, acting unfazed, shares an anecdote about her first film and how supportive her co-stars were. 'I would love to say that I'll be mimicking that support with Felix, but let's be honest, Felix doesn't need it. He's a pro and I'm not the least concerned.' She nudges my arm with her elbow, giving the impression of camaraderie to all those watching. 'I'm actually very much looking forward to everyone seeing a lighter side of this guy. Y'all are going to love it.' She raises a hand to her rounded mouth as if surprised. 'I guess Texas is already getting to me. That was my first y'all, y'all.'

Everyone chuckles, thinking her joke unpracticed.

With a confidence I don't feel, I adjust the smile I've perfected over the years while shaking my shoulders while I laugh, as if I too am caught off guard by Amanda's perfectly timed, Southern twang surprise.

A different reporter raises a hand, and once called on, steps forward in the crowd. There's a slight reshuffle, with the tall crew member from before sidestepping to make way for the journalist, my brain going into shock when the person standing behind him is revealed.

Anne.

Everything stops. My laugh, the din of the room, my ever-present smile.

Even with her head down, hunched over her phone, I know it's her. Hair up in a high ponytail, the end of it curls under her left ear and rests on her shoulder, giving me an unobstructed view of the pert nose she looked down at me with disdain just a few days earlier. Toned legs, one of which had emasculated me, extend from a pair of jean shorts in a firm stance.

'Mr Jones, what drew you to your role in *Countdown*?'

I barely hear the reporter, my eyes glued to the woman who's taken up the majority of my thoughts these past three days.

Why is she here? *How* is she here?

'Mr Jones?'

Only crew and press are allowed on site.

My hands feel clammy as I watch her thumbs fly over her phone screen.

She's a reporter.

The image of me, half-naked on the floor, curled around my balls, flashes before my eyes, this time next to various tabloid headlines, all written from a first-hand account. *Anne's* account.

Amanda's foot nudges my own, reminding me where I am.

'Well...' I replay the question one more time, hoping it looks like I'm giving the question serious thought rather than having a silent panic attack.

Clearing my throat and affecting a thoughtful tone, I meet the reporter's gaze. 'It was the depth of the story, the realness of the character.' I maintain eye contact with the reporter as I speak, hoping it will give my rather rote answer more credibility. 'I mean, what is life, without all its messy, funny, beautiful twists.'

Like having a one-night stand show up uninvited to your press junket.

As if hearing my thoughts, Anne looks up.

The dawning horror in her eyes as she realizes she's been discovered mirrors my own internal crisis.

But just when I'm about to do something stupid, something my lawyers, manager and even mother would advise me against – stand up and shout something, anything, to expel the growing swell of emotions inside of me at seeing my one-night stand holding the phone that took the scandalizing picture of me standing so close to reporters and cameras – someone beats me to it.

Someone loud, Southern and heavily pregnant.

6
LIZ

Fuck a duck.

Too late, I realize that Tall Guy has failed the one job I gave him (that he didn't know he had) – block me from view.

And now my numbing-cream nemesis is staring me straight in the eyes.

There's a spark of satisfaction from being proven right: he *is* handsome under that God-awful, unruly beard – freaking unfairly handsome. But that spark is quickly extinguished at the light of recognition illuminating his stupidly soulful, dark-brown eyes.

Feeling suddenly hot in the fully air-conditioned, hangar-like building, I fight the urge to shift under his intense stare while my annoyance at the situation, and myself, makes me want to scream, *Fuck you, limp dick* at him in front of all these people and cameras.

Not the most mature of urges, I'll admit. But one I'd like to think is understandable.

Because if I was standing in front of him as Elizabeth Anne Moore, former heiress to the largest American luxury retail conglomerate and charity princess, I'd be able to hold my own against anyone, including A-list celebrities with a penchant for anesthetized prophylactics.

However.

Right now, I am *not* Elizabeth Moore, I'm Anne Moore, a money-strapped grad student with scholarship requirements and a half-sister to meet. So as much as I'd like to tell the award-winning asshole staring me down to fuck off, I instead inhale for a count of three-two-one, filling my belly with breath, then exhale long and low. It's a trick I used whenever nerves got the best of me at public events and galas Stanley Moore insisted I attend. And a trick I use now in an attempt to stop myself from doing more physical harm to Felix Jones' junk.

Thankfully, when the first deep breath doesn't cure all my violent impulses, I'm saved by a woman with more shine than my t-shirt.

'Howdy, y'all!'

Everyone starts, including me, at a woman with strawberry-blonde hair blown out with enough volume to reach the heavens.

Blinking past the dryness from my stare down, my brain needs a moment to gawk at the newcomer's substantial pregnant belly which she has encased inside a fuchsia spandex jumpsuit. She's a technicolor vision in the otherwise black, white and gray building.

Just as entranced, the crowd parts to make room for her as she sashay-waddles closer in platform, high-top sneakers, coming to a stop with a slight pant of exertion.

'We made it.' She flips her hair back over one shoulder, her heaving chest on full display as she tucks her hand where her waist should be.

The 'we' she referred to must mean the shorter brunette beside her. A woman who, as she turns sideways to talk to Em, I realize is also pregnant. She doesn't seem as far along as the large-and-in-charge blonde, but it's hard to tell with her flowy, floral, ankle-length sundress.

That, and Em's amused smile, are all I register before my brain finally kicks into gear and I do the more mature thing and escape notice while I can.

But, just to make myself feel better, I itch my nose with my middle finger as I go.

* * *

Felix

As much as I'm dumbfounded by the pregnant duo before me, it doesn't stop me from noticing Anne turning to walk away in my peripheral.

And – I frown at her swishing ponytail – was she flipping me off?

Covering the microphone with my hand, I stand, drawing the attention of Amanda and Jack. 'I'll be right ba—'

'Audrey Cole!' Ron stands and circles around the table. 'I'm so glad you made it.'

'Oh.' Amanda turns back to the women. 'The writer's here.'

'See, I told you they were expecting us.' The blonde pregnant woman elbows the brunette.

While everyone is focused on the director greeting the author of *Countdown to Love*, Jack inches closer. 'What's wrong?'

I answer while keeping my eyes ahead and my smile in place. 'I saw Anne.'

'Here?' He isn't murmuring anymore.

Amanda turns to us. 'Everything okay?'

'Ah, I was just wondering who the newcomers are.' Jack nods at the two pregnant women who Ron is busy air-kissing.

'Oh.' Amanda points to the floral dress. 'That's the author of *Countdown to Love*.' She drops her hand, a bemused expression on her face. 'I'm not sure who the other woman is, though.'

Scanning the crowd for Anne, I catch the eye of the reporter from *Entertainment Daily* and force my gaze back to Ron and the pregnant duo. The last thing I need is for her to smell blood in the water on the first day of production.

There's a lull in the crowd's murmuring, allowing everyone to hear the writer introduce the woman beside her. 'This is my friend Rose.' She grimaces at Ron. 'The, uh, consultant I mentioned.'

'Hello.' Rose shakes Ron's outstretched hand with one arm and claps him on the back with the other.

It's the first time I've ever seen the veteran director startled.

Amanda rounds the table to walk over to them.

Jack motions for me to follow. 'Go greet the writer. I'll see if I can find your paparazzi Cinderella.'

I open my mouth to argue but Ron cuts me off.

'And this is our leading man, Felix Jones.'

I straighten under everyone's gaze and force my feet to move in the opposite direction they want to go. The direction Jack moves in.

I reach the group just as Amanda holds the blonde's hand under the overhead fluorescents. 'Great nail polish.'

Dragging my eyes away from Jack, I notice the gargantuan diamond on the pregnant woman's left ring finger before taking note of emerald glitter polish that perfectly matches her large, gemstone studs.

'See?' Rose throws the writer a satisfied look. 'I told you this polish wasn't too much.'

Audrey Cole rolls her eyes. 'I was talking about *you* being too much, not your nail polish.'

'Never mind that.' Em, seemingly popping out of nowhere, pinches the bridge of her nose and takes a visible, long, deep breath. Then, as if completely nonplussed, the PR manager straightens, her smile as blinding as her outfit.

She could teach young starlets a thing or two about image perception.

'Everyone—' Em's voice carried over the crowd '—this is Audrey Cole, the author of *Countdown to Love*.'

Fighting the urge to turn and follow Jack through the crowd, I hold out my hand like the good little Hollywood puppet I am. 'Pleasure, Ms Cole.' When she takes it, I hold hers in both of mine. 'I hope we do you and your book proud.'

'Damn.' Rose, next to Audrey Cole, gives me a long once-over that I'm pretty sure a married pregnant woman should not be giving men other than her husband.

I release the author's hand to offer my own to the blonde, but she steps back, both hands up as if in surrender.

'That's probably not wise.' Rose's sudden contrite look conflicts with the up-tilted corners of her mouth. 'I'm in a certain stage of my pregnancy that requires my husband's special attention at irregular, yet frequent times and —' she gives me a thorough assessment, one that makes me want to double-check that my fly isn't down '—now is definitely one of those times.' Then, pivoting on her platform sneakers, she hustle-waddles toward the building's exit, calling, 'Text me later.'

'I told you to be careful with that smile,' Amanda whispers next to me.

'She was already pregnant,' I mutter, pretending to follow the woman's exit from the building, while looking for a *different* blonde.

Audrey Cole smiles at everyone before pulling a folded fan from her purse. 'Nice to meet y'all.' She unfurls the fan – the same floral print as her dress – and flutters it, making the tendrils at her temples dance gently in its breeze. 'Audrey Cole is my pen name. Feel free to call me Trish.'

There's a pause from the press, like they're too stunned to attack. Normally, they'd jump on a new source, someone unused to choosing their answers with care to avoid having their words twisted later.

But perhaps as the new source of information is a pregnant woman who's seemingly acting out a scene from an eighteenth-century Georgian debutante ball in the middle of a state-of-the-art NASA training facility *after* her blonde counterpart strutted off on a mission to find her husband for sex, the press is too dumbfounded to pounce.

Even for Hollywood, it's a lot to take in.

***

Liz

'I can see you, you know.'

Sighing, I emerge from my hiding spot behind Iron Man. If Iron Man was white and gold robot with a NASA emblem on the center of his chest.

Peeking around the robot, I smile at Em, who, rather than smile back, is staring at my legs, clearly visible seeing as NASA's Iron Man is just a torso suspended from the ceiling by straps.

'I always sucked at hide and seek.'

The corner of Em's lips tilts up. 'And following directions?' She points at the red tape in front of her gold shoes. Red tape I clearly stepped over to reach my hiding spot.

My smile tightens. 'Uh, sorry?'

'Hmmm.' Em lifts one eyebrow.

She and my brother Thomas would get along like gangbusters.

Holding my bag close so as not to knock into anything, I move around the dissected Iron Man toward Em.

'The press junket is over, by the way.' Em watches my progress like a hawk. 'Has been for the past ten minutes.'

'Oh, ah, that's good.'

Em levels me a look that makes me stand up straight. 'Do I need to get involved?'

Playing dumb, I concentrate extra hard on stepping over the red tape. 'What do you mean?'

Shaking her head, Em turns, walking away from the robot and back toward the ISS mock-up. 'Your professor was looking for you.'

Despite my longer legs, I have to double-step to keep up with the petite PR manager. 'Oh, shoot, I—'

Em stops and I have to stutter-step to avoid crashing into her. 'And he told me about your problem.'

'Problem?' For a second, I think she means Felix Jones, before I remember that as my professor doesn't know, he couldn't tell her.

Em frowns. 'Your housing problem?'

'Oh, that.'

'Yes, that.' Her eyes narrow slightly as if trying to read my thoughts. Thankfully, she decides not to delve further and resumes walking. 'I found a place for you to stay nearby.'

Relief courses through me as I jog-step to catch up to her. 'You did?'

'Yes, but it comes with a price.'

'Oh.' I calculate the balance in my bank account and what I could save on hotel and car rental. 'How much?'

Em stops just outside the red tape laid out in front of the ISS mock-up where the director and my professor are talking.

Seeing me, my professor brightens. 'Liz...' His eyes widen at his mistake, probably mirroring mine. '...zzzANNE! There you are.' He waves me over. 'Come learn the first steps of storyboarding.'

I can feel Em's eyes burning a hole in the side of my face.

With an ebullience I do not feel, I smile and wave back. 'Be right there!' Keeping my smile in place, I look back at Em. 'Uh, you were saying about the cost of the place nearby?'

'Hmmm.' Her voice sounds as unimpressed as it did earlier, but her eyes seem to be holding back a smile. 'The cost is one sequined cat t-shirt.'

My surprised laugh bursts forth unexpectedly, echoing around the large building.

'Seriously?' I continue to chuckle, my amusement helping to release the long-held tension from the day. 'I'll get you ten t-shirts, if you want.'

At my surprised, genuine reaction, Em lets loose the smile. 'Just one will do.' She hands me a key connected to a cow keychain. '*Lizzanne*.'

7

FELIX

'I think you're starting to imagine things.' Jack pushes past me and into the five-star luxury hotel suite the studio provided that I've been calling home these past five days. 'Are you *sure* you saw your one-night stand at the press conference?'

For the hundredth time, I think back to the press junket day, clearly remembering Anne's blonde ponytail resting on the shoulder of her shiny, hairless cat t-shirt. 'Yes. She was definitely there.'

Jack, in shorts and a t-shirt rather than his usual power-suit, sits on one of the suite's chairs with a sigh. 'I have run through all the journalists invited to the event, scoured all crew contracts *and* double-checked with payroll and there is *no one* named Anne listed anywhere.'

For the past few days, I've remained holed up in the hotel, waiting. Waiting for the picture Anne took to fly through the tabloids. Waiting for Ron to release the film schedule so I can begin work. Waiting for Camilla Branson to spew more gossip that I'm unable to contradict.

I'm someone known for his action, I've had enough waiting.

Grabbing my key card off the coffee table, I mentally prepare myself to burn off my frustration in the hotel gym.

Jack, instead of standing to join, leans back his seat. 'There *was* an Anna*belle*.'

Surprised, the card falls from my fingers. 'And?'

'And unless you have a geriatric kink I am unaware of—' Jack smirks, looking a lot less LA and a lot more like the high school lacrosse player I remember from our lives pre-Hollywood '—I'm pretty sure Miss Bell, as the lovely sixty-eight-year-old catering chef goes by, is *not* our photo-taking culprit.'

Snagging the key card off the carpet, I flip Jack off with my other hand. Instantly, I'm reminded of Anne and her fuck-you nose scratch. 'She was there. I did not imagine it.'

'I believe you.' He sits forward. 'And we'll find her and take care of it, just like we'll take care of everything else. Just try and be patient.'

I scoff, and Jack joins me, both of us knowing that patience is not my strong suit.

Pushing off his knees, Jack stands with a groan. 'Go easy on me today, will you? I have to fly back to Los Angeles in a few hours and deal with those other problems.'

I pocket the key card, my body near vibrating from restless built-up energy. 'I make no promises.'

'Great. Thanks.' He grabs two water bottles from the mini fridge. 'Do me a favor?' He tosses me a bottle. 'No more women while I'm in LA.'

I press my hand over my heart. 'That, I can promise.'

Shaking his head, he moves past me, opening the heavy door. 'You better.' He checks to make sure the corridor is clear before waving me through. 'Your lawyers are busy enough as it is.'

I head toward the stairwell, wanting to avoid any potential interactions with fans in the elevator. 'What's the latest from them, anyway?'

'Not much, which is why I'm heading to LA.' His curse is masked by my hard shove of the stairwell door. 'I'm hoping to light a match under their asses by showing up in person.'

We both pad down the stairs in grim silence, our sneakers hitting the cement stairs at a fast clip.

Jack isn't going to like the workout that's rapidly developing in my head any better than any of the others I've tortured him with this week. With my main concern still unresolved, the fact that Anne remains unaccounted for has me wanting to go all out. Especially because, when I'm honest with myself, with every day the picture isn't published, my frustration stems more from wanting to simply talk to her again, rather than negotiate an NDA.

Disgusted with myself, I decide to sweat out my insanity with the Skills of Strength workout my trainer put me through for my airplane crash survivalist movie last year.

Jack will love that.

But when we open the door to the gym floor, all my sadistic workout plans go out the window, just like I wish I could, when I'm swarmed by a group of people.

'It's him!'

'Felix Jones!'

'Will you sign this?'

'Take my room key!'

'Did you really propose to Camilla?'

It's the last one that makes my blood boil. My eyes flash to Jack, who already has his phone out and is barking orders.

I do my best to smile as women snap pictures of me with their smart phones, one of whom I think is live streaming. By the time hotel security finally intervenes, I've signed multiple autographs, posed for various fan selfies and dodged a lot of uncomfortable questions about my supposed *fiancée*.

I may not have gotten my workout in, but by the time I'm back in my hotel room, I'm so exhausted by the ambush, I face plant on the bed.

Jack, still on the phone, continues issuing orders and asking questions for another twenty minutes before finally hanging up. 'I've got good news and bad news.'

I grunt in response.

'Bad news. Camilla Branson has spread rumors that you two are engaged.'

While I already guessed it from the fan's comment earlier, hearing Jack confirm that Camilla has started talking about me again feels like a punch to the gut.

'She didn't come out and say it herself, but she had one of her friends, that hotel heiress—' he stares at his phone, reading whatever's just been posted about me '—mention that she was in the market for a bridesmaid dress.' He scoffs. 'And when one of the reporters asked if it was for Camilla, she winked.'

Closing my eyes, I can see everything Jack just read play out. Probably at some stupid socialite function, or D-list celebrity outing, where those with money but lacking the fame they so desperately desire do and say anything to get noticed.

'Which,' Jack continues, as if I didn't already know, 'in Hollywood, is as good as a confirmation.'

This is why my lawyers are having trouble putting a gag order on Camilla. Besides the very first thing she asked for, she hasn't demanded or even publicly said or done anything that I can sue her for. She's been using her bevy of socialite friends to stir up trouble, all while holding personal information on me that she knows I don't want to see the light of day.

Forcing myself to roll over, I don't even twitch when a stem from one of my pillow's goose feathers jabs into my neck. 'Did you say you also had good news?'

Jack strides to the closet and pulls out my empty suitcase, tossing it on the bed next to me. 'I found you a better place to stay.'

* * *

Liz

Something bad is about to happen.

From my perch on the kitchen counter stool, I stare out over the morning sun glittering on the large expanse of water that my new condo overlooks with a sense of certain doom.

Too many good things have happened over the past few days since the press junket.

The place Em said I could stay? A large condo within walking distance of NASA.

My job as a storyboarder? Sit and draw all day. Alone.

The award-winning douchebag I was worried I'd run into? Haven't seen him.

Turns out storyboarders are part of pre-production. Our work is used to help the director and cast plan the set-up for each of the film's scenes. It's usually done ahead of the cast and crew showing up on location but since NASA only gave the studio permission to be on-site for a limited amount of time, some of the pre-production – like storyboarding – is happening in tandem with filming.

But not overlapping, thank God. Meaning I can continue to avoid the leading man.

I simply draw the set locations then turn them into my professor so he and Ron can plan camera angles and how the location visuals will interact with the script.

My phone buzzes with a notification telling me my grocery delivery is on its way. While I may not have a car, I have a phone, and it turns out that in Texas, you can have your groceries sans delivery fee. Meaning I've been able to supplement my catering table gorging without breaking the bank.

I should be happy in my twelfth-floor condo after a night of restful sleep on a bed that inclines, declines and adjusts firmness based on a person's weight while drinking fresh coffee and eating an apple rather than a dense catering muffin. Instead...

'Something's definitely going to happen,' I mutter, placing my phone back on the counter and watching sailboats and seagulls drift across the lake through the large living room window.

Even though I've been called a hippie quite a few times in my life, mostly by my asshole non-father, I've never believed in manifesting things with my thoughts until, not ten minutes after I voiced my certainty that things were going to take a turn for the worse, the doorbell rings.

'Fuck a duck.'

Sighing, I stare at the door, hoping that somehow my grocery delivery came early, while mentally preparing myself for an eviction notice or a pink slip – either or both delivered by some Hollywood gofer sent by Johnny Douchebag Felix Jones.

And yet, at no time before or after my Birkenstocks hit the wood floor and shuffled over to the door, did I manifest a man dressed like a city slicker off to the Hamptons – leather boat shoes, seersucker shorts and a white linen dress shirt – with a cat strapped to his chest.

'Chase?' I blink at my brother, confused by his presence and the beige lump under his chin. 'Mikey?'

'Hello, Lizzie.' His frosty tone makes me pause.

Pushing his Wayfarers up over his forehead, Chase struts into the condo looking like he's about to catch a ride on one of the sailboats outside my window.

'It's nice to know you're alive.' He holds Mikey to his chest with one hand while unhooking the baby carrier from around his waist, sliding it off him and the cat. It's a complicated maneuver that he makes look effortless thanks to how often he's done it.

'Uh, yeah.' Closing the door, I step toward him, wary of my brother's stiff demeanor. Chase has always been the fun brother. The one up for a joke or a laugh. The one always on my side, even if I'm on the other side of right.

It's usually Thomas I have to look out for.

I shift closer. 'Was there any doubt?'

Dropping the baby carrier on the floor, Chase slips something out of his back pocket before settling into the oversized reading chair in the condo's open-plan living room.

Chase crosses one leg, resting his ankle on the opposite knee, Mike, in all his hairless cat glory, perched on his lap.

I should've worn my flip-sequined t-shirt to match.

'You tell me?' He raises the hand holding the paper.

Slowly, I make my way over to the chair and take the folded document. The words *urgent care* catching my eye when I open it.

Fuck a fucking duck.

'Imagine my surprise when *that*—' Chase points to the insurance bill in my hand '—came in the mail.'

'What are you doing going through mom's mail?' Living in student housing before heading to Texas, any mail I get, from insurance or otherwise, gets sent to the Moore family residence in Manhattan – the 15,000 square foot mansion near Central Park I grew up in.

'Really.' Chase angles his chin down, his eyes boring into me. '*That's* what you want to go with?'

Sighing, I give in. Sort of. 'I ah, ate something that didn't agree with me.' Not technically a lie. 'I'm fine, really.'

He runs a hand down Mike's back, the saggy skin sliding over the feline's bones. 'A call would've been nice.'

I read over the medical insurance charge notice, thankful that it doesn't say what I was actually treated for. 'How did you know where I was?' While the urgent care's address is listed, it doesn't explain how he found me *here*.

'I could've called you, I guess,' Chase goes on, ignoring my questions. 'But would you have answered?'

I decide to circle back to my questions later, as it's becoming more and more apparent that not only was Chase seriously worried, but now, after seeing me hale and hearty with his own eyes, I'm very much on my brother's shit list.

Which I've never been on before.

In fact, with how happy-go-lucky and laid-back Chase always appears, it's surprising he even has one.

I scuff my sandal across the area rug. 'I would've answered.' Probably. At least by the third or fourth try. But as my brother's laugh lines are nowhere to be seen, I keep that to myself.

It's the silence that gets me. Chase and I are never silent. We tease each other. We laugh. We divert the other's attention from whatever gets them down. We spent our lives banded together, us against our father.

'Hey.' I nudge his boat shoe with my Birkenstock. 'Sorry.'

The cat breaks first.

'Meow.' Mike lifts one paw, asking to be paid attention too.

'Aw, you missed Aunt Lizzie, didn't you.' I bend over, scratching under Mike's chin. 'Yes, you did. You missed me, you little cunt.'

'Jesus.' Chase rolls his eyes, exactly the reaction I was going for. 'You can't say that.' Though his eyes crinkle while doing it. 'And especially not in baby talk.'

I add another hand, scratching behind Mike's ears. 'Why not?'

'It's crude.'

'So is your cat.'

We share a smile, and I know I'm forgiven.

'Here.' He grabs Mike around his ribcage with both hands and lifts him to me, the cat's back legs and private bits dangling. 'Take him.'

As I have a million times before, I reach for Mike, and, feeling like I'm holding a butterball turkey, I cradle him to my chest. For a cat that looks like skin and bones, Mike's rather dense.

'Now.' Chase leans back. 'Tell me about storyboarding.'

'Ah.' I nuzzle my nose against Mike's before sitting on the couch opposite my brother. 'My professor was the weak link.'

'Yes, well, go easy on him.' Chase spreads his arms across the back of the chair. 'He wasn't going to tell me where you were staying until I mentioned the urgent care thing and then suddenly, he was a flood of information and apologies.' Chase's brow pinches together. 'Something about a housing mix-up and car rental?'

Not meeting his eyes, I wave away his question. 'There was a bit of an issue, but it's been taken care of.' *Luckily*, I'd add, if I didn't think it would worry him. 'As you can see.' I gesture to the condo's floor-to-ceiling windows overlooking Clear Lake.

We spend the next twenty minutes catching up. Me telling him about my storyboard internship and my time at NASA, him bringing me up to speed on Moore's department store and regaling me with stories of our previously dour older brother Thomas whose now firmly wrapped around the little finger of a princess-loving nine-year-old.

'I wish I could see that.'

'Oh, you will.'

'I will?'

'Yep.' Chase lowers his foot and stands. 'I'm just a scout.'

I tilt my head, and Mike mirrors it. 'What do you mean?'

'What do you think I mean?'

I follow his movements as he picks up the cat carrier off the floor and drapes it over the arm of the chair, trying to put the pieces together.

But it isn't until he raises one eyebrow, looking very much like our older brother, that I figure it out.

I swivel on the couch toward the door. 'Thomas is here?'

'No, not yet.' Chase scoops up Mike from my lap, the cat unhelpfully limp. 'But he and the rest of the family will be.'

'Why?'

'Thomas gave you a year to "find yourself".' He adjusts Mike in one hand to air quote with the other. 'Honestly, I'm surprised he gave you that.' He shakes his head with a laugh. 'I'm surprised that *I* gave you that.' He turns Mikey's back into his chest. 'I know you wanted time to come to terms with everything that's happened but *time's up*, Lizzie.' He emphasizes his words by jabbing Mike's paw toward me.

There's an ominous rumble coming from the cat. Mike *hates* being used as a puppet. Something Chase is very much aware of but doesn't care.

No wonder he prefers Bell.

I refocus on my brother. 'When is he coming?'

He shrugs. 'I'm not sure.'

'Chase…' I sound alarmingly like our mother.

'I wouldn't want to spoil the surprise.' He lowers an unhappy Mike back to the floor. 'And as much fun as this last-minute day trip to Houston has been, I better get going.' He gestures for me to stand. 'I have a wife to get back to and a company to run.'

Once I'm on my feet, Chase engulfs me in a big hug. 'But if you're good,' he whispers, 'I might be willing to give you a heads up on the family's ETA.'

He steps back, petting my head like I'm a toddler.

I dodge him with a laugh. 'Uh huh, sure.' I learned my sarcasm from him.

It isn't until he's at the door that I notice what he's left behind. 'Um, aren't you forgetting something?'

When he turns, I point to Mike.

'Nope.' Chase smooths down the front of his cat-carrier free shirt. 'He's all yours.'

All the good feelings from seeing my brother leave. 'You're kidding me, right?'

He smiles wider.

I hustle over and heft Mike into my arm. 'You can't leave Mike here. This isn't my place. They probably don't even allow pets.'

'Actually, according to a woman named Emily, who your professor had a lovely chat with on my behalf, as long as it isn't another cow or a goat, she doesn't care what or who you bring into the condo.'

I frown, wondering if someone really tried to bring in a cow into the building.

But when Chase reaches for the doorknob, I quickly shake off the thought.

'Bell will kill you if you come home without Mikey.' Marching over to him, I thrust the cat in his direction and go for the jugular. 'She loves this cat more than you.'

I know I've hit a nerve when his eye twitches.

But instead of taking the bait, *or* the cat, Chase tucks his hands into his shorts' pockets. 'Which is exactly why I'm leaving him here.' He rocks back on the heels of his loafers. 'A little couple-time with my wife wouldn't be amiss.'

I glare and he smiles wider.

'But if you don't want Bell to worry and fly down here early, you better get better at communicating.' He sighs as if *he's* the one being put out. 'Because if Bell comes, then I'll come, and of course Thomas will want to come and the next thing you know, we'll *all* be here.' He tilts his chin down, catching my eyes with his. 'Interrupting whatever it is that you think you need to do all by yourself.'

I open my mouth to curse at my instigating brother, but Mike claws the air, not liking being held aloft. Curling him into my chest, I'm not hating how his saggy skin is warm against mine.

'Oh.' Chase, looking rather joyful at the turn of events, snaps his fingers. 'Almost forgot.' He walks back over to the baby carrier and slips something out of one of its pockets. 'Here.'

I lower Mike to the floor and take yet another folded piece of paper from my brother. This one a—

'Emotional Support Animal Certificate?' I blink at the professional, *notarized* certificate.

'Yeah, so you can take Mikey to work.'

'Wha—' I look at Mike, who's returned to basking in the sunlight and licking his balls, then down at the paper in my hands. 'I can't take him to work.'

'Yep, you can.' Chase looks positively gleeful. 'Just another thing your professor took care of in the name of apologizing for the housing mix-up.'

Chase flutters his lashes, looking about as innocent as kid with his hand in the cookie jar. 'You know how Mikey gets when left alone.'

'But I—'

Chase leans in and gives me a quick peck on the cheek. 'Love you, Lizzie.'

And then he's gone.

Leaving me with Mike Hunt.

8

FELIX

'There's a twenty-four-hour doorman and underground parking.' Jack stabs at the elevator button and glances at his watch.

After escaping through the hotel's service entrance to avoid any of the fans who had either snuck in or checked-in to the hotel to meet me, Jack had the limo take us back into the NASA area, where, in the midst of parks, neighborhoods and small commercial buildings, stood a thirteen-floor condo high-rise built on the shore of Clear Lake, looking like the answer to one of those 'what doesn't belong' puzzles.

'With Amanda still at the hotel, along with its ineffectual security, everyone will still think you're in Houston.' Jack fidgets in his sneakers, probably unused to being caught in public in anything less than a power tie. 'We're taking a gamble, but I'm pretty sure the press and your fans won't find you here.' He reaches out and tugs down the brim of my ball cap. 'But keep your head down just in case.'

Blinded, as he's lowered the brim over my eyes, I lift it back up. 'You're going to miss your flight.' I don't touch on the gamble we're taking.

I've been lucky thus far in my career that security's only been needed for events or crowd control. I've never felt threatened or unsafe in my own home or on location as long as I kept my head down. But today's ambush was different. With Camilla ramping up her lies about our relationship, and me not being able to publicly deny or confirm them, the fans and paparazzi are more rabid for my attention than usual.

Jack pulls out his phone, checking his Candy Crush score. He wanted to hire a bodyguard at the least, but I thought that would be like pointing a neon arrow to my location.

'I'll be fine.'

The elevator door dings.

Jack scoffs, the sound full of both sarcasm and rebuke, neither of which I can take offense to considering the latest turn of events.

'Seriously.' Dropping my hands on his shoulders, I lean in so we're eye to eye. 'Get out of here.'

'Fine.' He shrugs out from under my hands. 'I'll go once you're in the elevator.'

'Yes, Mother.'

We both pause at my inadvertent reminder as to why it's so important for him to get back to LA. Especially now that Camilla's lies have escalated rather than stopped as I hoped and she promised.

He plays the moment off by rolling his eyes, but Jack still waits until I'm inside the elevator and waving him goodbye before pocketing his phone and turning to leave.

As the floor numbers climb, I pull out my own phone to check the date.

Mom's scheduled to call tomorrow. And when she calls, I need to make sure she doesn't clue in to what's been going on.

I'm not sure if it's a Portuguese thing, or a woman thing, but Sofia Maria Santos-Jones has a hefty amount of determination and pride. The combination is both a strength and weakness. They helped her prove the naysayers wrong when, after Dad died, no one thought the daughter of Portuguese immigrants who spoke English as her second language would be able to raise a son on her own. But it is also why she has lived her life never asking for handouts or help, even when she really needed it.

And then, after years of sacrifices and support on her part, when it should've been my turn to take care of her, I failed.

Never again. I've got three weeks until she's scheduled to finish treatment at the exclusive facility I checked her into. Three weeks to make sure my mother comes home to nothing but rest and relaxation rather than drama and gossip.

I do the California to Texas time change in my head and double-check the shooting schedule on my phone, making sure I'll be available when she calls. Satisfied that I will be, I pocket my phone and pull out the key our recent astronaut escort Vance Bodaway had left for us with the concierge.

The elevator doors open, and I step out into a soft gray hallway lined every twenty feet or so with doors. I follow it down until it starts to curve, finding the condo number Jack gave me. Jack did some quick-thinking by calling Vance while I signed autographs for the trespassing fans. We lucked out that Vance had a friend in outer space with a vacant condo near NASA I could use.

Opening the condo door, I'm pleasantly surprised by the large, open-concept space. Floor-to-ceiling windows to my left where the living room is, a wall of cabinets to my right with a decent-sized island and counter stools make up the kitchen, and beyond that, a hallway that must lead to the bedrooms.

Catching sight of the lake view, I drop my bag by the door and head over to the window.

Focused on the stream of sunshine hitting my face, I don't notice the obstacle underfoot until it's too late. Foot caught under the surprisingly hefty weight of a beige sack, I stumble forward, my curse drowned out by an ear-piercing yowl, followed by the thud of my palms and face smacking against the window. There's only a second's pause before gravity wins and my face squeak-slides downward against the glass, stopping only when my ass hits the floor.

Caralho.

I'm not sure how much time passes as I lay there, eyes closed, body motionless and crumbled against the warm glass, but however long it would've taken to process what the hell just happened is cut short when something soft, wet and rough, drags against the side of my face *not* radiating in pain.

And when I finally open my eyes to see what new hell has found me, I'm met with the shriveled, shrunken face of the diablo himself.

Someone screams.

Sadly, it's me.

* * *

Liz

I lift my shopping bag laden arm and hit the button again, hoping the repeated action will magically make the service elevator move faster.

Ten minutes after Chase left, I was still standing there dumbfounded by the turn of events when the grocery delivery notification came, which I decided to collect myself as, directly after, the concierge called asking me to sign a pet waiver.

Too busy wondering when my previously lackadaisical brother started paying attention to details, I did something that anyone who has ever spent any time with my brother's pet knows not to do.

I left him alone in my apartment.

It wasn't until I scrawled my name on a document that made me liable for any damages that might occur due to said pet that my mistake hit me.

It's been a year since Mikey and I went on regularly scheduled outings to Central Park and I left behind the Best Cat Aunt mug Chase gave me for Christmas.

And while any normal cat would simply associate my smell with happy times and be content, in the 360 plus days that I have been absent from Mike's carefree and ball-licking life, I forgot one crucial thing – Mike is *not* a normal cat.

So while I left him basking in the sunlight like a nudist at the beach to decompress after his flight and abandonment by his owner, Mikey was more than likely thinking up various forms of retaliation for my long absence.

The elevator dings my floor's arrival, and I nearly dislocate my shoulders as I lumber out and down the hall toward my door. Concierge offered to get me a trolley, but I'd been too worried about the unattended, vindictive feline to wait.

And it's because of that unattended, vindictive feline that I'm not surprised when my struggle to open the door is rewarded with a high-pitched scream.

What *is* a surprise is that it's not mine.

The door bangs open just as the scream begins to wane and my eyes land on a man crumpled on the floor by the window staring at Mike Hunt.

The baseball cap the man's wearing hides most of his face, but what I do see of his mouth – slack-jawed and still emitting a low-pitched whine – tells me he's more scared to be in the condo than I am to find him there.

'Who…?' My groceries land on the floor with a cascading thud. My arms have a second's relief, followed by the sharp tingle of pins and needles as circulation restarts. But all that fades when my brain registers just who the baseball-cap-wearing intruder is. '*You.*' All the violent tendencies I surprised at the press junket come flaring back to life.

The Hollywood actor double-takes when he sees me, recognition replacing terror. Then his eyes, before large and round on Mike, narrow on me. '*You.*'

Meanwhile, Mikey, sits politely in front of my unfortunate one-night stand. The cat glances over his bare shoulder at me then back at the man in front of him as if awaiting introductions.

Eyes back on Mike, Felix struggles to his feet.

I clear my throat, trying for a less bewildered and more authoritative tone. It's annoying how I have to repress the thought of how good he looks in workout shorts and a t-shirt in order to do it. *Think of the urgent care bill.* 'Why are you here?'

Not looking at me, Felix carefully sidesteps the cat. At what he must feel is a safe enough distance, he locks eyes with me. 'Isn't that my line?'

'No.' I do my own maneuvering, abandoning my groceries and circling the island until I reach my phone that I left on the counter. 'This is my place.'

Please leave. Please leave. Please leave.

I don't know why he is here, but if I can manifest my brother and his hairless cat, maybe I can manifest Felix Jones out of my condo.

'What do you mean this is your place? I was…' He stops, shaking his head. 'Wait, never mind that.' He points at the phone in my hand. 'I want that picture.'

'What picture?'

A blend of annoyance and skepticism fill his gaze. 'You know what picture.'

I scoff. 'No, I don't.' Cursing my manifestation powers that seem to only work for evil, I slide my phone open, wondering if concierge can help me deal with a rogue Hollywood douchebag or if I'm going to have to call the police. I'd really rather not because once the police are involved...

Oh my God. The *police*.

I jerk my eyes up to his, realization dawning. I *do* know what picture he's talking about.

I can tell the moment he knows that I know. He folds his arms across his chest, his smile turning to a dark smirk. With his hair tousled, his gleaming brown eyes and his biceps bulging as they shift across his chest, he looks every bit the smoldering, sexy leading man that Google told me he was at the press junket.

And yet it's the memory of him curled up in the fetal position with a look of horror and pain on his mangy, bearded face as he holds his damaged junk that comes to mind. The memory I immortalized with my phone's camera before I left the hotel room that night.

I stifle a giggle, not wanting to poke the bull, as it were.

Even so, Felix's eye narrow as I fake-cough.

Mike, with his usual epic timing, chooses this precise moment to break wind. Audibly.

In seconds, *People* magazine's Sexiest Man Alive winner's normally handsome facial features are contorted into an expression of such contempt and revulsion, it's near savage. And almost identical to the face he makes when kneed in the nuts.

I give up and laugh.

* * *

Felix

My fists clench as the recent object of my desire and torment laughing at my expense.

Like, *really* laughs.

Head back, neck exposed, her spontaneous laugh echoes around us, just like it did at the bar.

And much to my annoyance, just like at the bar, my lower half reacts.

I almost bought her confusion. The knit of her eyebrows, the slight tilt to her head. All of it had me second-guessing if there even was a photograph. That maybe my nut-pain had somehow skewed my memory and that what I should really be focused on is finding out why Anne is in the condo Jack set up for me in the first place. And with her brother's cat no less.

My nose wrinkles at the smell emanating from said cat. Anne may have regaled me with hilarious stories, but no imagination, even an actor trained in improv, could do the real animal justice.

I didn't tell Anne that I have a slight... *aversion* to cats because it didn't seem relevant at the time. Mike Hunt was an abstract figure, an idea, not something tangible and flatulent that would one day be within clawing distance.

Slowly, too slowly, Anne's amusement fades. '*That's* why you're here? The picture?' She shakes her head. 'Isn't breaking and entering beneath you? I thought Hollywood stars had underlings for this sort of thing.'

'I didn't break in.' I reach into my pocket, pulling out what the concierge gave Jack and me. 'I have a key.' I dangle it between us.

Wrong move. Mike's shoulders drop, as if ready to pounce. Remembering what Anne said about his obsession with shiny objects, I toss the key a safe distance – across the kitchen and down the hall.

Mike scrambles after it.

Anne follows the cat, turning back to me, frowning. 'Why do you have a key?'

'Why did you take that picture?' I counter, feeling safer now that the cat is out of sight.

She giggles again. While I'm happy to bring the conversation back to my number-one priority, her continued amusement isn't helping my Portuguese temper.

Fueled more by embarrassment than any sense of justice, my tone hardens along with my body. 'I don't know what kind of deal you were hoping to make but I'm telling you right now, it won't be enough to cover the lawsuit I'll bring your way if you try and sell it.'

Her head jerks back, cutting her laugh short. I have a fleeting moment of satisfaction, until disdain colors her features.

She stalks toward me, looking far more threatening than the pouncing cat. When she's a foot away, I drop my hands in front of me, bracing for impact and trying to ignore the enchanting smattering of freckles visible on her flushed cheeks.

Instead of her knee, she lifts her hand, her index pointed at my sternum. 'Listen, *Johnny*.'

I flinch as her finger jabs forward, just shy of contact, while a wave of heat washes over me at the mention of my impromptu alias.

'If anyone should sue someone, it should be *me*—' she points back to herself before jabbing it once more at me '—suing *you*.'

This time, she makes contact, but I'm too afraid to move my hands from ball-protection duty. The sharp pain helps me cull the unhelpful buzz of attraction radiating from her touch.

Jesus, *sou patético*.

Rolling her eyes at what I can only guess is my rather comical expression, she crosses her arms. 'I only took that picture as evidence, in case I died, and the police needed a clue as to who killed me.'

Huh. I repeat what she just said in my head, letting it sink in.

As overly dramatic as her reasoning sounds, it also sounds valid. Which I hate. Because it makes my pent-up anger and judgement seem petty and unwarranted in the face of, well, her numbed face. 'Ah.'

'Yeah,' she scoffs, 'ah.'

'But...' I replay the last time I saw her. 'Why were you at NASA? Why did you run?'

'I was at work.' She shifts back on one foot. 'Same as you.'

'Jack checked the crew contracts.' I find her relaxed posture and flat expression more provoking than convincing. 'You weren't listed.'

Anne's stance doesn't change, nor her expression. 'I'm not crew.'

My head hurts. And my chest. Noting the face smears on the window, my pride is also pretty banged up.

Closing my eyes, I try and reset like I do when someone accidentally breaks character or the director wants to re-shoot a scene. Or when a girl has thrown me for so many loops at a time when I'm already playing tabloid gymnastics that I find myself too exhausted to jump anymore.

Unfortunately, when I reopen them, I'm still the same confused man I was seconds ago standing in front of a pissed-off woman with a penchant for nut maiming.

Risking said nuts, I raise my hand to pinch the bridge of my nose. 'Will you please explain?'

Her eyebrows shoot up, her shock at my sudden shift to politeness making me feel every inch the asshole Anne must think me.

'Fine.' Heaving a long sigh, she moves over toward the window and picks up Mike Hunt, who's returned with the key. 'I'm a storyboarder.'

I take a moment to appreciate the sunlight behind her casting a halo around her blonde hair, the vision marred by the odd-looking feline cradled against her chest, before refocusing. 'But you said you weren't—'

She holds up a hand, Mike listing to one side. 'Part of the crew. I know.' Her hand slides back under the cat, securing him to her. 'I'm not. I'm an intern. I work for my professor, David Morales, *not* the studio.'

I'm distracted by the folds of skin overlapping and moving against each other as the cat leans into her caress, its body relaxing. I'd be jealous if I wasn't too busy being creeped by his eyes, which remain fixed on me.

Unconcerned or unaware of my unease, Anne continues explaining. 'And I ran at the press junket because the guy I kneed in the nuts turned out to be a movie star who may or may not take out his anger on me by getting me fired.'

'I wouldn't—'

'What? Have me fired?' She snorts and lowers the cat back onto the carpeted patch of sunlight. 'And I'm supposed to know that after I was, one, catfished, two, poisoned and three—' she lifts a finger at each listing of my crimes '—barricaded in a hotel room when I attempted to leave to seek medical attention?'

I want to argue the poisoned comment, but wisely keep my mouth shut.

She flutters her lashes, her smile patronizing. 'It's a mystery how you've only won two People's Choice Awards.'

I could drown in the sarcasm dripping from her voice. And I have a feeling she wouldn't lend me a hand, or finger, to help if I did.

'You're right.' I hold my hands out between us like I've seen trainers do on set with wild animals. It's both for Anne and the cat. 'I'm sorry.'

Anne's detached, condescending expression flickers at my sincerity.

'Honest, I am.' All the tension I'd been feeling seems to leave me in one fell swoosh as I say the words I should've said from the start. And even though the cat is shifting uncomfortably closer, I make sure to maintain eye contact as I continue. 'It is not an excuse, but please know that being—' I flash her a small smile '—*Felix Jones*, can sometimes be difficult.'

Her lips twitch in an upward direction, helping me go on.

'I would like as much as possible to keep my personal life private. And when I thought you might...' I gesture wildly with my hand, unsure of how to phrase my concerns.

'Make it publicly known that the world's sexiest man suffers from erectile dysfunction?' Anne blinks innocently, smiling at the supposedly helpful suggestion.

'I don't—' I close my eyes and take a breath, deciding to fight that battle another day. 'Yeah, sure. That.'

The corners of her blue eyes crinkle. 'Honestly, I'd forgotten that I even took that picture.' She grabs her phone and slides the screen open. 'Here.' She leans in, showing me the screen.

Opening her photos, she taps on one, enlarging the picture of me frozen in pain on the hotel-room floor. Immediately, a thousand memes run through my head all featuring my face contorted in surprised pain.

'Damn.' I lean back, the image almost too painful to look at. 'You got me good.'

Catching each other's eyes, we share a smile. This one genuine. And slightly heated.

'Yeah, well.' Anne breaks away with a roll of her eyes. 'You were a dick.' With one more tap, she deletes the photo.

I *feel* like a dick for having imagined the worst of her, especially with how quick she is to delete it. I'd blame Camilla Branson for warping my sense of judgement, but that would be a cop-out.

I let my own anxieties guide my actions instead of doing what I usually strive to do. What my mother always taught me – *ser um cavalheiro*. Be a gentleman.

Which is kind of hard to do at the moment as my dick, probably in an attempt to save face after being unjustly shamed, has mistaken our verbal sparring as foreplay and wants to tag in.

'Okay.' Anne sets her phone back on the counter. 'Problem solved.' She waves me toward the door, unaware of the other problem happening behind the thin fabric of my exercise shorts. 'You can go now.'

I glance back at the door but don't move, my mind working furiously to figure out how best to broach our new, and more complicated, problem.

'Yo.' Anne's eyes narrow suspiciously. 'Why aren't you leaving?'

'Well…' Deciding it's best *not* to tell the woman who thinks I have erectile dysfunction that the most *prominent* reason for me being unable to leave is the cockstand I'm currently sporting behind my shorts, I inch closer to the island.

'Felix?'

There's a warning in her voice. One I'd really like to heed, but being without Jack, security or a mode of transportation, my smile stiffens as I brace for her reaction to the real reason why I'm standing before her Mike Hunt. 'So, the thing is…'

9

LIZ

'And *that's* when you walked in on me and Mike Hunt.'

It's a shame my brother isn't here to witness the fruits of his pet-naming efforts in action.

As it is, I need to hunch over the cutting board to hide how much that sentence, spoken in all seriousness from a man who just related today's absurd, snowball list of events that culminated with him screaming in the face of a hairless cat, amuses me.

Amuses me *and* confuses me. First, what kind of five-star hotel has such weak security? I've stayed in enough to know that things like that don't just happen. One or two fans, maybe. But a mob, lying in wait at the exact moment Felix went to the hotel gym? That smacks of outside interference.

Then there is the whole two-key situation. Maybe my New York City upbringing makes me more paranoid than most, but who gives away not one, but two sets of keys to their condo?

I'd call Em and ask if, one, I wasn't afraid she'd ask me to leave to make way for the more important Hollywood star in need of a crash pad, and two, I wasn't so preoccupied with the true surprise of the day—Felix Jones is cooking dinner.

Granted, I'm positive he only started cooking to distract me from kicking him out of the condo that *I* squatted in first, but still, as someone who is very much kitchen-averse, I appreciate his effort.

Putting the lid on a pot, he turns to me, his palm resting on the counter, his forearm muscles tensing from his weight. 'Since *I* can't go to a hotel, what if I paid for you and the cat to stay in the best, most luxurious hotel around?' Felix's large, brown eyes probe mine, as if looking for a trace of sympathy he can cling to.

Steeling myself against his heavy charm, I focus on the one kitchen task he gave me and press down on the knife, pushing the blade into the parsley. 'I mean—' I push harder when my first attempt to fails to cut '—what kind of blockbuster movie star can't book his own hotel room?'

'It's not about *ability*, it's about needing to maintain a low profile and...' Felix trails off as I lean my weight into the next press, the parsley looking more bruised than chopped. 'What are you doing?'

'Cutting the parsley?' Even I know to make that a question and not a statement.

He closes his eyes briefly, as if shoring up patience, before gently relieving me of the knife and using it to point to the stool on the other side of the island. 'Sit.'

I gladly acquiesce, moving a safe distance from both his forearm muscles and sharp objects, content to watch the movie star I was unable to kick to the literal curb mince the dented parsley in seconds, then move on to do that cool flip-stir thing with the frying pan.

If you had told me earlier that I'd find the guy I previously knew as Johnny douchebag disturbingly sexy as he moves around barefoot in my kitchen, I would've thought you certifiable.

I frown at Mike gazing at Felix with hearts in his beady blue eyes.

And yet here we are.

Felix's hair is sticking up at odd angles, a result of continually running his hands through it during his lengthy explanation. The resulting style makes him look more like John from the bar than Felix the movie star.

He throws me a smile over his shoulder that I'm sure causes rational women to throw panties at him. 'Room service, spa treatments, the works. On me.'

Thankfully, I've grown impervious to forced, exaggerated charm. One perk of my upbringing surrounded by people who have everything but still want something. 'No.'

His expression falls, and I'm annoyed to find his moue of disappointment much sexier than his mega-watt smile. 'Why not?'

Distracting myself, I grab Mikey from the floor as he readies to make another pounce towards Felix. I'm rewarded with a growl that sounds more human-sigh-like than I want to contemplate. 'Because *this* sweet boy—' I run my nose against Mike's as way of an apology '—still has PTSD from the last hotel suite he stayed in.' Not to mention the various payouts my brother had to make to some unfortunate Las Vegas male strippers. 'But mainly—' I level my bad-penny one-night stand a look I hope imbues imperviousness to bribery '—I 100 per cent don't want your money.'

Felix drops his forearms on the island, leaning in close across the counter. It's a move out of a movie I'm sure he's played the lead role in. It makes his biceps bulge, his shoulders look broader, and it brings me closer to the face which I'm sure could sell underwear just as well as his abs. 'Then what *do* you want?'

I know this move too. It's the move of someone who still wants something and is trying to feel out how far they'll need to go to get it. And while the move usually works, especially when practiced by someone as attractive as Felix Jones, it makes me realize just how much of the upper hand I have. Even without the photograph I deleted.

I lean forward, dragging my tongue across my lips, smirking when his eyes hone in on the movement. 'I want you...'

His Adam's apple bobs with a hard swallow.

'...out of my condo.'

It takes a second, but the joke lands.

His body visible deflates. 'Ha ha, very funny.'

I can't help but chuckle.

Mike stretches out a paw in Felix's direction. 'Meow.'

Felix jerks away, turning back toward the stove.

Mike slumps forward, resting his head on his paws on the counter.

'I don't get it.' I scratch behind Mike's flattened ears.

Felix doesn't pause in cooking. 'What?'

'Mike usually *hates* men.' My whole family knows that while Mike may tolerate men (including his owner, my brother), he is team girl all the way. Especially now that Bell, Alice and Mary are in his life.

Felix lowers the pan back on the burner, muttering. 'I wish he wasn't so fond of me.'

'You didn't seem so averse to cats when you laughed yourself to tears when I was relating Mike's antics at the bar.'

He glances back at Mike, whose head perks up at the attention. 'You wanna tell me cat stories or show me funny cat videos, sure, I'll laugh all day.' After holding Mike's gaze for a beat, he returns to the cooktop with a shiver. 'But being near a cat, or a part of those stories? No thank you.'

'So, it's not just that Mike's a little—' I cover Mike's ears '—unattractive? It's all cats?'

Mike shakes me off and glares at me, prompting me to give him extra belly rubs to prevent retaliation.

'I was mauled once.' Felix's t-shirt tightens, as if just recalling it has him stiffening. 'Never really got over it, I guess.'

'You were *mauled*?' Horrific images from long-ago watched episodes of *Animal Planet* run through my head. 'On a film set? By, like, a tiger or something?'

'No. This was before I started acting, when I was a kid.'

I frown, trying to make the pieces fit. From the little I've read, I know he was born and raised in California. 'Then where did you come across a wild animal?'

He stirs the pot with wide, slow circles. 'It was my neighbors' pet.'

'Your neighbor had a wild animal?' I know the ongoing stereotype is of west coasters being eccentric, but zoo animals as pets? Really?

Hunching over the pot more, he mumbles something that sounds like, 'Tabby.'

I lean closer, squishing Mike to my chest. 'I'm sorry, what?'

He sighs, as if resigning himself to the inevitable.

I'm about to apologize, not wanting him to share something if it brings up bad memories when he says, 'It was a *tabby* cat.'

I win the Herculean effort of not laughing in the silence that follows.

However, I must not do a good job with my facial expression, because when he turns to gauge my reaction, his body stiffens once more.

'It was a *large* tabby cat, okay?' He holds his arms out as wide as they'll stretch. 'The name doesn't do it justice. It was a mutant, I tell you.'

I fight the laughter. I fight it *really* hard. But when Mike makes one more attempt to reach out his paw toward Felix and the tough action star's feet come up off the kitchen floor, I lose. Badly.

So badly, I don't even realize it when Mike jumps off my lap, making a beeline to Felix.

I'm surprised when no one in the building reports hearing a woman being attacked in our condo.

* * *

Felix

Cracking two eggs in a small bowl, I pick up a fork and point it at the beast now strapped against Anne's chest. 'Thanks for confining the beast.'

'Thanks for dinner.' Anne's lips roll in before nodding at the bowls on the island. 'And thanks for making dessert.'

The cat sighs.

I beat the eggs, trying not to think about how Mike was finally able to rub his weirdly soft, hairless body against me, or how un-insulted I was when Anne laughed at my subsequent high-pitched cry.

Somehow between her laughing at the picture she took of me and her laughing at my tabby-cat confession, my ego has decided it's fine with being the butt of the joke as long as it's Anne doing the laughing.

Looking away from what I can only describe as the Benjamin Button-like cat in a baby carrier, I pour the eggs into the batter. 'I have a bit of a sweet tooth, anyway.'

'Yeah, but aren't you like Mr Action Hero?' The corners of her mouth kick up. 'You can't fight bad guys and save the damsel if you've got a cookie belly.'

I know she's simply waiting for Jack to land so I can call him and figure a way out of her condo, but I can't help but enjoy this time with her. I mean, now that I know she isn't a stalking paparazzi. 'I thought you didn't know anything about me?'

'I don't, not really.' She drops her chin over Mike's head, but not fast enough to hide the flush in her cheeks that makes my bruised ego heal. 'But the people at work seem to.'

And there go all the good feelings.

She must read something in my expression because she's quick to rush on. 'Not that I've heard much.' She shrugs, the movement shifting Mike's wrinkled skin. 'Storyboarders work alone. What I do know is from a quick search of your movies and a few things I overheard at the press junket.' She laughs, the sound easing my nerves more than all of Jack's PR meetings. 'All your, uh, *fans* were swooning over your large underwear ad billboard in Times Square.'

'Ugh.' I hang my head over the bowl, knowing the exact picture she's talking about. 'That was Jack's idea.'

It's odd how relieved I am when her smile kicks back up. 'The infamous Candy Crush addicted manager?'

I pause in scraping the dough off the sides of the bowl with the spatula, surprised by how much I shared over the past few hours with her. I should be nervous about it, but when she's looking at me with shiny, amused, blue eyes, I feel happy instead. 'Yeah, that Jack.' I slide the cookie sheet I found in a cabinet closer. 'I was doing so many survival-type action movies, he was afraid I'd get typecast as more of a Conan the Barbarian than a versatile leading man.' I roll my eyes, recalling the long and embarrassing underwear photo shoot. 'He thought the underwear campaign would help the public see me in a different light.'

'Well from what I heard, they see a lot more of you in *all* the lights now.' She waggles her eyebrows.

'Ha. Ha.' Dough ready, I scoop out a golf-ball-size amount with my hand and roll it between my palms into a five-inch-long snake.

'What kind of cookies are those?'

'*Biscoitos*.' I lay the snake down on the cookie sheet and bring the ends together to make a circle, pinching the ends together. 'It's like Portuguese shortbread.'

She props both elbows on the island counter, framing the cat, who looks at me the way one should the cookies, between them. 'Cool.'

I get through shaping the first six cookies when my phone rings. 'Shoot.' I drop the dough in my hands back in the bowl. 'It's probably Jack.' I move to retrieve my phone from my pocket, hesitating when I see my greasy hands.

'Don't worry.' Anne hops off her stool and circles the island. 'I'll get it.' Before I can think better of it, she reaches into my pocket. I stare long and deep into Mike Hunt's eyes to prevent my lower half from reacting to Anne's inadvertent grazing.

Phone retrieved, Anne slides her finger across the screen then taps on the speaker button before setting the phone down on the counter.

Anne points at the phone, then holds her finger over her lips, miming that she'll be quiet.

Like *that's* why I'm frozen, unable to speak.

'Felix?'

Clearing my throat, I turn back to my dough, needing a distraction and boner cover. 'Hey, man.' I glance at the clock. Between the time and the hum of a crowd in the background, I'm guessing he just got off the plane.

'How's the condo?'

I pick my discarded snake of dough out of the bowl. 'I don't think it's gonna work out.' Laying it on the cookie sheet, I pinch the ends. 'There's a problem.'

Anne's lips purse in amusement. Probably from being considered a problem.

'You've got to be kidding me.' Jack's sigh fills the phone with static. 'What's wrong with it?'

I open my mouth to explains, but Jack cuts me off before I can.

'Vance assured me that while the owner barely ever stays there, it's always kept clean and well-equipped. Something about her cowboy boyfriend being a neat freak who bakes.'

Anne and I both look at the cookie sheet and baking paraphernalia strewn across the island.

Jack mutters something to someone then speaks into the phone again. 'Something I figured you'd like as you like being in the kitchen.'

'The condo is fine, it's just that I don't think he—'

'It's gonna be hella awkward when we meet Vance and the rest of the astronaut crew for dinner after the filming is over if we reject his favor of a place to stay.'

Anne seems to freeze, and I wonder if she thinks I'll go back on my word to find a new place to stay. I won't, but I also don't want Jack to know she's the reason why I need to leave. He's dealing with enough at the moment. I don't want him to think there's another woman out to get me.

Ripping a paper towel off the holder, I begin making quick swipes at my hands, hoping to take the call off speaker before Anne can protest.

'Are you sure you can't stay there?' Jack asks, as if already resigning himself to the answer and the smoothing-over he'll need to do.

Hoping I'm clean enough to grab my phone, I toss the paper towel. 'The thing is—'

But Anne beats me to the phone, ending the call with one tap.

'Hey.' Hand still outstretched, I frown at her. 'Why did you—'

'I have a new deal for you.'

He drops his hand, sighing. 'Listen, I wasn't going to suddenly change my mind and try and kick you out. I'll leave, I promise. I just need to—'

The phone rings, and I sigh, tired of being repeatedly cut off. I reach for the phone again, lit up with Jack's name and picture.

Anne slides it out of reach. 'Listen.' She silences the call with a press of the phone's side button. 'I feel like it would be wrong to kick you out after you went to all this trouble to cook me dinner.'

I frown at her sudden one-eighty, my mind racing trying to figure out what changed between her threatening to call the police and now. 'It would?'

She nods solemnly. 'And with you not being much of a threat given your —' she waves her hands as if having trouble searching for the right words '—*regrettable* medical condition.'

'My what?'

Her eyes drop below my waist. 'It can happen to men your age.' She gives me what I assume she thinks is a sympathetic smile.

Understanding dawns and I swallow back my frustration. 'I'm only thirty-two.'

When her smile turns pained, I decide to show her just how threatening I and my dick can be. But before I can move one step around the counter, the cat meows and stretches a chicken-wing-looking arm toward me.

Pride makes way for safety, and I decide it's probably best for everyone if I and my dick stay where we are, well out of claw-swiping range.

I scoop another ball of dough and get back to forming my *biscoitos*. 'What deal?'

* * *

Liz

'*So.*' Ignoring the forearm flexing that happens when you roll Portuguese shortbread, I concentrate on sounding friendly to the man who attempted to bribe me out of a condo. 'I was thinking that you could stay here, in the guest room, if you wanted.' I flutter my eyelashes a few times, hoping they'll mask my tone and the stiffness of my smile that basically screams the truth behind the lie.

Because I don't want him to stay. I don't want his sexy, tousled hair, his hilarious aversion to Mike Hunt or his seductive smiles anywhere near me or the guest bedroom.

However.

I *do* want to go to that dinner. It is becoming readily apparent over the course of the last few days that, as a storyboarder who works early in the day to sketch out potential film sets before handing them off, I'm not in a position to coincidentally run into my sister at NASA.

'I'm confused.' Felix looks torn between laughing and complaining about my mentioning his erectile dysfunction.

And when his eyes fall to my chest where Mike is probably drooling over him, I sit on the bar stool and hunker down, trying to hide the triggering cat from view while I attempt to list all the reasons why my offer is so generous. 'This place is close to work, safe, has a fully equipped kitchen, *and*, as Jack said, the astronauts specifically called in this favor for you.'

'But I thought you were all about "finders keepers".'

I've never seen air quotes made with dough-laden hands. Or in such a derogatory manner.

He shakes his head in disbelief as he pinches another cookie together. 'You threatened to call the NASA's PR manager who gave you the key *and* the police if I didn't "get the hell out".'

'Well, I, uh...' My mind stalls on how to convince him to stay when I was so hard-pressed to get him to leave. I find inspiration when the oven dings, having reached the right temperature. I slam my hand down on the counter. 'I need a chef.' Ignoring the jolt of pain in my palm, I dodge Mike's paw swipe to my face.

Felix's eyebrows shoot up. 'A chef?'

'Yes.' I nod vigorously and straighten in my seat lest Mike retaliate later in ways I might not survive. 'I'm no use in the kitchen and having you around will be helpful.' I gesture to the cookie sheet and dough bowl, so Felix doesn't home in on the cat again.

Following my hands, Felix scans the island and then the rest of the condo. When he meets my eyes again, instead of looking convinced, he seems wary of my sanity.

Giving up the façade, I duck my head while giving an apology scratch to Mike, too embarrassed to meet Felix eyes. 'And it would be cool if you wanted to maybe take me to the astronaut dinner.'

There's a pregnant pause after I admitted just how the tables have turned.

'Big fan of astronauts, are we?' As expected, his expression is both amused and smug.

'Maybe.' Not a lie. I could be. At least of one astronaut in particular. But he doesn't need to know that. The more information one has, the more they can use against you. Stanley Moore taught me that.

'So let me get this straight.' He braces his hands on either side of the cookie sheet, his contracting upper torso muscles contradicting his self-proclaimed sweet tooth. 'You'll let me stay as long as I cook for you and take you out on dates?'

'Don't be ridiculous,' I rush on, worried I've just shot myself in the foot. 'I'm saying I want *one* date.' I hold up my finger. 'One specific date to the astronaut dinner.' I drop my finger and scratch Mike's head. 'An invite, really. Not a date.' I nod at the cookies. 'And the chef thing.'

His nostrils flare, and I can't tell if it's from annoyance or amusement.

'What do you say?' Taking a chance, I stick my arm across the counter. 'Deal?'

10

LIZ

I am not expecting the condo to smell so delicious when I open my bedroom door at five in the morning.

But it does.

I also didn't expect my new roommate to be awake, but as the guest bedroom/office door is open beside mine, I'm guessing the Hollywood interloper is taking his chef duties more seriously than I'd intended.

Either that or his bed, aka the guest room futon, wasn't very conducive to a Hollywood A-lister's sleep.

But just in case I'm wrong and Felix *is* sleeping, I hook my messenger bag on my shoulder and tiptoe past his door like a ninja.

Unlike a ninja, I'm thrown off balance by a cantankerous pussy sprinting past me. My bag, heavy with my work tablet and cat treats, swings forward, casting me into the wall with a thud that causes the framed picture of a baby cow to tilt on its hook.

As Mikey bounds out of sight, I brace for a scream. Or a whimper. Or whatever it is that a person suffering from tabby-cat PTSD does when greeted by Mike Hunt first thing in the morning.

Strangely, I hear nothing but the soft hiss of cooking as I straighten the odd choice of wall decor.

Re-hefting my bag, I quick-step the rest of the way down the hall, only to come to a stop at the sight that greets me.

My roommate is naked.

Nearly naked.

Ignoring the thread of disappointment at the sight of Felix's low-slung shorts, I let my bag slide off my shoulder as I stare at his exposed back, shoulders and biceps. I point at Mike, who's sitting on his haunches next to me at the mouth of the hallway, and whose expression I'm worried mirrors my own. 'Behave.'

The cat gives me side-eye.

We both know I wasn't talking to him.

Hearing me, Felix turns, spatula in hand. 'Morning.'

'Morning.' I fake a yawn, surreptitiously checking for drool. 'You didn't have to get up this morning. I can make myself breakfast or grab something from the catering table later.'

He shrugs, the movement doing things to his abs. Tantalizing things. Things I want to feel with my hands.

Things I *have* felt with my hands.

Unaware of my pervy thoughts, Felix continues to move fluidly in the kitchen. 'I'm used to waking up early. I work out in the mornings.'

His bicep muscles flex as he opens the refrigerator door. *Yeah you do.*

The bastard's lips twitch.

'Ah, yes. I see.' In an attempt to reset my brain, I pick up Mikey, using him as a human shield before walking over to my new designated spot – the island stool positioned across from the cooktop where Felix earns his keep. 'I usually work out in the morning too.' When I'm not having to go to NASA before the sun rises, that is.

My next yawn isn't faked.

Felix grabs two plates from the cabinet behind him and sets them on the counter in front and beside me before plating the food.

Sautéed bell peppers and scrambled eggs on toast, topped with a side of fruit.

It's all stuff from my grocery order, but cooked.

Which may seem insignificant to most, but considering all I was going to do was eat shabbily cut raw veggies and pray to the chicken gods that my eggs didn't burn when I tried to hard-boil them, I'm feeling better about the absurd deal I made with the Portuguese Don Juan last night.

He hands me a fork before circling the island to sit next to me.

I lower Mike on the floor between us, as if that will somehow diminish my awareness of the lack of space between his bare torso and my current overheated one.

As I hoped, he keeps his eyes on the cat who, for once, is sitting politely on the floor. When Mikey remains still, Felix takes his first bite.

I follow suit, the taste of breakfast enough of a distraction to help me block out all the visible skin beside me. Felix's and Mike's. 'Where'd you learn how to cook, anyway?'

'My mother.' He lifts the open-faced toast, taking a large bite.

'Yeah?' A stab of jealousy hits me. I've never cooked with my mom. Not because she wouldn't if I asked, but I never did, knowing full well that my father was of the opinion that cooking wasn't something New York City society queens and princesses did. We had *staff* for that.

I swallow another bite as I watch his lips roll as he chews his. 'What else did she teach you?'

'Most everything.' He licks the crumbs from his lips. 'My dad died in a car accident when I was young, so she raised me on her own.'

My fork pauses on the plate. 'I'm sorry.'

Felix's shoulders lift in a smooth, well-practiced response. 'I don't really remember him.' His brows knit together for a fleeting moment. 'I've never been sure if that's a good thing or a bad thing considering how torn up my mom always seemed whenever I asked about him.' He forks a strawberry then pauses, as if considering what he just shared.

I stab my own strawberry, angry at myself for asking. 'You don't need to talk about it if you don't want to. I didn't mean to pry or anything.' I chew hard, knowing full well what it's like to have daddy-issues, then pick up my toast.

'No.' Felix straightens in his seat. 'It's not that.' Lowering his fork to the plate, he gives me a small smile. 'I was just thinking how long it's been since I had to tell anyone about myself like this.' He huffs a laugh. 'Usually people already know all these things before they even meet me.'

'Sorry.' I pause my next bite, the eggs on my toast wobbling as I shrug. 'Not a big movie buff.'

'Don't apologize.' His small smile transforms into a full-blow grin. 'It's great, actually.'

His happy expression is more genuine than all the professional smiles he flashed at the press junket. It reminds me of Johnny from the bar, except the effect is ten times as powerful without an atrocious beard in the way. Strong enough to have me shifting in my seat.

Shoveling the rest of the food in my face, I jump off the stool and bring the plate to the sink. I have it loaded in the dishwasher before I've even finished chewing. 'I better get going.'

He glances out the still dark window. 'Already?'

'Yep.' Internally cringing at how disturbingly perky I sound, I hustle back to my room to brush my teeth so I can get the hell out of here.

It's just for a little while. I only need to put up with the Hollywood sex symbol long enough to meet my sister. After which I'll be able to figure out who I am. To become anchored after a year of feeling adrift.

Even with my little pep talk running through my head while I move the brush fast and furiously around my mouth, it still takes me reminding myself that while the upper part of Felix Jones is hot, heavy and hard, the bottom half is only two of those things.

So don't start acting dumb now.

* * *

Felix

Why am I so dumb?

I continue to berate my intelligence as I watch Anne's jean-clad backside retreat to her room.

I'm cold, tired and my back hurts, and yet, thanks to the reflective microwave door, my large, goofy grin is proof positive that I've lost a few thousand brain cells between here and the guest room.

I'm equally disgusted with myself and dumbfounded by my situation as I get up to wipe down the counters.

Ripping off a paper towel and grabbing the cleaner from under the sink, I scrub harder than necessary while I contemplate all the ways in which I'm dumb.

I didn't lie when I said I'm an early riser. I am. But I also never set my alarm when I don't have to be on set until the afternoon. Something I did last night after Anne informed me what time she'd be leaving for work today.

I reasoned that if Anne only granted me permission to stay because she couldn't cook – and her weird thing for astronauts – then I had better get up and cook.

And just ignore how easily I was able to convince myself that staying with Anne was my only option.

Finished with the counters, I rinse and load the cutting board and other utensils I used into the dishwasher. Saving the still-hot pan for later, I make a wide berth around Mike Hunt, who's watching me from a spot on the floor near the corner of the island, and pad over to the living area.

My t-shirt from yesterday lays on the top of the couch from where I threw it this morning. I grabbed it from on top of my bag when I woke up this morning, knowing from cooking dinner last night that the air-conditioning vent blows directly over the kitchen. And yet, instead of tugging it over my head as I walked down the hall, I tossed it here instead before making breakfast.

I told myself it was so I didn't get anything on it while I cooked, but I'm pretty sure me and my ego know better.

Goosebumps on prominent display, I grab the shirt and shrug it on before plopping down on the couch. Even sprawled back on the cushions, my muscles refuse to unknot after a poor night's sleep.

I haven't slept on a futon since my auditioning days when Jack and I shared a tiny studio apartment. But instead of rejecting Anne's roommate offer last night and burdening Jack with setting me up with new security and a comfortable bed at a nearby hotel, I dumbly agreed.

Because... well, reasons.

Reasons that, if I allowed myself to think about, probably have more to do with a pretty girl's perverted sense of humor and attractive, loud laugh than keeping a low profile from the press and Camilla. But I'm not thinking about that.

I prove my dumbness by smiling at the way Anne pretended not to look at my chest, arms and abs as we ate breakfast.

A smile that dips as the couch does when Mike jumps up beside me, making the knots in my back coil tighter.

I have no idea why this cat is so enamored with me, but at least he seems intelligent enough to know that the feeling is not mutual. He leaves a two-inch gap between us as he lays down beside the length of my thigh.

That gap and the fact that I covered most of my exposed skin enables me to remain still and silent while Mike gets comfortable. A feat I most likely appear visibly proud of when Anne re-enters the room, grabbing her bag off the floor. She looks the same as she did a few minutes ago – fresh-faced and charming in her jeans, t-shirt and Birkenstocks. Like the quintessential young twenty-something off to class or work.

Her features are pretty, no doubt. Beautiful, even. But it's her expressions that get me. Her humor. Her blatant dismissal of my fame and my dick.

Damn, I'm dumb.

I see the moment she notices my shirt and fight a smile over the look of relief that passes over her face before her eyebrows jump at seeing Mike beside me.

Knowing last night's tabby-cat confession has left me in a less than manly light, I try and play off this sudden turn of events with a shrug. 'He's all right, I guess.' Which would've been more believable if I didn't suddenly jerk my arm back when Mike's tail touches it.

'Uh huh.' Walking over to the chair across from me, Anne lowers her bag and grabs a pile of straps and fabric off its seat. 'You're a regular cat-lover now.' She begins inserting herself into the contraption, first one arm, then her head then the other arm.

A baby carrier.

'What do you need that for?'

She snaps a buckle then points to Mike.

'Wait.' I glance back and forth between her and the feline. 'You're taking *Mike* to NASA?'

'I can't leave him.' Her chin drops as she gives a light roll of her baby blues. 'Not when my Hollywood, high-maintenance house guest suffers from ailurophobia.'

'Ailuro-what now?'

'Ailurophobia.' She smirks. 'Fear of pussies.'

My lips twitch, warring between amusement and embarrassment. 'Can't you just keep him in your room?'

Anne answers with a defeated sigh, her ponytail swinging forward. 'Unfortunately, no.' She points to Mike, who has managed to close the gap between us to one inch while I wasn't looking. 'Sphinxes are social creatures. It's why they're usually adopted in pairs.' She wraps a strap around her and clicks it to the front. 'I'm not sure if it's because he's a lone sphinx or he's just a cunt—'

I sputter over her choice of vernacular.

'—but Mikey gets up to some serious mischief if he's left somewhere strange and without a person in sight.' She gives the carrier a final tug.

Then I watch, horrified, as she gets the cat ready to leave.

The first thing she pulls from her bag is sunscreen. For the cat.

'I mean, I know that people are supposed to wear sunscreen everyday no matter what, but is it really necessary for a cat?'

Anne sits on the coffee table, facing Mike. 'Sphinxes have sensitive skin.' She sprays the SPF onto her hands then reaches out and rubs down Mike's head and ears. 'And the sun may not be out too much now, but it will be this afternoon when I walk back.'

'Wait.' I shift on the couch, too disturbed to be worried when Mike's body sinks against mine. 'You're *walking*?' I glance at the cat, the carrier and the heavy work bag.

Anne shrugs, continuing to grease up the cat. 'It's just down the road.'

A busy, two-way, triple-lane road.

Finished protecting Mike from the hole in the ozone layer, Anne drops the sunscreen back in the bag. 'Snacks, harness, leash, sweater—'

'Sweater?'

She nods, closing the bag. 'For the polar-like air conditioning NASA pumps into the buildings.' She lifts Mike, then slides his greased-up body in the baby carrier. 'He might get a chill.'

'Meow.'

'Oh. Sorry Mike.' She reaches in and turns him so that he's facing out. 'I forgot you like to see where we're going.'

It's like the cat *is* a baby.

'All right then.' She stands with a grunt and hikes her the bag's strap on her shoulder. 'Enjoy your workout.'

She waddles two steps before I'm off the couch. 'Hold up.' I jog back to my room, snag a pair of socks and return in seconds. 'I'll walk you.'

I'm too busy pulling on socks and jamming my feet into sneakers to look, but I can hear the frown in her voice. 'You don't have to. I'm fine.'

'Yeah, well, I was going that way anyway.' I slam my foot down to push my heel into it, then stomp over to her and grab her bag from off her shoulder. 'Part of my cardio.'

The looks she gives me is far from grateful and mirrors my exact thoughts.

I'm so dumb.

11

FELIX

'You want to tell me what's going on?' Jack's voice snaps in my earbuds while I finish up my preacher curls in the condo's gym.

'I don't know what you're talking about.' Extending my arms, I reset the weights and stand from the machine.

The building manager was right when he said the gym is usually deserted between the hours of ten and three. I've been here for thirty minutes so far, and no one's come in. It's way more relaxing than a hotel gym where people are constantly in and out.

'You don't know what I'm talking about?'

Sigh. Jack is super annoying when he does the whole repeat-what-I-just-said-as-a-question thing.

'Nope.' But I can be just as annoying when playing dumb.

An act I seem unable to drop since this morning.

'First, you hang up on me last night.'

'I told you.' I check the list of exercises my trainer sent me on my phone. 'I accidentally hit the off button.'

Or Anne did. On purpose.

Thinking of Anne reminds me that I need to order more than yesterday's sad assortment of groceries and I shoot off a text asking her when she'll be home today so I know when to have it delivered.

'And now you cancel your meal service?'

Pocketing my phone, I heft a fifty-five-pound plate off the rack. 'Like you said last night, the condo has a well-equipped kitchen. And I like cooking.' Sliding the weight onto the bar, I secure it with a clamp. 'It's relaxing.'

'Cooking.' He draws out the word. I can just imagine him in his office, narrowing his eyes, trying to see all the angles.

As astute as my friend and manager is, I don't think it ever occurred to him that I'd be so excited about getting back into the kitchen. Especially when it didn't occur to me until the job of chef was foisted upon me.

I grab another plate and add it to the other side to balance the weight, then grab my phone, once more texting Anne to ask about food allergies.

Text sent, I settle back on the bench and wrap my gloved hands around the metal bar, squinting against the bright morning sun coming through the floor-to-ceiling windows.

Earlier this morning, even with the sun just rising, I nearly sweated my balls off walking a mile and a half to NASA's security gate carrying a twenty-something pound computer bag full of cat treats.

Meanwhile, Anne hadn't complained once. Even with the heavy feline furnace strapped to her chest. Which means *I* couldn't, not unless I wanted to look even less like a man in front of the woman who knows I'm afraid of house cats and thinks my dick is broken.

But it also doesn't mean I can't try and proactively prevent myself from experiencing it again. Because while I managed to escort Anne to NASA unharmed this morning, I was right in thinking that NASA Road 1, which connects our condo building to NASA's security entrance on Saturn Lane, is one busy street. Even at six in the morning.

I grunt as I lift the bar.

I'm annoyed that it bothers me. Obviously, Anne has been walking the same commute before I arrived and has remained unharmed. Why I suddenly need to interject myself into the situation is as infuriating as my decision not to wear a t-shirt this morning.

It's like I've forgotten what happened the last time I let a woman get too close.

Not that Anne and I are close.

Jack, apparently giving up on me explaining further, breathes heavily into the phone. 'You're making me burn through my daily Candy Crush allowance that much faster, you know that, right?'

Which is exactly why I stop myself from mentioning the idea of renting my own car instead of using the studio's chauffeur service. I can only imagine the screen time uptick that idea would cause.

'*Especially* now that it seems I need to stay in Los Angeles longer than I'd planned.'

I pause mid bench press. 'Everything okay?'

'Yeah, man. Nothing's wrong, but the lawyers are hopeful they found a way to shut down Camilla's plans.' His calm tone helps me finish my set and heft the bar back onto its cradle.

If there was a real issue, he would've started the conversation with it.

'The lawyers just need time to go over all the details, make sure the option is viable.'

I crunch up and head back to the weight rack. 'That would be amazing.' Deciding to lift heavier, I pick up two twenty-pound plates and slide them on the ends of the bar.

I don't need to bulk up for this movie. I always maintain a decent fitness level, and I've enjoyed taking it relatively easy for this role. Usually, a medium-weight routine coupled with pre-packaged meals from my nutritionist is enough to keep me in leading-man shape for a film that doesn't require me to free solo rock climb or BASE jump skyscrapers.

But now that I'm cooking, I'd much rather burn off the extra calories with more exercise than deprive myself of all the meals I've been planning since I saw Anne's expression as she bit into a simple breakfast of eggs and toast.

Exercise that doesn't include fainting and falling into oncoming morning rush hour traffic due to heat stroke.

'Their plan might involve you endorsing a company that was planning on collaborating with Camilla on a new fashion line, but it's a reputable company. I don't see any downsides to working with them.'

I snort, my grip nearly slipping on the twenty-pound plate I grab. 'Except they have no problem working with Camilla.'

'To be fair, we're probably two of the few people who know what a horrible person she is.'

I concede his point with a grunt and secure the weight to the bar. 'All right. Keep me informed.'

'Will do.' He pauses for a beat. 'And since I'll be here longer, I'll check in on Mama Jones.'

He makes the switch from manager to friend seamless, making me feel like a dick for lying to him about my roommate situation. 'I appreciate that.'

Twenty minutes later, workout complete, I sit poolside under an umbrella/mister, sunglasses on and my ball cap pulled low over my eyes.

My muscles are relaxed from fatigue, the guilt from being here instead of nearer my mother has been lessened by Jack's planned visit, and besides an older gentleman swimming laps, there is no one here to recognize me or disrupt my peaceful solitude.

And yet.

My thoughts keep going to Anne and her walk back to the condo in what my weather app tells me is Houston's hottest summer in the past five years.

Distracting myself, I download an app I never thought I'd find use for – Pinterest – and lose myself in finding recipes comparable to the ones my mother used to make.

I make it twenty minutes, three boards and fifty pins before I switch apps and get out my wallet.

* * *

Liz

My phone buzzes for the umpteenth time today.

Ignoring it, I continue to rest my eyes. I've been finished with my drawings of Mission Control for about an hour, and yet I'm making use of the quiet space to gather enough energy and determination to go back to the condo.

I'd like to blame my exhaustion on the lack of sleep from my unexpected roommate last night, but honestly, the walk to NASA this morning nearly killed me. I still feel sweaty in places I'd rather not even after four hours of sitting in arctic-like air conditioning.

Another buzz.

I don't need to look to know who it is.

Even my family isn't this relentless.

After I woke to Felix Jones making me breakfast, even though he didn't need to be up until much later, I felt bad enough. But now that he's spending his morning asking me about any food allergies I may have, my spice level preference and even sending me recipes to yay or nay, I feel particularly troubled.

Or at least I would if my mental energy hadn't been turned into physical energy and flittered away on my mile and a half walk through hell carrying a twelve-pound brimstone.

I didn't admit to him that on my previous commutes over the past few days, I frequently stopped and rested. Or that today, on Mike's first outing, I was planning to make Mike walk on a leash when he got too heavy for me to carry.

It was a hell of a lot of pride and my sheer determination not to look weak in front of Mr Action Star that kept my feet moving and my mouth shut. Even then, I don't think I would've made it if Felix hadn't carried my computer bag for me.

But all that went out the window once we reached the security gate and Felix turned around to *jog* back to the condo like our morning's slog through heavy humidity was nothing. I cursed and complained the whole time to Mike while I stumbled from bench to bench along the remaining distance to building five, stopping multiple times just to stretch out my back and wipe sweat – and probably tears – from my eyes.

So much for being a hardened New Yorker who can walk blocks upon city blocks in a day. All that goes out the window when you add in the Texas weather and a hairless pussy.

'What is that?'

My body jerks, the stylus still in my hand skidding across my open tablet. Shifting in my seat in the back room of Mission Control – an elevated room with a glass wall that overlooks the larger communications room – I open my eyes to see a horrified Em gazing down at me and the previously mentioned brimstone, who I'm planning to put on a strict diet, in the chair next to mine.

'This is Mike Hunt.'

She chokes on air. 'I'm sorry, what?'

My brother really is a perverted genius.

I fight to dim my smile. 'This is the cat you were warned about.'

Em squints, leaning over me to get a better look at Mikey, who's laid out diagonally on the seat, his back left leg dangling off the edge. 'That's a cat?'

At her incredulous tone, Mikey lifts the skin wrinkle above his left eye.

'Oh. Wow.' Em tiptoes closer. 'It is.'

The only good thing about the hot walk to work is that it seems to have zapped Mike's energy along with mine. The ball of tension that was lodged in my chest from me imagining the kinds of chaos Mike could cause in a government secure facility was thankfully unwarranted, as he's spent the past few days laying limp under an air-conditioning vent while I draw. He hasn't so much as even licked himself, probably disgusted by the taste of feline sunscreen.

'Just so you know—' I summon up the energy I've reserved for the even hotter trek home and pull out the notarized emotional support certificate from my bag '—my brother wasn't lying when he said he's certified.'

I've already shown the certificate to both the security guard at NASA's front gate and to the appropriately horrified public relations personnel who had the awesome job of escorting me into the security badge entry only building this morning. I was sure that, after staring at me and Mikey's sweaty, wrinkled face peeking out from the baby carrier like I was Sigourney Weaver in *Alien*, they would've marched straight off to tell Em all about me and my alien-looking cat.

But it seems not.

As Em has walked me to and from buildings with more regularity than anyone else from public relations since I started my storyboarding internship, I've begun to think of her as more of a friend than security protocol. But that doesn't mean I want to take advantage of her any more than I already have with the condo.

However, ignoring my outstretched hand holding the certificate, Em circles around my chair to sit next to Mike. 'Hey there, little guy.'

I brace for Mike's retaliation from Em's earlier skepticism but relax when he allows her to scratch behind his ears without baring teeth or claws.

Either Mikey is mellowing in his old age, or the rhinestone brooch pinned to Em's button-down blouse is enough to hypnotize him from retribution.

My money's on the latter. That, and residual heat exhaustion.

'I have three cats.' Em's fingertips rub down Mike's back. 'But I've never petted a sphinx before.'

With Mike properly engrossed and my sketch done (after one tap of the undo button from my startled stylus mark), I lean back and close my eyes. 'Have at it.'

Another buzz.

For a Hollywood superstar, the man has too much time on his hands.

If it weren't for his extreme cat aversion, I'd leave Mike with him tomorrow just to keep him on his toes and off his phone.

And me with a much *lighter* commute.

While I wouldn't have called the last few days' walks to NASA pleasant thanks to the heat and the weight of my work tablet in my bag, I never dreaded the walk back as much as I am today.

Another buzz.

'You going to get that?'

'Hmmm?' Jarred from my thoughts, I open my eyes.

Em's head is tilted in the direction of my phone, laying on the seat next to Mike. 'JD really seems like he needs to know your thoughts on *polvo guisado*.'

My face heats in the frigid room. 'Oh, ah, yeah.' I grab my phone, thankful I used Johnny Douchebag's initials rather than his real name when he asked to exchange numbers this morning.

I agreed because he made a good case about needing it if there was an emergency. But when I open my phone and read over the eleven new text messages, I'm thinking maybe I should lay some ground rules on what constitutes an emergency.

For now, I tap, *polvo guisado is fine*, into my phone and turn off my notifications.

Honestly, I haven't a clue what *polvo guisado* is. But as it's something that I don't have to cook, I'm sure it's great.

I wish I could say that after a year of being on my own, I've become self-sufficient in all areas, but after multiple attempts, fires, knife nicks and upset stomachs, I feel it best to play to my strengths by *not* cooking.

So while boring, I have made do with simple, pre-packaged things—fruits, vegetables, yogurt, hummus, etc.

Growing up as Stanley Winston Moore's daughter had certain privileges. Unlimited access to Moore's retail, an on-call chauffeur, home gym and the best art supplies money could buy.

And yet, besides my mother and brothers, the thing I miss the most, even over free clothes and a bottomless bank account, is the family's personal chef.

Before I can click my phone off, Felix sends me a link to a recipe. Tapping it, I'm taken to a website where a woman in a blue, ruffled apron stands holding a bowl and a whisk.

I snort a laugh, imagining Felix in the apron instead. My smile falls as my mind goes into the gutter, my image of him evolving into him wearing *only* the blue frilly apron.

'You okay?'

'Hmmm?' I click the side of the phone, blacking out the screen and the NSFW picture in my head. 'Ah, yes.' Deciding to take my chances in the heat, I start collecting my things.

Em watches me reapply Mike's sunscreen with a look of fascination, before walking me out of Mission Control's back room and down into the lobby.

We say goodbye before I take a deep breath and prepare for the onslaught of Texas' afternoon heat.

But it isn't the sun that blinds me.

There, leaning against a new, shiny, black Land Rover, is the reason I'm grateful for my phone's unlimited texting – Felix Jones.

Unfortunately, there isn't a blue, ruffled apron in sight.

12

LIZ

'Dinner is fucked.'

My hand pauses over my sketch as I turn to my disgruntled, movie-star roommate in the kitchen. Something I've been actively trying *not* to do since I sat on the couch and began drawing Mike Hunt.

Two days ago, after Felix saved Mike and me from the melting walk back to the condo, and I threw myself at him in an impromptu hug – making a sandwich out of poor Mike – I retreated to my room, thinking that space would be the best thing for my hero roommate. My plan was to hole up in my room and lose my thoughts in art.

Specifically, my superfluous, roommate-centric thoughts.

And yet.

My thoughts proved themselves dirty when, startled out of a mental art fog by Felix knocking on my door to tell me dinner was ready, I found myself further shocked by what I'd drawn.

Felix.

Naked, except for a blue, ruffled apron.

My sudden inspiration is frustrating on multiple levels. I haven't felt moved to draw from my imagination since leaving New York. I'm rarely not drawing, something that used to vex my father a great deal, but it was always from pictures, arranged still lifes or land and urban scapes.

When I was younger, after I had my after-school snack, I'd hole up in my bedroom, sitting on the window seat, and sketch out fantasy worlds. The people walking outside through Central Park would transform into characters, making my sketch pad an impromptu picture-book telling fantastical stories. Happy stories.

It's been a long time since I've been able to do that.

So, while it's a relief to know that my ability to create from my imagination hasn't left me for good, my current muse is wrecking hell on my common sense.

As in, it's common sense not to get worked up over your celebrity roommate/co-worker. Especially as I have other things to focus on beside his bulging biceps. Like a half-sister to introduce myself to.

A forlorn sigh escapes as I glance from sketch book to real-life model. I never would have thought I'd be grateful for erectile dysfunction, and yet here I am, disappointed but thankful I can't act on my inconvenient imaginations even if I wanted to.

The sad victim of ED throws his hands in the air like a forlorn housewife. 'The avocados are hard.' His face is the definition of toddler-tantrum over poor produce selection.

It takes all I have not to laugh.

Hair on end, Felix moves around the small kitchen, his movements unnecessarily aggressive.

Almost without thinking, I flip the page on my sketch book, my hands making quick movements across the paper—

His hands as he grabs an apple.

His shoulders as he rips a banana from the bunch.

His expression as he tosses them in a paper bag along with the offending avocados.

The line of his spine as he stands, hands on hips, staring daggers at the counter.

'Meow.' Mike, probably perturbed at having his modeling ignored, splays his legs out – his favorite way to warm his nether regions in sunlight.

My hand, interrupted by Mike's whine, flexes around the graphite, eager to keep moving. So much for thinking I'd be too conscious of Felix to draw him if we were in the same room together.

That real Felix would be safer than my imaginative one.

Because if I'm honest with myself, which I haven't been very often in the last year, my opinion of the real Felix Jones has altered significantly ever since I saw him scream like a peacock in the face of Mike Hunt.

And his attitude, after realizing I *wasn't* out to sell nude photos of him, has been... charming.

I close my eyes, cutting off the view of my inappropriate muse, the last two days playing out in my head.

He's cooked for me. He's walked me to work. And then arrived like a knight in shining armor riding in a black SUV, saving Mike and me from potential sunstroke.

My anger and pride have mellowed. Mellowed enough that I can now look back on our unfortunate night together and see Felix's reaction to my wanting medical attention for what it really was – panic.

On top of which, he never asked for an apology for my own act of panic that night. That of kneeing him in his Hollywood jewels.

All this adds up to a possibility that's hard to swallow, *especially* as, if true, it isn't going to help me with my new erotic artistic imaginings.

Felix Jones might be a nice guy.

'How can we have avocado cilantro dressing without ripe avocados?' the newly anointed nice guy murmurs to himself while loading the sink with small dishes, knives and utensils. 'This is why grocery delivery services can't be trusted. You need to *feel* the avocados.' He picks up the cantaloupe that was delivered yesterday off the island counter. '*Smell* the melons.'

At that, I finally lose hold of my laughter.

Startled, he looks up, his annoyed expression melting to amusement when he realizes what he said. 'What?' He shrugs, smile still in place. 'I like ripe melons.'

I make a show of rolling my eyes before closing my sketch book. 'You might not be ready to play Casanova, but I think you're a cinch if Hollywood ever makes a Gordon Ramsay biopic.'

He snorts. 'Yeah, you've mentioned my less than stellar pick-up game before.'

Our eyes meet and a rush of heat hits as I remember the night we met. And not just the pre-face-numbing bedroom part. The conversation. The shared laughter. The chemistry between us when I thought he was just a regular cowboy.

Regular cowboy.

As my idea takes hold, I toss my sketch pad aside and stand, clapping my hands for attention. 'You want ripe melons?'

I roll my eyes again when Felix's drop to my chest.

Mike licks himself.

Disregarding the two perverted males in my life, and the secret satisfaction they bring, I pull my phone out from my pocket and open the navigation app. 'Then ripe melons you shall have.'

* * *

'Jack is going to kill me.'

I lift the cowboy hat off the nearby mannequin and place it on Felix's head. 'Isn't he already going to kill you for renting a car?'

His eyes meet mine under the large, cream, ten-gallon hat.

Almost as if he's embarrassed, Felix turns to the nearby full-length mirror. 'Yeah, but getting caught looking like *this*—' he gestures at his reflection '—would make him want to kill me even more.'

Ignoring how trim his waist is after he tucked in his plain, black t-shirt, I decide the contrast of the cream felt is too noticeable. 'Dead is dead, JD.'

He rolls his eyes with a smile. 'Why do you keep calling me that?'

I glance around the shop. 'Would you rather me use your real name?' While not particularly crowded, it isn't empty.

'Hell no.' His eyes cut to the nearest person, the cashier at the counter who's busy rearranging belt buckles in the glass case. 'But I am curious over your choice.'

Grabbing a black hat, I swap it for the cream. 'It's not my choice.' I step back and consider the difference. '*You're* the one who introduced yourself as John to start.'

While he looks annoyingly sexy in both the cream and black, the darker color and slightly smaller brim suit him better. 'And the D?'

I grab a belt off the nearby rack as he adjusts the hat. 'Douchebag.'

His amused expression deadpans. 'Nice.'

'Yeah.' I shrug, holding out the belt for him to take. 'I thought so.'

He stares at the buckle, twice the size of a credit card, and doesn't take it.

With a sigh, I step closer, threading the belt through the belt loops myself.

I realize my mistake halfway through when my front becomes flush with his. I'm close enough to hear his hard swallow before we both step back, clearing our throats.

I haven't felt this awkward since I cut Brandon Harrison III's lip with my braces in eighth grade during a scandalous game of spin the bottle at his parents' black tie anniversary party in the Hamptons.

Felix drops his head, the hat affectingly shielding his expression as he grabs the ends of the belt. 'I can, uh, take it from here.'

Though he can't see me, I nod, still too flustered to speak.

When the buckle clasps, he takes stock of his appearance in the mirror.

So do I. And my lustful artistic drive very much likes the fact that my muse looks like the Portuguese love child of James Dean and Scott Eastwood.

Eyes traveling over his reflection, it's no surprise that he's an A-list movie star.

Felix has... something. Something illusive. Something frustratingly intangible. A simmering charm that underscores the cheekbones, cut muscles and blinding smile.

I hate it.

With that lie firmly planted in my mind, I avert my eyes. 'You should head back to the car while I buy these.' Reaching up, I rip the price tag off the black hat, then snag the one off the belt.

'Whoa.' He reaches for his back pocket. 'I have my wallet.'

Breathing through the urge to rip more than just tags off his body, I step out of reach. *My* reach. 'As you've insisted on buying all the groceries, it's only fair to use my now defunct food budget to buy a disguise that ensures you ripe melons.'

The smile he flashes me makes me glad for the distance.

'Besides. We've already been gone forty minutes.' I turn toward the counter, throwing the next sentence over my shoulder. 'Who knows what Mike's done to the concierge by now?'

* * *

Felix

My eyes feel as big as Anne's melons. 'What *is* this place?'

'It's a supermarket chain called H-E-B.' Like an immature teenager, Anne waggles her brows while weighing two melons in her hands – at chest level.

It's jarring.

Not the melons, but the fact that, even counting the hairless cat, I'm having fun. In fact, I've had more fun in the past few days than I've had in all my red-carpet appearances over the last few years.

Finally done handling the melons, Anne rests one back on the pile. 'My sister-in-law says H-E-B is the one thing she'd take to New York with her if she could. Even more so than snow-free winters.' She hands me the other. 'And she *hates* the cold.'

There's a beat of silence while I file the Texan sister-in-law comment under *things I know about Anne*.

When I picked her up from work, opening the passenger door for her like my mother taught me, I watched, intrigued as she entered the car more gracefully with a hairless cat strapped to her chest than the well-practiced stars limo hopping during awards season.

Yet, over texts, meals and commuting, I discovered a crucial difference that separates Anne from the typical Hollywood crowd I'm used to. Something besides her frugality and her disinterest in counting calories before eating.

Anne *hates* talking about herself.

'Well?' She nods at the melon. 'Is it ripe?'

Smiling at her interest, I lift the melon to my nose and inhale. 'Nope.'

Her deflated enthusiasm is adorable.

I gesture her closer and lift the melon toward her. 'What do you smell?'

Anne sniffs, frowning. 'Nothing.'

'Exactly.' I place the melon back and grab another, one that looks less green. 'What about this one?'

Anne's arms brush mine as she leans closer. 'Oh.' She straightens, blasting me with a smile. 'It's sweet.'

I feel that smile below my massive belt buckle.

A woman pauses her cart pushing to reach for a cantaloupe. 'Excuse me.'

I sidestep out of her way. 'Ma'am.' Tipping my head down, the brim of my hat blocks my face from view.

The woman doesn't even look up. Just nods back and grabs a melon before moving on.

Anne takes the ripe melon out of my hands, a satisfied smile on her face. 'See. I told you no one would recognize you.' She places the melon in our cart and steers it toward the avocados. 'Come on, JD.' She struts, her ass moving in tandem to her swinging ponytail. 'Not only am I getting hungry, but we've got a pussy to pick-up.'

All shoppers turn to Anne who, seemingly oblivious, stops to grab a few apples.

Awed at how relaxed I am in public, even with Anne's mouth drawing attention, I do as she commands and amble after. 'Yes, ma'am.'

* * *

'I feel like I just bought Mike Hunt the feline equivalent of a blow-up doll.'

Anne, sitting next to me at the kitchen island, rolls her lips, her nostrils flaring.

She's trying not to laugh. She's been trying and failing throughout most of dinner.

I might be laughing too, if I wasn't so busy trying to figure out how Mike managed to open a zippered backpack, pull out a limited-edition action figure – which, to me, looked more like a pornographic Japanese Barbie doll – and humped it until its head popped off.

A giggle escapes Anne's mouth as she spears another bite of the avocado-topped chicken breast with her fork.

One of many giggles she's been unable to contain since we got home to find our impromptu concierge cat-sitter in tears of despair, rocking himself in the living room chair as he watched Mike defile what appeared to be a prized possession, apparently too scared to wrestle it from the enamored feline after his first attempt was met with a claw swipe and a 'tiger-like growl'.

I scrape the remaining salad into a pile on my plate with my fork. 'Why would someone pay that much for a doll?' While Anne calmed the guy down with tissues and pats on the back, I searched the cost of the doll on my phone, shocked at the prices listed for these so-called action figures.

My limited-edition Ken doll made in my likeness isn't even close to this obscure manga character's figurine price.

I ended up giving the distraught concierge everything in my wallet just to cover the ruined doll and his cat-sitting fee. *Plus*, a promise for an autographed picture once filming was done to ease his emotional trauma.

I scoop the salad up with a tortilla chip, chewing hard.

'Collector's item.' Anne wipes her mouth with a napkin before hopping off her stool.

My eyes water when a jagged piece of chip slides down my throat. 'What?' I wheeze out.

Shaking her head with another chuckle, Anne grabs her plate and moves around the island to the sink. 'They're called collector's items.'

I clear my throat with a cough. 'It's a doll.' Standing, I grab my plate and follow her to the sink. 'A minuscule *porn* doll.'

Anne snorts. 'Collectors get very snippy if you call them dolls or toys.'

'How would you know?'

'My brothers' middle school's headmaster collected *Star Wars* memorabilia.' She rinses her plate in the sink before opening the dishwasher.

My hair, no doubt smashed awkwardly from wearing a cowboy hat earlier, flops to the side as I tilt my head toward Anne. 'A what now?'

'A *Star Wars* collector.' Anne, having mistaken my interest for the headmaster's hobby rather than the fact that her brothers *had* a headmaster and not a principal, takes my plate from me and rinses it. 'He made Stephen the concierge's meltdown look downright stoic compared to his reaction when, years ago, he found my brother Chase playing with his previously mint-in box Darth Vader and Luke Skywalker action figures in his office.'

I watch her awkwardly loading the dishwasher from the front and wonder if it's simply East Coast vernacular to call a principal headmaster, or if I'm right in thinking a headmaster is the title for those who run *private* schools.

But before I can press my luck and push Anne for answers, tonight's man-meltdown instigator pipes up.

'Meow.'

Anne and I lift our eyes to the living area where Mike is sitting curled around the decapitated collector's item, looking very much like the cat who got the cream.

Or, in his case, an expensive humping doll.

13

FELIX

Too much happened this past week for someone who is supposed to be lying low. Too many ways that things could've gone horribly wrong or caused my career more problems.

However, as I rest my head on the back of an oversized armchair and wait for my mother to call while listening to the distant sound of Anne's shower running, I can't find it in me to regret a damn thing.

Even when I'm not under strict do-not-be-seen orders from Jack, I'm usually quick to covet my downtime. Probably because moments of solitude are rare when you're at the top of your game in Hollywood.

The constant need to pretend to be other people – both in front of the camera and in public – is exhausting enough to want to be left alone.

But tonight, as I have over the past few nights, even after filming started, I was perfectly content to share my precious alone time with a funny, beautiful woman who all but ignored me while sketching just a few feet away from where I stood cooking.

And instead of eating in silence, I voluntarily asked about feline sunscreen and the surprisingly detailed grooming requirements for sphinxes.

The sphinx in question snores softly from his perch on the back of the couch opposite me. His collector's item ladylove, which cost me a mint just a few days ago, left forgotten on the cushion below him.

Heartless bastard.

My phone, lying screen up on the coffee table, illuminates with a picture of my mother and me back when I was in high school, standing in the sand on the coast of California.

I pick it up, a surge of relief hitting me when the call opens to my mother's smiling face.

'*Mãe*.' My heart swells at my mother's smoothed updo, red lips and wrinkle-free blouse under the blush-colored cashmere cardigan I bought her last Mother's Day. Sofia Maria Santos-Jones looks like her usual self as opposed to the gaunt, unkept version of herself I held in my arms as I checked her in to the state-of-the-art rehab facility in Rancho Mirage. 'How are you?'

'I'm fine, *coração*.' She must be using the iPad I got her, the wide screen giving me a view of her plain, but high-end room. 'Jack came by.' Her happy smile makes me feel guilty for not being the one to visit. 'He said you finally stopped those cardboard meals.'

I chuckle at her description of the costly nutritionist-designed, pre-planned meal delivery that has been my usual for the past few years. 'Yes, I've been cooking.'

Her smile grows, making me feel prouder than when I was offered a multi-million-dollar brand ambassador contract on the heels of my first successful movie.

Earlier this year, when I had been out enjoying the life of a celebrity, dating socialites and having my picture taken, my mother had been suffering from an opioid addiction stemming from a recent shoulder surgery.

She'd torn her rotator cuff when she fell after tripping over a parking lot median. Jack and I mobilized a renowned surgeon, an at-home post-surgery aid, and a top-tier physical therapist that would make house calls.

All the best that my money could afford.

But none of that mattered when I failed to notice the tell-tale signs of addiction.

I came to visit after wrapping my biggest budget film to date to find my mother, a woman who prides herself on her well-kept appearance and house-cleaning skills, disheveled and staring vacantly in her recliner, her house cluttered and dirty.

Apparently, she'd been able to hide her addiction long enough to get through the aid's help and physical therapy, but for some reason – for which I initially hired my pack of lawyers – the doctor's office kept signing off on prescription painkillers well after the recovery period.

The working theory from my lawyers is that as she's my mother, the doctor probably thought she was giving her pills to me, a not uncommon thing for celebrities to do in Hollywood.

In short, *I'm* the reason my mother became additive to opioids.

Ignoring my own emotional turmoil, I add, 'I even made *biscoitos* the other night.'

'*Bom.*' She sniffs, looking every bit the strong, proud Latina woman who raised me. 'Maybe you'll put on a few pounds and those silly women will stop asking you to take your clothes off.'

With the dinner I just made laying heavy in my stomach, her wish is more than likely to be granted. 'Yes, *Mãe*.'

'*Deixa eu te falar, coração.*' She tsks, her lips pursing. 'They don't even *know* you.'

'I know, *Mãe*.' My response is the same as it has been the several other times we've had this conversation.

While she's never said a word against me being an actor, my mother has had more than a few things to say about the pretty overt come-ons she's witnessed whenever I've taken her as my date to events. And then there's the lustful fan comments she reads online and on my social media posts.

Which is probably why, with everything going on with Camilla, I'm glad for the social media ban the rehab facility has in place for those undergoing treatment.

Deciding to circle back to what I know will make her happy, I lift the phone up higher and lean back on the chair's cushions. 'I'm finally putting all your cooking lessons to use.'

'Ah.' Another smile. 'What else have you been making?'

We chat happily for a while, the call feeling more natural since she's finished the hardest part of her treatment – detox. We discuss recipes and reminisce over my early years in the kitchen when I was as bad at cooking as Anne is now.

Thinking of Anne…

'You would love the grocery stores here.' I chuckle, remembering Anne's melons. 'Texans don't mess around when it comes to food.'

'You went to a grocery store? Yourself?' Her brows draw together. 'I thought Jack said you didn't have security with you?'

Damn it, Jack.

I wave away her concerns. 'I wasn't alone, so don't worry.' I keep talking before she can ask more questions. 'It's called H-E-B.'

'Heb?' She speaks the word.

'No, I wasn't spelling it. I mean, I was, but you actually say the le—' Something warm and leathery brushes against my calf, causing me to jerk my leg, my shin whacking into the underside of the coffee table with a loud crack. '*Merda!*' The phone falls from my hands as I grab my leg, the pain making it nearly impossible to recognize that Mike, uncurled from his hump-doll, ventured over to my side of the room.

'*Coração.*' My mom's voice from the phone now muted from its spot on the floor. 'Are you okay? Should I—*oh.*'

Mike looms over my upturned phone on the floor, his wrinkled face taking up the entire screen.

'Is that a movie prop?' Her voice is slow, as if trying to process what she's seeing. 'I thought this space movie was contemporary, not sci-fi.'

Worried he'll understand that my mother just mistook him for an alien puppet, I carefully reach beneath Mike's head to slide my phone out from under it. 'No,' I say once I'm looking into the camera again. 'That was a cat.'

My mother appears more shocked than when she first saw my underwear advertisement billboard. 'A *gato*?'

Before I can explain, Anne, frazzled, wet and near naked, runs into the room. 'What happened?' Her right hand holding the ends of what I'm guessing is a bath towel, but which looks more like an oversized hand towel, together in a fist above her right breast.

My response to her questions is swallowed as a drop of water slides off the end of her wet hair and down between the valley of her breasts.

'Felix?' Mistaking my speechlessness for fear, Anne comes over, using the hand not holding up her towel to grab my shoulder. 'Are you okay?'

Another droplet follows the first, but I manage to nod in answer.

Someone clears their throat.

Anne's hand tightens on my shoulder before slowly turning toward my phone.

I know the exact moment she sees my mother on the screen because the skin under the water droplets pinks in embarrassment.

'Uh, hello.'

'Who are you?' My mother's voice is laced with a tone I only ever heard her use when, in my teenage stupidity, I thought I was entitled to an opinion on how I should be raised.

It's enough to break my sudden fascination with water droplets. '*Mãe*, this is my roommate, Anne Moore.' Turning to Anne, I gesture to my phone. 'Anne, this is my mother, Sofia Maria Santos-Jones.'

Anne's hand, probably from shock, loosens, her towel sliding down an inch.

'You have a roommate, *coração*?' My mother's eyes drop to the corner of the screen as if trying to see Mike. 'With a *gato*?' She seems more incredulous over the last, even though I've never shared a room with anyone on set before. Even Jack gets his own place when he visits.

'*Sim*.' I nod firmly, determined not to deceive her any more than all the lies of omission I've made over the past few weeks.

'Jack didn't mention a roommate,' my mother murmurs, her eyes as fixated on Anne's face as mine are on her towel. 'Or a cat.'

'Don't worry.' Anne drops her hand from my shoulder and squares up to the phone. 'I'm usually good about keeping him away from your son, knowing his fear of house cats.'

My mother lets out an indelicate snort. 'He told you about Fluffy?'

Anne bites down hard on her bottom lip.

Kill me now.

'He told me about the, uh—' she studiously avoids my eyes '—cat who scratched him, yes.'

Adding to my embarrassment, Mike decides to groom himself, loudly, at my feet.

I can only hope my phone's audio isn't able to pick up on the slurping.

Anne tugs her towel up. 'His name is Mike, by the way. The cat.' She grimaces, looking down at herself. 'And, uh, sorry for the towel.'

My mother smiles and nods, having seemingly become charmed by Anne.

A feeling I know well.

There's a beat of slurping awkwardness I rush to fill. 'Anne's the one who got me to cook again.'

'Did you?' *Mãe*'s expression brightens.

Mike stops licking. I don't have time to be thankful since he only does so to jump up on my chair's armrest.

Anne smiles and shakes her head. 'That was the cost of your son staying here.' Seeing Mike reach out his paw toward me, she scoops him up with the hand not holding her towel. 'And I'm lucky your son is such a great cook. I'm definitely getting the better end of the deal.'

I can't help but smile at the compliment.

Seeing my pleased expression, Anne rolls her eyes. 'In fact, I told him he'd make a better cook than actor.'

My mother chuckles, a sound I haven't heard near enough lately. 'And you, Anne? What do you do?'

Anne adjusts her hold on Mike, whose back legs dangle at her side. 'I'm interning as a storyboarder as part of my master's degree in digital art.'

'Master's degree?' She cuts her eyes to me. 'Impressive.'

Anne flushes.

'*Mãe*...' It's a Hail Mary attempt to curb my mother's blatant interest. If Sofia Maria Santos-Jones wants to look at Anne as a potential future daughter-in-law, I can't stop her. The best I can do is pray for subtlety.

'Is that how you two met?' Mother leans into the camera. 'On set?'

Anne and I share a look. One filled with memories of our bar conversation and the hotel after. Memories I'd rather my mother not know about, even if it means another lie of omission.

There are some things a mother really shouldn't know.

Clearing her throat, Anne turns back to the camera. 'Actually, it wasn't until your son showed up and screamed high and loud enough to break glass that I realized I was getting a roommate.'

Mãe laughs. Really laughs.

It's a great moment. A weird moment. Me sitting in an oversized armchair, Anne standing in just a towel with a hairless demon in her arms, both of us smiling at each other while my mother, watching avidly from hundreds of miles away, laughs.

And, unsurprisingly, Mike Hunt goes and ruins it.

No doubt uncomfortable with his awkward hold, Mike curls his back legs forward, the momentum loosening Anne's grip. Gravity takes hold, swinging his hairless body like a pendulum until he and his claws entangle in Anne's damp towel.

There's a collective chorus – Anne's exclaimed obscenity, Mike's hiss, and my inadvertent gasp – as the towel is torn from Anne's body, leaving her naked and wet while Mike lands a perfect dismount on the arm of my chair.

It's only a second. Maybe even shorter, before Anne dives to the floor, but it's enough for the dick Anne thinks of as impotent to stand strong and proud under my exercise shorts.

Thankfully, with Anne ducking out of the camera's view and my phone's raised position, my body's reaction remains hidden.

Re-covered in her towel, Anne stays hunched on the floor, opting to crawl toward the hallway rather than stand again. 'I'm so sorry!'

I'm not sure if she's talking to me or my mother but neither of us say anything as my mother stares at me staring at Anne's half-visible backside peeking out from her towel as she slinks out of the room on all fours.

My mother breaks the silence. 'I like her.'

'Yeah.' As if in a daze, I drag my eyes away from where Anne just disappeared and stare into my mother's all-too-knowing smile. 'Me too.'

It isn't until I look back at the small square of myself on the phone screen that I realize I'm not only smiling back, but I'm also scratching Mike behind his ears.

14

LIZ

'Places, everyone.' Ron, the director, claps his hands, the sound echoing in the massive building, as he sits behind the camera focused on Felix, who looks handsome as ever in a plaid button-down, jeans and boots.

Felix's character, Holden, is a cowboy who falls in love with an astronaut. And while I've seen him dressed as a cowboy to go produce shopping, something about the way the wardrobe team has cut the line of his shirt and molded the denim to the curve of his ass has me appreciating Texas in a way I never did before.

If Thomas were here, he'd poach the wardrobe team for Moore's tailoring department.

'Where's Amanda?' David asks, looking around for Felix's co-star.

With the pre-approved time to film at NASA so tight, Ron's been leaning on my professor to help with more of the pre-production work than just storyboarding.

One of the crew members points to a side door. 'I saw her go that way.'

Ron's expression flattens. There's only so much time before NASA kicks the Hollywood interlopers out. There's no time for retakes, let alone running over the film's schedule.

Today's scene, filmed poolside in the Neutral Buoyancy Lab, where

NASA trains its astronauts in what is as close to micro-gravity as you can get on Earth – water.

And a lot of it.

The NBL has one of the world's largest indoor pools that contains full-scale mock-ups of the International Space Station and visiting vehicles like SpaceX Dragon and the European Space Agency ATV.

And with that comes the heavy scent of chlorine saturating the humid air.

Mike's already wrinkled face contorts with multiple sneezes. On the fourth, he bats at his own face with his paw as if attempting to expel the heavy, chorine-saturated air out of his nose.

Today is my last day as a storyboarder and the film's quickest turn-around time on any given NASA location. Usually, after I hand in a storyboard, there's a day or two where Ron can review the locations via my artwork before arriving on set to film. Time to plan lighting, camera angles and actor marks. But with the added insurance needed to film near such a large amount of water and the astronauts' tight training schedule, there's only one day to get it all done.

Mike sneezes again and I fight the urge to pick him up and cuddle him. The less attention I bring my way, the better.

'Um...' Amanda's manager stares at the door the crew member pointed to, fidgeting when his client fails to appear. 'I'll go get her.'

With a heavy sigh, Ron slides off his seat and walks toward Felix. 'Let's take this time to go over the scene.'

Felix nods, looking more apt student than devil-may-care leading man.

It's annoyingly attractive.

'In this scene, you're being pushed to overcome your fears.' Ron pauses, staring at Felix but as if seeing him as his character. 'Fear that's become a crutch after losing your father in a car accident.' He lowers both hands onto Felix's shoulders. 'And now that fear is keeping you from what you really want. What you *need*.'

A plethora of expressions flicker over Felix's face in rapid succession as if he's trying on and shedding various emotions, determining which ones fit his motivation.

It's entrancing.

'Jennifer is going to push you,' Ron continues, speaking of Amanda's character. 'And you'll want to fight it. But you love her. And love is what allows you to be fearless.'

A few crew members sigh.

While I hold back on sighing, I do find myself nodding. Without love, I'm pretty sure Chase would still be playing the spare to the heir card by speed dating and refusing to live up to his potential while my other brother Thomas would still be a workaholic with a soul as empty as my bank account after Stanley Moore got done with it.

But then again, love is also why my mother married Stanley Winston Moore. A decision I'm sure she regrets.

I guess that means that while love can make stupid people do smart things, it can also make smart people do really stupid things.

Things like accepting my professor's invitation to stay and watch filming when I could be home, alone, and free to draw whatever my little heart and imagination desires.

Not that Felix and I are in love. Or even a relationship. A *friend*ship, maybe. But definitely not love.

I shake my head as if to emphasize that fact, accidentally scribbling over my latest drawing. Curiosity. Yes. I'm simply *curious* over all the hubbub I've heard about Felix's acting skills.

That's all. That why I'm here.

'You know electronics are forbidden on set, right?' Coral Halter Top, aka Sylvie, who I also remember from the press junket, taps her foot in front of me. But instead of a coral halter top, today she's wearing a white tube top sans bra, noticeable thanks to the puckered circles visible through the spandex.

'It's studio approved. I'm a storyboarder.' I tilt the tablet toward my chest, not wanting her to see the obvious not-work-related drawing of Mike lovingly riding a rocket into space to hunt for mice-eating moon cheese.

'Huh.' She crosses her arms, a half-smirk on her glossy lips. 'That's right, you're the *intern*.' She says *intern* like it's an insult.

'Yep.' My cheeks feel tight as I smile. 'That's me. Intern.'

She shakes her head, the rhinestone clip in her hair catching the overhead lights.

Mike lunges, but my hold on his leash keeps him from jumping.

Boobs jostling as she takes a step back, Sylvie points at Mike. 'What's *that*?' As usual, Mike's presence startles the unsuspecting.

'Oh, this?' I slide my tablet in my bag then pick Mike up. 'This is an emotional support sphinx.'

Mike's eyes never leave the woman's hair.

Giving me full-on *Mean Girls* vibes, Sylvie curls her lip. 'Ew.' She recoils further when Mike stretches a paw toward her. 'Keep that rat away from me.'

Feeling very much like a protective older sibling, I step toward her. *I may be able to call him all sorts of names, but that's because I love him. I'll be damned if I'm going to let some big-boobed, try-hard slander my brother's cunt.* 'He's *not* a rat.'

Her eyes widen in surprise. I guess she isn't used to a lot of back-talk. Bullies never are. I learned that in boarding school.

'And if you don't want his attention, hide your hair clip.' I smile when both her hands shoot to her head. 'He loves clawing shiny things.'

With one last glare, she spins on her heel and hustles back to the crew.

The large amount of satisfaction I feel when she pockets her hair clip is sad.

Mike meows his disappointment.

'Let's just get a crew member to step in for Amanda.' Ron, apparently done waiting for his leading lady, draws my attention back to the crew as he points between the jib crane and the edge of the pool.

'Yes.' David nods, his expression focused. 'Good idea.'

As if rewarding me for my loyalty, Mike rubs his nose against mine and purrs.

I nuzzle him back. 'I love you too, buddy.' He's been especially affectionate since he caused my indecent exposure in front of Felix's mother.

And Felix and I have been especially awkward in front of each other since then as well.

I undo the scribble on my tablet, and, using the shape tool, change Mike's pupils to hearts.

'I'll do it!' Sylvie nearly pops her top thrusting her arm in the air. 'I volunteer.'

'Sorry.' David shakes his head. 'We can't use a crew member.'

Nearly all of Sylvie deflates.

'It might cause problems with the union,' David adds.

Ron pinches the bridge of his nose. 'Then who the hell—'

'I got this.' David scans the crowd, pausing when he catches sight of me. 'Anne!'

Fuck a duck.

Hands together, as if in prayer, David points them toward me and smiles. 'May I borrow you for a moment?'

Reluctance threads its way through me as I force a thin smile and lower Mike to the concrete floor. 'Sure.'

'Great.' If David notes the reluctance in my voice, he doesn't show it.

Felix, standing behind David, covers his mouth with one hand, his shaking shoulders telling me he did *not* miss my lack of enthusiasm.

'Anne isn't a studio worker, she's my intern,' David explains to Ron.

Sylvie doesn't look as superior as she had before at the mention of my title.

Under her glare, I drag my feet as David gestures me forward.

The crew parts like the Red Sea allowing Moses Mike and me through, their murmurs of shock and awe causing Mike to make the most of his catwalk.

As I move past the crew, Ron glances at me and shrugs. 'Fine.' Then he goes back to looking over his clipboard. I'm not sure if he doesn't notice Mike or just doesn't care.

Circling on his leash, Mikey faces me, holding up his tail and giving Ron the perfect view of his hairless arsehole. Thankfully, Ron doesn't look.

I bite my lip, coughing to cover a laugh when my eyes catch sight of Felix, his lips twisting to the side. Our shared amusement over Mike's antics strangely making me feel less nervous about all the unwanted attention.

Placing my work bag on the ground, I pretend not to notice Sylvie eviscerating me with her eyes as I tie the end of Mike's leash to the leg of a crane that's bolted into the ground. Satisfied I've properly thwarted Mikey's genius-level Houdini skills, I scratch him between the ears. 'Be a good boy, okay?'

Thus far, Mike has defied the odds by *not* causing a federal incident while at NASA. A miracle that might have to do with the tight leash and baby carrier always keeping him restricted. Or, and probably the most likely, his good behavior stems from a constant stream of treats.

I pat his side, noticeably thicker since Chase left him with me.

'This way.' David waves me over once more, hurrying me along.

For added insurance, I give Mikey another treat before standing.

'Now then, Anne,' David says once I reach him and Felix by the crane, 'we just need to block out the scene, make sure the angles are good before we start filming.' David holds up the storyboard I created, the details from the script coming back to me as I look it over.

Oh crap.

I cut my eyes to Felix, who, from the smirk on his face, knows exactly what the two characters are supposed to do in this scene.

'Stand.' Ron gestures to a blue taped X on the ground.

Like a soldier obeying orders, I do, my Birkenstocks dragging across the textured poolside concrete.

'In this scene, the two leads are talking,' Ron explains. 'Then Jennifer, Amanda's character, walks over to Holden, Felix's character.' Ron looks at me, and whatever expression I'm making has him adding, 'You're standing in for Amanda's character.'

Felix's eyes glitter like the pool water under the fluorescent lights.

'Got it.' I nod, looking anywhere but at the man standing on the other blue X a few feet in front of me.

To Felix, I'm probably getting my just deserts. I've spent the past few days since flashing his mother avoiding him as much as possible. Kind of hard to do when you live together, but I've given it my best shot.

And now here we are, publicly thrust together, about to be closer than we have since that night at the bar.

Because what Ron didn't say, but Felix and I know, is that this scene doesn't end with Julia walking to Holden.

It ends when they kiss.

* * *

Felix

My mother's prayers must've been answered.

'All right people, places!' Ron shouts, waving people back behind the floor lines the crew taped up earlier.

Because I'm sure she's spent the last few days since meeting Anne praying to whomever the saint of matchmaking is for them to intervene between Anne and me. She said so in no uncertain terms before she hung up the other night.

And while all week Anne's done her best to limit her interactions with me, and thus thwart my mother's not-so-secret plans, it seems today the patron saints finally pulled through.

Not that I want them to.

I pull at my collar, tight in the humid room.

It's just that Anne's awkward, near-silent treatment is getting a little old.

I mean, she sends me thank you notes whenever I call the chauffeur service and leave the car for her to take to work whenever our schedules don't align. And she still sketches when I cook and eats with me when I'm home, though that hasn't been often since filming started.

But it's obvious that she's still embarrassed from dropping her towel in front of my mother, even though I told her she didn't need to be. However, it probably hadn't helped that I was laughing at the time.

Anne's eyes narrow and I realize I'm chuckling even now as I remember her peach-shaped ass peeking out from under the bottom of her bath towel as she crawled across the living area and down the hall.

But at least she's looking at me.

'Walk when you hear "action",' Ron instructs.

If possible, Anne stiffens further, and a flash of sympathy hits me. She *really* doesn't like being center stage.

'Action.'

She doesn't even get halfway across the ten feet between us when Ron shouts, 'Cut,' stopping her robotic movements.

Before Ron can yell further, David slides an arm around her shoulders, corralling her back to the starting point. He whispers something in her ear that has her looking sharply at him. But then she nods, kicks off her sandals and turns on her mark to face me.

'She's got it now,' David tells Ron.

Ron's expression remains skeptical, but he motions the crew to be quiet.

And in the few seconds it takes for the crew to focus all their attention on Anne, and before Ron even yells 'action', something happens.

Anne rolls her shoulders back, lifts onto her toes as if wearing heels, and cocks her hip to the side. She appears taller, confident, and quite frankly, every inch the leading lady.

'Action.'

It's my turn to stiffen – *everywhere* – as Anne saunters, not walks, toward me, hips swaying, ponytail swinging, stopping a mere breath away.

She grabs the front of my shirt with both hands twisting into the fabric, tugging me closer until my chest presses against hers, until her breath caresses my lips.

'Hey, cowboy.' Her husky whisper echoes in the large space, the line spoken with a sultry sexiness that nearly makes me forget my reply.

'Hey there, space cadet.' My voice lower than it needs to be for filming.

But just when Ron is about to yell cut, to go over the stand-in spacing to ensure the camera angles are set for filming, Anne presses her lips to mine.

I should stop her. Tell her what she doesn't seem to know. That blocking is just for going through the motions, not acting out the entire scene.

I don't. Instead, I do just what romance novelist Audrey Cole thinks any hot-blooded cowboy would do with a spitfire astronaut in their arms – I kiss her back.

But it isn't a Hollywood kiss, and this isn't an astronaut in my arms. It's Anne, the woman who didn't hesitate to knee me in the nuts but took the time to ensure I'm not triggered by her brother's ugly-ass cat. Anne, who can't cook but who went out of her way to disguise me so I'd be safe selecting my own fresh produce. Anne, who could not be less impressed by my celebrity but who nearly imploded from embarrassment when she accidentally exposed herself my mother.

I wrap my arms around her, pulling her flush against me, her arms releasing their hold on my shirt to slide up into my hair. And when I lap my tongue against hers, her nails drag against my scalp.

Someone yells cut. Someone else whistles. Another person catcalls.

Neither one of us pulls back, our breath melding together along with our lips.

I'm not thinking about the crew, my public image, or how being so lost to reason will only stir the shitstorm surrounding my life. I'm thinking about Anne and how good she feels in my arms. How I never want to stop kissing her. Having her. Being with her.

In fact, I'm not sure we ever would've stopped kissing.

If it wasn't for the blood-curdling scream.

15

FELIX

'Jesus H Christ!' Ron's voice booms across the pool. 'Get it off me!'

Anne and I jerk apart, her looking deliciously confused, me 100 per cent certain of what 'it' is.

And sure enough, when I'm able to focus beyond Anne's lips, I catch sight of Mike, looking like an obese, hairless flying squirrel, attacking Ron's backside.

How he attached himself to the back of a middle-aged man's cargo shorts, I have no idea, but there he is, digging into Ron's rear end with all the frantic pawing of a dog searching for a bone.

Anne's hand encircles my forearm in a vice-like grip when she catches sight of the chaos. 'Mike Hunt!'

If there was anything that would get more attention than a hairless cat attacking the ass of one of the foremost revered directors in all of Hollywood, it would be Mike's full name screamed in a secured, government facility.

Especially as it's shouted in a lull between Ron's stunned curses.

Half the crew focuses on Anne.

'What did she just say?'

'She can't possibly mean—'

'I thought only British people used that word?'

'What the—fuck!' Ron's face goes white and David reaches out a hand to steady him.

Oblivious to everything but Mike on Ron, Anne rushes forward, arms out. 'Mikey, let go!'

'His claws…' Ron drops his hands to the front of his shorts and every male winces in sympathy from Mike digging a little too deep.

David grabs hold of Ron's shoulders, stiff with pain, while Anne grabs ahold of Mike's ribcage. A tug of war ensues with David pulling one way and Anne pulling the other.

Fabric renders.

Anne's bare feet grip the wet cement, as she just manages to maintain her hold on Mike.

Ron's sneakers aren't so lucky. He pinwheels back into David, both sliding perilously close to the water's edge.

I snap to my senses just in time to prevent them from capsizing into the pool, pulling them forward by Ron's t-shirt.

More fabric renders.

'What—' Ron's pants echo over the shocked, silent crew '—the hell?'

Bent over from exertion, the crew bears witness to their director's white briefs, revealed behind shredded cargo shorts.

Briefs and… frowning, I reach out and unhook an object from Ron's back belt loop. 'Is this a hair thing?'

'Who the fuck cares what that is?' Ron snatches the hair accessory from my hand, pointing it at Mike. 'The real question is what the hell is *that* and who the *fuck* allowed it on my set?' The silver, rhinestoned claw catches sparkles under the many fluorescent overhead lights.

Mike's shoulders shimmy, his eyes narrowing on Ron's hand.

'No, buddy.' Anne struggles to contain him, but Mikey's leash is nowhere in sight. 'Don't you do it.' But it's too late. Anne loses her grip and Mikey pounces.

Ron, horror struck once more, steps back, throwing his hands, and the hair accessory, trying to ward off the attack.

Anne steps forward, hand outstretched. 'Mikey!'

But it's too late.

The hair clip arcs over his head. And, like an acrobat, Mike climbs the director's body, using Ron's shoulders as a launching pad to dive after the sparkling accessory.

And dive he does – right into NASA's swimming pool.

There's a splash, then silence. Everyone's eyes fixated on the circle of ripples wavering above the submerged International Space Station mock-up.

'Mikey?' Anne's voice, stunned and anxious, breaks me from my stupor.

I tug off my boots.

'Don't even think about it, Jones.' Ron has one hand on his ass, the other at the torn neck of his t-shirt and his voice brokers no argument.

So I don't argue.

Because I always listen to my director. I'm known for it. And, if I'm asked later, I will insist that I'd listened to him now. Because there's no way I'd be doing exactly what I'm doing now, if I'd been thinking about it at all.

I jump in.

'Damn it, Jones!' Ron's voice carries underwater.

Just to prove how much I hadn't been thinking about my actions, as soon as I hit the water, I realize cannonballing into the pool was *not* the smartest course of action.

For so many reasons.

Like, having closed my eyes, I get turned around in the unfamiliar pool. And with the pool so deep, I'm unable to push off the bottom, leaving me kicking to the surface, which is slow and exhausting thanks to my soaked jeans.

But the main reason jumping into the pool after Mike was a bad idea is because the force from all 212 pounds of me has caused a surge of waves that have pushed the skinny-dipping feline farther and farther away.

'Mikey!'

Ignoring the sting of chlorine from the water in my eyes, I squint up at Anne, whose bare toes are over the edge of the pool, looking like she's about to man-overboard alongside me.

'I've got him.' At least, I hope I do. 'Stay there.'

She gives me a quick glance and a shaky nod before pointing toward the middle of the pool.

I begin swimming in that direction, huffing what seems like equal amounts of water and air.

'Fucking hell!'

I'm pretty sure that's Ron, but I'm too focused on the task before me to turn back and check.

'Mike.' I catch a glimpse of his ears as I push my hands out and back in a breaststroke, the heavy weight of wet denim making my legs almost useless. 'Come here, man.'

While the waves I made pushed Mike a few feet away, his intense kitty-paddling is taking him even farther over the International Space Station and middle of the 200-foot-long pool.

Validating my feline aversion, Mike continues pawing the water in front of him – away from me.

I hear another splash, but I'm too focused on catching up to Mike that I don't check who else is dumb enough to join my cat crusade.

I just hope it isn't Anne.

Finally, I snag an arm around Mike. He must've gotten a hold of the hair clip just before I grabbed him because it's in his front paws but he's batting it around making it hard to keep hold of him.

'Chill, man.'

Struggling to keep him and me above water, it hits that I'm now a hundred feet from the edge of a pool with no shallow end. And now, with Mike in my arms, I'll need to swim back one handed.

I shift him to my chest so I can give us a moment's rest by floating on my back, but the heavy soaked denim around my legs doesn't allow me more than a few seconds before I need to kick out if I don't want us pulled under.

'I promise...' My pleading's staggered from struggling to stay above water. 'I'll buy you... a disco ball... if you just... stop moving.'

Hair accessory secure in his mouth, Mike listens.

And yet, in typical Mike fashion, he listens by digging his claws in the wet flannel covering my chest so he can use me like his personal flotation device.

Taking a moment to recoup, I close my eyes against the bright overhead lights above the pool and focus on keeping the top of my body above water.

I also question the validity of my trainer.

I'm a fit guy. The whole country can testify to that, or at least the ones who watch my movies. I do most of my own stunts and I work out nearly every day. Some might even say I'm cut.

The act of swimming, fully clothed, after a naked cat has become my Everest, and I've found myself up shit mountain without a sherpa.

I'm fucking exhausted.

'I've got you.'

Either my ears are waterlogged, making Anne's voice deeper, or there's someone else willing to jump in after Mike Hunt.

Someone with heavily muscled arms and solid shoulders.

Tilting my head back against one of the shoulders now propping my head up, I find myself staring into dark-brown eyes ringed with vivid green. 'Hold on to the, uh, cat, and just let your body relax as I pull you in.'

I might be suffering from oxygen deprivation. Or muscle fatigue. Or quite possibly my brain hasn't recovered from Anne's reality-altering kiss. But whatever it is, as the muscular man with pretty eyes floats me to safety, I have the strange thought that I might want to start looking into damsels-in-distress roles.

Because being rescued isn't half bad.

Mike shifts, clawing my nipple.

Minus the cat, of course.

* * *

Liz

'What in the ever-loving fuck just happened?' Ron's temper, momentarily checked when his leading man jumped into a pool to save an ass-assaulting hairless cat, explodes once more.

Felix winces before giving him one of the two towels that someone handed him and the guy next to him. The guy who helped save him and Mike.

Too overcome with relief to be concerned with Ron's implosion, I cuddle a wet and weakened Mike Hunt to my chest while the crew scurries to find more towels.

Mike nuzzles me, something hard and pointy digging into my shirt. Pulling back, my eyes narrow on the hair clip clenched between his chattering jaw.

Feeling murderous, I search the crew for a white tank top.

'Someone get more towels.'

'Call wardrobe for a new outfit.'

'Where the *hell* is Amanda?'

The crew, formerly frozen in shock, jumps into action. I can't find Sylvie among them. If she ran, she's smart. Because if I catch hold of her now, feeling like this, I'd end up doing something truly horrific.

Something worse than a quick punch to the implant. Or some impromptu water boarding in front of her movie-star crush.

No, I'd do something that would scar her for life – both mentally *and* physically.

Something demonic like spraying her with edible glitter and locking her in a room with a disco ball and a catnip-drugged Mike Hunt whilst Tom Jones' 'What's New Pussycat?' played on repeat.

I'm startled out of my vengeance planning when the guy who helped Felix and Mike catches my eye. Having been so concerned with Mike, I failed to notice how attractive he is. Or how shirtless. Standing in a pair of board shorts, he looks like a wet, muscular K-Pop idol Ken doll come to life.

'Everything all right?'

It takes a second for his words to compute. Oddly, it's the same amount of time it takes to stop staring at his abs.

'Um, yes. Yes, it is.' I hug Mike closer to my chest. 'I can't thank you enough.'

'Yeah.' Felix flares out the new towel someone tossed him and wraps it around me, obscuring my view of K-Pop Ken. 'Thanks for the help.' Pulling me closer to him, he peers over my shoulder to see Mike. 'How's the little guy doing?'

Mike slow blinks while using my boob as his pillow, the maniacal feline already starting to doze. Which isn't surprising considering he's gotten more physical activity in the last five minutes than he probably has all year.

With the tube-topped object of my anger not here to rage against, the tears of relief that have threatened since Felix managed to catch up to Mike in the dead center of the pool are harder to hold back. 'Fine, I—' I clear my throat. 'Fine, I think.'

Felix's eyes catch mine.

A drop of water slides down his temple, close to his mouth, and his breath hitches.

As does mine.

'Felix, I—'

'Excuse me?' Ron's New Balance sneakers smack to a stop next to us. 'Can someone tell me how the *hell* we're supposed to film our next scene with one actor missing and the other soaking fucking wet?'

For a man with his tighty-whities half exposed, Ron is surprisingly frightening.

'Sorry, Ron.' Felix shifts, the odd moment gone. 'I'll find wardrobe and—'

'Who are you?' Ron points to K-pop Ken, who steps up on my other side, his ab muscles glistening under the nearby camera lights.

Felix pulls me back.

'Park In-Su.' He holds his hand out to Ron.

As if out of habit, Ron grasps it.

Park smiles.

The director blinks, momentarily stunned just like I'd been. 'Are you an actor?' Ron sounds hopeful.

'No.' Park chuckles. 'I'm an astronaut.'

At 'astronaut', I glance across to where Park had jumped into the pool and where a few NASA employees have gathered to see what all the Hollywood commotion is about.

Thankfully, I don't see a blonde with black glasses. As much as I want to see my sister, I definitely don't want to be holding Mike Hunt, about to be fired, the first time we meet.

Park gestures to his co-workers. 'I just happened to see what was going on as I was exiting the locker rooms.' He chuckles at Mike. 'Man, the others are not going to believe me when I tell them what happened.'

Hopefully by 'others', he doesn't mean my sister.

Park's smile brightens. 'I'll just have to see if I can get a copy of the footage.'

'What footage?' My voice cracks at the end.

Mikey nuzzles my boob.

Park points into the pool. 'There are cameras lined along the pool's walls.' He crosses his fingers. 'Let's hope they were on just now.'

Ron closes his eyes and takes a deep breath, as if trying to fend off a mental breakdown. 'David?' His voice much lower and calmer than before.

My professor is at his side in an instant. 'Yeah, Ron?'

'Why does your intern have a cat?' The undercurrent of his question a lot darker than all his previous shouting. 'And why is it on set?'

David jerks his head to me, then back to Ron. 'Ah, well you see...'

'Mike's an emotional support animal,' I offer, my voice a lot higher than I'd like. Water droplets that I can't blame on the pool, sliding down my temples.

As if knowing he's the topic of conversation, Mike flops his head back to aim an upside-down glare at Ron. I juggle his weight, trying to show Mike in a better light. If such a thing is possible. 'After I cleared it with NASA, I thought—'

'Why wasn't it cleared with *me*?' Ron, looking less than impressed with Mike and his (probably forged) credentials, crosses him arms.

The crew stills once more, all eyes on me. Judging eyes.

Heat rushes to my face and I feel like I'm seventeen again, standing in front of my 'father', who's furious because I had the audacity to ask to go to an art institute rather than an Ivy League college.

David, sensing my discomfort as he did during the scene blocking, opens his mouth.

I cut him off with a look, not wanting to jeopardize his comeback to film or his friendship with Ron over something that is very much my fault. I should've gone home. I should've said no to being a stand-in. And I most assuredly should not have had Mike on set with me surrounded by all these people and various temptations to cause mischief and mayhem.

Consoling myself with the thought that I'll still have an opportunity to meet my sister at the astronaut dinner, I take a deep breath and prepare to be fired. 'I'm—'

'Because I didn't tell her to.' Felix takes a step forward, drawing Ron's attention.

Ron pulls back. 'And why would you be talking to her?' He frowns at Felix, and, if possible, his eyes narrow further. 'She's an intern.'

Man. Hollywood really doesn't like interns.

'Because I hired her.' Felix thumbs over his shoulder at Mike, now snoring like a top-of-the-line espresso maker in my arms. 'To look after my emotional support animal.'

My mouth, along with all the others', drops.

'That's *your* animal?' Ron's voice rises again, this time at a higher pitch.

In my peripheral vision, I notice Park's shoulders shaking.

'Yeah.' Felix crosses his arms, looking every inch the kick-ass-and-take-names action hero he is. 'Is it a problem to take care of your mental health?'

The vein at Ron's temple pulses.

'Sorry about that.' Amanda, looking badass in a blue NASA jumpsuit, struts through the gathered crew. Her million-dollar smile fading as she comes full stop next to David, her eyes ping-ponging between her soggy co-star, the half-naked astronaut and the apocalyptic expression on her director's face. 'Um…' Settling on me, she raises an eyebrow at Mike. 'What'd I miss?'

16

LIZ

I feel horrible.

Dropping my forehead on the steering wheel in front of me, I fail to muster up the will to vacate Felix's rental and head upstairs to the condo. It seems the drive to the parking garage, that I made as if on autopilot, has drained whatever energy I had left after watching my brother's cat almost drown, my roommate go full-on Tom Hanks in *Castaway*, followed by my inability to take responsibility for the clusterfuck that is Mike Hunt.

Not to mention that *kiss*.

The clusterfuck himself paws the inside of the driver's side door of the SUV, giving the impression that he's fully recovered from his skinny-dipping ordeal.

It seems I'm the only one stuck in traumatization mode.

Even Felix rebounded to normalcy once everyone else got back to the job of movie making. He asked me if *I* was okay as he steered me toward the exit of the Neutral Buoyancy Lab. And when I nodded in response, lamely I might add, he *smiled* before handing me the keys to his rental car.

As if he wasn't upset, or angry, or even annoyed over the drama I caused between him and Ron, the director who gave Felix a chance by casting him in his first non-action role. He's mentioned his desire to step out of his normal shoot-'em-up roles, and I can tell by the amount of prep work I've seen him doing – script reading, NASA research, scene blocking – that he's taking this role very seriously.

And after I fucked it up, Felix seemed more concerned about my emotional state than his career.

It could be that Felix is an exceptional actor. And yet, while that still may be true, I think the real reason is something else. Something I previously suspected the first time Felix chopped parsley at the kitchen island.

Felix Jones is a nice guy. A guy who made a horrible first impression, but has since proven himself a man that goes above and beyond. Even when it doesn't benefit him. And even when, like today, it actually hurts him.

And what have I done aside from deleting a photo I was never going to sell?

I've flashed his mother, drawn him in NSFW poses and paraded a feline PTSD trigger around our shared living space like an American flag on the Fourth of July. And now, with the help of Mike Hunt, I damaged his professional reputation and possibly his future movie options.

Leaning back against the leather seat, I close my eyes. 'God, I'm the worst.'

Mike, as if agreeing, head butts my shoulder.

It should've been the one to jump in after Mike. But I'd been too... too... *something* after that kiss to think straight.

Obviously, Felix did not have that problem. He's used to kissing women on set. It's his job. In fact, he's probably kissing Amanda right now in the same place he kissed me.

Stupid Amanda.

Ugh. No. Amanda is great. *I'm* the worst.

I may have continued wallowing in the safety of Felix's luxury SUV if it wasn't for my phone ringing with a familiar New York number.

My sister-in-law wants to FaceTime.

'Meow.' Mikey paws the air in front of my phone.

'Okay, okay.' Sliding the call open, I angle the camera toward Mike. 'Hey, Bell.'

Ignoring my greeting, Bell goes full-on cat momma. 'Oh, there's my sweet boy! There's my darling.' Bell's baby-talk has me rolling my eyes. 'Do you miss your mama? Because your mama misses you.'

Mike rolls onto his back, his junk lewdly on display.

'Wow.' Feeling like I'm shooting cat porn, I turn the camera towards me. 'I guess he's mad you ditched him.'

Bell pouts. 'I didn't *ditch* him. I allowed my husband to offer Mike a strategically timed vacation with his Aunt Lizzie.' She leans back, her surroundings coming into focus.

'You're at Moore's?' I recognize Chase's desk chair and view out the window behind her. After Stanley Winston Moore was ousted from his luxury conglomerate throne in Manhattan and sent to jail, I helped Bell and Alice redecorate his office, splitting the massive one into two – one for each brother.

No one mentioned splitting it three ways. Not that I wanted an office. Or even to work there. But I remember wondering if the lack of invite had less to do with my career goals and more to do with me no longer being a legitimate Moore.

'Yes, it's the only place Chase lets me get any work done.'

I blink out of my funk. 'Really?'

'Yeah, since I told him I was working from home today.' She smirks. 'Moore's would be the last place he'd look.'

I nod, continually impressed with my sister-in-law's business and marriage savvy. 'Smart move.'

She flips her red hair back off her shoulder. 'I know.'

'My brother and Moore's would be lost without you.'

Her red lips kick up on one side. 'I know that too.'

Chuckling, I decide to take the opportunity to distract myself with something non cat or Felix related. 'So what are you working on?'

'Moore's has hired my firm to handle new marketing materials for an in-house fashion collaboration they have lined up.' Bell shuffles some papers in front of her. 'Camilla Branson.'

I frown, the name somewhat familiar. Probably another actor. I guess I should watch more mainstream movies if I ever did decide to work at Moore's. 'Who's that?'

When my brothers took over Moore's, they modernized the outdated sales plan and revamped the stores offerings with plans for celebrity-collaborated capsule collections that Moore's themselves would manufacture. It's an exciting direction for a store that used to only sell other brands' designs.

'A Hollywood socialite. Did a reality TV show recently and became quite famous for her style.'

I scoff, all too familiar with the people who claim celebrity just because they're rich. *'That's* enough to get her a collaboration with Moore's?' Though it explains why the name sounds familiar. It was probably one of many on the various invitee lists I helped my mother put together over the years when she was busy being New York City's charity queen.

Bell considers the question. 'Well, not usually, but lately she's been linked to—'

'Whoa, dude.' Not liking being ignored, especially by his mama, Mike climbs onto my lap, insinuating himself between me and the phone.

'Aw, baby.' Bell clasps her hands under her chin. 'You *do* miss me.'

Tuning out my sister-in-law's lovey-dovey nonsense, I get back to contemplating the Felix situation. Between the grudge holding, the kiss and today's Mike-foolery, damage control is needed.

And yet, if I come clean to Ron about Mike being *my* cat, that might make things worse for Felix. And being unable to take responsibility means I'm left with executing one hell of an apology. Words won't be enough.

But I have no clue what to do for him. Even if I dipped into my unused account, Felix is just like my brothers – impossible to shop for. What do you get someone who already has the means to buy themselves whatever they want?

'What's with the long face?'

'Hmm?' I blink back into the phone screen.

'You look sad.' Bell's brows knit together. 'What's wrong and who do I have to hurt?'

Chuckling at the 180-degree emotional turn that took her from cooing to murderous, I do something I haven't done much of this past year. Open up. 'I'm trying to think of how to say, "I'm sorry" to someone.'

While still frowning, the deadly intent leaves her face. 'Want me to send them something from Moore's?'

'Nah.' I stare at the Gucci sports bag that Felix left on the floor in front of the passenger's seat. 'This person is sort of like Chase and Thomas. They have everything they want, or if they don't, they can easily get it themselves.' I shake my head. 'And as with my brothers, I feel like whatever I get them won't be meaningful enough.'

'Are you kidding me?' Bell's snort draws back my attention.

'What?'

'I *wish* I had your ability for gift giving.'

Pushing Mike's head out of the way, I shift in closer to the middle console so we can share the screen. 'What are you talking about?'

'Ummmm...' Bell widens her eyes like the point she's about to make is obvious. 'The Mike Hunt printed dress socks you gave Chase for his birthday last year? Or how 'bout the family calendar you made for Thomas with King Richard in different poses for each month?'

I snort, remembering Thomas' face when Alice hung the calendar on his office wall.

'Or the paint-by-number you made for Mary from the picture of her on her first day of school?' Bell levels her expression. 'Alice *cried*.'

My face heats remembering how emotional my other sister-in-law became when her and my brother's adoptive daughter Mary opened the present. 'But they didn't cost anything, really.' I turn up the SUV's air conditioning. 'They were just simple things.'

Bell looks like she wants to smack me. 'I don't know what's so simple about somehow segmenting a photograph, then labeling each shape with a number that coordinates to a color, but—' she rolls her eyes '—whatever.'

I fiddle with Mike's collar.

'And you should know, growing up like you did, that the best things to receive aren't necessarily large or expensive. They're meaningful.' One of Bell's eyebrows arches. 'Like all the family dinners you orchestrated in the hopes of bringing your family closer together.' A small smile plays on her lips. 'Thomas and Chase agree that a huge part of them burying the hatchet and making amends was *you*. You arranging the dinners. You calling them, keeping tabs on them. Inviting them places – *together*.'

Suddenly, all my brother's phone calls this past year don't seem as troublesome.

Bell scoffs at whatever expression I'm making. 'What did you do that you have to apologize for anyway?'

The past week flashes through my mind. 'A lot of things.'

'That's surprising.' Her auburn brows pinch together. 'I mean, I know I'm biased, but honestly, Lizzie you're one of the most thoughtful people I know.' She blows me a kiss. 'I love you, you know.'

'I love you too, Bell.' I angle my face toward the blasting air-conditioning vent to help dry my watering eyes. 'I—*oomph*.'

Mike head butts me.

'Jesus, Mikey.' Properly scolded for daring to turn the camera away from him, I refocus my phone on the wrinkled terror.

Distracted once more by her feline baby, Bell feigns a speech impediment recounting all the various ways she loves Mike Hunt while I contemplate why, if I'm such a thoughtful person, I've been anything but to Felix Jones.

'Oh, shoot. I got to go.' Bell, voice back to normal, leans back in my brother's desk chair. 'I have a virtual meeting to run for the new campaign.'

'All right—' I give Mike a hug for her benefit, his skin sliding up over his ribcage as I do '—talk soon.'

It isn't until after I hang up that Bell's stunned expression when I mentioned we'd talk soon registers.

Maybe it isn't just Felix I need to apologize to. I may have thought I needed this past year to 'find myself' after discovering the truth about my parentage, but today made me realize that all I've seemed to do is avoid the people who already know me. The people who care about me.

I need to plan more family dinners when I get home.

Dinner.

I let the idea take hold.

Unlike arranging the Moore family dinner – aka asking the chef to cook – I'd have to make this one. Which, if I did, would make for a very unpredictable outcome for an apology that I was hoping to make worthy of Felix's actions today. And making dinner wouldn't be expensive either. Felix already did the shopping.

But maybe he'd find meaning in me taking over what I essentially blackmailed him into doing for me so that I wouldn't kick his homeless Hollywood ass to the curb.

It's just, with my below-basic kitchen skills, I might end up needing to apologize for my apology gift.

Still undecided, I push the ignition button and gather up my belongings.

But as Mike and I are about to get out of the car, a phone rings.

And this time, it isn't mine.

* * *

Felix

Ding.

With my head low, I enter the condo building's elevator, thankful it's empty.

Merde, what a day.

Earlier, once I ushered Anne and Mike off set and out the door, everyone got back to work. The crew reset the scene while I donned a *dry* duplicate outfit from wardrobe and the hair and make-up team redid the work I washed away in NASA's pool.

Through it all, Ron grumbled about high-maintenance actors and their emotional support animals, stopping every few seconds to palm the back of his torn shorts as if making sure it was cat-free. It's obvious he wanted to rip into me. But with the tight deadline and the NASA onlookers, he kept himself in check.

It was good that Anne hadn't argued when I gave her my rental keys.

One, because we didn't need Mike causing any more trouble, and two, Anne probably would've tried to come clean about who Mike belonged to, which would've meant me explaining why I lied – an explanation I don't have.

And three, I would've been too distracted to shoot the scene if Anne had been watching.

The last of which is dumb. I kiss people all the time in movies. Most actors do. Even married actors. Yet, for some reason, the thought of Anne watching me kiss someone else bothers me.

Probably because as soon as Amanda's lips met mine, I stopped pretending Amanda was her character, Julia, and started pretending Amanda was Anne.

Still, it was probably due to that inappropriate imagining that Amanda and I managed to shoot the scene in one take, keeping the film on schedule and giving the crew time to pack up to cede the pool to Park In-Su and his fellow astronauts.

Which – *thank God* – made Ron happy again. Or happy-ish.

He was truly happy after Park and his cohort of NASA employees invited Ron to watch the footage of Mike Hunt's undercarriage floating over the International Space Station. Nothing like having a feline's buoyant nether regions save one's career.

Ding.

Shuffling out of the elevator, I duck my head as a man sidesteps his way on, then make my way toward the condo door. I forgot my bag with both my phone and baseball cap in the car. Without a disguise or an Uber to call, I ended up having to ask Amanda for a ride home.

It was an awkward ten-minute drive. Her trying not to pry but wanting the details about the infamous emotional support hairless cat, the hot astronaut everyone gawked over and me pretending not to know much about the former or care about the latter. Except that I was very much aware of the latter and how Anne was one of the many looking at astronaut Park In-Su as if *he* were the leading man in a romantic comedy.

Merde, I'm pathetic.

Shaking my head at myself, I knock on the door, my key to the condo having been attached to my rental keys. I'm prepared to wait the few minutes it'll take Anne to get from her bedroom to the door. Especially now, with our kiss and Mike's *cat*astrophe putting her center stage – something Anne *hates* – I'm betting she's past awkward avoidance and now fully committed to using her room as a concealment bunker.

So I'm surprised when, before I can even lower my arm, my hair is blown back from a gust of air conditioning as the door opens wide.

'Hi.' Anne greets me with a smile that's brilliant, if a bit crazed, before spinning away and hustling into the kitchen.

The door swings back to close and, on reflex, I throw out my arm to stop it.

'Come in,' Anne calls over her shoulder as my feet remain planted in the hallway, too shocked by what I'm seeing to move.

Cabinet doors open. Fridge ajar. Wafts of steam and the sounds of bubbling coming from the stove top.

And Anne, her topknot off-kilter, a sheen of sweat on her brow and an oil splatter on her t-shirt, twirling one way and then another between the cooktop and the island.

'I made dinner.' Anne cracks an egg on the side of the pan, leaving a trail of egg white sliding down the side.

'I see.' I also see what appears to be every pot, pan, bowl and utensil in the condo strewn out over the countertops, all in various states of use.

Wiping her forehead with her forearm, Anne wipes one egg-covered hand on the tea towel before grabbing one of two spatulas laying on the counter. 'I think it's done.'

If going by the blackened nature of whatever meat is laid out on the plate next to the stove, I'd say it was done quite some time ago.

'Don't look at that.' Anne points to the plate. 'That was my first try.'

My eyebrows shoot up. *First?* How many tries were there?

'*Meow.*' The forlorn sound emanates from the opposite side of the room, where Mike, as if keenly aware of our impending doom, burrows his head in the sofa until only his naked, wrinkled butt is visible between the cushions.

Scanning the empty jar of tomato sauce on the countertop, the half-mangled shallot with the skin somehow still intact on the cutting board, and the open bottle of white distilled vinegar near the stove, I fight the urge to cross myself before entering.

With her free hand, Anne grabs a plate from the cabinet, one of the few things still in there, then gestures to the bar stools with the spatula in her other hand. 'Sit down.' Specks of rice arch off the utensil and onto the floor.

She doesn't notice.

Tentatively, I cross the threshold, closing the door behind me while Anne turns back to the stove and flips the eggs.

Feeling like a passer-by at a car wreck, I'm unable to look away as the yolk breaks and flecks of shell float in the white.

She must not notice that either because she scrapes it out of the pan and onto the plate of rice. *Pink* rice.

Anne places the plate in front of me and steps back to make jazz hands. 'Ta-da!'

I ignore the foreboding churn in my stomach.

'It's tomato rice.' Anne's smile falters. 'You like tomato rice, right?'

'Yes. I like it.' Not that I would classify what's before me as tomato rice, which is usually red, or the egg as fried. More like barely scrambled.

'Good.' Anne heaves a sigh of relieve. 'Your mom said it's supposed to be served with chicken, but, ah—' she eyes the plate of charred meat by the stove '—I figured eggs would be a good protein substitute.'

'Eggs are fi—wait.' My shoulders tighten when what she said registers. 'My mother?' Dread, having to do with the meal before me, coils in my stomach.

'Yeah, you left your phone in the bag in the car.' Anne circles the island to sit next to me. 'She called and since I wanted to apologize to her for the boob incident, I thought it would be okay to answer.' She glances at me and what's left of her smile vanishes. 'No?'

Avoiding her eyes, I pick up my fork. 'What did, uh, you two talk about?'

Out of the corner of my eye, Anne shrugs. 'Not much. I apologized to her and then shamelessly asked her to tell me what you liked to eat so I could cook you dinner.' She ducks her head, adjusting the utensils on the counter. 'I told her I wanted to thank you for helping me out today. And that she raised a soh she should be proud of.'

My stomach tightens, but not from the prospect the dinner before me. Rather, the unsuspecting swell of emotions I'm having trouble controlling.

Anne's lips twist the side. 'She said she's always proud of you but would be even prouder if you stopped taking your clothes off for money.'

I laugh, choking on the lump that had been forming in my throat. 'Yeah, she isn't a fan of my recent underwear campaign.'

We smile at each other, warmth filling my chest where dread had been just moments ago.

Anne fiddles with her utensils. 'My first attempt was piri-piri, but when that didn't turn out, she suggested tomato rice instead.'

It's the first dish my mother had me make as well.

'Tomato rice is great. Thanks.' I glance around at the mess. 'But you didn't have to go to so much trouble.'

'Yes.' Anne locks eyes with me. 'I did. I—' she goes back to fiddling with her fork '—well, I just wanted to say sorry and that, um, you don't need to be my cook or anything to stay here. We're friends now and friends help each other out.'

'Friends?' My gaze drops to her lips, remembering our kiss.

When I lift my eyes to hers again, Anne looks away, a flush on her cheeks. 'But you know, I'd still like to go to the astronaut dinner.'

Laughing, I return my attention to the rice. 'No problem.' I stab/shovel rice and cooked yolk onto my fork, lifting it to my mouth. 'I've already told Vance I'm bringing a plus one.'

Eyes on my fork, Anne watches me take a bite.

Action heroes get a lot of flak for being meatheads who can't act. We're better known for our ab muscles than our acting muscles. And while I have enough self-confidence to know I'm a good actor, and also because Ron wouldn't have hired me for his romantic comedy lead if I wasn't, any doubts I may have had about said acting skills are put to rest when I manage to chew, swallow and smile, not even flinching when my teeth crunch over eggshell. 'It's great.'

'Really?' Her eyebrows shoot up, as if my answer surprises her. 'I mean, I wasn't expecting much, with, you know, my previous attempts in the kitchen—' she laughs nervously '—but I was hoping it was at least palatable.'

She's cute, trying to appear nonchalant but I can tell by the way she won't meet my eyes and the flush deepening across her skin that she isn't as unaffected by her cooking gesture as she'd like me to think.

It makes me want to hug her. Kiss her. Eat more eggshell.

Instead, I wait until she lifts her eyes to mine. 'Really.'

Her answering smile, natural and bright, is nearly enough for me to not notice the overcooked, gelatinous-like texture of the rice.

Nearly.

As she flits between the sink and stove fixing her own plate, I catch sight of my reflection in the microwave door across the way, and the goofy smile I'm wearing.

Somewhere between Anne's numb face and my unexpected water rescue, Anne has me feeling something I never thought I could feel again, especially not while dealing with the aftermath of the last woman I got involved with.

Content. Happy, even.

Even with my mother still in treatment. Even with Camilla's threats still unchecked. Even with living with the most cantankerous and diabolical feline known to man.

I'm happy thanks to a woman whom I don't know near enough about but still can't help wanting all the same.

And I can't help but look at the mess around me as evidence of how hard she tried to say thank you and I think that maybe, just maybe, Anne feels the same.

Having retaken her seat and apparently a bite of her dinner, Anne struggles to chew, her eyes watering.

Worried, I stand, about to thump her on the back. Not realizing until she manages to swallow that she isn't choking but laughing.

'Felix Jones.' Grabbing a napkin, she dabs her eyes. 'You are *such* a fucking liar.'

Then again, maybe she doesn't feel the same.

'I cannot believe you would eat that.' She double facepalms herself. 'That's just what I need – Ron coming after me for giving his lead actor food poisoning.'

'It isn't *that* bad.'

Dropping her hands, she stares at me, her brow furrowed, but her lips twitching. Like she can't decide if she wants to laugh or yell at me. 'Really?' Reaching over, she plucks a large chunk of eggshell from my plate, then drops it back down.

I bite my lip to keep from laughing.

Snorting, she wipes her hands on her napkin. 'Why in the world would you eat that?'

The answer to that is the same as the answer to why, weeks ago, despite Jack's logical warnings, I followed Anne from a bar to a hotel. The same answer to why I wanted to stay in this condo, with her, rather than a five-star hotel. And it's the same answer to why I couldn't stand by and watch Anne get yelled at today, despite the repercussions it may have had on my career.

And while I'm well versed in improv and could probably romance a soliloquy that would make men and women weep like they do at my movie's happy endings, a good actor knows when to talk, and when to take action.

Leaning towards her, I grab her chin in my hand and do what I did this afternoon by the pool, what I've been dying to do since she first laughed at my beard in the bar.

I kiss her.

17

LIZ

He tastes like tomato.

And while that taste made me gag a second ago, I find it damn delicious on Felix's lips. 'Hmmm.'

Yet, just as I lean into the kiss, he pulls back, his eyes moving back and forth between mine. '"Hmmm" as in keep going, or "Hmmm" as in stop?'

Thus far, I've managed to use drawing slightly pornographic pictures of him as an outlet for my built-up attraction. But after today's scripted poolside kiss and now his impromptu one, I'm not about to hold back. Not after he was willing to poison himself rather than hurt my feelings.

I slide off my stool, then fist my hands in his shirt to yank him off his. '"Hmmm" as in let's do this, Hollywood.'

Eye wide, he laughs. 'Hollywood?'

Smoothing out his t-shirt, I run my palms over his chest. 'You prefer Johnny Douchebag?'

His expression flattens. 'Definitely not.'

'Well then.' With only my fingers curling over his shoulders as a warning, I jump, straddling him, unsurprised when Felix's hands instinctively cup my ass to hold me. 'Let's do this.'

He manages to sidestep out between the stools and walk down the hall with me attacking his neck, ears and face like a starved octopus.

And I am.

Not an octopus. But starved.

I never denied I was attracted to him. I just denied myself action. Which I only managed to do because I held onto the numbing cream grudge for far too long.

It took Mike Hunt and eggshells in rice to finally break down the barriers I'd built around my libido.

In a few strong strides, we're in my room, and I'm dropped on the bed. With the floodgates now open, my hands have his belt unbuckled before my ass stops bouncing.

Felix chuckles. 'You in a rush?'

I answer by nearly whipping myself in the face with the leather strap as I move it aside to get to his button. 'Well—' I nod at the bulge below my hands '—you're hard.' I pop the button and lower the zipper.

Shoving his jeans to the floor, I reach for his boxer briefs. They're red.

'Um, yeah.' Felix huffs a laugh. 'Why wouldn't I be hard?'

I stare, transfixed, as his ab muscles clench and retract in tandem as my index fingers slide back and forth under the waistband.

It's well known that women have a thing for grey, but honestly, that's only because they haven't seen Felix Jones in red. I make a mental note to write to the Calvin Klein marketing people about this so they can rectify his billboard.

Felix reaches out a hand, trailing one finger down the side of my jaw, breaking my concentration.

Narrowing my eyes on his rather smug face, I pull the waistband out and let it snap back, smirking when he winces. 'Well, with your *situation*, it's best to take action as soon as possible before...'

Belying the erectile issues I was about to mention, his dick – long and hard – does what the belt did not.

Smacks me in the face.

I pull back, blinking. 'Oh.'

One eyebrow quirks over his doubly self-satisfied expression. 'Before what now?'

Face hot, I refocus on his glorious dick. 'Shut up.'

Chuckling, Felix crosses his arms over his chest, seemingly at ease with his hard-on half an inch from eye-maiming me. 'No, really.'

Really, I am seriously horny.

But *he* seriously needs to shut up.

His smile forms a playful curve. 'I'd *love* to hear what you were saying about my situa—'

I fill my mouth in order to close his, taking his cock as deep as I can.

'Ahhh.' His hands drop to my head, fisting in my hair.

My plan works.

'*Caramba, isso é bom.*'

Kind of. But at least now he's saying what I want to hear. In the language I want him to speak.

His fingers tighten, then release, as if worried he's going to hurt me. I grab his ass and pull him closer, letting him know I'm okay.

He allows his body to rock forward an inch, but I know he's holding himself in check.

Releasing one ass cheek, I use that hand to hold the base of his dick, sliding it up and down as I bob, trying to keep my mouth loose enough to lap my tongue underneath but still suck hard enough to make him groan.

'*Adoro a tua boca.*'

I don't have much time to feel victorious before his hands find the hem of my shirt and lift, my mouth popping off his hard-on and my shirt off my body.

Feeling helpful, I take care of my bra before Felix grips my ribcage and tosses me further up the bed.

'Now who's in a hurry?' My tease is met with a growl before he begins the awkward action of toeing off his shoes under the pants bunched around his ankles.

It's endearing.

The awkwardness, not the growl.

The growl is straight-up sexy and makes the panties I start shimmying out of extra wet.

Finally freeing himself of pants, Felix tosses a condom he must've retrieved from his pocket beside me on the bed.

Not hesitating, I grab it and begin reading the small print on the back.

'It's normal.' Felix raises a hand, crossing a finger over his heart. 'Promise.'

It's hilarious how he thinks magnums are normal. But as he's already hard and smug, I don't mention it.

Having confirmed there's zero benzocaine in the condom, I drop it next to me and crook my finger. 'You need me to yell action?'

Scoffing, he places both hands on the foot of the bed and crawls over me, caging me in. 'You can direct me anytime.'

Maybe it's because this isn't our first rodeo (so to speak). Or maybe it's all the time we've spent living together. Or maybe it's just part of the instant attraction I felt the moment I clapped eyes on that mange-worthy beard of his. But it hits me how *comfortable* I am with Felix.

Some people might think comfortable is synonymous with passionless. Not me.

I'm comfortable in that I'm not worried I might do something Felix might not like. Nor am I scared of not living up to his expectations, or him mine. And I find feeling comfortable enough to both care about his pleasure and be self-assured enough to demand my own incredibly hot.

Especially when I realize that, up until now, I've never had both.

Huh.

Leaving that thought for another day, I examine Felix's heated expression as I grab his hand and direct it to my clit.

'So wet.' Bracing his weight on one hand above my shoulder, he circles my clit with his other, dipping his fingers inside me. '*Tão quente.*'

His thumb stays pressed against my clit, and first one, then two fingers thrust inside.

I arch back. 'Hmm, yes.'

The pressure changes, lightens as his thumb moves back and forth in short, fast motions, almost like a vibration.

'Oh God. That's good.' I spread my legs further, my thigh muscles clenching, my clit pulsing. 'Do that. Keep doing that.'

He does. And it's a testament to his workouts that he's able to remain balanced above me on one arm as I wrap my legs around his waist.

Yet it's the crook of his fingers that finally does it.

'I'm coming.' Tensing around him, my heels dig into his ass.

The touching and massaging of my spot continue as the lapping waves of pleasure swell.

'Fuck, I'm coming.' Cresting the tsunami-like orgasm, my body spasms and lifts off the bed.

Still his arm holds strong as I ride out my orgasm, clinging to him like some kind of spider monkey in heat.

It isn't until the last ebbs of heat fade, and I drop back to the mattress that he moves the hand between my legs and pushes himself back, grabbing the condom as he goes.

Through half-mast eyes, I watch him tear open the foil packet with his teeth.

Condom in one hand, he wraps his other around the base of his cock, stroking it as he stares between my legs. Watching him watch me makes me wetter. Hotter. But just as I'm about to reach for him, I have a sudden thought.

Maybe there's another reason – besides making me wet – for the self-stroking.

Wanting to be as considerate to him as he is to me, I lift on my elbows and meet his eyes, wanting to give him, and not just his dick, my full attention.

Felix frowns, his cock-stroking hand pausing.

'Just know—' taking a breath, I attempt to rid myself of the impatient desire that Felix has stoked high and hot inside me '—that if you need to stop at any point, or if there is something I can do to keep—' my eyes drop to his erection still hard and long in his fist '—everything in working order, just let me know.' I nod, satisfied that we can have this kind of conversation even in the heat of the moment. 'I'll help however I can.'

I smile, pleased with how comfortable we are with each other.

And yet Felix does not look comfortable. His mouth flattens and his eyes narrow. He looks... vexed. 'Are you fucking serious right now?'

Extremely horny but vexed.

'Uh...' I guess just because *I'm* comfortable doesn't mean Felix is.

Guys are weirdly sensitive about the working order of their dicks.

'Sorry.' I strive for a look of understanding, but seeing as I don't really understand, I'm sure I don't quite nail it.

Felix holds my eyes with his narrowed gaze and rolls on the condom.

'I didn't mean to spoil the mood.' I try for a smile for it feels awkward. 'I just wanted you to know that you don't have to push yourself.'

His nostrils flare twice before I'm unceremoniously flipped on my stomach. I have just enough time to push up onto my hands and knees before Felix thrusts inside.

Then I break out into song.

Not really. Maybe. I'm not sure.

But the pressure, hot and heavy and pushing deep inside me, makes me feel fucking lyrical.

* * *

Felix

'How's *that* for pushing myself?'

'Good.' She gasps as I swivel my hips. 'So good.'

Her voice is high, and weirdly sing-songy. But the words are all I need to keep going.

To show her that the numbing condom was never needed. That her concern over my erection, while thoughtful, is completely unfounded.

And that there is absolutely nothing fucking wrong with my dick.

Digging my fingers into her hips, I pull back and slam my dick inside, the way smooth thanks to her thick arousal.

'Ahhh.' She drops her head to the mattress, her heart-shaped ass rising in my hands.

Her moans sound like music notes. And with each thrust, I can hear her desire sucking me in. The sounds together make the sweetest song I've ever heard.

'Felix...'

I take that back. My name on her lips is the sweetest.

Pausing my thrusts, I curl around her, sliding my hands up and then under – teasing her nipples until they're peaked and hard. '*Sim, gatinha?*'

'More.'

My lips, resting against her back, smile at her whispered demand.

Moving my hands farther up, I hook them over her shoulders, pulling back until we're both upright, her back against my front.

'*Fuuuuck.*' The drawn-out curse, said in unison, echoes in the room as my cock settles even deeper.

I turn my head into her neck, inhaling her scent, kissing my way down her shoulder. In the mirror beside the bed, I catch sight of her – blonde hair draped over my shoulder, pebbled nipples, her strong, lean legs straddling my thighs as my cock burrows inside her.

'Meow.'

Both Anne and I tense as Mike jumps onto the bed in front of us.

I don't even flinch as Mike reaches a paw toward my thigh. 'No.' Instead, I draw on all my past action movie experience and engage in the villain before me in an epic stare down. 'Absolutely not.'

He lowers his paw to the bed. 'Meow.' Somehow, Mike manages to imbue both hurt and menace into his cry.

Pointing an arm at the door, I hold firm, making a mental note to ensure the door is securely locked before falling asleep tonight if I want to avoid retribution maiming while I sleep. 'Out.'

He turns tail, but instead of bounding down the way he came, he lands first on Anne's side table, knocking over her sketch pad before jumping down to the floor.

'Wow—' Anne shifts suggestively on my lap, causing a spark of pleasure to shoot down my spine '—it was kind of hot when you got all domineering like that.'

At any other time, on any other day, I would be 100 per cent consumed with what makes Anne hot, but right now, I'm too captivated by the sketch book lying open on the floor.

'Is that me?'

Anne follows my line of sight to the floor. 'Is what yo—' She claps a hand over my eyes. 'Oh shit.'

I wince behind her palm. 'I take that as a yes.'

'It's not what it looks like.'

Pulling her hand away, I trap it at her side, then do the same with her other by locking an arm around her mid-section. I flex, both arms – one across her chest, the other over her abdomen – holding her trapped against me and take a good long look at the proof that Anne has not been as unaffected by me as she made out. 'It *looks* like I need to tell my stylist to invest in blue ruffle ensembles.'

Her skin, flushed from desire, goes red. 'I—'

I thrust. She moans.

Lifting my ass off my heels, I make short, strong movements as my arms hold her in place. With her legs spread out over my thighs, and her arms trapped beside her body, all she can do is take it. 'It looks like you've been thinking some pretty kinky things.'

Thrust. Thrust. Thrust.

Each thrust brings another moan, vindication for my new-found need to punish in the bedroom. Never have I wanted such control. Such dominion. But then again, never have I felt so out of control with a woman. From the very first moment we met, she's had me breaking all my rules. Left me feeling like a cat on a leash.

Thrust. Thrust. Thrust.

It's only fair she gives me this.

'Oh my God.' Her hands, still trapped at her sides, reach for me, claw at my sides. 'I'm gonna come, I'm gonna—'

I watch in the mirror as her mouth opens, her body jerks, helpless under my hold. No sound, just a breathtakingly beautiful silent scream of pleasure as I continue to move.

Thrust. Thrust. Thrust.

On a ragged inhale, she starts to cry. 'Wait, Felix. I just—*fuck*.'

We have waited. I feel like we've waited forever.

Thrust. Thrust. Thrust.

'Something's—I... oh, oh God.' Her head, the only thing free to move, twists and turns, her hair flying out in every direction. Bathing me in her scent.

Citrus. Sweet but tart. Just like her.

'*Apanhei-te.*' I don't have her. Not really. And the knowledge makes me thrust harder, faster, as if punishing her for not giving me everything I want. Things I didn't know I wanted until right now. '*Deixar ir, gatinha,*' I whisper. 'Let go.'

'I'm coming...' Her nails dig deep. 'Oh God.' She writhes again, her head now in the direction of the mirror. Our eyes meet. 'Felix...'

Thrust.

This time, her orgasm isn't silent, and she doesn't feel it alone. Both of us, sweaty, loud and shaking, come together.

Her – eyes closed, a tear trailing down her cheek only to merge into the beads of sweat spreading across her body.

Me – chest heaving from the best workout of my life and eyes fixated on the open sketch book.

Moments tick by as both of us calm down, our breathing evening out. Only then do I find the strength to lift her off my dick and lay her gently on the bed.

I step into the bathroom as she basks in the afterglow, a small Mona Lisa smile on her lips.

When I return, her smile's still in place but her eyes are fully closed. Thinking she's sleeping, I move to retrieve her sketch book. But just as I bend beside the bed, Mike shoots out from underneath it and plops his bare ass on top of my face. The face Anne drew.

The feline's expression is the definition of defiance. I recognize retribution when I see it.

'Touché, Mike.' I nod, acknowledging his move. 'Touché.'

Leaving Mike to his revenge, I climb in next to Anne, spooning behind her.

A picture is worth a thousand words.

And if that's true, it's almost enough to keep me from sleep thinking about what I'd give to hear just a few of those words from Anne.

Almost.

18

LIZ

'We really have to stop meeting like this.'

Sitting cross-legged on the foot of the bed, sketch book on my lap, I watch Felix wake up to the glorious sight of Mike Hunt inches from his face.

'Meow.' Mike's wrinkled face retracts a few inches. '*Meow.*' He sits on his haunches, like he's disappointed in Felix's reaction.

Felix stretches out on his back, eyes closed. 'Just be glad I didn't scream.'

Mike tilts his head as if processing what Felix said.

This is followed by a grumble/growl that honestly could've come from either of them. Though I'm guessing it was Felix's stomach.

We *did* skip dinner last night, after all.

Eyes still closed, Felix reaches a hand toward Mike, and color me surprised when Mike closes the last remaining inch of distance by touching his nose to it and Felix doesn't flinch.

I turn the page in my sketch book and attack the clean sheet.

'Anne?' Felix's sleep-filled voice stills my pencil.

My middle name, familiar since I assumed it last year, hits me differently the morning after our night together.

It's just a name.

Shucking off the guilt, I resume my sketch, wanting to capture the soft morning light bathing Felix – and Mike – in its glow. 'Don't move.'

'You taking advantage of my body again?' There's a smile in his voice.

Not looking up from my quick line sketching, I smile back. 'The cat's out of the bag so to speak—' Felix snorts '—so I thought I'd make the most of a live model.'

'I hate to break it to you, but this live model isn't going to be alive much longer if he doesn't get something to eat.' As if to prove his point, his stomach emits another loud growl.

Frowning at the thought of losing my model, I think of the box of Bisquick I saw in the pantry. 'I could make pancakes.'

'No.' His answer is so violent, Mike takes offense and leaps off the bed.

'Well, then.' I feign hurt feelings. 'See if I ever cook for you again.'

The war of emotions cascading over his face is so easy to read, I can't contain my laughter. 'Don't worry, I *promise* never to cook for you again. How's that?'

Returning my smile, he pushes himself to a seated position and throws back the covers. '*I'll* make pancakes.'

I hold out my pencil, measuring his proportions.

His body really is beautiful. Even without the blue, ruffled apron of my imagination.

Especially without it.

'Stay there a sec,' he says as he leaves the room, his well-defined muscles twitching and stretching as he walks.

I figure he's gone to get dressed but when he gets back, he's holding a yogurt cup and a spoon in one hand and an apple in the other.

'Here.' He places the yogurt next to me, then takes a standing position at the foot of the bed before taking a large bite out of his apple. 'Have at it.' He turns his shoulders and poses, the only thing moving his jaw.

'I thought you wanted pancakes?'

Still looking off to the side, he swallows his bite. 'I will, but this will tide us over until you answer your muse's call—' he flexes his pecs '—and I can get to the store.' He gives me side-eye. '*Someone* used all the eggs last night.'

Heat rises in my cheeks, and I dip my chin back to my sketch pad. I don't even heckle him about calling himself my muse.

Hard to heckle when it's true.

Time ticks by, enough for him to finish his apple as my pencil flies over the parchment, the varying shhhh sounds familiar and calming.

What isn't as calming is the tall, muscular man in front of me, yet I find myself just as comfortable today – showing him the side of myself my 'father' deemed worthless – as I was in bed with him last night.

I continue making quick glances, ensuring my lines are correct, my eyes fighting to linger longer over his body, wanting to do more than catalogue proportions and shadows. Especially when a certain part of him starts moving.

Rising, if you will.

I've taken a lot of art classes. Mostly in secret to keep Stanley Moore from giving me a hard time. And I've drawn a lot of nude models. Even male models whose bodies may have involuntarily reacted to being stared at. I've always remained professional. I've never been disrespectful.

Today, I shift in my seat, my legs wanting to uncross and press together. Wanting to soothe the damp ache growing beneath my sketch pad.

When I find myself re-tracing the lines of his hard-on more than once, I decide to call it quits and get the poor man something to eat.

Closing my sketch book, I uncurl my legs. 'Just give me a sec to get dressed and I'll come with you.' I slide to the edge of the bed, stopped from standing when Felix bends over and kisses my forehead.

'No, you stay.' He pops back up, his dick bouncing. 'Artists shouldn't waste inspiration.' His tone is more self-satisfied than I'd like, but as I'm going to need to change my panties before getting dressed, I stay quiet.

He steps into the bathroom and tosses the apple core, re-entering the room cock first.

'You sure?' Managing to keep my eyes above his shoulders, I take in his well-known features. 'What if someone recognizes you?' Even with bed hair and scruff, Felix looks every inch the leading man right now.

Thinking of inches, my eyes drop to his hard-on, and I can't help but note that our positions are very much like the ones last night when I put his cock in my mouth.

I lick my lips.

'Ah.' Felix, not looking as lustful as I feel, holds up a finger before leaving the room again.

The man is hungry, Liz. Just let him eat, then you can jump his bone.

He comes back mid-pep talk, this time with his cowboy hat in hand. 'I have this as a disguise, remember?' Felix dons the Stetson I bought him.

Yeah. Felix is just going to have to starve.

Standing, I push down my panties and yank off my shirt. 'I'm really glad you finished that apple.'

Felix's Adam's apple bobs. 'And why's that?'

Plucking his hat off his head by the crown, I drop it on my own.

'Because you're gonna need your energy.'

A slow, delicious smile curls up the sides of his scruffy face, his dark eyes twinkling.

I tip the brim of the hat. 'This cowgirl needs a ride.'

His hard-on rises higher.

And then, in one smooth move, he jumps past me, turning as he falls, landing cock up on the mattress. Hands behind his head, wearing nothing but a smug smile, he waggles his eyebrows. 'Ride 'em, cowgirl.'

Straddling him, I grab his dick with both hands, squeezing as I pump.

He groans. 'You're my favorite lone rider.'

Laughing, I continue teasing him with one hand while bringing the other to the ache between my legs. I'm so wet and very ready. 'Condom?'

He stills. 'Shit.'

I stop my ministrations and press my palms down flat on his abs. 'Seriously?'

His eyes close, his mouth pursed in disappointment. 'Yesterday's was the only one I had on me. My emergency wallet condom.' He peeks at me with one eye. 'The only other condoms I have are the—'

'Nope.' I cross my arms under my breasts. 'Don't even think about it.' Like I want any numbing cream mishaps on the day I finally meet my sister.

'Yeah.' Felix's sigh is forlorn. 'Didn't think so.'

Sighing back at him, I move to dismount, but stop when his hands grab hold of my thighs.

'Oh no you don't.'

'Hey.' I settle back on top of him. 'I hate to break it to you, but I'm not riding bareback. Even if we both declared ourselves clean and good to go.' I pause, thinking that over. 'Which I am by the way.'

Felix lifts his hands. 'Me too. Studio physical says so.'

'Good.' I nod, pleased that the answers to the question we each should've asked each other last night are favorable. 'Even so—' I press a hand to my chest '—*I'm* not on birth control.'

He opens his mouth but I cut him off by slicing my hands across the air. 'And the pull-out method is *not* a legitimate form of birth control.'

Felix rolls his eyes. 'I know that.' Using his considerable strength, he slides me up and over his dick, stopping only when my ass rests on his chest and his chin is a few inches away from my clit. 'What I was *going to* say before I was so rudely interrupted, is that there's more than one way to ride a horse.'

He sticks his tongue out, moving it in a way I should find perverted and mood killing, and yet somehow makes me laugh.

I'm not a virgin, or a prude. But I've never sat on a guy's face before. It always seemed... impolite. And I was nothing if not polite in all my past relationships.

'Please?' Felix begs like a kid at a candy store, dissolving all the arguments I may have tried to make. But honestly, when a man like Felix Jones asks you to ride his face – you ride his face.

Reading the answer in my expression, Felix flashes a wicked smile and slaps my ass. 'Giddy-up, then.'

Biting my lip, I hold off on moving so I can assess the least awkward way forward, when Felix, having lost patience, moves me himself. He has me lifted up and him shifting down in seconds. Until his mouth gets what it wants.

Me.

His tongue slides around and over my clit, the heat from his mouth compounding my desire.

While his tongue works, his hands snake up my body, caressing my breasts, tweaking my nipples.

It feels good. So good. And yet, as good as it feels, and as comfortable as I am with Felix, I can't help but brace my weight on my knees, worried I might crush him. The effort taking a concentration that pushes any future orgasm further and further out of reach.

But then his tongue, vertical and deft, is inside me. His scruff teases my sensitive skin as he moves his head back and forth.

In a position where I'm supposed to be riding him, I feel like I'm being devoured.

I love it.

His mouth closes over my clit and sucks.

'Whoa.' I sway forward, my fingers grabbing fistfuls of his hair.

Felix's laugh is smothered, and by the time I realize he's laughing at my unintended horseback riding pun, I'm too interested in his mouth service to care.

I stop holding myself up. Stop holding myself back. And I let go.

* * *

Felix

'What in the name of Marlon-fucking-Brando is going on?'

My blissful, post-sex feelings evaporate in H.E.B.'s dairy section as nearby customers turn toward Jack's sharp tone booming from my phone.

Switching my phone to the eardrum Jack didn't burst, I whisper back. 'Stop shouting.' I peek out from under my hat, relieved to see everyone already back to their grocery shopping. 'I'm in public.'

I place a carton of Happy Eggs into my shopping cart, making a mental note to have my personal shopper switch over to the organic, small-farm brand when I get back to Los Angeles. Expensive, but worth it.

Lost in produce thoughts, it takes a second to register Jack's ongoing lecture now that he's speaking at a lower volume.

'...emotional support animal? When *the fuck* did you need an emotional support animal and why *the hell* is it a cat? You *hate* cats.'

Sighing, I grab the milk on the next shelf. 'Who called you?'

The answering silence has me checking to see if the call dropped.

'Who?' Jack's voice isn't loud, but it's definitely not as calm as before. 'The who should've been you.'

I've seen Jack lose his shit before, which is what usually happens after he sounds as dark and menacing as he does right now, but he's never lost his shit on me. Even after Camilla showed her true colors.

'*Especially* as I'm over here in LA spending all my time fighting with one set of lawyers, collaborating with another all while still trying to handle incoming contracts and scripts from various producers and you don't even call to tell me that you have a cat *and* a fucking roommate!'

The last makes me blanche.

How did Jack find out about Anne? A sick feeling twists in my stomach when my first thought is that Anne sold information to the press.

No. She wouldn't do that. She's not Camilla.

Shouldering my phone, I maneuver the cart around the corner into a lesser trafficked aisle lined with paper plates and garbage bags. 'Who told you about Anne?'

'Again—' I can practically hear him rolling his eyes '—it should've been you. But thankfully, your mother filled me in when I went to see her this morning.'

Relief, then guilt, hits me. '*Mãe.*'

'Dude.' Jack sounds drained, making me feel like the worst kind of friend. 'What the hell is going on?'

'I can explain.' I act interested in unscented garbage bags as a woman pushing a cart with a toddler in it passes by. 'Just not right now.'

Jack scoffs.

'No, really.' I lower my voice. 'I'll call you as soon as I'm done grocery shopping.'

'*Grocery shopping!*'

The women's head whips toward Jack's voice.

I hang up, pocketing my phone. 'Ma'am.' I lower my head and infuse as much Southern boy charm into the word as possible.

It seems to work, as when I peek under my brim, she's smiling back before being immediately distracted by her kid grabbing a box of plastic forks and shaking it like a rattle.

Not wasting time, I move my cowboy boots at a fast clip to the self-checkout line where I make quick work of scanning and bagging before heading to my car.

My phone never stops buzzing in my pocket.

Groceries loaded and air conditioning blasting, I use Bluetooth to accept Jack's next call.

'Explain.'

And, as promised, I do. I tell my friend and manager everything that's happened from the moment he left me in the condo lobby up until this morning's grocery run. I leave out the part about us sleeping together, but I can tell from Jack's tone that he knows exactly what I've left out.

The conversation takes a while. Because with each moment I recount since he left, Jack follows with twenty questions.

Questions about my sanity. Questions about Anne. Questions I don't have answers for.

* * *

'Let me get this straight.' Anne, palms pressed down on the kitchen countertop, stares wide-eyed at me from her seat on the other side of the island. 'You want to leave my brother's cat, the cat who attacked your director's ass before skinny-dipping in NASA's pool, home, *alone*, in someone else's condo?'

My hair, no doubt smashed awkwardly from wearing a cowboy hat earlier when I went to the store, falls forward as I slice strawberries on the cutting board. 'You got a better idea?'

The ten-minute ride home felt oppressive after Jack's call, and yet, entering the condo to Anne practicing yoga while Mike played on his back with a strip of curled drawing paper, eased the heavy weight of apprehension from my shoulders.

The yoga pants may have helped.

Anne, looking far less pleased than she had in downward dog when I arrived back with all the ingredients to make pancakes – from scratch – and fruit salad, shakes her head at me in disbelief. 'I'm telling you—' she points at Mike sunbathing innocently in front of the living-room windows '—that demon nearly crumbled the Bellagio in Vegas with nothing more than a blow job shot and a penis candle.'

I nearly slice my finger off.

Anne leans forward, her narrowed eyes eerily similar to Mike's before he pounces. 'You do *not* want to leave that pussy to his own devices.'

Finishing with the strawberries, I toss them in the bowl with the grapes I plucked off the vine and grab an orange. 'You sound like Mrs Slocombe from *Are You Being Served?* when you say pussy.'

If I needed any more proof for how gone I am over Anne, the semi that sprouts just from peeling an orange would do it. I wonder if all citrus fruits will get me hard in the future now that I associate the smell with Anne and sex.

'OMG.' Anne's arms and jaw drop.

I look down, wondering if she noticed my hard-on.

'You know the television show *Are You Being Served?*?'

Stepping closer to the island, I shrug. 'Unfortunately.' I manage to make a few small digs in the peel before remembering a citrus hack I saw on a cooking show once.

'What do you mean *unfortunately*?' Anne snags a grape from the bowl between us.

Bracing my thumbs at the rounded top of the orange half, and my fingers along the sliced edge, I turn the orange inside out, the halved, segmented pieces falling into the bowl.

'Cool.' Anne nods appreciatively.

I smile at the compliment, embarrassed by how much her praise affects me.

Shaking her head, Anne regroups. 'Anyway, *Are You Being Served?* was like, the *best* show.'

Out of all the interesting tidbits I've accumulated about Anne, which according to Jack aren't *near* enough, her familiarity with an obscure and dated British comedy show may be the most intriguing yet.

Well, beside her love of drawing pornographic images of *me*.

I grab the other orange half. 'My mother watched TV after work to improve her English. And since we couldn't afford cable at the time, television meant the local PBS station which aired a whole lot of older British sitcoms.' Dropping the rest of the orange pieces in the bowl, I toss the orange peel and reach for the pineapple and watermelon chunks that I bought pre-sliced at the store. 'What's your excuse?'

'Our chef was British.' Anne shrugs, her eyes fixated on my hands. 'Always had the TV on in the kitchen.'

I stand corrected. *That* is the most intriguing bit of information yet.

Forcing myself not to react, seeing as Anne has yet to realize what she just gave away, I select a few chunks of fruit from each container to cut into smaller pieces. 'Your chef was British?'

Anne frowns at the bowl as I mix the fruit like my mom taught me – with my hands. 'Yeah.'

I'm not sure if it was the nonchalant tone of my question or how wet and sticky my hands are from fruit juice, but Anne appears successfully distracted.

'Did your family always have a chef?' I toss the fruit with more fanfare than required.

She nods. 'Mmhmm.'

The plan works too well as I become the one more distracted when, her eyes still on my hands, Anne slowly licks her lips.

By the time her tongue travels from one corner of her mouth to the other, my dick is close to knocking on the lower cabinets.

Switching tactics to alleviate the ah, *tension*, I stop tossing the fruit and shake my hands off over the bowl. 'That explains it, then.'

Anne blinks out of her stare when I turn on the faucet and wash my hands. 'Explains what?'

I dry my hands on the tea towel. 'Why you can't cook.' When she just frowns, I make a show of rolling my eyes before throwing the towel at her. 'An *English* chef.'

'Hey.' She catches it, laughing. 'I take major offense to that on Curtis' behalf.' Stealing another grape, she pops it into her mouth and then points at me accusingly. 'I dare you to try and make Yorkshire pudding better than old Curt.' She settles back in the stool and crosses her arms. 'He was a right legend.'

She says the last with an English accent. A perfectly posh one, which I know from experience is hard to slip into and not sound like a caricature. Unless you've had a dialect coach or spent a good deal of time in the affluent areas in London.

Neither of which makes sense. *She* doesn't make sense.

Jack's questions replay in my ear. And for the first time, I ask my own.

Why would someone who grew up with a personal chef need a free place to stay? And why would an artist, who has no interest in Hollywood, take an unpaid internship as a storyboarder?

With no answers to be had, or fruit to toss to distract her, I give the pancake batter I made one last whisk before scooping it onto the hot griddle pan.

'Meow.' Having enough sun, Mike reaches his front paws up Anne's stool and stretches.

'Hey, buddy.' Anne picks him up under his arms like a child and settles him on her lap. 'Wanna treat?'

I eye the cat and his increasing rolls over the island. 'Isn't he getting too many treats lately?'

'Oh, be quiet.' Anne waves away my words and selects a small slice of strawberry.

Mike laps it into his mouth before motor-boating Anne in thanks.

Selecting a piece of pineapple for herself, Anne pops it in her mouth, moving it to the side like a chipmunk. 'Back to the matter at hand.'

'Hmmm?' Distracted by suddenly wanting to *be* Mike Hunt, I refocus on flipping my pancakes.

'The astronaut dinner.' Pausing to chew her fruit, Anne uses both hands to scratch Mike's neck, still stuck between her breasts. 'I can think of only one way to deal with Mike while we're at dinner.'

She sighs, but the glint in her eyes belies her reluctance.

I'm both apprehensive and intrigued.

As I always am with Anne.

I turn off the griddle and grab the spatula. 'And what's that?'

'We use the lie you so kindly made on my behalf about my being your emotional support animal sitter.'

I nearly drop the pancakes.

'That way, no one gets the wrong idea about us, and best of all,' Anne raises the chubby feline's front paw, 'Mike Hunt can come.'

19

LIZ

Why am I such a fool?

Checking myself out in the mirror, first turning one way and then the other, I study my face as if seeing it for the first time.

It would be easy to paint on my society face like I used to – carefully contoured cheekbones, neutral eye make-up, subtle blush. All blended and blended and then blended some more. Just as I was drilled into doing since I was sixteen.

But I don't want to look like that version of myself. Not when I'm about to meet my sister.

On the other hand, besides my brothers' weddings where there was a make-up artist on hand, I haven't had to get ready for any special occasions since I decided it wasn't my right to *be* Elizabeth Moore anymore.

I fan out the sides of my short silk robe, trying to stop the stress sweat from pooling under my arms.

Then, ignoring the line-up of cosmetics, I give myself a sharp look. 'Get a grip, Lizzie.'

First things, first, I apply an extra layer of deodorant.

Feeling better – and dryer – I re-order my make-up by application. Face, eyes, cheeks, lips.

I bypass the foundation, having never liked the feel of it on my skin, and grab liquid eyeliner. Even though I bought it because it looks and feels just like one of my artist pens, I never wore it to a society event.

Stanley Moore thought liquid eyeliner whore-ish.

With a mental *fuck you, Stanley*, I apply it now, my familiarity with drawing helping me flick it up at the ends in a subtle cat-eye.

Feeling more confident, I add mascara before grabbing a coral lip gloss, quelling the inner voice telling me the color is too bright. A voice that sounds very much like Stanley Winston Moore.

'Fuck you.'

'Excuse me?'

I jump, my eyes shift in the mirror, catching Felix staring at me from the doorway. 'Oh. Hey.' I gesture stupidly to the mirror. 'I was, uh, just talking to myself.' Or my absent, incarcerated not-father. But whatever.

'I'm not sure why you sound so angry.' His eyes travel from my bare feet to the top of my head where my hair is clipped up in a messy bun, out of the way of my make-up application. 'Because you look fucking fantastic.'

My glossed lips curve into a smile. 'You know I'm not dressed yet, right?'

He shrugs, the move doing incredible things for his white button-down shirt. 'You look even better not dressed.'

'Well.' I fan my face, my current hot flash having nothing to do with stress. 'Aren't you the charmer?'

'Of course.' Holding my eyes in the mirror, he pushes off the door frame, slipping his arms around me from behind. 'If you read the gossip columns, you'd know all about it.'

'Good thing I don't read the gossip columns then, huh?'

'Yeah.' His eyes turn oddly serious. 'Good thing.'

Before I can ask after that comment, he dips his head and kisses my shoulder. When he raises his head again, the serious expression is gone, replaced with a smile and roaming hands.

'Excuse me, sir.' I grab the hand squeezing my ass and dodge out of his hold. 'Some of us have to finish getting ready or we're gonna be late.'

He shrugs. 'So we'll be late.' He tries dragging me closer again. 'No big deal.'

I dodge him again. 'It *is* a big deal.' Pushing at the back of his shoulders, I evict him from my bathroom. 'I want to make a good impression.'

He pouts. 'On Park In-Su?'

'Who?' The K-pop astronaut floats to mind. 'Oh. The hot astronaut who saved you?'

'He didn't save me.' His crossed arms, added to the pout, making him look like a mutinous toddler. 'He helped me save Mike.'

'Yes, of course.' I fail to fight my smile, causing Felix's eyes to narrow.

I know I shouldn't, because obviously Felix is upset, but I find his blatant jealousy kind of thrilling. No one has ever been jealous over my attention before, unless you count Mike Hunt. Previous boyfriends may have been jealous over my family's holdings, or others may have been jealous over not having me on their arm. But not because it was *me*. The girl I see smiling in the mirror right now. They wouldn't have cared less about me if it weren't for my name and everything it came with.

Felix wants *me*.

And oddly enough, in this moment, I want to tell him who I really am.

I chuckle, correcting myself. He knows who I am. Probably better than I do. He knows I can hold a grudge. He knows I can be vindictive. He's seen me sunscreen a cat without a hint of shame and he's seen me fail in the kitchen.

He's seen me at my worst, seen all the things I've always had to hide as Elizabeth Moore.

He knows me.

And still, he wants me.

'Felix, I—'

'What's so great about astronauts anyway?' If possible, his bottom lip gets fuller. 'I mean, sure, they're smart and all, but I—'

'I like you.'

His pouty lip drops.

It isn't what I was going to say, but now that I've said it, it's what I needed to say. More so than my real name. 'I like you.' Forcing myself to hold his gaze, I step forward. 'I like you a lot, actually. And I was thinking that maybe, after the filming, if you wanted, maybe we could…' My courage only goes so far before anxiety makes me second-guess every word coming out of my mouth. A quick glance tells me Felix is still trying to recover from my confession. 'Uh, never mind, I—'

'I like you too.' His words fall fast from his lips, his hand cupping the side of my cheek. My *face* cheek this time.

I snort, trying to hide the well of emotion and relief with a laugh. 'We sound like a couple of teenagers.'

'You make me feel like one.' He waggles his eyebrows, his eyes dropping to the deep V of my robe.

Laughing outright, I allow the tension from the moment to ease. There's a lot more I could say. But right now is not the time. It might lead to more sex or fifty questions, and we don't have time for either.

'Meow.' With unusual perfect timing, Mike jumps up on my bed, visible through the open bathroom door.

Distracted by the call, Felix turns. 'Is he wearing a tuxedo?'

'Yes.' I take the opportunity to guide Felix the rest of the way out the door. 'But he still needs his rhinestone collar.'

With heavy steps, Felix allows me to push him toward the bed and its occupant. 'I thought he was staying in the limo? I paid extra for a driver who doesn't mind looking after cats.'

'Yes, but Mikey's feelings will be hurt if we don't dress him for the occasion.' Or so my brother says. Grabbing the collar from my nightstand, I dangle it on one finger between us. 'Be a dear, will you?'

'What?' Felix's horrified expression ping-pongs between Mike and my hand. 'You're kidding, right?'

I toss the collar next to Mike, then lean up on my tiptoes to plant a glossy kiss on Felix's cheek. 'Go get 'em, cowboy.'

* * *

Ten minutes later, I step out around the corner of the hallway and into the living room where Felix is waiting. Along with a properly collared Mike Hunt.

Taking a breath, I hold my hands out. 'What do you think?'

Felix looks up from his phone, his eyes going wide. 'Damn.' But as he looks me up and down, from my gladiator heeled sandals to my tangerine lace dress and up to my hair brushed and braided to one side, Felix's expression flattens.

'You don't like it?' I smooth my hands over the long-sleeved, minidress. I hadn't packed much in the way of dinner party outfits, but I had prepared to look nice in case I managed to arrange a meeting with my sister. It's a dress my mother's personal shopper sent to me right before I flew to Houston.

So while I know it's stylish – because Susan, the head of womenswear at Moore's wouldn't send me anything less than the latest fashion – I wonder if Felix is worried that the color is too much, or that the slip underneath isn't demure enough under the open-work lace. I touch the hem that hits me at mid-thigh. Or maybe he thinks it's too short?

I fight back the sick feeling of self-consciousness that I'm all too familiar with.

No. Felix isn't like my father. He wouldn't be worried that my appearance or actions will reflect badly on him. He likes me. The real me. He said so.

I peek back up at him, and when I do, he's smiling.

Huh. I must be letting my insecurities get to me.

Standing, Felix's navy slacks drape perfectly over his burnished brown dress shoes. 'You look beautiful.'

'Thank you.' Annoyed at myself for being so needy, I clear my throat and give him an exaggerated once-over. His well-cut trousers and textured white button-down remind me of my brothers and their impeccable style. Though Felix leans more towards Chase's laid-back elegance rather than Thomas' exacting formality. 'You clean up nice yourself.'

He chuckles, but it doesn't seem to reach his eyes. 'All part of the job.'

Still feeling oddly tense, I nod. 'Yeah, I get that.'

He tilts his head, eyes on mine. 'You do?'

'Yeah, I—' Having stepped forward, I pull up short, stopping myself physically and verbally. I'd been about to mention the many galas I've attended and hosted over the years. And explain about all the dresses I've worn that have felt like costumes. The enumerable feigned smiles and forced laughs that were all part of an act to keep my father happy. To fit in as a Moore. 'I just do,' I finish lamely, tossing my hands up and dropping them back to my sides, promising myself that tonight, after dinner, when I have more time, I'll tell him how I understand. Tell him my name and what that name means in certain New York circles.

I should've told him *before* we slept together, but now that we have, I definitely need to. I want to.

I'll even tell him about my sister. And my father. My *real* father.

Decision made, I feel lighter than I have in a long time.

I continue forward again, this time to wrap my arms around him, when Felix's phone rings.

Phone still in hand, he looks at the screen before glancing at me. 'My mother.'

'Oh.' It will be nice to say hi again. Show Sofia a more put-together version of myself. 'Let's—'

'I'll take it in my room.' With a smile just as stiff as his walk, he moves past me.

'Uh, okay.' But by the time I recover enough to speak, the door to his room has already closed.

* * *

Felix

Three thousand nine hundred and ninety dollars.

That's how much Anne's dress costs.

'Thank you so much for having me.' Anne smiles brightly at astronaut Vance Bodaway, our host for the night, as he ushers us into his home. 'I hadn't known until we pulled into the driveway that the dinner was at your house.' She looks around at the not-quite-a-mansion-but-more-than-a-house. 'Which is stunning, by the way.'

'Thanks. The credit all goes to my wife, Rose.' Vance takes Anne's hand in both of his. 'I've heard a lot about you.' He steps back and scans the floor around our feet. 'But where's the infamous cat?'

Anne's eyes cut to mine, but I ignore them just as I've avoided her gaze since we left the condo. 'I thought it best if we left Mike with the chauffeur and simply went out to check on him once in a while. I didn't want any, uh, problems occurring in your home.' She glances at me again, but my eyes remain fixed on Vance.

On the ride over, I avoided her by feigning interest in my phone while she held Mike on her lap. And while a thread of guilt wound its way around the knot of suspicion already lodged in my chest, I covertly scanned social media for any new leaked information or gossip.

'He'd be no problem at all.' Vance leads us through the twenty-something-foot ceilinged foyer and into an open living room/kitchen. 'We put our dogs out back, and no one's said they're afraid of itty-bitty house cats—' he laughs like the very idea's preposterous '—so if you wanted to bring Mike inside later, that would be fine.'

I glare at the marble floor, mumbling under my breath. 'I wouldn't exactly call Mike itty-bitty.'

Anne, the only one who seems to have heard, rolls her lips before nodding at Vance. 'Thank you.'

'Howdy!'

Anne and I start at the woman reclining on a white sofa.

'Felix, I think you've met my wife, Rose.' Vance moves toward Rose when she outstretches both arms in the air.

'Yes.' I stay put, remembering the last time I offered her my hand at the press junket.

Vance grabs a hold of his wife's hands in his and steps one foot back as if to brace himself. 'And Rose, this is Anne.' He grunts Rose to her feet. Her bare feet.

Anne steps forward once Rose gains her balance, the large pregnant belly jutting over her small, bare feet making it hard to do. 'You were at the press junket a few weeks ago, weren't you?'

'Yep, that was me.' Rose, looking pleased at being remembered, attempts to tug the hem of her dress down.

As if anyone could forget a pregnant woman wearing a fuchsia spandex jumpsuit. And while tonight's dress is yellow, it's just as bright and tight as her onesie had been.

Seeing Rose struggle to maneuver around her baby boulder, Anne steps forward to help her tug. 'Love your dress.'

'Thanks!' With her dress pulled back down to a decent length, Rose sticks out her foot, wiggling her toes. 'While I can manage the dress with help—' she winks at Anne '—I draw the line at heels these days.' She rolls her eyes. 'But when Trish gets here, I bet she's in stilettos.' At Anne's blank look, Rose explains. 'The other pregnant woman at the press junket that day.'

'Trish is the author of *Countdown to Love*,' I add, forgetting my reticence. Another thread of guilt hitting me when my explanation, the first words I've directed at her since we left the condo, makes Anne beam.

Rose runs her eyes up and down Anne and whistles. 'But speaking of dresses, yours is fabulous. And the color—' she makes a chef's kiss '—perfection.'

'Thank you, I—'

'May I use your restroom?' My tone, harsher than I'd meant, has everyone turning.

The following silence breaks Vance's besotted stare, which was focused on his wife's rear end. 'Uh, yeah.' He points back where we came. 'Around the corner, first door on your left.'

I leave before the talking resumes. I don't want to hear anything more about that damn dress. I don't even want to look at it. It brings up too many questions. Too many memories.

Slipping into the half-bath under the stairs, I close the door and sit, bracing my elbows on my knees, my head in my hands. Even the best actors need to break character, and the role I donned of unaffected man after seeing Anne in that dress is wearing thin fast.

Three thousand nine hundred and ninety dollars.

That's what this season's Oscar de la Renta cocktail dress cost a few months ago. The dress I bought Camilla. The dress that started my fall into blackmail.

Running my hands down my face, I lean back against the tank, unable to break free from my regrets. Regrets over my mother. Regrets over Camilla. Regrets that are now bleeding into my perception of Anne.

I snort, annoyed with myself. That I'm back to questioning the women in my life.

Camilla entered my life in a typical Hollywood way. A friend of a friend of a friend heard that she was interested in me and asked if I'd like to take her out. Camilla is pretty, fashionable and had seemed like a nice person the one time we'd met at a mutual friend's screening, so I hadn't seen a problem.

The problems came later.

At first, Camilla and I had, if not fun, a decent time. She may have seemed immature when she'd stop in the middle of our dates to pose for selfies I hadn't wanted to take, but I hadn't wanted to be judgmental in a town where even the most acclaimed can act like emotionally stunted children clamoring for attention.

We 'dated' for a month. The few times we met up solo were oddly well documented in the papers the days following our dates. As if the paparazzi had been tipped off ahead of time. She had seemed annoyed by it, like me, so I hadn't thought to question her.

It was also when my mother's condition became glaringly apparent.

The one and only time I invited her into my house was for the sole purpose of telling her I didn't see it working out between us. There was no drama. In fact, Camilla laughed and nodded in agreement, making me feel as if my opinion of the two of us was mutual.

She wished me well. She hugged me. She asked if she could use the bathroom before she left.

The next day, after my mother's first allowed call from rehab, Camilla texted me a link to a three-thousand-nine-hundred-and-ninety-dollar dress.

The very dress Anne is wearing in Vance Broadway's living room right now.

Confused, and busy with my mother, I ignored her. A few days later, she sent me a photo she'd taken of my mother's prescription bottles. Bottles I'd hidden away, along with my mother's admission papers into an exclusive rehab center, before Camilla came over that night.

Too busy trying to help my mother, I bought Camilla the dress, hoping it was her weird way of collecting some sort of break-up alimony. Like maybe that's how celebrities and socialites say they're sorry.

I should've known better.

It was as if the dress was Camilla's test, and once I passed (or failed, depending on how you look at it), she felt free to do and say whatever she wanted.

When she wore the dress, she told everyone I bought it for her. I couldn't deny it. This led the press to believe that we were still together.

Her next demand was that Jack get her a job in show business, but I ignored it. Soon after, pictures of me meeting with a previous co-star, a woman currently in the middle of a nasty divorce, were sent to all the newspapers.

'Felix Jones: Cheater and Home Wrecker' headlined all the gossip rags that week.

Still, I couldn't say anything. Because the truth was my friend had graciously met with me during a troubling time to give me the benefit of her experience after she had to admit her soon to be ex-husband into rehab earlier that year.

The only smart decision I made was to confide in Jack. Because when I did, he did three things – got Camilla a part in a popular reality TV show, hired a ferocious gang of lawyers, and did not blame me. For Camilla or my mother.

But he should've.

Pushing off my knees, I stand, staring into the bathroom's oval mirror.

Knock. Knock. 'You okay?' Anne's soft voice barely travels through the thick wood door.

'Be right out.' I wash my hands to stall some more, then re-don the role of unaffected man.

Taking a breath, I open the door.

'You okay?' She repeats the question I never answered.

Flashing her a dimmer version of my red-carpet smile, I begin my act. 'Fine.' The small smile is part of the expression I use whenever I'm asked something I don't want to answer. The one that usually gets me out of tough spots.

Yet I'm not surprised when Anne's frown doesn't clear. Like she can see right through me. Like she's used to people gaslighting her.

Folding her arms across her chest, skepticism written all over her expression. 'Uh huh.' But after a moment, when I remain quiet, the suspicion morphs into concern. 'Oh my God.' She grabs hold of my arm. 'Did something happen with your mom?' Her grip tightens. 'Is that what the phone call was about?'

Earlier, before I braved my childhood fears and collared a cat in rhinestones, I would've thought Anne's questions sweet. That she cared, not only for me, but for my mother. But now, with her cheerful lace albatross of a dress staring me dead in the eye, I can't help but see her questions as probing. Her grip as desperate. And I wonder if the real reason she told me she liked me was because her internship is at an end and that was the only way to prolong her connection to information she could use later?

One more question I don't have the answer to.

Someone's laugh echoes down the hall.

The sound, loud and carefree, much like Anne's on the night we first met, makes me determined to get answers to that question, and to all my others. Even if the answers aren't what I want to hear.

'Felix?' Anne's eyes, wide and blue, probe mine.

Summoning my skills, I wash my expression and answer Anne like I would an interviewer asking questions I don't want to answer. 'Everything is fine.' I gesture down the hall. 'Shall we go meet your astronauts?'

20

LIZ

Something's wrong.

And I don't mean the fact that my sister is apparently not coming. Although that *should* be my main concern.

'Holt, that brisket was fantastic.' Felix wipes his mouth with his napkin, avoiding my eyes as he's done the entire meal despite the fact that I'm sitting directly across from him.

'Hear, hear, bro.' Rose, sitting to my left at the end of the table, raises her iced tea glass. 'Although you could've just cooked it all here.'

Holt, Rose's brother, shrugs. 'I like my kitchen.'

A little over an hour ago, Holt sauntered into his sister's house with covered containers full of meat and side dishes.

'Besides, I wanted to use my new smoker.'

'Is that how you cooked it?' Amanda asks, her hand falling on Felix's shoulder next to her as she leans forward to catch Holt's eyes. 'It was delicious.'

I smile in agreement, while thinking rude, appendage-slapping thoughts.

Felix nods, asking Holt more about his smoker, not seeming to care that Amanda's hand stays where it is.

My face hurts. My smile unnatural since I asked Felix about his mother not long after we arrived.

I hadn't thought much of Felix's silence on the drive over to Vance and Rose's house, having been too preoccupied with the nerves multiplying in my belly the closer I got to meeting my sister. But when he avoided my touch after I got out of the car, I thought maybe the problem was Mike. That despite their slow-burn bromance, between his latent fear of house cats and the latest Neutral Buoyancy Lab debacle, Felix wasn't comfortable having Mike here, even if he was in the car.

So instead of letting Mike free-range in the limo as I'd planned, I double knotted his leash to one of the seat belts and piled a mound of treats beside him. On top of which, I had the chauffeur promise me – in front of Felix – that he would keep the partition down so he could keep an eye on Mike at all times.

Still, Felix's smile remained dimmer than usual and the space between us glaringly wide.

Leading me to believe that if it isn't his mother or Mike that's the problem, it's me.

And between having been so consumed with wondering what I did wrong, and going out to the car to check on Mike, I haven't had time to mourn the profound disappointment that my sister isn't here.

'So Anne.' Beautiful as always in a simple, blue shift dress, Amanda shifts her attention to me. 'I've heard your internship is over.'

My eyes cut to Felix, still arguing the merits of braising versus smoking with Holt before zeroing back on Amanda's hand still lingering on Felix's shoulder. 'Yes.'

Amanda blinks at my less than inviting tone, her eyes following mine to her hand. 'Oh.' Straightening, her hand *finally* falls to her side.

The relief coursing through me is grating.

'Since filming at NASA is wrapping up, the pre-production team is leaving, right?' Amanda's smile is kind. 'Did you enjoy working as a storyboarder?'

'Yes.' I take a breath, attempting to quell my petulant thoughts and feelings. 'It was an interesting experience.'

'I've seen lots of storyboards before, but yours really came together like a complete story.' She looks at Felix, as if to corroborate her opinion, but he's moved on, now laughing with Vance.

'What's a storyboard?' Trish, the author of *Countdown to Love* and the second pregnant woman I saw at the press junket, chimes in with her *Steel Magnolias*' accent.

'Kind of like an illustrator.' Amanda turns back to me looking hopeful. 'You have to take the adapted screenplay and transcribe it into pictures, right?'

Pulling my concentration away from Felix, I mull over Amanda's assessment. 'Yeah, I guess that's true.'

'You're looking for an illustrator, aren't you?' Ian Kincaid, Trish's handsome husband and the son of a state senator, says as he places another slice of corn bread on her plate.

I'm lucky that all the political fundraisers the Moores have attended or contributed to have been north of the Mason Dixon Line.

Trish takes a large bite before answering with a nod. 'Hmm mmm.'

'Oh, that's great.' Rose, sitting opposite Vance at the end of the table, lifts her large mass of blonde hair off her neck and holds it to her head as if trying to cool down. 'Now Trish can finally go about creating those pornos she's been wanting to publish.'

That gets everyone's attention. Even Felix's.

Vance excuses himself from the table.

'They aren't *porn*.' Trish pouts after swallowing her corn bread. 'I'm looking to create *mature* web comics from my romance novels.' She shoves another big piece in her mouth, still sulking.

Ian leans over and kisses her full, chipmunk cheek.

'Relax.' Rose lowers one hand from her head to take a long pull from her iced tea. Finished, she holds the cold glass to her neck. 'I meant porno in the best possible way.' She scans the table. 'I mean, who doesn't like a little spice in their stories?'

'Amen,' I say before I can think better of it.

Rose laughs. 'I like you.'

When she winks at me, some of the hurt from Felix's avoidance and disappointment from my sister's absence wanes.

Vance comes in with a portable fan, plugging it in near his wife. Flipping it on, he hands her a hair clip.

Eyes closed to the breeze now blowing her way, Rose secures her hair with the clip. 'I knew there was a reason I married you.'

Holt snorts, getting up from his spot next to Rose. 'I'll get the pie.'

'There's pie?' Trish and Rose both ask, eyes gleaming.

The table chuckles.

'While they couldn't make dinner, a few more guests should be coming for dessert.' Vance, still standing by his wife, slides his phone out of his pocket. 'I'll let them know it's—'

The doorbell chimes.

'Ah.' Smiling, Vance re-pockets his phone. 'I bet that's them.'

Heart beating faster, my eyes stay glued to the dining room's archway. Maybe my sister will come. Maybe then I can stop thinking about Felix and...

All maybes die a gruesome, violent death when the chauffeur, not my sister, walks into the dining room.

He's holding a black satin leash attached to a rhinestone collar.

An *empty* rhinestone collar.

* * *

'What do you mean, Mike Hunt's escaped?'

Rose drops her pie fork, Ian chokes on his coffee and the slice of pie Holt was in the middle of serving plops onto the tablecloth.

As the chauffeur relays the absurd and yet unsurprising story of the cat's Houdini act through the open sunroof, I toss my napkin and push back my chair. 'Did you see where he went?'

'Her cunt's a dude?' Rose whispers.

'Rose West.' Holt admonishes. 'That's too much, even for you.'

Rose snorts. 'Please. I'm the definition of *too much*. I should probably make "cunt"—' she air quotes '—my go-to curse word.'

'Please don't.' There's desperation in Vance's plea that I'd find amusing if it wasn't for the thing *besides* my brother's missing cat catching my attention.

'Rose West?' I glance at Holt before landing on Rose. 'I thought your name was Bodaway?'

'West is my maiden name,' Rose says.

My heart feels like its beating out of my chest. 'So that means your brother—'

'Holt?' Rose frowns at the man holding the pie server.

'Ah, no.' Maybe I'm wrong. Maybe the world isn't this small. 'I mean, do you have another brother? Married to—'

'Um, ma'am?' The chauffeur holds out the leash and collar in his hands.

Shaking off the urge to ask more questions, I grab the leash, winning the battle when I notice the collar is set to the second to last largest hole even though there's a very distinct indentation where the collar *should* be belted, three holes smaller.

Apprehension, disappointment, and frustration funnel into anger as I glare at Felix. 'Why did you make it so loose?'

Felix's brows lower while Amanda's shoot up.

But before he can answer, or Amanda can ask why a storyboarder/emotional support animal sitter is taking such a sharp tone with her employer, I hustle to the front door.

I should've never left Mikey in the damn car. I should've checked on him more. I should've told Felix to fuck off with his douchebag attitude and co-star flirtation and brought Mike inside with me as planned. And I most definitely should not have let my previous privilege assume tonight's dinner would be a larger gathering that included *all* current astronauts.

At the very least, I should've asked for a freaking guest list.

Felix catches up to me as I reach for the front door's handle. 'I'll help look for him.'

'Don't bother.' My jaw is clenched as tight as my hand on the collar.

He leans against the front door, preventing me from opening it. 'Look, I'm sorry about the collar. I hadn't wanted to choke him.' When I don't respond, he leans in. '*You're* the one who had me put the collar on him in the first place.'

Dropping my hand, I square up to him. 'So now it's *my* fault?' Resentment and tears threaten to spill over.

'No, I—'

Pushing back the tears, I lean into the resentment. 'So *sorry* the safety of my cat has once again damaged your all-important image.' It seems my resentment manifests as sarcasm. 'Heaven forbid this lowly intern get in the way when there are so many more *important* people to impress.'

And there it is. The real reason I haven't been able to concentrate on anything other than Felix tonight. It started with me second-guessing my dress, then every action I took since we arrived as I watched Felix smile and converse with those with more important titles at the table.

Felix is acting just like my 'father' did at the thousands of dinners I spent my lifetime attending as a dress-up doll that was only to be seen and spoken to when I was of benefit.

And I've let it bother me. Consume me. Just like I did with Stanley Moore.

Finally, a *real* expression crosses over Felix's Hollywood features. Confusion.

Well, welcome to the club, Johnny Douchebag.

'Listen, Anne, I—'

Knock. Knock.

Felix and I startle before he steps back and I swing the door open wide.

I'm half-expecting to see Mike Hunt sitting on his haunches, paw outstretched on the other side, acting impatient over the two seconds it took me to greet him.

And while it *is* Mike Hunt, he isn't twitching his tail on the doormat.

He's cuddled-up in the arms of a woman.

* * *

Felix

'Em.' Anne looks more surprised to see the public relations manager than she is to see Mike in her arms.

I nod at the man next to Em. 'Park.'

Anne mutters something that sounds like 'guest list' under her breath.

The astronaut nods back, his annoyingly memorable smile flashing. 'Found this little guy wandering around the bushes on our way in.'

'Hey, Em.' Vance comes up behind Anne and me, looking over the newcomers. 'Park.' He leans between us. 'Is this the infamous cat?'

'Yes.' Anne slides the collar over Mike's neck before tightening it. 'This is Mike.' Collar secure, Anne takes Mike from Emily's arms. 'Thanks so much for finding him.'

'To be fair, he found me.' Em points to her silk sleeves dress with rhinestone buttons down the front. 'I think he liked my buttons.'

'He's a bit of a handful, isn't he?' Park turns his smile on Anne.

Even more annoying than his smile is the effect it appears to have on Anne – all the tension between her brows, tension that's been there all night, vanishes.

'Yes.' Smiling back, she lowers Mike to the floor. 'If you don't know how to handle him.'

Even not looking at me, the dig lands.

'Hey there.' Vance pulls up his pant legs and squats down to Mike's level.

Anne's grip on the leash whitens when Vance reaches out to pet him, sighing in relief when Mike melts into Vance's hand, purring.

Then, as if embracing the formality of his tuxedo, Mike leads everyone inside, sashaying into the foyer with his nose up, tail curled.

'What a sweet guy.' Vance follows, fascinated. 'I bet he's a great emotional support animal when he isn't running away.'

It takes me a minute to realize he's talking to me, because Mike is supposed to be *my* emotional support animal. 'He can be.'

'Yeah.' Park chuckles. 'Not at all the alien menace he looks like on the NBL's pool footage.' He holds up a thumb drive. 'Which I brought, by the way.'

My smile feels more feral than Mike Hunt. 'Great.'

* * *

Twenty minutes after everyone witnessed Mike Hunt's skinny-dip in NASA's foremost state-of-the-art micro-gravity training pool, played out on Vance and Rose's big screen TV, the star of the show is cuddled like a baby in Park In-Su's arms.

'Jules is going to be sad she missed Mike,' Trish says, eating her second piece of pie on the couch next to Park. 'She's become quite the animal lover since she adopted Cookie.'

Mike purrs against Park's chest like the fly-by-night playboy he is.

Anne, next to Park, breaks her astronaut-infatuated trance. 'Cookie?'

Trish nods. 'Her pet cow.'

'Then there's her dog, Rocket,' Rose adds, facing the fan Vance moved to the side table next to her. 'I call him Red for short.'

Holt, beer in hand, rolls his eyes. He seems to be one of the only people here not enamored with the hairless beast. 'I don't regret our cow or dog, but I do question my sanity over our goat every morning when I wake up to it bleating before the damn rooster crows.'

I frown at Holt. 'Our?'

'You didn't know?' Vance asks. 'Holt is married to Julie Starr.'

'And our *other* brother—' Rose gestures between herself and Holt '—is married to Dr Jackie Darling Lee.'

Anne goes still.

Rose shrugs. 'It seems the Wests have a kink for astronauts.'

'Wow.' Amanda nods, looking impressed. 'That's one astronomical kink.'

Trish snorts. 'Good one.'

'Is she coming?' Anne asks, her voice at half volume.

'Who?' Vance asks.

'Dr Jackie Darling Lee.' Anne clears her throat. 'Is she coming tonight?'

'Sadly—' Rose tilts her face back into the fan's airstream '—Jackie is nerding out tonight at an interactive virtual reality thing.'

'Did you want to meet Jackie?' Trish asks, catching Anne's disappointment.

'Oh, um, yes.' Her face flushes. 'I'm a big fan of Dr Lee's.'

'Uh oh.' Park leans his arm against Anne's beside him. 'I thought *I* was your favorite astronaut.'

Distracting myself from the pinprick of jealousy, I grab one of the cookies off the plate Holt set on the coffee table earlier. 'These are great. Glad to know I'm not the only guy who can bake.'

Holt nods with a smile. 'Which makes me happy that you're the one staying in Jules' condo. All the cooking equipment I bought her will finally get some use.'

Anne's wide eyes bore into me, as if in warning.

'Wait.' Em shifts on the couch, frowning at me. '*You're* staying in Jules' condo?'

'Yeah.' Vance snags a cookie for himself. 'I gave Felix the key when his hotel was infiltrated by fans.'

'And I appreciate it.' I speak slowly, not understanding Anne's reaction or Em's pointed interest.

Until Em's next statement.

'But I gave *Anne* the key.'

Merde.

21

FELIX

'Did you and Anne *really* meet by showing up at the same condo?' Amanda leans her elbow on the car door's armrest, her laugh laced with disbelief. 'And just like that—' she snaps her fingers '—you hired her to watch over your emotional support animal?'

I glance at the chauffer in front of us, surprised Amanda would ask me something like that with him in easy listening distance.

Back at Vance's house, when Anne and my shared living arrangements were outed, Anne saved us with a we-made-the-best-of-the-situation lie. Explaining how we hadn't wanted to trouble Vance and Em, who had already gone out of their way to help us.

It was obvious Em wanted to follow up with more questions, but whether out of courtesy or the fact that Park dropped Mike Hunt in her arms to hold, everyone went back to petting my emotional support animal.

Amanda's eyebrows lift, waiting for an answer.

It seems not everyone is so easily distracted.

I give her a small nod. 'Thanks for the ride, Amanda. I appreciate it.'

She's silent for a second, as if debating whether or not to accept my abrupt change of subject.

For the first time, I'm uncomfortable around her. But as soon as the thought forms, it vanishes when she shrugs and smiles. 'Not a problem.'

I blame Anne for my sudden distrust of everyone. Every woman.

In the moment, I was grateful for Anne's quick thinking, but now I'm starting to think of it as a quick lie. And instead of just wondering what I don't know about Anne, I'm questioning everything I do as well.

I close my eyes against the southbound oncoming traffic lights on interstate forty-five, my head hurting.

Hopefully, Jack has a good reason for calling and insisting I not go to the condo, but instead meet him at the hotel.

Walking to the car with Anne, I'd pulled my phone out, ready to use it as a shield between us until we got to the condo and I could unleash all the questions I've stored up over the past weeks with her. That's when I saw all the missed calls from Jack. He'd been calling and texting all night, but I had turned off my phone when dinner started, not wanting to be rude. His last message was to inform me that he was boarding a plane for Houston and wanted a face-to-face tonight, even though he'd be arriving late.

I'd hesitated for a moment, not wanting to put off the inquisition that I've already put off for far too long. But one more look at Anne in that dress made me think that it might be best to regroup and reorganize my thoughts before we started that conversation.

And honestly, a petty part of me felt vindicated at Anne's shocked expression when I told her I'd text her later and asked Amanda to give me a ride to the hotel so I could meet up with my manager.

'Hey.' Amanda lays a hand on my arm. 'You okay?'

'Hmmm.' I drop my head against the headrest. 'Headache.'

'Ugh, that sucks.' There's riffling, like she's checking her purse. 'I don't have any on me, but I have some Motrin in my room. I'll get it for you when we arrive.'

'Thanks.'

The rest of the ride downtown is quiet.

Except for the constant throbbing of my head that weirdly echoes the one in my heart.

* * *

'Here.' Amanda emerges from her hotel room bathroom, two pills in her outstretched palm.

I toss them back with a long chug from one of the room's bottles of water. 'Thanks.' I check my phone again, even though I know Jack isn't due to land for another hour.

'Why don't you stay here until Jack arrives?' Amanda offers, kicking off her heels. 'It's better than waiting alone in your hotel room.'

She must read the hesitation on my face because she picks up the remote. 'We can watch a movie neither of us are in and be mean and judgy about the actors in it.'

That gets a small laugh from me. 'If you don't mind.' Distracting myself for a while might help my headache and keep me from doing what I really want to do – call or text Anne.

'Not at all.' She sits on the end of the suite's sofa, legs tucked under. 'What should we watch?'

Setting my phone, screen up on the coffee table, I take the other side of the sofa, releasing some of my tension with a long sigh. 'You pick.'

* * *

Liz

'Felix didn't come home last night.'

Mike stares at me from his spot on the chair opposite the condo's couch.

'You're right. He's a grown ass man.' I toss the phone I've held in my hand since I woke at five in the morning onto the cushion beside me. 'I'm sure he's fine.'

Mike turns on his side, his front and back paws crossed.

'But, you know, it's weird.' The foot resting over my knee vibrates. 'For someone who had proven himself to be such a nice guy, it's odd that he hasn't texted or called like he said he would.'

Then again, he hadn't seemed himself last night.

'Maybe I should text him?'

Mike remains motionless in the morning stream of sunlight coming in through the windows.

'Yeah, not a good idea.' As much as I'd like to simultaneously ask if he's okay and chew him out for leaving with his co-worker last night, it would reek of desperation. Plus, I'd already asked if he was okay, and he said everything was fine.

My foot shakes faster, remembering how Felix ignored me, spent more time talking to Amanda than me, then sent me home alone under the guise of having to meet with his manager.

Fuck a duck.

With a large yawn, Mike stretches and gets to his feet.

'Is this how my mother felt during all those years with Stanley?' Sympathy for my mother, which I haven't let myself feel much of this past year, wells up inside me.

Bounding from chair to coffee table to couch, Mike settles in next to me, his warmth immediately stilling my foot and soothing my inner agitation.

Maybe the whole emotional support animal isn't such a stretch after all.

My phone dings and it's embarrassing how fast I grab it.

> This is your warning

Fuck a huge fucking duck. I stare at my brother Chase's text, wondering how things went from great to shit in the matter of a day.

First, I build up my courage and decide to come clean to Felix about everything, but then Johnny Douchebag takes over Felix's body again. And now my family decides that this is the perfect time to ambush me.

I mean, I guess I should feel lucky that they waited until after my storyboard duties were over. But it would've been nice to meet my sister before coming clean to my brothers about what I've been up to.

Even so, what with everything that's happened and everything that I've learned these past few weeks, I've realized I need to stop pushing my family away. Even if that means telling them why I did so in the first place.

I snap a picture of Mike curled up next to me on the couch and text it to Chase, giving him both proof of life and letting him know that I got his warning.

But just as I'm about to put my phone down, it buzzes with a text from an unknown number.

> This is Trish.
>
> From last night.

I chuckle, wondering how many Trish's she thinks I know.

> I got your number from Em. Hope that's OK.

With nothing better to do other than whittle away time before I either kiss or kill Felix and then get swarmed by Moores, I call Trish instead of texting.

'Hey there,' Trish's Georgian accent sing-songs over the phone.

I put it on speaker so I can cuddle Mike closer. 'Hey Trish from last night.'

She snorts. 'Did you get home okay? Has Mike recovered from his adventures?'

Mike flicks his tail with acknowledgment of his name being called.

I nuzzle the top of his head. 'Yeah, that was just another day in the life of Mike Hunt.'

Her laugh sounds like bells. 'I see.' There's some murmuring in the background.

Remembering her questions on illustration last night, I ask, 'Is there something I can help you with?'

'Um, actually, yes. I was wondering if we could meet?'

'Now?' I glance at the clock.

'I was thinking brunch. I know we talked about how webcomics are created last night, but I wanted to look over your sketches and discuss maybe *you* creating the webcomic for me.'

My mind pauses, then fast-forwards with a million thoughts. The most pronounced is *awesome*. 'You know I've never made a webcomic, right?' My self-doubt can't help but pipe up. 'I just read them and can draw.'

'Yes, but Amanda said that storyboarding is similar.'

Damn Amanda. It's hard to dislike her when she talked me up so well. 'That's true.'

'And plus, I invited Jackie to brunch.'

Fuck a duck. My brain stutters again as her words sink in.

'You can meet your favorite astronaut.' Trish says the last as if trying to bribe Mike Hunt off his humping doll. 'You looked so disappointed last night when Rose said she wasn't coming. And since us girls usually have brunch together anyway, I thought you and I meeting up today would be great for everyone.'

'Yes.' I nod my head, nearly bashing Mike with my chin. 'I can meet.'

More bells. 'Great. I'll send you the link to the restaurant. Is ten o'clock okay?'

I have just two hours to put together a portfolio from the work I have saved on my tablet and get ready to meet my sister. 'Perfect.'

'Okay, sugar. See you soon.'

22

FELIX

A loud trilling invades my dream.

It trills twice, just long enough for my brain to start functioning. In the following silence, a low murmured conversation starts lulling me back to sleep.

'Felix.'

Someone nudges my shoulder.

'Wake up.'

Another nudge and my head falls to the side, jarring me.

'Hmmm...?' Blinking, I wake to Amanda, one knee resting on the sofa cushion next to me, leaning in.

'Jack's looking for you.'

'What—' I clear my throat, wincing as I look around for my manager. I'm still in Amanda's suite, sitting on the sofa, just as I was when we started watching the movie. 'What time is it?'

'Eight.'

I pause in stretching my stiff neck. 'In the morning?' I mean, it must be considering we didn't get to the hotel until midnight. But still, I slept here all night?

My mind goes to Anne. I never texted or called like I said I would.

Amanda grimaces. 'You fell asleep at the start of the movie, and I hadn't wanted to wake you what with you having a headache and all.'

'Fuck.' I struggle to my feet, reaching for my phone. Dead.

'So sorry.' Amanda's chin sinks between her shoulders.

Shaking off my exhaustion, I take a deep breath. 'Not your fault.' I stare at my blank phone screen. 'But where's Jack? And how do you know he's looking for me?'

'I guess when you didn't answer your phone, he called around.' She points to the suite's phone on the nearby desk. 'He's waiting in the suite the studio booked for you at the start of filming.'

The one I left to escape paparazzi and fans. Jack must've assumed keeping the room in my name would trick people into thinking I'm still staying here.

'All right.' I pocket my phone and pull out my wallet, thankful I never threw out the room key. 'Thanks for the ibuprofen and letting me crash here last night, Amanda. I appreciate it.'

She cuts her eyes to the side with a weak smile. 'No problem.'

* * *

'Why *the fuck* were you in Amanda Willis' room?'

The heavy suite door clunks to a close. 'I fell asleep.'

At Jack's incredulous look, I raise both hands, one still holding the hotel room's card key. 'Honest.' Turning to the door, I latch the inside lock. 'I was waiting for you to arrive, and I fell asleep on the couch. Nothing happened.'

'Fine.' Jack sinks back into the chair I found him in when I entered the room. 'That's the least of our problems anyway.'

I toss my key card on the suite's entry table. 'What do you mean?'

He points to his bags on the bed. 'Grab the file in the front pocket of my briefcase.'

Exhaustion drags my feet as I walk across the room. Despite almost eight hours of sleep, I feel groggy. I guess no one feels well rested after spending the night sleeping upright.

'First—' Jack pinches the bridge of his nose as I pull out the file '—I want to apologize.'

That pulls me up short. 'What do you mean?' I glance at the plain manilla folder in my hands. 'What do you have to apologize for?'

'I haven't been doing a good job as your manager.'

I scoff. 'You're a great manager.'

'No.' His resolve sobers my amusement. 'If I was, I would've intervened with Camilla sooner. Or at least vetted her before you went out.' He shakes his head, sighing. 'But I was thinking as your friend, not wanting to overstep into your personal life.'

My fingers tighten on the folder. 'Is this about her? Did she do something else?'

Damn my dead phone battery. I haven't been able to check the headlines this morning.

'No.' Jack shakes his head. 'This is about Elizabeth.'

Huh. 'Who's Elizabeth?'

He points to the folder in my hands. 'The *real* name of the condom woman from the hotel. The woman I should've been more concerned with finding.'

My brows pinch together, the headache from last night threatening to resurface. 'That's not her name, her name is—'

'Elizabeth.' Jack pushes off his knees and stands. 'Elizabeth Anne Moore.' Sidestepping the coffee table, Jack walks over to me, taking the folder from my hands. Opening it, he turns it back to me.

I take it, confused as I stare at a photo of Anne. Except it's not Anne. Not really.

It's a woman who looks like her, but different. This woman has her blonde hair pulled back and sprayed in a formal updo. And her features, while similar, have been contoured and masked with make-up, making her look airbrushed and flawless. No freckles. No natural flush. No expression.

There are diamonds in her ears and around her neck and wrists. Her body is clad in head-to-toe designer. Reminding me of red-carpet events I've attended.

But it isn't how she looks that's the most jarring part of this being Anne. It's who's with her in the picture.

She's standing front and center in a group of women, all of whom look eerily similar to each other. All holding a champagne glass, all posing for the camera.

And she's standing next to Camilla Branson.

* * *

Liz

I never thought I'd be back in Boondoggles, but here I am. Once more sweating from my trudge through the hot, crowded parking lot as I approach the hostess stand.

'Hi, I'm looking for—'

'Yoo hoo!' I glance over the hostess' shoulder to see Trish waving like a beauty queen. 'Hey there, sugar.' She flops back down in her seat, the effort of holding a half-stand half-squat probably too much for a pregnant woman. 'Over here.'

With a smile at the hostess, I move through the crowded restaurant part of Boondoggle's, toward a semi-private table set up inside a huge, old-fashioned fireplace. The semicircle of brick walls remains while the flue is covered and hearth has been removed to fit a table inside.

When I reach the table, the loud noise of the restaurant becomes a more manageable din thanks to the brick walls acting as a barrier to the sound. 'I hope you weren't waiting long.'

'Nope. Just got here.' Trish notices me looking at the empty chairs. 'Don't worry. Rose and Jackie are coming in about—' she checks the thin Cartier watch on her wrist '—thirty minutes or so.' Lowering her arm, she sits straight, looking like a pregnant beauty pageant queen. 'I asked you to come a little earlier so we can get work talk out of the way.' She smiles kindly at me. 'That way, you'll be free to ask Jackie all your astronaut questions.'

My return smile feels awkward as I second-guess my decision to wear jeans, a t-shirt, and my standard ponytail. After hiding treats around the condo in the hope that the food hunt would keep Mike from causing chaos while I went to brunch, I hadn't much time left to get ready.

As I grabbed Felix's rental keys from the counter, I told myself this was an opportunity to meet my sister without all the trappings of a Moore. That I should simply come as I am and not burden myself or her by attempting to be overly impressive. But now, toes wiggling in my Birkenstocks, I'm thinking maybe I should've at least worn some make-up.

Assuming my hesitation has to do with which seat I should take, Trish pats the one next to her.

Pushing my self-doubt aside, I sit while Trish pulls a laptop out of her bag hanging from the back of her chair.

'Ron was sweet enough to send me your storyboards that Amanda had mentioned.'

I blink at her, unable to imagine curse-my-cat-out Ron being sweet to anyone. 'Oh.'

'Hope you don't mind.' Trish sets the computer between us and flips it open. 'I didn't wanna put you on the spot asking you for them because I wasn't sure if you were legally allowed to, so—' she lifts her slim shoulders '—I went straight to the source.' She turns the laptop to me, my storyboards already on screen. 'I *love* them.'

My chest, feeling battered after everything that happened with Felix since last night and shaky from nerves, warms at her compliment.

'I'm a bit of an Asian pop culture nerd. I love all the graphic novels that have come out recently. They remind me of manga, even though the modern ones are all in color.' Pulling out romance book after romance book from her bag, she stacks them on the table. 'I'm interested in turning *all* my romance novels into webcomics. And when I saw your work—' she pauses to point to the computer screen '—I *knew* I wanted you to do it.'

I eye the considerable stack of books, feeling both excited and overwhelmed. 'Me?'

'Yes.' Finished, Trish resituates herself on her chair. 'Whew.' She exhales a long breath, resting both palms on her belly. 'Being pregnant really takes a lot out of you.'

Flagging down a waitress, I ask for water to be brought to the table.

'Thanks.' Seemingly recovered enough to resume talking, Trish points to her computer again. 'I think what you did with the storyboards is *exactly* what I had in mind for the manga.'

Looking at my work from a different perspective, I can see what Trish means. While the compositions were driven by required camera angles and the finished storyboards aren't as clean of a finished project as I would normally make, they do tell a story. Trish's story. 'I never considered being a webcomic artist.'

'Well, now that you have—' Trish props one elbow on the table, leaning toward me '—what do you think about it?' Her elbow slips off the edge, her belly having prevented her from sitting close enough to the table. 'Oops.' She giggles her jingle-bell laugh.

I can't help but smile with her.

I like Trish. She's genuine. Nice. And a talented writer. And now that she's planted the idea of being a webcomic artist, it feels... *right*.

Although I haven't enjoyed the Hollywood nonsense involved in my internship, I *have* enjoyed the work. Drawing all day and getting paid for it. Creating art from words on a page. It made me feel like the talent I have, the talent that Stanley Moore always said was useless, is actually worth something.

My smile, unrestrained and engaging every muscle in my face, stretches the corners of my mouth. 'I think I would really, really like it.'

Trish claps. 'Great!'

The two of us spend the next thirty minutes discussing her books, timelines, and costs. Afterwards, she insists I take all of her romances home. She even signs them for me.

Pulling my tablet out of my bag to make room for the books, I lay it on the table. 'I don't have my hard copy portfolio with me, but I save most of my work on this.' I click the screen open and hand it to her. 'I know you liked the style of what I did with the storyboards, but you can compare it to the other things I've done in case you see something else you like.'

Trish lights up over the drawing I did of my niece Mary holding King Richard. 'I should start implementing more animal sidekicks into my novels.' She swipes right, moving through the images I've saved.

Still lifes, portraits, the cartoon I made of Mike Hunt in space.

She snorts at the one with Mike on the spaceship. 'These are great.'

Feeling a little embarrassed over the praise, I busy myself and take a sip of water.

'Oh.' Her fingers pause over the screen, her brown eyes meeting mine over my water glass. 'I *really* like this one.' She sounds like she's holding back laughter.

Placing the glass back on the table, I lean forward. And when I see what's there, my mouth drops.

Felix in his blue apron.

I'm surprised there's no smoke pouring from my lips because my insides are combusting from embarrassment.

I'd forgotten that I used my tablet to take pictures of my sketch book. I transfer the drawings I've done into my illustration app to save time online work when I want to convert the sketches into a digital file.

Which is why Trish, looking more amused than shocked, is holding a tablet showcasing my deprived inner fantasies of a Hollywood action star.

'I love how the sky blue of his apron contrasts with the deeper, olive tones of his skin,' Trish says, turning the tablet back to her. 'You have a gift for color.'

'I, ah…'

Trish laughs at whatever expression I'm making. 'I take it you didn't mean for me to see this?' She pats my hand. 'Don't worry, I'll pretend I didn't.' Returning to the tablet, she swipes again. 'Oh.' Trish's cheeks match her lips. 'Maybe I should just hand this back to you.'

She clicks the screen off, but not before I remember what else I transferred to my tablet.

Nude Felix.

My hands shake as I take the tablet from her.

'Don't be embarrassed. Art is art.' Trish waves the air like she can somehow cool the embarrassment choking the words from my mouth. 'And it answers the *other* question I needed to ask before we start working together.'

Clearing my throat, I try and not sound like one of Mikey's squeaky toys. 'And what is that?'

'If you'd have a problem drawing sex scenes.' Her mouth kicks up on one side. 'Because, as Rose mentioned last night, I want the webcomics to be rated mature.'

'Porn. I said porn.'

Trish and I – along with quite a few nearby tables – startle and turn toward Rose, standing at the table, hands where her hips would normally be if it weren't for her belly.

'It's hotter than balls outside.' Rose blows Trish a kiss, then me before waving both hands at her cheeks. 'I can't tell you how much I regret these damn leggings.'

My gaze drops to her bright-red, leopard-print embossed maternity leggings under a NASA emblem t-shirt.

'But honestly, I couldn't do another dress after all the thigh chafing from last night.' Asking a passing waiter to turn the ceiling fans on high, she pulls out the chair beside me. 'I also resorted to slipping the hostess a hundred-dollar bill and asking her to pump the AC as high as it'll go.' She points, moving her finger back and forth between Trish and me. 'So if your nipples start puckering—' she shrugs '—sorry, not sorry.'

'Where's Jackie?' Trish asks, saving me from doing it myself.

'She dropped me off at the entrance so I didn't have to waddle through the parking lot.' Rose pours herself a glass of water from the pitcher the waitress left on the table. 'That's true friendship.' She downs the glass in one go, wiping a drop of water off her chin when she's done. 'But enough about me.'

'That's something I never thought I'd hear her say,' Trish murmurs, shooting me an amused smile.

Rose ignores her with a wave, before staring into my eyes. 'How are *you* doing?'

Her sudden concerned tone has me exchanging frowning glances with Trish.

'What do you mean?' I ask.

'The whole thing that blew up this morning with Felix and Amanda,' Rose asks, scanning the TVs hung around the restaurant. 'I mean, I know you're just his pet sitter, but I'm sure his whole team has been in an uproar.'

I stare blankly at the back of her head.

'There.' Rose having found what she wanted, points to one of the TVs in the corner. One of the only ones not playing ESPN. 'See what I mean, everyone's talking about Felix and Aman—' She stills. 'Oh fuck.'

The split screen of Felix and Amanda's headshots fade, replaced with a different picture.

'Is that you?' Trish asks.

Wordless, I nod, my eyes staring at a photo of Felix and me at the Neutral Buoyancy Lab. Kissing.

'That was for work, I, uh, had to stand in. For the scene.' My stammers are met with sympathetic stares.

Rose pats my hand. 'That's good. It's bad enough that he's cheating on his fiancée by having an affair with his co-worker. I wouldn't have wanted to like a guy who was also sleeping w—'

'I'm sorry?' My brain still doesn't seem to be working. 'Fiancée?'

A pinch forms between Rose's brows. 'I mean, he didn't bring it up last night, so I didn't, but I thought he just got engaged to Camilla Branson not too long ago.'

'Engaged.' The word falls from my lips, sounding foreign and dangerous.

Rose nods and pours herself another glass of water.

'Um, Rose?' Trish's eyes bounce between me and the TV screen.

Not seeming to hear her, Rose points at the screen. 'Someone at the hotel last night said Felix entered Amanda's room and didn't leave until this morning.'

'Is that so?' My voice sounds very far away.

'Yeah, and I consider myself a good judge of people and I didn't get a hint of cheater from Felix last ni—'

'Rose!'

'Huh?' The pitcher slips in Rose's hand, water sloshing on the table. 'What?'

'*Read the room.*' Trish's Georgian accent hardens.

Catching my expression, Rose stills. 'Oh.' She bites her lip. 'Fuck.' She mutters something about Vance, super sperm and pregnancy brain. 'I should've put it together sooner.'

'Anne?' Trish's hand covers mine on the table. 'Are you okay?'

'Fine.' I nod, plastering a smile on my face. Feeling very much like my old society doll self as the television shows a woman with white-blonde hair, tanned skin and perfectly contoured cheekbones dabbing her dry eyes with a tissue. The closed captions flashing words like, *Camilla Branson. Fiancée. Other woman. Home wrecker.*

'Um, just so you know,' Rose offers, 'you can't really trust anything you read on the internet.'

'Yes, sugar.' Trish pats my hands again. 'I'm sure Felix's management team will be right on this.'

I concentrate on tilting the corners of my lips up, just enough to give the appearance of grace and poise in the face of my worst fears coming to life.

But when the TV screen flashes a picture of Felix's mom with the question, *Where is Sofia Jones?* my old façade cracks.

My hand, under Trish's, contracts into a fist. 'Fuck. A. Duck.'

Rose shares a mother glance with Trish before frowning at me. 'Fuck a what, now?'

'A duck. A motherfucking duck.' I grab my tablet and my bag of books.

'Yep.' Rose nods. 'That's what I thought you said.'

I stand, shouldering my bag. 'I have to go.'

And when they continue to glance uneasily at each other, I pull a trick from Douchebag Felix's playbook – 'Everything's fine' – before excusing myself from the table.

Passing my sister on the way out.

23

FELIX

I should pick up a Candy Crush addiction.

, Playing a mindless phone game right now would be infinitely better than being caught in a mindless loop of self-recrimination and loathing while staring down a hairless cat.

Mike's tail curls one way and then the other from his perch on the chair opposite my sofa.

Normally, he'd be taking my distraction as an opportunity to inch closer. To sneak beside me as I stare vacantly at the front door, waiting for Anne to return with my rental car keys.

But either Mike knows what the packed bag at my feet means, or he's more in tune to emotional undercurrents than I've given him credit for in the past.

Forcing my gaze away from his beady-eyed focus, I click open my phone. However, instead of the smart thing – downloading my manager's favorite app – I do the dumb thing and look over the Hollywood news feeds and scroll through my social media accounts.

Cheater. Playboy. Addiction. Missing mother.

It's the last that guts me.

An hour or so earlier, after having finally digested who Anne, *Elizabeth*, is, Jack's phone blew up from various news agencies asking to know if it all was true. That I've been cheating on my fiancée with various women while my mother's been missing from her normal social life.

It's Camilla's last warning.

A text flashes above the picture of my mother and me attending the Golden Globes last year that a tabloid is using in their 'exposé':

> Are you sure you don't want me to come up?

While Jack knew there were things to collect from the condo, he had wanted to do it for me. But as the location hadn't been leaked yet, I felt it a good idea to do it myself. To get some of the answers I should've insisted on from the start of my relationship with An—Elizabeth.

I just hadn't expected her not to be here when I arrived. Or that she would've taken my rental car.

'Meow.' Mike bats a hidden treat from under the couch toward him.

I also hadn't expected her to have left Mike alone in the apartment.

The sound of keys rattling against the door jerks my attention to the left.

Not wanting to be at a disadvantage, I stand, preparing myself to hear things I don't want to but *need* to.

Yet even with all my mental preparation, my heart isn't prepared for when Anne walks into the condo.

Her hair is a halo of frizzy flyways from her ponytail, her skin flushed and damp from the heat, her expression somehow stunning and murderous at the same time.

'Elizabeth.' Not Anne, I remind myself.

She stutter steps in her Birkenstocks as the door swings shut behind her. Then, as if my knowing her lies doesn't faze her, she continues toward me, dropping her bag with a thud just a few feet away from mine by me feet. 'Douchebag.'

I balk, her anger at me unexpected, like so many other things about her. 'Excuse me?'

'You heard me.' She tosses my rental keys on the coffee table between us. 'As you're already packed—' she thumbs over her shoulder '—get out.'

My hands fist at my sides. 'That's how you want to play this?'

'Play what?'

'Play this whole act you started, trying to get close to me for a story.'

'Wait.' She laughs unkindly. 'You're going to blame *your* cheating on *me*?' She shakes her head. 'You made me the other woman and then spent the night with your co-worker?' Tears well in her eyes. 'I *promised* myself I would never get involved with someone like...' She trails off, her fists pressing against her eyes. 'Jesus, your poor fiancée.'

'Poor fiancée?' I sneer. 'So your friend Camilla got you to believe her lies too, huh?'

'Friend?' She lowers her hands, confusion in her watery eyes. 'I don't even know Camilla.'

'Sure.' As much as it hurts, I'm almost happy to catch her in one of her lies. Pulling the image Jack printed out from my back pocket, I hand it to her. 'How would you explain this then?'

She stares at the photo, a deep V between her brows. 'Where...?' Taking it from my outstretched hand, she continues to study the photo of her and Camilla, their combined outfits and accessories probably more than the average person's yearly salary, as if genuinely confused. 'This... this must have been a few years ago.'

She's a good actor. I'll give her that. But I'm done living a fantasy. I only ever wanted to work in make-believe, not live it.

'Sure. And I guess you'll tell me you didn't know your family is currently working with Camilla on her own fashion line?'

A light of recognition clicks in Anne's – *Elizabeth's* – eyes. 'That's not me. I don't have anything to do with Moore's.'

'Just stop.'

Not as aggressive now that I have proof, she holds up both hands. 'Look, I don't know what you're accusing me of, but the only thing I did was not tell you my first name.' She crosses her arms over her chest. 'You're the one cheating and carrying on. And what is this about your mother? You told me last night that nothing—'

'Don't even *think* of bringing my mother into this.'

She steps back from the force of my words.

'You're the one who did this to her.' I swallow back the emotion attempting to erupt from my chest. 'Threatening to make her struggle public.'

'What are you talking about?'

I'm not sure if she really deserves an Oscar or if she really had no idea what Camilla was going to do with the information Elizabeth gave her, but I decide to lay out for her. Let her know the true consequences of her selfish actions. 'Your dear friend Camilla is a blackmailer. As soon as you gave her proof that I wasn't living up to her lie of us being engaged, she retaliated. Got the whole world to hate me while being sympathetic to her.'

The lines between Elizabeth's brows deepen. 'I don't understand, what proof? And what is she blackmailing you with?'

I choose to believe her confusion, only because if I don't, I don't think I could recover. It isn't until coming face to face with her, knowing what she's been hiding and me still having to fight the urge to hold her, kiss her, look to her for comfort that I realize just how far I've fallen.

For Anne. Elizabeth. Whoever the person was who brought me back to the man I was before the fame.

'My mother is in a rehabilitation program for drug addiction.'

Elizabeth's head rears back, her eyes and mouth wide.

Clearing my throat, I explain. 'My mother is getting the help she needs after being prescribed too much pain medication after a recent surgery.' I take a breath. 'She didn't know. The doctor just kept giving her meds, thinking that she was really getting them for me, her movie star son who probably gets high for fun.' I run a shaky hand through my hair. 'She was just following doctor's orders and then because of me...'

'Felix.' Elizabeth reaches out, but I jerk away, causing her compassion to fade and her shoulders to square. 'I didn't know about your mother. I swear. And even if I did, I would *never* be friends with *anyone* who would use something like that against another person.'

'Yeah, then how did they get this then?' I cut her off, not wanting to hear how much she cares about the woman she helped hurt. Raising my phone, flashing her the picture of us kissing at NASA. 'Who else could've sent this to Camilla?'

'How could I have taken that picture?' She shakes her head, crossing her arms. 'I'm in it.'

'You probably got someone else to take it for you.' I pause, a memory hitting me. 'Is that what David was whispering to you about before you kissed me?'

She frowns, as if thinking over my question. 'No.'

'Then what did he say before you kissed me in front of the whole crew even when everyone knows stand-ins aren't supposed to act out the scene?'

'First of all, I'm not everyone. I don't work in Hollywood, and I didn't know I wasn't supposed to kiss you.' Her cheeks darken, from embarrassment or anger I'm not sure. 'And David was just trying to help me relax. He told me to—' she sighs, some of the fight leaving her '—he told me to pretend like I was arriving at one of the galas I attended in the past. The ones I was forced to attend by my father.' She shrugs, her eyes cutting to the side. 'I always had to pretend to be someone else. That's what I meant when I said I knew how you felt the other night.'

I scoff, too afraid to believe anything she says.

'That picture—' she points to the one of her next to Camilla '—was taken at one of those events. And while that is me next to Camilla, I don't know her. I don't know any of those people in that picture. It's just a coincidence. I swear.'

Looking at the photo of Elizabeth next to Camilla only serves to propel my anger. 'Oh, it's just a *coincidence*, huh?' My smile is not warm or genuine. 'Just like you *coincidentally* forgot to tell me your real name? Or how you *coincidentally* showed up in the condo Jack secured for me?'

Elizabeth's jaw clenches. 'I told you, I was here f—'

'Was sleeping with me a coincidence too, or was that part of the plan?'

A sharp satisfaction courses through me when her whole body flinches. But it's short lived, turning bittersweet in the following silence.

Mike rises on his perch, his beady eyes narrowed on mine. Raising his tail, Mike readies to pounce.

I brace for impact, but he's stayed when Elizabeth rests a hand on his back.

Breaking free of his judgmental stare, the weaker part of me still needing answers.

'Why?' The question sounding more broken than I'd like.

Her continued silence grates.

'Why now?' Rising anger strengthens my voice. My resolve. 'Why not use the picture you took of me in the hotel when you had it?'

'I deleted it.' The words are forced between clenched teeth.

'Really?' Contempt drips off the word.

'You saw me.'

'I saw you delete a copy. You could've saved it somewhere else while you were busy getting me to play chef while ruining my career and getting me to take you to dinner.'

'I didn't—'

'The dinner.' I tilt my head, reassessing her request to be my date. 'Yeah, you needed me to take you to the astronaut dinner.'

Her eyes widen, only for a moment, but I see it, recognizing it as confirmation.

'Why?' I step closer, only a foot between us.

Mike hisses.

I step back, but when Elizabeth's hand remains on his back, I press on with my questions. 'Why was it so important to go to that dinner?'

She blinks, her eyes shiny. 'I can't say.'

I laugh unkindly. 'Well, isn't that the story of our entire relationship?'

Blonde lashes falling over pale cheeks. 'Listen.' When she reopens them, the blue is brighter and more intense than usual. 'I know you're mad and hurt right now.' The hand not holding Mike back rests against her chest. '*I'm* confused too. But I didn't do any of what you're accusing me of.'

I drop my gaze to her shoulder, unable to fight the tempting lies in her eyes.

She takes a deep breath, as if shoring up patience. 'I may have not told you my first name, just as *you* didn't.' She pauses to let her point sink in. 'But I never lied.'

I want to dismiss her claim, but the truth of that particular argument makes it impossible. Which only pains me more.

'This is pointless.' Exhausted, I pocket my phone and pick up my bag. 'I don't know what I was expecting from this conversation with you.'

But I do know.

I expected my questions to be answered with something that would give me hope. Hope that it wasn't all fake. That I wasn't as shallow or clueless as the film critics like to assume because of the movies I've made. Or, at the very least, I expected guilt, shame and regret to mar her bewitching natural beauty. A reaction that would make the hole in my chest feel a little less torn and ragged.

I walk away from them both.

Reaching the door, I open it, turning back one last time. 'What is it that makes me such an easy mark for talentless women wanting to make a name for themselves?' It takes all my strength to hold her gaze.

And while her eyes don't waver, her mouth remains closed.

Her unwillingness to answer yet another question has me lashing out one final time. 'I guess that's just what happens when you don't have one yourself. At least not a legitimate one, anyway.'

Elizabeth's blank expression contorts into a pain that's almost palpable.

There it is. Just what I wanted.

And yet, the vindication I expected to feel is strangely absent. Instead, the void inside my chest grows, more battered and oppressive than before.

Disappointed in myself, I turn to leave, pulling up short when something large blocks my path.

I have a moment to register the sparkle of sequins in the shape of a cat, before a fist slams into my face.

* * *

Liz

Felix falls like deadweight to the floor.

My eldest brother Thomas stands over him.

'Thomas!' Alice, my sister-in-law, grabs her husband by the waist when he reaches down to grab the front of Felix's shirt, other arm cocked back.

'Hit him again, T-money.' Chase pushes past Thomas and through the door, his attempt to kick Felix while he's down impeded by my other sister-in-law, Bell, jumping on his back.

'Fight!' Mary, my niece, pokes her head around the door frame and into the room behind Thomas, only for an arm with multiple diamond tennis bracelets to pull her back before she can slip through.

Mother.

I witness all of this as if my internal pause button has been pushed.

'What the fuck?'

'Who the hell are you?'

'Stop!'

'Let me see!'

'Don't you ever talk to my sister like that.'

'Calm down.'

'Get 'em, Daddy!'

Chaos revolves around me as I remain rooted to the floor, the only other sound penetrating is the echoing thump in my hollow chest.

Then a new voice enters the fray, yelling about lawsuits. Another few whacks that are probably landed punches. And then, silence.

Until slender hands grip my shoulders, their touch gentle. 'Elizabeth?' A light squeeze. 'Lizzie, dear?'

Mother.

Something smooth and warm winds its way around my legs. *Mike.*

Slowly, I come back to the moment. To myself. To a sequined cat t-shirt – half King Dick Moore, half Mike Hunt.

I blink, raising my eyes until the details of my mother's face come into focus. 'Mom?'

Thomas steps up beside her, his lip split. 'Hello, Elizabeth.' His sequined shirt flipped to King Dick Moore.

'Hey, Lizzie.' Chase takes Mom's other side, making small jazz hands. 'Surprise.' His shirt, unsurprisingly flipped to Mike Hunt.

My eyes cut toward the doorway where Bell, Alice, and Mary are gathered. Each wearing their own sequined cat t-shirt that I'd sent them. Half of them flipped to Mike Hunt. The other half King Dick Moore.

'The t-shirts.' My smile feels wobbly. 'You're wearing them.' My eyes blurry.

Everyone but Mother glances down at their chest, as if trying to figure out why that, of all things, is what I've chosen to focus on.

Mother keeps her eyes on me. 'I've missed you, my sweet Lizzie.'

It's then that the floodgates open. The hurt, the guilt, the shame, even the love and loss that I've kept at bay over the past year surging in, filling my chest until I can't hold onto it any longer.

And as the tears fall, I'm held tight by a group of sequined pussies.

24

LIZ

'Who did Daddy punch?'

Mary's question breaks through the strangely comfortable silence that my family has kept after Felix went full douchebag and Thomas went full *Fight Club*.

Bell, part of the protective sequined cat cocoon hugging me, breaks off to answer my nine-year-old niece playing Barbies on the floor nearby. 'I'm pretty sure that was a movie star.'

'No shit?' Chase is the next to step back, Bell slapping his arm.

'Don't curse in front of your niece.'

'It's OK, Aunt Bell.' Mary lowers the astronaut Barbie while keeping Prince Charming Ken upright. 'Daddy says I should only listen to half of what Uncle Chase says—' she moves Ken as she talks, as if he's the one saying it '—and repeat none of it.'

Thomas winks at his daughter, looking smug.

Chase shrugs. 'That's pretty sound advice, actually.'

'Thomas.' Alice tilts her head back to look at her husband. 'Did you know that was a celebrity when you punched him?'

His smile flattens. 'No.'

'I see.' She tilts her head. 'And now that you have punched him, and in front of our daughter no less, are you feeling any kind of remorse or regret?'

The only change in his expression is a slight flare to his nostrils. 'Only that I didn't hit him harder.'

'Damn, T-money.' Chase claps Thomas on the back. 'That's so gangster of you.'

Alice, probably attempting to look disappointed, rolls her lips. 'Well then, I'm sure the ensuing lawsuit won't feel quite so challenging as long as you have no regrets.'

'If he's going to sue anyone,' I manage without tears, my voice raw, 'he'll probably sue me.' Especially as Felix's lawyer-slash-manager arrived in time to pull his client out of the condo and away from Thomas' fists.

Sinking onto the sofa, I jerk my head at Mary and pat the cushion next to me.

Taking her cue, and her Barbies, Mary saddles up next to me, Mother taking the other side.

As if gathering around for a bedtime story, Chase drags two kitchen stools into the living room for himself and Bell. Thomas sits on the chair with Alice perching on the armrest beside him.

Mike Hunt and King Dick Moore cuddle in the sunlight.

'So.' Wrapping one arm around Mary and resting the other on my mom's knee, I take a deep breath to clear the remnants of my emotional tsunami. 'In the past year, I have gained enough credits to graduate with a master's in digital art, become a certified yoga instructor, taken an internship as a storyboarder, fallen in love with a movie star and found out I have a half-sister.' I look around the room, meeting everyone's shocked eyes before asking, 'What would you like to hear about first?'

* * *

'Hey Mom?'

Having shocked my family – or most of my family – with the reason why I came to Houston and all that's happened since I got here, I was persuaded to pack up and leave the condo.

A good choice seeing as the paparazzi are now swarming the building and I hadn't wanted to stay anywhere that reminded me of douchebag Felix.

Mom, unpacking her Louis Vuitton roller bag into The Post Oak Hotel's three-bedroom suite dresser, turns to me. 'Yes, dear?'

'Why didn't you tell me about my dad earlier?'

I know about my half-sister because my mom told me about her and who my real father was after my brothers discovered that the man who raised me used my illegitimacy as a reason to steal my inheritance. But I never asked any questions afterwards, too busy reeling from the news.

Now, having purged myself both emotionally and verbally, I sit cross-legged on the bed feeling strong enough to hear the answers I've spent the past year running from.

I tilt my head up to hers. 'About who my *real* dad was, I mean?'

She sighs, her gaze fixed on the perfectly folded clothes she places in the drawer. 'I want to make something crystal clear before I begin.' Closing the drawer, she faces me, holding my eyes until I register her conviction before continuing. 'When I say the affair was a mistake, I am in no way referring to *you*.' She moves forward, sinking elegantly onto the foot of the bed. 'You are one of the very best and most precious things in my life and I wouldn't change anything if it meant not having you.'

Swallowing back more tears, I nod.

Sighing, she smooths her hand across the bedspread. 'Believe it or not, your fath—I mean, *Stanley* and I used to get along.'

I do find that hard to believe, but I keep that to myself.

'And when things got rocky between us, I should've fought for our marriage instead of ignoring my problems.' She smiles sadly. 'I wasn't as brave as you.'

'Me?' I sit up on my elbow. 'Brave?'

'Oh yes.' Her smile deepens. 'I've always looked at you in awe as you sat at the dinner table, fighting your entire childhood for our family to get along. I was amazed by how you were mature enough to hold back but brave enough to move forward at just the right times.' She stretches her hand out, capturing mine and squeezing it. 'And when you set off for a whole year without the security of the Moore name or your inheritance behind you and still managed to blossom into the capable, strong woman you are...'

Her pink lips twist to the side. 'Your brothers thought I didn't want them chasing after you because I felt guilty.' She tilts her head as if considering. 'And maybe there's some truth to that.' She squeezes my hand again. 'But I also wanted to give you space. Not because it was the easy thing to do, because it was most definitely the hardest, but because I respected your choice to leave, the choice I could never make.' She lets go, lines creasing her normally smooth forehead. 'Even though it killed me not to talk to you. Not to explain.'

I scoot forward, retaking her hand, waiting for her to continue.

But just when I think she's said as much as she can, she clears her throat with a delicate cough. 'I met your father, your *real* father, after I finished hosting a charity luncheon. One of the many charity lunches I kept myself busy with once I became aware of Stanley's affairs.' Her sigh is half self-recrimination, half weary acceptance. 'I was sitting in the hotel bar when he came in, looking handsome but a little unkempt with his tie hanging crooked and his hair windswept and uncombed.' A small, wistful smile plays on her lips. 'He was so unlike the men I grew up with. So passionate and real.'

I'm shocked by how young my mother looks remembering the moment. Her eyes bright, her cheeks flushed.

'Though he had only stopped in the bar to wait for his room to be ready, we ended up spending the whole afternoon talking. He was in New York on business, his first trip away from his daughter after his wife had passed away from cancer two years earlier.'

I flinch, pained by the idea of the sister I never knew losing her mother so young.

'And after we talked...' Mom's slim shoulders lift, unable to say the words. 'And later, when I realized I was pregnant with you, I chose to pretend he and I never happened. To keep living the life of Eleanor Moore, wife of Stanley Winston Moore, head of one of the most prominent families in New York, if not the country.' The lines deepen between her brows. 'I told myself that it was all for the best, but I never asked myself who it was the best for.' Her eyes, now watery, meet mine. 'And I'm sorry. I'm so sorry for not telling you sooner. I'm sorry for so many things.'

Slipping my hand out of hers, I scramble to my knees and hug my mom. Squeezing me tight, she whispers in my ear, 'I love you and I'm of proud of you, and I'm so happy that you're my daughter. You're everything I always wished I could be, and you did that all on your own.'

Head on her shoulder, I let the minutes tick by as I play with the soft cashmere fabric of her cardigan. Because of course Eleanor Moore wears cashmere even in the humid hell of south-east Texas.

'I'm not sure if I'm really all that you think I am, Mom.' I bury my face in her sweater.

She leans back, holding my face to hers with both hands. 'And why would you say that?'

'Thomas is a brilliant businessman and Chase is a savvy investor, both of them not only running the family business, but making it more successful than it has been in years.' I drop my eyes to her pearl necklace. 'I'm just someone who can draw.'

'First—' she kisses both my cheeks before releasing me '—I want to say that I love all my children equally. *However*.' She eyes me, looking every inch the socialite matron she is. 'Thomas is a bit of a dick.'

I choke on my next breath.

'And Chase, well, he's ridiculous, really.' She looks down at her t-shirt between her open cardigan, which, like Mary, is flipped half Mike Hunt, half King Dick Moore. 'And he has been an unfortunate influence on you and your sense of humor.'

We share a smile.

'So don't think—' Mom reaches up, brushing back the hair escaping from my ponytail '—that just because they have good business sense that they are somehow more successful or better than you.'

Her words reach a part of me that has been lame and wounded since I found out I didn't share 100 per cent of my brothers' DNA.

Mom's lips press together, a slight twitch on one corner. 'And I'd pay serious money to see either one of them try and make it a whole year without their inheritance. Because don't forget, Thomas was handed the business simply by being born first. And Chase's principal investment came from his inheritance, even though he paid it back with the profits.' She cups my cheek once more. '*You*, my dear sweet girl, walked away from all of that privilege to take on college loans and work part-time jobs, all so that you could be true to who you are and hone your extremely impressive artistic talent.' She exhales a soft laugh. 'Could you even image Thomas or Chase doing that?'

The question conjures up an image of Thomas and Chase leading one of my yoga classes, making me chuckle.

She laughs with me. 'Thomas would've been fired for calling a customer an idiot.'

'Oh my God.' I laugh harder. 'I can *so* see that.'

'And Chase would've spent all his money on trying to impress women rather than pay off tuition bills.' She pauses, thinking over what she said. 'That's if Bell wasn't in the picture.'

'Alice too?' I ask, thinking of the softening effect she has on Thomas.

Mom dismissing that idea with a wave of her hand. 'Even with Alice's saintly influence, Thomas still calls people idiots.' She heaves a long sigh, the sequins on her t-shirt catching the light. 'George is forever earning his yearly bonuses by smoothing things over for him.'

I chuckle again thinking of Thomas' long-suffering secretary.

Mom slips her arm around my shoulders. 'So don't ever think you are not as talented or as loved as your brothers.' She pulls me in tight. 'Because honestly,' she whispers, '*you're* the most impressive.'

I squeeze her back. 'Thanks, Mom.'

'Yes, well.' She retracts her arm, swiping her glossy polished fingers under her eyes. 'What is not impressive is your plan to meet your sister.'

I wince at the hard truth.

'It doesn't seem like you planned anything, actually.' She stands, smoothing down her pencil skirt that somehow looks classic and chic even with her two-faced cat sequined t-shirt peeking out from her cashmere cardigan. 'It's like you just showed up and hoped to run into her.'

Meeting my mother's less-than-dazzled gaze, I grimace. 'I just thought if our meeting was random, if she and I just *happened* to meet, then she wouldn't have time to—' I sink into my shoulders '—I don't know, be disappointed or upset, maybe?'

Mom holds my gaze, not an ounce of sympathy in hers. 'Please tell me you are hearing how asinine that sounds now that you've said it out loud?'

I sigh, scooting forward on the bed until my feet drop to the floor and my head rests on her stomach. 'Yes.' Wrapping my arms around her, I mumble against her sequins. 'I hear it.'

'Good.' Placing both hands on my shoulders, she waits until my eyes meet hers. 'Then, shall I call your father?' At my bewildered expression, she gives me a withering glare that rivals Thomas'. 'No, not *that* asshat.'

Apparently, I'm not the only one Chase has been a bad influence on now that the 'asshat' Stanley Moore is no longer around.

The sunlight streaming in from the bedroom suite's window highlights my mother's pale-blonde hair. 'I'm talking about your *real* father, Dr Gerald Howard Lee.'

Goosebumps appear at the name I've only read in the research I did after discovering my true parentage. 'You—' I grip my knees with my hands '—have his number?'

'Yes.' She straightens her pearl necklace. 'I've never used it, but I've always made sure I had it.' Hand still resting on her pearls, a mix of regret and guilt flit over my mother's refined features. 'I was waiting for you to decide how you wanted to tell them, or even if you wanted to, before I acted.'

'Oh.' The hollow spot Felix left in my chest warms. 'Thanks, Mom.'

She opens her mouth, then pauses, as if second-guessing what she was about to say.

I purse my lips, wondering what else she has to surprise me with. 'What?'

'May I ask why you were so hell-bent on seeing your half-sister before seeing your father?'

I grimace, knowing the answer is going to make me seem lamer than my haphazard attempts to see my sister. 'I, uh, just figured I seem to have more luck with siblings than fathers—' I shrug, not meeting Mom's eyes '—so, um, I thought Jackie the safer option.'

'Please remember that Stanley Winston Moore is the exception, not the rule.' She holds my gaze, her soft eyes looking harder than I ever remember seeing them. 'That goes for *all* men. Because *anyone* worth *anything* would consider themselves the luckiest man alive to have you in their life.'

I nod, once more unable to talk, knowing full well she isn't talking about either of my two dads anymore.

25

FELIX

Having your ass chewed out verbally by someone who blames you for their ass being chewed out literally is *not* fun. Two days later, I'm still reeling.

I drop my head back on the Four Seasons suite's sofa, exhausted from the day's long and, thankfully, final shoot.

As expected, Ron lost his mind after the Hollywood rumor mill began attacking his two co-stars. Phrases like, 'Unacceptable and unprofessional behavior', 'Keep it in your pants' and, 'There will be hell to pay' were banded about until David, Anne's professor talked Ron down.

He wasn't even mad about the bad press, either. Just the black eye. Everything to Ron is inconsequential against the shooting schedule. And seeing as, even after Hollywood make-up magic was shellacked on my face, Ron still had to rearrange the shoot to hide the swelling around my eye, I'm one mistake away from being on Ron's blacklist.

Especially when you add in the constant re-shoots from Amanda missing her marks and forgetting her lines – all from being a victim the cheating rumor Camilla spread about us, no doubt.

Our PR firms mutually denied the affair, issuing a joint statement: *It is unfortunate in this day and age that two people of opposite sex cannot share a ride back to their hotel without the public assuming something more than friendship.*

Amanda and Felix are simply friends and colleagues who share the utmost respect for each other personally and professionally.

Thankfully, the studio issued their own statement in regard to the picture of Elizabeth and me kissing, shutting down any further inquiries: *As cell phones, tablets and cameras are contractually forbidden, not only on set, but inside the government facility, we will be taking legal action to get to the bottom of the leak.*

Even so, the news outlets have commented on the glaring absence of my own statement in regard to my supposed relationship with Camilla Branson or the whereabouts of my mother.

The phone in my hand vibrates.

Rubbing my tired eyes, I take a deep breath and smile before sliding my phone open. 'Hi, *Mā*—'

'What's wrong?' She leans forward, studying my picture on her iPad, noticing the swelling under the make-up I left on for her call. 'Did you get hurt on set?'

'No, I—'

'I knew it.' She leans back, throwing her hands up and letting them fall on the table in front of her with a smack. 'All those years doing such dangerous stunts and you hurt yourself on a romantic comedy.'

'It's just a black eye. It doesn't hurt.' It doesn't hurt *now*, but it hurt like a bitch when it first happened. I'm just thankful as hell that Jack showed up when he did, stopping Elizabeth's brother from bashing in the other side of my face.

'There's something else besides your eye.' She tilts her head, still assessing my face. 'What else is wrong?'

I flinch, wondering how the women I care about can see through me so easily.

Woman. Singular. Anne/Elizabeth doesn't count anymore.

'I—' I pause, emotion suddenly choking me now that it's time to confess.

Jack and I agreed that as Camilla has already gotten people focused on my mother, whether she leaked the news or not, it would be better to brace Mom for the possibility of people finding out she's in rehab before she finishes the program and checks out of the facility next week. That way, she can set up more sessions with the in-house counselors to help her manage any anxiety the attention may bring.

'*Coração*—' The word falls softly over the call '—you can tell me anything.'

'I'm sorry, *Mãe*.' I press my index finger and thumb against my eyelids, trying to ease the sting. 'It's my fault.'

'What's your fault, *meu filho*?'

Holding up my phone, I stare down at the floor between my legs. 'Someone knows you're in rehab.' I'm wearing the cowboy boots Anne/Elizabeth bought me. 'I'm doing my best, but the press may find out and—'

'So?' My mother's relieved laugh draws my eyes up. 'Who cares if they know?'

Shocked silent by her reaction, I look at my mother, *really* look at her. Shoulders back, spine straight, her usual vibrant red lipstick a flat, prideful slash against the darker olive hue of a healthy complexion. Not a trace of the broken woman I checked in to rehab a few months ago.

'Did you think I wasn't going to tell anyone? That I should hide it?' She scoffs at whatever expression I'm making, her eyes narrowing. 'Are you ashamed of me?'

'*No*.' The word falls hard and fast from my mouth. 'Not at all. I just didn't think—'

'That it would be good for your image to have an addict as a mother?' She crosses her arms over her chest, the stance she's shown me many times over the years as she took me to task.

'But you're not an addict, Mom. It's just because the doctor knew you were my—'

'I *am* an addict, *coração*.' Her voice is as strong and steady as her expression. 'And my addiction has nothing to do with you.' Staring at my no-doubt bewildered expression, my mother's eyes soften. '*I* was the one who asked for more pain pills. And *I* was the one who took them. I was also the one who hid the fact that I was taking them.' She uncrosses her arms, laying her palms flat on the table to lean forward. 'I, Sofia Maria Santos-Jones, am an addict.'

I swallow hard as my mother smiles despite her words, my mind failing to reconcile itself with that fact. 'But, if it weren't for me—'

'Then I would never have gotten such great care.' She gestures to the room around her. 'And I wouldn't have a strong drive to get better.' She shakes her head at me. 'You had nothing to do with this, *meu filho*.'

Tears I can't press back spill over. 'If I had just been there, though. If I had noticed sooner—'

'If, if, if...' Mom waves away my guilt with a flutter of her hand. 'If I hadn't fallen in love with your father, if you hadn't gotten your first big break, if you hadn't been scratched by the neighbor's cat when you were little.'

She smirks at the last, surprising a laugh from me as memories of the first time I met Mike Hunt pop into my mind.

'So many ifs, so many ways life could've gone.' She holds my eyes. '*Não se pode viver assim*. The ifs mean nothing. They *change* nothing.'

I stare at the woman before me. A woman who's spent her whole life overcoming challenges. Losing her husband, being a single mom, and now, an opioid addiction, and I wonder why I ever thought that she needed me to fight her battles.

Maybe my acting roles have gone to my head. Because she's the real hero.

'Now.' Mother shimmies in her seat, her face lighting up expectantly as her eyes roam over the screen as if trying to see past me. 'Where is Anne?' She purses her lips. 'You didn't let me talk to her last time.'

Merde.

I run a hand through my hair, flinching when the move pulls on the swollen skin around my eye. 'She's, uh, not here.' I point to the ceiling as if she can see it. 'I'm back in the hotel.'

Recrossing her arms, my mother settles back into her seat. 'And why is that?' She looks more upset over this than her addiction going public.

'Because she isn't who she said she was.' My tone less concrete and more petulant than I'd like.

She discounts my reason with a roll of her eyes. 'Neither are you half the time.'

I shake my head, unwilling to budge on this. 'This isn't a movie, Mom. She *lied* to me.'

'I lied to you.' Mom shrugs. 'You still love me, don't you?'

My breath leaving me on a gasp of surprise, I choke out the words. 'Of course I do, *Mãe*.'

'Well?' she asks as if she's proved her point.

'This is different.' My fingers grip the phone harder. '*Elizabeth* Anne Moore is different.'

Instead of asking about what I mean, she shrugs. 'Love is love, *coração*.' Looking off to the side, my mother's lips curl as if lost in a happy thought before meeting my eyes again. 'Just because your current movie is pretending love is all hearts and flowers doesn't mean that's the way it is in real life.'

In the smaller screen in the corner of my phone, my expression remains as mutinous as I feel. 'I never said I loved her.'

'And I've never once called you dumb—' she lowers her hands, palms up '—but here we are.'

'You think I'm dumb?'

'What's that movie you like so much, the one with Tom Hanks?'

I frown, failing to keep up with my mother's train of thought. '*Forrest Gump*?'

'*Sim*, that one.' She points at me. 'That quote I like.'

I sigh, suddenly realizing why she brought up my favorite movie. 'Stupid is as stupid does?'

She nods softly. '*Um ótimo conselho*.'

Hunching over, I switch hands holding the phone so I can use my left hand to hold my head up by the side *not* bruised and swollen. 'So you're saying I'm not dumb, I'm just acting dumb?'

Mother smiles, her dark lips a stunning contrast to her bright, knowing smile. 'Why don't you think it over and tell me, *meu filho*?'

* * *

Liz

'Why are men so dumb, Mikey?' I cuddle the uncomfortable sack of bones closer and bury my face in his soft, leathery skin as one of Felix's movies plays on mute on the hotel suite's television.

Having settled things with my mother, she left me to decide whether or not I want her to call my father, or if I should bite the bullet and ask Trish and Rose for another meet-up to see my sister. That was two days ago.

Instead, I tried to distract myself by sightseeing with my family, my thoughts still filled with a dumb, handsome, Hollywood douchebag who broke my heart.

Mike allows my hug for ten seconds before wiggling free and sitting up on his haunches. He drops his head to one side, eyes narrowed on me.

I feel judged. 'What?'

He tilts his head the other way.

'Um, you're supposed to be on *my* side.' I rest my hand over my heart. '*I* love you. Felix only tolerated you.' At Mike's continued stare, I flop back on my pillow. 'All right, so he *saved* you, too.'

Even though he's afraid of house cats. Hilariously afraid, but afraid, nonetheless.

I lean over the side of the bed and slide out the container I stole from the condo. A container once full of Felix's *biscoito* cookies. Two left.

I pick one up, studying the small indents of Felix's fingerprints baked into the dough. 'And he can cook.'

'Meow.'

Turning, I prop my head on my elbow and glare right back into his ice-blue eyes. 'He called me talentless.' Snapping my jaw over the cookie, I make quick work of its annihilation. 'He thinks I sold him out.' I close my eyes, feeling nauseous even as my taste buds sing happily.

Felix BASE jumps off a skyscraper on the television.

Mike continues his statue game.

'Okay, so I should've told him my real name before we slept together.' I grab another pillow, holding this one to my chest seeing as Mike has met his cuddle allowance for the day. 'That was wrong of me.'

'Meow.'

'And I *may* have called him a douchebag and a cheater before I knew about the Camilla-mother-blackmail thing.' I wince thinking of Felix's charming mother and all she's been going through. All Felix has been going through.

'*Meow.*'

'Still.' I lower the pillow, glaring the worst pity-party wingman in existence. 'After everything he said, you want me to what? Feel bad for the guy? Forgive him?'

Mike's answer is a paw to the face.

'Did you...' I raise my hand to my scraped cheek. 'Did you just paw slap me?'

'Meow.' And with that, Mike gets up on all fours, turns tail, and butthole to my face, sashays off the bed.

Never I have felt so thoroughly told off in all my life as I watch him disappear out of the bedroom and into the suite's living area.

'So, *I'm* so dumb?'

Silence is my only answer, and it isn't the one I want.

Apparently, I'm not smart enough to figure out what comes next. In life or at work. So I do something I told myself I wouldn't do when I left to figure things out last year. Something I didn't do when I needed money for tuition. Something I didn't even do when I needed medical attention thanks to lidocaine-lined condoms.

Something a dumb girl does when a dumb boy finds his dumb way into her even dumber heart.

I ask for help.

* * *

'I don't like it.'

My eldest brother Thomas, having traded his sequined cat t-shirt for one with a NASA emblem on it, stands like an ancient immovable oak at the end of the coffee table in front of the suite's glass balcony doors overlooking the prestigious cityscape of Houston's Galleria area.

I'm not sure if it's Thomas' innate sense of superiority that allows him to find the best vantage point during any negotiation, or his position just gives him his preferred distance from Chase, who's across the room rocking Mike Hunt while humming an Elvis tune.

Mother gives her opinion to my suggestion by ignoring Thomas and kissing my cheek before heading to my bedroom to make the phone call I asked her to make.

'I think it's the right thing to do.' I tell Thomas, knowing full well it won't persuade him that my idea to help mitigate the damage and hopefully stop any more miscommunication is a good one.

'I still don't like it,' Thomas says, proving me right.

'To be fair Tommy-kins—' Bell leans back on the couch '—you don't like much of anything.'

'Except Alice,' Mary chimes in, not looking up from her spot on the floor between my legs, wearing her new astronaut jumpsuit and building the Lego set Thomas bought her during our trip to Space Center Houston.

Thomas' eyebrow does its usual imperious lift, but a smile plays on his lips as his gaze drops to his daughter. 'And you, little one.'

Mary, still engrossed in her Lego, rolls her eyes. 'Duh.'

Alice, beside Bell on the sofa, rolls her lips in as she pets King Dick Moore on her lap.

I bend over, wrapping my arms around my genius niece and pulling her in for a long, tight hug.

'So—' Chase, still trying to console Mike after having cut down on his food due to his recent weight gain, points at Thomas '—what exactly is it that you don't like about Lizzie's plan?'

The look Thomas gives Chase is withering.

Which, in Thomas' normal suit and tie, would be intimidating. But now that I've seen him in a sequined cat t-shirt, khaki shorts and a split lip looking more like a rowdy fraternity brother at a pride rally than the CEO of a luxury retail conglomerate, the look has lost some of its power.

'From my research, it is always the man who makes the effort. The *grand gesture*.' Thomas turns to me, his softened eyes threatening the stranglehold I have on my emotions. 'After what I heard that di—' his eyes drop to Mary '—decidedly rude man say, *he* should be groveling to *you*.'

King Dick Moore lifts his head from Alice's lap, as if to second his master's opinion.

Chase and I share a look at our proper brother almost resorting to vulgarity in front of his daughter. It's a side of Thomas neither one of us are used to.

And while I know that he's right, and that 99 per cent of what Felix accused me of is wrong, just remembering Felix's expression when he mentioned his mother serves to dissolve most of my righteous indignation. 'Yes, but I did lie to him.'

Thomas shrugs as if that's a moot point.

'And as he's being blackmailed, then I can understand why he doesn't believe me.' Unfortunately, giving reason to Felix's lack of trust in me doesn't help ease the pain.

'I can't believe we were going to work with someone like Camilla Branson,' Bell mutters, leaning over Chase's arm to nuzzle Mike's round belly.

Chase turns to Thomas. 'I want to know more about this research you did, T-money.' He fights Mike's attempt to escape his hold.

Alice, cat in hand, stands and walks over to Thomas, placing King Dick Moore in his arms.

Instantly, my brother's rigid posture softens.

Encircling her arms around Thomas' waist, Alice leans her cheek on his shoulder. 'He's been reading my romance novels.'

Chase's mouth and arms drop, freeing Mike to stalk into the kitchen looking for scraps.

Thomas sniffs in the resulting silence, his fingers combing through King Dick Moore's long fur.

I have a fleeting thought that maybe it wasn't my father that Thomas learned his expressions and quirks from, but rather Captain Peacock from *Are You Being Served*?

Testing the waters, I don a posh, exaggerated British accent, a la Mrs Slocombe. 'Mr Humphries, are you free?'

Not missing a beat, Chase raises his hand and overturns his palm in a campy, flamboyant gesture. '*I'm free.*' His voice melodious and playful.

My battered heart warming, I peek at Thomas, whose expression remains aloof even after my reference to the show the three of us used to watch after school while eating snacks our chef Curtis prepared for us. 'And you, Captain Peacock?' I lean into the sweetly condescending tone from our childhood. 'Are *you* free?'

There's a pause, and I swear Chase holds his breath right along with me, until our older brother once more raises his left eyebrow, looks left then right just as Captain Peacock did on the show, before answering with an imperious English accent. 'I'm free.'

Chase and I lose it, cackling until tears stream down our faces. Until Mother, finished with her phone call, comes out of my room to check on us. Until I know Thomas has given his blessing to my plan and Bell, Alice and Mary look at us like we're crazy.

And we are. A crazy awesome family.

26

LIZ

'I really appreciate everything you've done.'

Em, standing next to me in the glassed-in viewing platform, turns away from our birds-eye view of my family walking through the International Space Station mock-up in building nine. A mock-up clearly set behind the red tape still marking the off-limit areas.

She arranged for my family to get VIP access on their NASA tour today, something that made me a hero in my niece's eyes. But still, I opted to stay back in and watch her skip from one module to another, more comfortable in the non-VIP tour area.

'It's no problem really.' Em shrugs. 'Truth be told, the mock-up isn't really that off-limits to visitors. I just didn't trust the crew not to wander.' The look she gives me clearly telling me she remembers when she caught *me* wandering.

Embarrassed, I chuckle sheepishly and return to watching Mary skipping beside Park In-Su. 'Well, yes, thanks for arranging the tour.' I smirk at my brothers' obvious jealous expressions as they look at Bell and Alice, who are watching the handsome astronaut pick Mary up so she can reach the buttons on the next module. 'But also, for keeping my secret this whole time.'

Em was the opposite of surprised when I called her, telling her who I was and then having the audacity to ask her for favors.

Her 'did you really think NASA gave out security badges without doing background checks?' made me question how I was smart enough to graduate college.

I nudge her shoulder with mine. '*And* for letting me look over the Neutral Buoyancy Lab footage.'

The second of the favors I asked of her.

Thankfully, I was right in thinking that if the NBL kept underwater cameras running, it probably had above water cameras running as well.

'No problem.' Em leans against the railing. 'It made for an entertaining lunch break.'

I smirk, the footage of Sylvie, aka Coral Halter Top, attaching her sparkling hair clip to Ron's back belt loop and the resulting aftermath was vindicating, if unsurprising.

'So.' Em's eyes meet mine with unspoken support. 'Are you gonna tell him?'

I don't have to ask to know she isn't talking about Coral Halter Top. Having sat next to me when the NBL security footage played, Emily bore witness to both the proof I expected along with something I hadn't.

'Maybe.' I look through the glass once more, something moving fast through the leftover film crew catching my eye. 'I guess, first I have to decide what to do about—' Recognition hits as I narrow in on the quick-moving person below. 'Is that Ron?' Anxious sweat blooms on my forehead as I scan the rest of the large building, both worried and hoping to see dark, wavy hair, my hand fluttering near my jean pocket where my phone with its three missed calls from Felix rests. He didn't leave a message or send any texts, so I don't know if he was calling to rip me a new one or apologize but him reaching out made me oddly feel better.

However, I only asked Emily for the VIP tour after confirming with David that the principal cast had finished and left for California.

Running into Felix is not part of my plan. Not only am I not ready to talk to him, but I'm also worried that with my family here, someone might realize the woman Felix Jones kissed on set was none other than Elizabeth Anne Moore, a socialite to rival his supposed fiancée. And while I'm no longer hiding who I am, I don't want to chance giving Camilla a reason to spread more lies or make good on her threats about Felix's mom.

Em watches the deceptively quick director cut through crew breaking down equipment, a look of expectation in her eyes. 'Ron stayed to make sure they had what they needed to recreate sets as accurately as possible back in the studio.' She cuts her eyes to me. 'But all the actors left.'

Dropping my damp forehead on the glass in front of me in relief, I watch Ron come to a stop in front of the very person I was planning to speak to later.

With gestures as violent as they'd been when Mike was attacking his rear end, Ron confronts Sylvie. Even from my position twenty-plus feet overhead, and without the benefit of sound, I can tell Ron is not happy. And that Sylvie is totally fired.

'Did you do this?'

Em's eyes remain laser focused on the drama below. 'You ever heard of the saying, don't mess with Texas?'

I push off the glass, the expression on Em's face right now, one of an evil mastermind watching their villainous plan unfolding, is a bit frightening. 'Uh, yeah.'

Her smile grows, causing me to return my attention to the government security agents escorting a crying Sylvie out of the building.

Apparently satisfied, Em dismisses the scene below with a flutter of her lashes. 'Well, you don't mess with NASA. Not while I'm around.' She nudges my shoulder. 'And you don't mess with my friends, either.'

I gaze in admiration at the petite public relations manager. 'You're pretty awesome, you know that?'

'I know.' Not a hint of conceit in her voice. Just pure confidence. 'And you're pretty awesome yourself.'

'Yeah.' I nod, for once accepting the compliment. 'I am.'

* * *

Felix

'We need to talk.'

Head down over my phone on the way to my car, I startle at Jack's greeting. And then at the person standing in front of his Tesla parked in my drive. 'Amanda?'

'Hi, Felix.' She looks gaunt, nothing like the sparkling girl-next-door romcom queen I'm used to.

'Hey.' Squinting against the bright, but not sweltering, California sun, my eyes ping-pong between Jack, his arms resting on the roof of his Tesla, and Amanda, her hands clasped in front of her, her fingers twisting together.

About to call Elizabeth again, I click my phone off and slide it into my pocket. Elizabeth isn't answering her phone. Or more than likely, doesn't *want* to answer her phone. I've been trying to call her ever since I landed in California the day after talking to my mother.

'What's going on?' I might be running a few minutes late to my 8 a.m. set call time, thanks to another restless night of me replaying and regretting all the things I said to Elizabeth and then berating myself for regretting them, but Jack's never worried about my timetable before. And he's *never* brought someone to my place without asking.

'Get in.' Pushing off the roof, Jack opens the driver side door and slides behind the wheel.

Wondering what the hell is going on, I don't immediately move.

It isn't until Amanda slides into the back seat that I open the passenger side door.

'Tell him.' Jack clicks the gate remote clipped to his sun visor and guns the Tesla.

I brace my hand on the door, the electric car's pick-up always surprising. 'Tell me what?'

Jack's eyes flick to his rearview mirror.

Shifting in my seat, I turn to Amanda, who is looking anywhere but at me.

Her hands, clasped in her lap, turn white. 'I'm the one who took the picture of you and Anne kissing and sent it to Camilla.'

The car jerks to a hard stop, Jack checking the road for traffic before pulling out.

I barely notice the whiplash. 'What?'

'Camilla...' She meets my eyes for a moment before dropping them again.

My gut churns. 'Don't tell me she's blackmailing you too?'

Amanda nods. 'My girlfriend is an old sorority sister of hers from college.'

I cut my eyes to Jack, but from his non-surprise, I take it he already knew that Hollywood's romcom queen is dating a woman.

'She showed up at my girlfriend's house one day and we...' Amanda sighs. 'She seemed totally nonplussed at first. But then when I started *Countdown*, Camilla contacted me and said if I didn't keep tabs on you while you were in Houston, she'd go to the press.'

'So what?' My voice rough. 'You didn't want anyone to find out that you're gay, so you took a picture of me and—' I stop myself from continuing, unsure who I'm really angry at.

Amanda? Camilla? Myself?

I'm the one who blamed Elizabeth for the picture. Even when her taking or spreading the photo didn't make sense. She lied about her name, and without listening to her reasons, I believed the worst.

'I'm so sorry.' Amanda drops her head in her hands. 'I've actually been wanting to come out, even before Camilla found out. I'm tired of the hiding and the secrets.' She lets out a small, hysterical laugh. 'I even went so far as to guilt trip my girlfriend, bullying her into coming out with me. Telling her that if she really loved me, she'd do it.' She raises her head, a haunting look on her face. 'But then, when Camilla blackmailed me, I realized how selfish I'd been. That if you love someone, you don't force them to do things they aren't ready for.'

My chest aches thinking of how I did the same thing to Elizabeth. All because she wouldn't open up to me in the way I wanted her to, and because of that, I questioned her feelings and ignored my own.

Ron's directorial guidance on set at the Neutral Buoyance Lab was spot on. But for me, rather than my character. I chose fear, not love.

Reaching back between the two front seats, I take hold of Amanda's hand and squeeze. I don't say it will be all right, or that I forgive her. But I do understand all too well what she's feeling.

She returns my squeeze, using her other hand to brush tears from her eyes. 'I promise I was going to tell you even without Elizabeth sending me the security footage.'

I drop her hand. 'Wait, what?'

'It came this morning,' Jack says, weaving in and out of traffic.

'Elizabeth caught me out.' Amanda shakes her head, a weak smile on her lips. 'And instead of taking the security footage of me with a camera on set to the studio or telling the papers, she sent it to Jack and asked him to talk to me about it. Said that she believed I was a good person and that I must've had my reasons.'

'And I did.' Jack's eyes meet mine for a brief moment before returning to the road. 'I drove her straight here afterwards.'

Amanda's small laugh is rife with bemused disbelief. 'I'm not sure how she could be so forgiving, but I'm just so thankful that she is. Especially knowing who her family is. It's a miracle she grew up like Camilla and still turned out so wonderful.'

We sit in silence while Jack puts his Tesla to the test against LA traffic.

Mother was right. As usual. I'm a dumbass.

'These also came by courier this morning.' Jack pulls a hefty file from his door side pocket, handing them to me before veering onto the interstate.

I flip through the folder of documents, stopping on a signed page. One of many signed pages if the number of yellow tabs is anything to go by.

Elizabeth Anne Moore. Even her signature is a scrawl of artistic lines.

'Elizabeth signed an NDA?'

'Everything's been timestamped and notarized, all dates from this past week.'

My mind whirls as he optimistically sets his cruise control, as if LA traffic isn't going to force him to repeatedly stop-and-go for the one hour it takes to go fifteen miles. 'How—'

'I had our lawyers look it over,' Jack continues. 'We all agreed that no self-respecting lawyer would draw up, let alone allow their client to sign a document like this unless they were specifically asked to.' His eyes cut to me. 'Not only has Elizabeth agreed never to initiate contact, either in person or by phone or mail, she's agreed to a substantial penalty if she ever breaches said agreement.'

More silence as I stare at the pages in my hands.

'I don't know if this means anything to you,' Amanda says from the back, looking a little less haggard now that she's unburdened herself. 'But my girlfriend also knows Elizabeth.' She holds up her hands. 'Not well, but well enough that when I confessed to what I did and why, she wasn't surprised by Elizabeth's actions. Saying that out of all the people she met during her society upbringing, Elizabeth Moore always seemed the most genuine.'

Jack crosses two lanes of traffic before unclicking cruise control and squeezing in front of a beat-up taxi. 'Something else came this morning.'

'Jesus.' I close the folder and squeeze my eyes shut, not sure I can handle something else. 'What now?'

He points to the glove compartment.

Opening it, I find a letter with *Felix Jones only, please* scrawled on the envelope in the same handwriting as Elizabeth's signature.

'She said this would be her final communication with you now that she's signed the non-disclosure agreement.' For someone who was so against me having any sort of contact with any women, Jack doesn't look pleased at that piece of news.

With hands less steady that I'd like, I unfold the letter.

Felix,

I wasn't able to tell you this at the time because I was protecting someone. At least, that's what I told myself. And while partially true, I can see now that I was mainly protecting myself.

As you insinuated the last time we spoke, the man who raised me is not my father. I was only made aware of this last year along with the public when Stanley Winston Moore was arrested. My biological father is a scientist named Dr Gerald Howard Lee, who has a daughter, a few years older than me — NASA astronaut Dr Jackie Darling Lee.

As of the time of this letter, I have not yet worked up the courage to meet them. Until that time, or perhaps even after, I would please ask that you not mention this to anyone, as I'm unsure if they would want our connection public.

That's why I wanted to go to the astronaut dinner. Because I was too nervous and unsure to introduce myself properly. I guess it was karma that she happened not to be there that night.

I am so very sorry my insecurities jeopardized your career and your mother's wellbeing. Please know that I'm working to fix that.

Your Anne.

I stare at the last line, wondering how two words can make such an impact.

Underneath the letter, a small sketch slips out. It's Mike, lazing in the sun on his favorite spot in the condo.

Clearing my throat, I refold the letter, slipping it back into the envelope.

'I haven't read it.' Jack answers before I can ask. 'It's the only thing she asked for in return for—' he gestures at the paperwork in my lap '—all that.' He heaves a long, heavy sigh. 'So even though the manager in me really, really wanted to read it, I didn't.'

I smile at my friend. 'You're a good guy, Jack.'

'I know.' He merges onto an exit ramp. 'Which is why you're going to give me a raise and let me hire an assistant.'

'Whatever you want...' I trail off, noticing our surroundings. 'This isn't the way to the studio.'

With a smile much less grim than before, he maneuvers through the slower airport traffic.

'Here.' Amanda leans forward, handing me a first-class ticket to New York. 'Tell her I'm sorry, will you?'

'Yeah.' My head whips back as Jack pulls to a stop at passenger drop-off. 'But not before I do.'

27

FELIX

I never imagined it would be so hard to apologize.

Not that I thought it would be easy. Or that I'd be forgiven. I mean, if I were Elizabeth, I'd nut kick me at first sight before telling me to fuck off.

'Camilla dear, I'm so glad you could make it.' Elizabeth's voice, stiff and lilting, filters through the cracked-open secret door built between the Moore brothers' offices.

The door I'm standing behind, wedged in between the brother who punched me and the brother who thought Mike Hunt a good name for a hairless cat.

The brothers who have denied me the opportunity to beg for forgiveness since I landed in New York an hour ago.

'*Elizabeth.*' Camilla's surprise is quickly followed by two loud air kisses.

'I knew the secret door would come in handy,' Chase whispers.

Thomas doesn't respond. He doesn't have to. He shuts his younger brother up *and* wipes the satisfied expression off his face with a single raised eyebrow.

I make note to try and imitate it if I ever play a mafia boss.

Before Jack left me at the airport, he said a car would be waiting for me when I landed in New York. That it would take me where I needed to go.

That it was all part of the plan. Not having time to ask questions, I ran full speed through the airport to make my last-minute flight, hopeful that the plan Jack mentioned was Elizabeth's.

In fact, I was so hopeful, I didn't even care about missing my call time. Or that Ron was going to have the one more mistake he needed to officially place me on his blacklist. Not wasting a moment, I spent the entire five-hour flight rehearsing ways to apologize to Elizabeth for the awful things I'd said and almost believed. To find the words to encourage her to introduce herself to her father and sister. To help her realize how lucky they would be to have her in their lives. How lucky I would be if she gave me another chance.

I may have overheard the flight attendants muttering that I was either practicing for a movie or had cracked under the recent tabloid stories.

Landing, my hope was further bolstered by the chauffeur who met me at the arrival gate holding a sign with *Johnny Douchebag* scrawled across in black marker.

However, when I was driven into a basement garage and escorted by security up a private elevator only to be deposited into a chair situated in front of a large desk which Thomas Moore sat behind, all hope met a quick and violent death.

After his secretary, part of the office escort crew, mentioned Chase Moore's imminent arrival, Thomas and I waited – alone – in tense silence.

Me noting how, despite being dressed in an impeccably tailored three-piece suit, the eldest Moore child looked no less savage than he had while swinging his fist while wearing a sequined kitty-cat t-shirt. Him, probably debating the various places he could hide my body.

So when Chase finally waltzed in wearing a smile and Mike Hunt strapped to his chest, I felt something akin to relief. Which then dissipated when the younger Moore decided to bypass my outstretched hand and instead greeted me with a hard, passive-aggressive slap/punch on my back, followed by Mike's complete refusal to even acknowledge my presence.

It was the cat's silent treatment that truly hurt.

Now out of his carrier, Mike's been grooming his left testicle for the last five minutes.

Between the flight, navigating intense animosity from two polar opposite brothers, being rejected by a hairless pussy and now hearing Elizabeth's and then Camilla's voice next door, I have lived an entire lifetime of emotions in the span of six hours.

Ignoring the two men who want to maim if not kill me, I lean forward toward the bookcase-camouflaged door to better hear the conversation happening in Chase's neighboring office.

'What an unexpected surprise.' Camilla's over-annunciated syllables grate on my nerves. 'I didn't know you *worked* at Moore's.' She says the word like it's beneath her.

'It is my family's company, after all.' Elizabeth sounds unaffected by the condescension.

'Hmmm.' There's a wealth of insinuation in that sound.

'I'm here as the final step between you and your collaboration with Moore's.'

'Final step?' Camilla's voice sharpens. 'The contracts are signed. I was told I was here for product selection.'

'That was before.'

'Before what?'

'Before you started blackmailing people.'

I hold my breath, fists clenched.

'I—I don't know what you mean.'

'Listen, Cammie.' Elizabeth's voice softens, having heard the tell-tale stutter. 'I know what it's like.'

'Know what what's like?'

'I know what it's like to be put in a box. Told what to do and when to do it. Not knowing if your choices are your own or what others want from you.'

Thomas' eye twitches. Chase's foot bounces up and down.

My heart aches.

'But you don't have to find your way like this.' Papers shuffle. 'By signing these, you can start fresh. Stop hurting people and work with Moore's to—'

Camilla laughs. 'Are you under the impression that I did what I did because I feel trapped?' She snorts. 'You know, I hadn't heard much from you since the whole mishap with your father.' Camilla pauses. 'I mean the man you *thought* was your father.'

The three of us start.

Mike pauses his licking.

'But it seems that your whole sabbatical from *real life* has made you delusional.'

There's a pause.

'I see.' Elizabeth sounds disappointed, yet unsurprised.

'Now, if you don't mind, I would like to continue on with what I came here for.'

'Certainly.' There's a click and then, 'You can send them in.'

I glance to either side of me, but neither Thomas nor Chase gives any indication of what's happening next.

'Here we are,' a different woman calls out, entering the room.

'Our mother,' Chase whispers.

'I was just treating Mr Branson to a late lunch.'

'The treat was all mine, Eleanor,' a man, Mr Branson I'm guessing, replies.

Elizabeth's mother titters. 'Oh, stop it.'

'Daddy?' Camilla's voice sounds strangled. 'What are you doing here?'

'I was invited, of course. The Moores have given an interest in donating to the Branson Foundation.'

'They have?' Camilla sounds as confused as I feel.

'Yes, but, just as we were getting to the nitty-gritty, Thomas had to leave.' His voice turns arctic. 'Something about rumors involving your dealings with Felix Jones and Amanda Willis?'

My heart speeds up.

'Oh, ah, that's nothing, Daddy. Just a—a misunderstanding.'

'Well now—' Mr Branson bounces back to his previous jovial tone '—that's settled then. You can just sign these and then Eleanor and I can get back to that donation they've been wanting to make.'

'But—but Dad, this isn't what I agreed to. This is just a series of non-disclosure agreements.'

'Yes. They are.' Goosebumps break out on my arms over Mr Branson's emotionless tone. 'And you will sign them, in addition to the dissolution contract ending your previous collaboration agreement.'

'But—'

'*Or* you can consider yourself cut off. *Permanently*. Do I make myself clear?'

We all three lean forward, foreheads nearly touching the bookcase, to hear Camilla's forlorn capitulation. 'Yes, Daddy.'

I might have felt a sliver of sympathy toward Camilla if I wasn't champing at the bit to get to Elizabeth. To thank her. To apologize. To grovel.

To do *all* the things.

But as I reach for the hidden latch, just after hearing everyone move to exit Chase's office, Thomas rests a heavy hand on my shoulder, stopping me. Again.

'Why don't we reconvene tomorrow, Mr Branson?'

I turn toward the non-secret door, where Eleanor's voice rises then fades as she walks past.

'Now that the papers are signed, we can schedule a lunch to discuss the charitable…'

I move to follow, but Chase blocks my path.

I'm getting really fucking tired of their interference.

His smile now threatening in conjunction with his aggressive stance. 'We didn't invite you here to reconcile with our sister.'

Disappointment flares. '*You* invited me?'

Thomas nods, moving beside his brother. 'We invited you here so you could understand just how much you don't deserve her.' His tone deceptively bored. 'The money Elizabeth had Mother donate to the Branson Foundation? It's hers. She insisted.'

Chase crosses his arms over his chest. 'Her inheritance. Money she hasn't touched ever since she found out that she isn't our father's daughter. Money we were hoping she'd use for *her*, not you.'

Thomas' left eyebrow arches. 'She's too good for you.'

I swallow, feeling sick over the money, the effort Elizabeth has made. Effort I don't deserve. 'You're right.' Fighting back nausea over my asshole actions, I gauge the distance between here and the door, more motivated than ever to get to Elizabeth. 'I was dumb and scared, and I screwed up.' I take turns looking both brothers in the eye. 'But I love her.'

Feeling very much like one of the many action heroes I've played, I assess which brother I might have to incapacitate first if I want to reach Elizabeth. It's two against one, but as they're encumbered in perfectly fitted business suits and I'm still in California casual – shorts and a t-shirt – I've got mobility on my side.

'And if there's even a chance she's dumb enough to love me back—' I sidestep, making note of Chase mirroring my move, while Thomas inches closer '—then I'm going to do everything I can to spend the rest of my life apologizing for my lack of intelligence while thanking God for hers.' Giving up on stealth, I raise my fists and brace for impact. 'Including fighting the two of you if I have to.'

Yet, instead of throwing the first punch, the two brothers do something far more chilling. They share a look – Chase for once grim, Thomas for once smiling – before turning their attention back to me.

I've never felt so imperiled in my entire life. Not even before BASE jumping Shanghai Tower.

Knock. Knock.

My eyes shift hopefully to the secret door between Chase and Thomas.

'Don't kill him!'

'We're here to help!'

Like a child whose playtime was interrupted by chores, Chase sighs and gestures me back.

Not asking twice, I retreat to the center of the room as two women push themselves through the bookcase door.

Thomas reaches out a hand to the smaller blonde. Chase pats the redhead's butt.

'Hi.' The blonde steps forward but is held back by Thomas. Rolling her eyes in the face of his grimness, she smiles. 'I'm Alice. Thomas' wife.'

Looking between the two, I could not ask for a more prime example of the grump and sunshine trope popular in so many famous romantic comedies.

The redhead swats at Chase's hand and waves. 'And I'm Bell.' She has a slight Southern accent that reminds me of Texas.

Raising my hand in answer, I feel like the odd man out. 'I'm Felix.' I glance behind them at the office that mirrors the one we're all standing in. 'Were you in there with Elizabeth during the meeting?'

'Oh no,' Alice answers. 'We were listening from the bathroom.'

'The Moores tend to eavesdrop a lot.' Bell leans forward, giving my arm a playful punch. 'You'll get used to it.'

Ignoring Chase's laser focus on where Bell just touched me, I replay what his wife just said. 'I'll get used to it?'

'Yes.' A genuine, bright smile lights up Alice's brown eyes. She tilts her head up and back to stare at Thomas. 'Because we all decided that we're going to respect Elizabeth's feelings and think about what she would want, right?' She speaks slow and loud, making me think she's talking more to Thomas than to me.

Amazingly, Thomas nods in answer. 'As I was saying, we didn't *just* invite you here to show you how much you don't deserve Elizabeth.'

Alice's smile wavers.

Avoiding his wife's eyes, Thomas continues. 'We also decided to aid you in coming up with an apology worthy of our sister.'

With a satisfied shimmy, Alice returns her attention to me.

'Since apparently, you can't do it yourself,' Thomas mutters.

Either Alice doesn't hear him or she's has made the wise decision to ignore him.

'My apology?'

Thomas glowers harder, if that's possible. 'Were you not going to apologize?'

'I've been *trying* to—' I stop, pausing to taking a breath and release my mounting frustration. '*Of course* I'm going to apologize. I've been trying to call but she hasn't been answering her phone.'

Rather than looking appeased, Thomas seems satisfied. 'Yes. I had her change her phone number.'

'Because of the press?'

He tilts his head, considering. 'There's that. But also because I didn't want to make it so easy for you.'

I can tell Thomas and I are going to be fast friends.

I close my eyes for a moment, reminding myself that while right now, they are a huge pain in my ass, it's great that Elizabeth has such caring brothers. 'Listen, I flew here with the sole purpose of apologizing.' I wave towards the secret door. 'So while the thing with Camilla was great, I don't need it. I just need Elizabeth.' I focus on my hardest critics, Thomas and Chase. 'Who *you* just kept me from.'

Neither brother looks regretful.

'Tell me something.' Bell draws my attention. 'Did you call her before or after she sent you that video of your co-star selling you out?' She folds her arms across her chest, looking more formidable than her husband as he reaches down to pick up a thoroughly nut-clean Mike Hunt.

'Before.' I open my phone and bring up my call history. 'I regretted what I said the moment I said it. I just... my mom...'

Bell's expression softens. 'Yeah, I get it. If someone threatened my mom, I would've lost it.'

'Me too!'

Pivoting toward the office entrance – the non-secret one – I'm greeted by a cat in a stroller being pushed by a girl wearing an astronaut helmet and a glitter-speckled tutu.

The cat – who from his hairy nature, I can only assume is the regal King Dick Moore – yawns under his lace bonnet.

'I'd get mad if someone was mean to my mommy.'

Alice seems to melt at the little girl's words. 'Thank you, Mary.'

Thomas strides to the little girl, bending down to kiss her nose before closing her visor.

Mary giggles, flipping her visor back open. 'Did you figure out how to get him to tell Aunt Liz that he loves her, yet?' She looks expectantly at Thomas.

'Not yet.'

She pouts at his reply before pushing the stroller and cat toward the couch. 'Did you show him the list?' With a grunt, Mary lifts Dick out of the stroller, lowering him to one side of the couch.

Mike abandons Chase, leaping from his arms and bounding up onto the cushion next to Dick's.

'The list.' Alice rocks back on her heels, clapping her hands. 'I almost forgot.' She hurries across the large Oriental rug and out the door.

I address the only one who seems to know what's going on. 'You made a list?'

Mary nods, settling herself between the two cats. 'In case you had trouble coming up with ideas for the gesture.'

'Gesture?'

'Here it is!' Alice re-enters the office, pushing a rolling whiteboard into the room.

Studying the many colored Post-it notes arranged in a grid-like pattern on the board, I move closer to read one. 'Thread golf balls in arch over new Gucci golf bags.'

'Oh no.' Alice places both hands on my arm to guide me back a few steps so she has room to flip the whiteboard over.

Thomas incinerates my arm with his eyes.

'*This* is the list.'

I stare at the wobbly letters written in all-caps and in alternating colors.

'I wrote it,' Mary chimes in, somehow having procured a tea set which she's set up on the coffee table, cups in front of her, Mike and King Dick.

Even the best Hollywood scriptwriters couldn't make this stuff up.

Forcing my attention back to the board, I read the first line out loud. 'Hang a billboard saying, "I'm sorry" in Times Square.'

'Simple and effective.' Bell's face lights up. 'Plus, I know all the marketing people in New York.' She snaps her fingers. 'I could get this done tonight, no problem.'

Navigating her idea as I would any writer pitching me a role I *don't* want, I try for diplomacy. 'Why, I think that's a *great* idea, and I thank you *so* much for offering to help, but I'm having trouble seeing how that would appeal to Elizabeth.'

Bell's expression flattens.

'Elizabeth hates being the center of attention,' I explain. 'I'm not sure drawing all of New York's and probably the country's attention to her is the best idea.'

Her lips twist to the side, muttering, 'Well, we could always just post the picture of you and your apron.'

Chase jerks his eyes to his wife. 'What was that?'

'Hmmm?' Bell flutters her lashes at him. 'What was what?'

Ignoring the marital squabble, and the knowledge that Bell has seen Elizabeth's sketch book, I read the next line. 'Set up meeting with her real dad and my new aunt to meet her.'

Thomas nods, resolute. 'Elizabeth wants to meet them.'

'Yes.' I draw out the words, wondering how diplomatic I have to be to not get punched. 'But shouldn't *Elizabeth* be the one to decide if, when and where she meets them?' I glance at Alice, my biggest cheerleader and ally against my biggest nemesis. 'We shouldn't take that decision away from her, right?'

As I hoped, Alice nods. 'That's a good point, Felix.'

Thomas, nostrils flaring, is at my side in two strides.

I brace for impact, but instead of attacking me, he aggressively wipes his suggestion off the board with his hand, like a child throwing a mini tantrum.

Alice studies her shoes for a beat before lifting her head with a carefully arranged neutral expression, and helps Thomas wipe dry erase marker remnants off his fingers with his handkerchief.

Having dodged a bullet, or more accurately, a fist, I return to the board, reading under Thomas' half-smeared suggestion. 'Hold a family dinner.'

'That would be my idea.' Eleanor Moore waltzes into the room.

I lean back, searching for Elizabeth, but she doesn't appear.

'Sorry, Felix, but I sent her home.' She gestures to her sons in a what-can-you-do kind of way, looking elegant and regal as she does.

A battle was lost, but not the war, I tell myself as Eleanor continues.

'Elizabeth was forever gathering us around the dinner table, even when she was a child.'

'Even when we wanted to kill each other,' Chase adds.

Thomas shakes out his handkerchief before folding it twice into the perfect square and sliding it into his pocket. 'Even when we were less than appreciative.'

The three Moores share a look, this one filled with love and happy memories. Making me remember that most of all, the moments where Elizabeth seemed to open up to me were over the simple, shared meals I made for us in the condo.

'I love that idea, Eleanor.'

Elizabeth's mother's smile rivals her diamonds.

'However.'

'Oh God.' Chase collapses in a huff, laying his forehead on her shoulder. 'Now what's wrong?'

I grimace, not knowing exactly how to explain, even though my mother clearly said she didn't mind people knowing about her addiction. 'My mother really cares for Elizabeth, even after only talking to her a few times on the phone. And I was hoping that the first family dinner we had would include my mother.' I shrug one shoulder. 'But she won't be available until next week because she's…'

Eleanor's slim hand drops on my raised shoulder, easing it back down. 'Because she is currently doing the brave and healthy thing by taking the time to recover and deal with her illness.'

I nod, grateful for Eleanor's phrasing. 'I won't pick her up for a week.' I stare Thomas in the eye. 'And I don't want to wait that long. I can't.'

The silence that follows is interrupted by the clink of plasticware.

'Have you told her that you love her?' Mary, helmet visor up, pours Dick an imaginary cup of tea.

As unaffected as I am by hundreds of people staring at me while I'm performing – both in front of a camera and on the red carpet – my skin has never felt so hot as it does now when all Moores turn to stare at me, the same straightforward question in their eyes.

'Um, no.'

Mary shakes her head, her astronaut helmet twisting as she does. 'I go to a feelings doctor.' Alice smiles at her daughter. 'And my feelings doctor says that whenever you feel stuck, you should talk about your feelings.' She pretends to pour Mike Hunt tea.

Mike hovers over his cup, meowing in disappointment to find it empty.

Lowering the plastic teapot to the table, Mary straightens her helmet. 'Why don't you just talk to Elizabeth?'

Wide, brown eyes have never made me feel so small or so dumb.

And I can't help but think about what my mother said to me on our last phone call, and the advice she always gave me, whether it was in reference to cooking, acting or life – 'Simple is best.'

'But simple is boring,' Chase complains.

Ignoring him, I continue to think out loud. 'Elizabeth doesn't like flash.' Alice and Bell nod in tandem.

'She is completely unimpressed by materialistic things.'

Thomas and Chase join their wives in nonverbal agreement, if grudgingly.

'And above all,' I think back to the letter she wrote me, 'with everything Elizabeth's been through, she just wants to know she's loved.'

Mary raises her teacup to me and I hurry over to grab the extra fourth cup. Lifting it, pinky out, I clink it to hers. 'You're a genius.'

Looking very much like her father, one eyebrow disappears behind the top of her helmet. 'Yes. I am.'

I'm about to get up and go do what I should've done much, much earlier, when Mike's meow pauses me in my tracks.

Placing my teacup back on its plastic and heart-stickered saucer, I stretch my fist out towards Mike. He stares at me, as if assessing my worthiness, before touching his paw to it.

'I'll be damned,' Chase breathes.

You know you're stupidly in love when you find hope in advice from a nine-year-old dressed as an astronaut ballerina and reassurance in a fist-bump from a hairless pussy.

* * *

Liz

Fuck a duck.

I forgot how hard this stuff is to get off. Scrubbing harder, I rub the make-up remover wipe across my face, my skin feeling both abused and rejuvenated with each pass.

Back at home, my skin isn't the only thing feeling rejuvenated. While I really wanted to give Camilla the benefit of the doubt, I wasn't all that surprised when she laughed at my offer to let her choose to be a better person.

Tossing the completely covered wipe into the trash, I reach for another. There's probably some metaphor to be found in my appearance—half my face make-up-free, half looking airbrushed and contoured to perfection, dressed in a plain white robe. Maybe something about the year I spent trying to decide between my past and present selves.

Laughing at myself, I attack the eye still caked with make-up, pausing when it hits me that my metaphorical thought wasn't followed by Stanley's voice in my head, berating me for having such new-age, hippie-like thoughts.

Progress.

Knock. Knock.

I start, poking my eye with my make-up-wipe-covered finger. 'Jesus, fuck, my eye!'

'*Merde.*'

A hand touches my arm and I slap it away.

'*Desculpa, meu amor.*'

'Who the hell?' Squeezing my injured eye shut, I try seeing out of my other eye, watering from the sting of smeared make-up.

'It's me, Felix.'

Even though his voice, language and blurry shape all add up to that being true, my brain is having trouble acknowledging that the man reaching for me is, in fact, Felix Jones.

One, because Felix is still working in California. And two, because there is no reason for the dark-brown-haired, darker-eyed celebrity with the sexy jawline – all details quickly coming into focus the more I blink – to be physically standing in the Moores' New York City mansion.

Attempting to give me further reassurance, Felix gestures to himself. 'It's me, Johnny Douchebag.'

My laugh surprises me and I end up having a coughing fit while holding my eye, completing the whole hot-mess package I've got going on.

'Should I get you some water?'

If I could roll my eyes, I would.

Reaching over to the faucet just a foot away, I turn on the tap, rinsing my face and taking a few cold sips of water. When I've cleaned off all the make-up and stalled as long as possible in an attempt to regroup, I turn off the water and reach for a—

'Here.' Felix rips the hand towel off the hook and hands it to me.

Taking it, I pat my face dry while coming to terms with the fact that Felix Jones is very much standing in my bathroom now that my vision isn't impeded by pain or make-up. 'What are you doing here?'

'Your brothers invited me.' He looks proud of this.

I lean to the side, searching for Chase and Thomas in my bedroom. No brothers. I frown at Felix. 'They invited you to my bathroom?' I speak slowly, trying to make sense of things as I talk.

'No.' He closes his eyes, pinching the bridge of his nose. 'To the house.'

'Okay.' I draw out the word, feeling very much not okay.

'This is probably why they were so hell-bent on the gesture.'

'Who's they?' I toss the towel on the counter. 'What gesture?'

'A *grand* gesture.'

My heart thumps. 'My brothers are forcing you to make a grand gesture?'

If the tile could crack and suck me under right now, that would be great.

'No.' Hands on my shoulders, he dips low to catch my eyes. 'They were *helping* me think of a way to apologize. I *wanted* to…' He stops, as if rethinking his words. 'Well, no, I didn't want to do what *they* suggested.'

'What'd they suggest?'

He scoffs, rolling his eyes. 'For starters, a Times Square billboard.' He steps back, triumphantly pointing at my expression. 'See. You'd *hate* that, wouldn't you?'

I nod emphatically, just the thought of all those people knowing my business making me break out in a sweat.

Felix drops his hand, radiating self-satisfaction. 'That's why I agreed with Mary.'

'My niece?' I'm more confused by the minute.

'Yes.'

By the look on his face, I can tell Mary added another man to her tally of those wrapped around her finger.

'And she's brilliant for someone being so enamored of your psychopath brother, Mike Hunt and King Dick.'

I snort, biting my lip to quell the echoing noise.

'But now that I'm here—' he looks around at the white marble bathroom, running a hand through his hair '—I'm realizing I don't do so well without a script.' His laugh suddenly unsure. 'Maybe I should've written out the way to say I'm sorry before charging in here.'

'Oh.' Hope that I hadn't known I had that his presence meant something more than *I'm sorry* squeezes at my chest. 'So Amanda told you?'

'Yes.' He closes his eyes, as if replaying the moment. 'I can't tell you how sorry I am for blaming you.'

'It's okay, I know you were—'

'It is *not* okay, Elizabeth.' Felix looks more serious than when his melons were hard. 'I knew you didn't – *wouldn't* – do something like that, but I, I was just so scared. There so many things I didn't know that made me—'

'I'm sorry I didn't—'

'No. Don't apologize. Please.' He runs a hand through his hair, reminding me of the man I met at the bar. 'You've done more than enough for me when I didn't deserve it.'

'I really didn't do much.'

He skewers me with a look that rivals my older brother. 'Just so you know, I wrote the check for the Branson Foundation.'

I open my mouth to protest, but he cuts me off.

'I 100 per cent appreciate what you did, but that money is yours.'

'Not really.'

'Yes. It is.' He places his hands on my shoulders. 'You are your mother's daughter. Your brothers' sister. That is money that your family, your real family, wants you to have. Money that I would rather you use to go meet the rest of your family, so you'll have even more people to love you as much as you deserve to be loved.'

I bite my lip, the pain and tang of soap helping me keep my emotions in check.

'I'm so sorry I didn't believe you. That I said... that I said...' He lets loose a string of Portuguese that I can only guess by his expression aren't PG. 'Elizabeth, I—'

'I accept your apology.' I clear my throat, drowning out the imaginary lecture in my head from my brothers about giving in too easily. Because while my brothers may have my best interests at heart, having grown up with them, they are also the reason why I know just how dumb men can be.

'And I like it when my friends call me Liz.' Feeling awkward and hopeful once more, I reach my hand out between us. 'I'm Liz.'

He stares at my outstretched hand, his eyes wide, the tension previously etched into his face softening. And when his brown eyes, lit with a smile, look into mine, my hope grows.

Hope that Felix and I can start over. Try again.

But instead of taking my hand, he lowers it. 'I don't want to be friends.'

Dropping my gaze, I stare at my toes embedded in the plush bathmat. 'Ah, yeah. Um, sure. Of course.' Blinking rapidly, I try and suppress the hurt and disappointment threatening to overwhelm me. 'I mean, yeah, I totally get it. I—'

Felix finger rests under my chin. 'I can't be friends with someone I love.' With a gentle touch, he lifts my eyes to his. '*E eu amo-te*, Liz. Anne. Elizabeth.' He steps forward. 'I love all of you.'

'Wait.' I hold up both hands, my palms resting on his chest as I struggle to process *that* piece of information. 'You love me?'

'Oh, yes.' Felix's brown eyes hold mine. 'So much, *meu coração*.'

'But...' I glance at the mirror and, as if having caught his previous uncertainty like a common cold, my hands touch on my scrubbed face, before dropping to the bow of my robe's belt, feeling all the ways in which I am physically unprepared for this moment. 'I'm not even dressed.'

His brows pinch together. 'Does that matter?'

'I don't know.' A hysterical laugh replaces the sob in my chest. 'Does it?'

Laughing with me, a sexy chuckle rather than a hyena-like explosion, Felix brings my hands back to his chest. 'You're always lovable.' His finger traces my jawline. 'Your face, your body, but mostly—' his fingertips graze my chest '—here.'

'My boob?' I blurt out, face heating.

Rolling his eyes, Felix taps again. 'Your *heart*.'

'Sorry.' I stare at my hands, my palms pulsing from the hard beat of his heart. 'I've never, uh, been confessed to.' Admitting that sad fact does not help my embarrassment.

Instead of looking amused, his eyes darken. 'That's okay, *meu tesouro*. I'll help you take your own advice.'

I meet his eyes, the heat in them warming my cold agitation. '*My advice?*'

He leans down, his nearness hitching my next breath. 'The night we first met.'

I frown, the first thing that comes to mind popping out of my mouth. 'When I told you to go fuck yourself?'

He rolls his lips. 'Before that.' His finger nudges the neck of my robe wider.

'When I told you not to use serendipitous as a pick-up...' My thoughts scatter at his lips on my shoulder.

'After that,' he murmurs, making his way up my neck, his breath tickling my ear.

'I don't remember.' The sleeves of my robe slide back as I raise my hands to hold on to his shoulders.

'Sure you do.' His hands slip under the edges of silk. 'You said it makes perfect.'

'Perfect...' I rake my fingers up and into his hair, tugging, not so gently.

'Mmmhmmm.'

The pinch to my nipple runs through me like lightning. '*Practice.*'

'*Boa rapariga, meu amor.*' He rubs over the sting with his thumb. '*Sim*, we need to practice.'

Our lips meet, our breath flowing into each other, our bodies aligning in that perfect way that sets my toes curling into the bathroom rug.

Lips, tongue, touch – it's a great kiss. Our best yet.

If this is practice, mark me down as an A-plus student.

Fully invested in our practice, I can't help but whimper when he pulls away before I've had my fill.

His eyes bore into mine, serious and hot and brimming with promised practice. '*Eu amo-te.*'

I'm too dazed from desire to be embarrassed.

'*Eu amo-te*,' he repeats, his hands cupping my cheeks, his forehead dropping to rest on mine. 'No matter what your name. No matter Mike Hunt. No matter how many times your brothers punch me, or how many times I deserve it—' he pulls back, once more holding my eyes with his '—I love you.'

I swallow. Or try to. It's kind of hard at the moment.

As if sensing that, he kisses first one eye, 'I love you,' then the other, 'I love you.'

Moving across my body, Felix kisses my skin, inch by inch, each touch of his lips followed by the words, 'I love you.'

Until I'm physically too riled up to feel emotionally insecure. Until the dampness between my bare thighs demands action rather than words. Until my hands find his shirt and dig in, dragging his face to mine.

'I love you too, Douchebag.'

28

FELIX

I had needed to talk to her. I had hoped to be forgiven. Even so, I hadn't thought to acknowledge my want of being loved in return. It had seemed too much to ask. Of the universe. Of her.

So for all my waiting and rehearsing, I'm solely unprepared for the words when they come.

Taking advantage of my silence, Elizabeth pushes against my chest.

Eyes on hers, I stumble over the bathroom threshold, walking in reverse until my calves hit back into something and I trust fall on top of her bed.

Behind her, on either side of the bathroom door, are pictures. Elizabeth as a little girl, holding hands with her mother. Teen Elizabeth in between two suits – one smiling, one not. Recent Elizabeth, standing in a group surrounding Thomas and Alice in their wedding attire. Art awards, sketches – some framed, some not. Everywhere I look, there's Elizabeth. The Elizabeth that was and the Elizabeth that is, crawling on top of me.

'*Também te amo.*' Her smile the most beautiful thing in the room. A smile Michelangelo himself could not recreate.

Laying on her bed, in the middle of her room filled with memories, art and insights into the woman I love, I'm amazed all over again. 'You learned Portuguese?'

She shrugs, her cheeks pinking. 'A little.'

My eyes home in on the parting white fabric of her robe as she straddles me. 'Your brothers are right.'

Her smile turns down as she tugs on one end of the robe's silk belt. 'My brothers?'

Swallowing, I have trouble finding the words as her skin, soft and toned, is revealed. 'They said I don't deserve you.'

'They're overprotective.' She sounds like she's rolling her eyes, but I wouldn't know, too focused on her wet arousal hovering over my lap.

'No. They're right.' In a daze, I lift one hand to touch her, then still, my mind faltering. 'But don't tell them that, okay?'

This time, I do see her roll her eyes. 'I promise.'

My love is adorable. I touch my fingertip below her belly button, the skin pebbling with goosebumps at my light graze. My love is soft.

'Oh.' I pause again, my mind now inundated with all the things I never thought I'd get to say and do now that she's forgiven me. 'I want to take you to meet my mother.'

Her mouth drops. 'Now?' Her voice squeaks.

'No, no.' I drop my hand to my stomach and force my eyes to stay on hers, trying to concentrate. 'Next week. When she gets out of rehab.' I'll book us both first class tickets. Her mother too. Maybe even her brothers.

'Okay.' She fidgets on my lap, making it very hard to keep my eyes above shoulder level and my mind on doing all the things I can to show her how much I love her. 'We can have a big family dinner. Your mother said—'

'Felix.' She presses both hands over my mouth, her eyes, once dazed with desire now hard and serious. 'You said you loved me, right?'

I frown, wondering why she needs to ask when I'm in the middle of trying to prove it. 'I do.' My answer is muffled by her palms.

She nods. 'Then stop talking about our families and *show* me you love me.' My lips smile under her palms before she lifts them. Grabbing my hand on my stomach, she brings it between her legs, sighing when my fingertips meet her wet flesh.

Pressing firmly against her with one hand, I tip an imaginary cowboy hat with my other, my mind going back to that first night we had together. 'Yes, ma'am.'

But this time, I'm going to make it worth her while. I'm going to drive her crazy with how much I love her.

I delve my fingers deeper inside, a whimper of relief passing her lips. Stroking, rubbing, petting, she grinds until her thighs begin to tense. Until her fingertips dig into my abs.

Just before she comes, I slip my fingers from inside her.

Her mouth opens with a sob.

Before she can glare at me again, I shift under her, placing the ridge of my cock just where she needs it before holding onto her hips. 'Use me, *meu coração*.' My fingers dig into her flesh to pull her forward an inch, then push back, setting the pace for her to climb. '*Assim mesmo, meu amor.*'

She arches her back, her robes sliding off her shoulders, her breasts swaying with her movements. 'So good.'

'*Sim.*' I fight back a groan, worried that if I let go now, I'll be too caught up in my own desire to fully show her how much I want her. Cherish her. Love her. '*Tão bom.*'

* * *

Liz

Felix loves me.

Maybe that's the reason my body feels electric. Feels hot and sensitive and so, so good right now.

Then again, it could be the workout shorts.

The thin, barely there material dampens with my arousal and generates just enough friction to tantalize my clit as I move back and forth over Felix's long, hard cock.

'*Minha querida.*' Felix palms my breasts, heavy with desire, squeezing them, easing the ache. '*Amo-te.*' His thumbs graze my nipples in a rough caress.

I'm close. So close. I grind harder as I rock, chasing the heat, craving the release.

Just as the orgasm starts to gather, Felix flips me onto my back.

'No.' I draw out the word, sounding half petulant, half crazed. Because I am.

Felix answers my complaint by reaching over his shoulder and grabbing a fistful of his t-shirt, one handedly pulling it over his head.

I barely see the six-pack that usually has me so enraptured. '*Felix.*' Shifting on the bed, I whine, the unreleased desire built inside of me stripping my ability to speak coherently.

Lifting one of my ankles, Felix pulls me closer to him, the silk of my robe pooled under me easing the way. 'Ah, *meu coração*.' He continues murmuring in Portuguese as he kisses and caresses first one leg, and then the other.

And while I've only learned a few basic phrases over our time apart, I don't need a translation to know what he's saying. To feel the difference between our past selves and now.

The want, desire, attraction – it's all still there. But now, after the hurt, the apologies and the hard truths, there's something more between us, something that at first seemed idle but now, as Felix's lips reach the apex of my thighs only to bypass it for my belly, kissing my soft and panting skin, I see it for what it is.

Love.

This isn't fleeting. This doesn't need to be rushed. We have time.

Felix is loving me.

Tears blur my vision.

'*És tão bonita.*' He moves his mouth across my ribcage. '*Meu amor.*' One hand slides up and down my leg. '*Tão doce.*' His other palming my breast. '*Tão deslumbrante.*' His tongue laves at my nipple. '*Eu não te mereço.*'

Even knowing what he's doing, what he's trying to show me, I can't help but writhe on the bed, whimpering, my body near expiring from the passion he's stoked.

Light touches, delicate kisses, a tease of tongue. The sounds coming from me are desperate and needy. As is the throbbing in my heart.

'Come for me, *meu amor*.' His mouth closes over the tight bud, pulling just as his other hand presses against my clit.

I do.

My mouth opens in a wide, soundless scream as sparks and waves collide inside me. My back arches, my heels dig into the mattress and my hands fist in his hair. I'm pulled tighter and tighter still until tears stream down my face, the strums of my pleasure breaking me.

Felix continues to kiss, soothe and love my body as I sob in the afterglow of my release. '*Sentes o quanto te amo?*'

I'm not sure what he's asking. But I know what I want. 'Yes.' I find the strength to urge him over me. 'More.' Reaching my hands between us, I lower the waistband of his shorts.

His dick free, I revel at the soft skin pulled tight over his erection as I pump him up and down.

'*Merde.*' He grabs my forearm like he's going to stop me but doesn't do anything else, enjoying my handiwork.

'Nightstand.' My vague command is immediately followed as he reaches over and opens the drawer, taking out a condom.

He rips the packet open with his teeth and I take it from him, but don't immediately put it on.

Up and down, then a soft tickle of my fingertips over his testicles – drawn high and tight – then back up to grasp his cock.

I do it again. Then again.

He drops his head, his groan deep and long, reverberating under my touch. 'Is this payback?'

I smile, his recent confession and my orgasm making me feel powerful and playful. 'Maybe.'

But when Felix raises his head, his eyes glittering darkly on mine, I realize my orgasm wasn't the only thing Felix was holding back all this time.

In seconds, the condom is on and I'm lifted onto his lap.

In one powerful thrust, I'm impaled by his cock and shouting and shuddering with renewed pleasure.

'Fuck.' Felix wraps his arms around me, holding me tight against him.

'Yes.' I nod, my chin digging into his shoulder. 'Yes. Fuck.'

Lifting on his haunches, he drops fast, impaling me over and over again. Whereas before he was slow and methodical, now he seems crazed and out of control.

I love it. I love him.

'Wrap your legs around me, *meu coração*.'

I do it without thinking, still focusing on the radiating waves of pleasure building once more inside me.

Felix's abs tighten as he lifts again, a smile that contradicts the aggressive passion I've unleashed. 'I love you.'

He thrusts just as what he says registers and my next shout of pleasure comes between a smile of my own.

I've never done this before. I've never experienced mixing love with sex. Because I've never loved before.

It's slow. Fast. Too close. Too far away. It's safe and secure, yet terrifying.

It's everything.

Digging my fingers into his back, I rock myself on him as he continues to thrust, his dick hitting my G-spot, his pelvis rubbing my clit.

He dips me back to pull my nipple between his lips.

'Ahhh.' I rock faster but I've lost my rhythm, the build-up too good to concentrate.

I bite my lips, claw his shoulders. But his pause in thrusting continues as he sucks, pleasuring my breast.

I whimper. He moves to the other breast.

Unhooking my leg, I place my heels on the mattress, trying for more leverage.

'No.' Felix stops me with a nibble. 'Like this.'

'But... I need...' I try to bounce but can't.

'Shhh, *meu amor*.' He blows cool air over my hardened nipples. 'I've got you.' He takes over, rocking me against him.

It's good, so good. But not enough.

'Felix, I need more.' Fire licks at my clit. 'I need you.' Black dots shadow my vision. '*Please*.'

'Tell me.' He dips me lower, his cock sliding farther out of me. 'Tell me, *meu doce*.'

I don't need to concentrate to understand the question, the words pour out of me as I reach the edge of the cliff he's taken me to. 'I love you.' My voice breaks on a sob as I cling to him, my back hovering inches off the mattress. 'I love you. I love you. I love—'

Felix lifts me only to let me fall upon his dick, the pound breaking me. Ravages me.

I scream as I fall over the edge.

My mind blanks, my muscles tighten and spasm as Felix continues with hard and fast thrusts, chasing his own release. It seems like minutes; it could be seconds. Time is nothing but pleasure until Felix stills, pushing me down hard on his cock that's deep and pulsing inside of me.

And when the pleasure subsides. When we're lying on my bed, sweaty, chilled and spent. When it's just the two of us basking in what we've said to each other with both our words and our bodies. I've never felt more loved in my life.

EPILOGUE
FELIX

'How do I look?' I lift my chin left, then right, studying my reflection in the mirror. 'Is my beard okay?'

Elizabeth slides one foot into her Birkenstocks, pausing to shake her head at me. 'You are oddly insecure about your looks for the man recently voted "world's sexiest".'

I roll my eyes, while not-so-secretly pleased. The yearly title of World's Sexiest Man is just another nonsense award given by the tabloids to random Hollywood celebrities, but it has made for some hilarious comebacks against my new frenemies, Chase and Thomas. 'I was voted that *before* I grew my beard out, *meu tesouro*.'

Toeing on her other sandal, Elizabeth double-checks the gift bag by the door, ensuring for the third time that the pastel portrait she made of Jackie is still there. 'Aren't you always the one telling me that the sexiest part of a person is their heart?'

'Yes, yes.' I push away from the vanity, grabbing my cowboy hat off the bed as I go. 'But this is different. I made one hell of a mess the first time I met your brothers and mother. I'd rather try to start off on the right foot with your father and sister.'

'From what my mother tells me about my father and from what Rose and Trish have told me about my sister, they don't seem like those kinds of people.' She pulls at the front of her t-shirt dress, billowing the material as if to cool off.

'I just can't believe that my natural beard is finally okayed by wardrobe for a role and now I have to meet your father looking like a shipwrecked cowboy.'

She laughs, continuing to pull at her dress.

Considering the hotel room is set to a chilly sixty-eight degrees, I'm thinking she's trying to cool the anxiety currently boiling inside her.

I lift her hair off her neck, helping her cool down.

It's been three months since the end of my filming obligations for *Countdown*. During that time, I was offered a role, not by Ron, still upset over me missing two days of filming due to my impromptu trip to New York, but by another prominent director. A *Broadway* director.

Now the beard that had kept me from being recognized is plastered all over New York billboards, having been declared 'perfect' by wardrobe for my role as the twisted shipwrecked Duke of Milan, Prospero, in Shakespeare's play, *The Tempest*.

On hiatus thanks to *Countdown*'s premiere happening this weekend at Space Center Houston, I asked Elizabeth to be my date. I know she doesn't like being the center of attention, but I had hoped she'd use it as an excuse to finally make a date to meet her biological father and sister.

My hopes paid off.

I kiss her neck before lowering her hair, enjoying the spread of goosebumps that I'm pretty sure have nothing to do with the air conditioning.

'Thanks.' Liz reaches up, scratching my cheek. 'And thanks for coming with me.'

'Gimmie some practice?'

Liz's smile grows, more confident and easy than when we first started this game. 'I love you.'

I reward her with a light kiss. '*Também*.' Then step back with a swat at her ass. 'Now get.'

Laughing, she grabs her gift, before allowing me to carry it for her. Still looking flushed, but a whole lot cooler.

* * *

Liz

This is it. No big deal. Just finally going to meet my father and sister. A renowned scientist and an honest-to-God astronaut.

I cut my eyes to the gift in Felix's hands as we walk up the driveway to my sister's house, the temperature a cool eighty-two degrees. Cool if you compare it to the triple digits I endured the last time I was in Houston.

Second, triple and quadruple guessing the portrait I made, I'm glad Felix is here to smack my hand away if I tried to grab it and run it back to the car.

Glad that he's here in general.

'I love you.'

My words halt him in the middle of the walkway. The sun, just starting to set, glowing around his tangle of facial hair.

God, that's one ugly beard.

'I think you're nailing this practice thing.' He tips the brim of his cowboy hat up with his index finger before bending down to brush his lips against mine.

He doesn't say it this time, but it doesn't matter. I know I'm loved.

Practice does indeed make perfect.

We continue walking toward the front door, me leaning on his arm.

I've done a lot of thinking over the past few months. *Good* thinking, not just the avoidance of thinking like I did before Felix. I started working on Trish's manga, designed logos for Bell's marketing company and even joined Mary in seeing a feelings doctor.

My life is full. I'm happy. I'm excited about what's to come.

And yet...

I pause at the door, Felix waiting for me to ring the bell.

'We can go if you're not ready,' he offers. 'But we're leaving the picture.' He raises the gift bag. 'It's too good to not share.'

Pushing off him, I stand on my own and take a deep breath. Then I ring the bell.

It feels like a few seconds as well as an eternity before someone opens the door with an aggressive yank.

Blonde ponytail swishing from the force of the door, large brown eyes, the shape of which is eerily familiar, staring behind thick, black-framed glasses. Eyes that look me up and down as I do the same to her.

She's wearing an *I need my Space* t-shirt with a NASA logo in place of the A, fitted, denim blue jeans and worn, white Converse.

'I'm Elizabeth.' I throw out my hand, nearly punching her in the stomach. 'You can call me Liz.'

She grabs hold of my hand with both of hers, pumping it hard. 'I'm Jackie.' She keeps pumping. 'You can call me, uh—' she stops pumping and laughs '—Jackie, I guess.'

Her nervousness settles my own, and I feel so, so good.

Even better when two men appear behind her.

'Hello, Elizabeth.' A man with Jackie's kind eyes steps up beside my sister.

My eyes.

'I'm Gerald.'

I manage a lame wave.

'And I'm Flynn, Jackie's husband.'

Flynn's introduction seems to break the spell, and I swing both arms to the side, whacking Felix with one, the gift bag with the other. 'This is Felix.'

As expected, Jackie's mouth drops as she turns to the man she didn't seem to realize was standing there. Unexpectedly, it isn't his celebrity she comments on. 'Holy Mercury, that is one ugly beard.'

At Felix's fallen expression, barely visible from the scraggly of hair, I burst out laughing, as does everyone else.

And when the laughter ebbs and we're ushered into the house, Felix by my side, I can't help feeling like I found another place to call home.

ABOUT THE AUTHOR

Sara L. Hudson is a bestselling romantic comedy author living in Houston, whose books include the hilarious Space series, featuring the men and women of NASA and their panty-melting happily-ever-afters.

Sign up to Sara L. Hudson's mailing list for news, competitions and updates on future books.

Visit Sara's website: www.saralhudson.com

Follow Sara L. Hudson on social media here:

- facebook.com/SaraLHudsonWriter
- x.com/_SaraLHudson
- instagram.com/sara_l_hudson

ALSO BY SARA L. HUDSON

Anyone But You Series
Anyone But The Billionaire
Anyone But The Boss
Anyone But The Superstar

LOVE NOTES
LOVE IN EVERY CHAPTER

WHERE ALL YOUR ROMANCE DREAMS COME TRUE!

THE HOME OF BESTSELLING ROMANCE AND WOMEN'S FICTION

WARNING:
MAY CONTAIN SPICE

SIGN UP TO OUR NEWSLETTER

https://bit.ly/Lovenotesnews

Boldwood

Boldwood Books is an award-winning fiction publishing company seeking out the best stories from around the world.

Find out more at www.boldwoodbooks.com

Join our reader community for brilliant books, competitions and offers!

Follow us
@BoldwoodBooks
@TheBoldBookClub

Sign up to our weekly deals newsletter

https://bit.ly/BoldwoodBNewsletter